Passion and seduction outside
the nine-to-five!

HER
Mediterranean
BOSS

Complete your collection with
all four books!

In April: *Her Billionaire Boss*
In May: *Her Outback Boss*
In June: *Her Playboy Boss*

The professional is about to get very, very personal!

Four fabulous collections of stories from your favourite authors

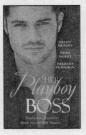

HER
Mediterranean
BOSS

HELEN BROOKS
BARBARA McMAHON
TRISH MOREY

*M&B™ and M&B™ with the Rose Device
are trademarks of the publisher.
Harlequin Mills & Boon Limited, Eton House,
18-24 Paradise Road, Richmond, Surrey TW9 1SR*

HER MEDITERRANEAN BOSS
© by Harlequin Books S.A. 2009

A Spanish Affair © Helen Brooks 2001
Her Spanish Boss © Barbara McMahon 2004
The Greek Boss's Demand © Trish Morey 2004

ISBN: 978 0 263 86894 4

010-0309

*Printed and bound in Spain
by Litografia Rosés S.A., Barcelona*

A SPANISH AFFAIR

HELEN BROOKS

Helen Brooks lives in Northamptonshire and is married with three children. As she is a committed Christian, busy housewife and mother, her spare time is at a premium, but her hobbies include reading, swimming, gardening and walking her old faithful dog. Her long-cherished aspiration to write became a reality when she put pen to paper on reaching the age of forty, and sent the result off to Mills & Boon.

CHAPTER ONE

'THINGS are really that bad? But why on earth didn't you tell me?' Georgie's sea-green eyes were wide with shock as she stared into her brother's troubled face. 'I could have helped in some way.'

'How?' Robert Millett shook his blond head slowly. 'You couldn't have done anything, Georgie, no one could, and there was still an element of hope before that last contract was pulled out from under our feet. Old man Sanderson really ducked and dived for that one. But, as he's so fond of saying, all's fair in love and war.'

Georgie's smooth brow wrinkled in an angry frown. Mike Sanderson was a mean old man and she wouldn't trust him as far as she could throw him, and as she was a tiny, slender five foot four to Mike's burly six foot that wouldn't be far! 'He's an out-and-out crook,' she stated tightly. 'I just don't know how he can sleep at night with some of the tricks he pulls.'

'Georgie, Georgie, Georgie.' Robert pulled his sister into his arms and hugged her for a moment before pushing her away and looking down into her flushed face. 'We both know Mike's not to blame for the mess I'm in. I had to make some choices over the last months when Sandra was so ill, and even now I know I made the right ones. I don't regret a thing. If the business fails, it fails.'

'Oh, Robert.' This was so *unfair*. When Robert had discovered his beloved wife, Sandra, was suffering from a rare blood disorder that meant she only had a few months to live, he had devoted himself to making her last days happy ones, and taking care of their seven-year-old twins, David and Annie, and trying to shield them from as much pain as possible as their mother slowly faded away. Sandra and Robert had told no one the true state of affairs—not even Georgie had known Sandra's illness was terminal until four weeks before she had died.

That had been six months ago, and immediately she had understood what was happening. Georgie had packed her bags and left her wonderful, well-paid job in advertising and high-tailed it back to the family home to take some of Robert's burden in the last traumatic weeks of Sandra's illness.

She hadn't had to think twice about such a step—Robert and Sandra had opened their arms to her when, as a bewildered little girl of ten and newly orphaned, she had needed love and care. Now, thirteen years later, it was her turn to repay the tenderness and warmth they had lavished on her, which hadn't diminished a jot when their own children were born.

'What about the de Capistrano deal? They've already offered us the contract, haven't they? And the rewards would be brilliant.' Sandra had run the office side of Robert's building firm before she had become ill, and after a succession of temps had muddled through Georgie had had her work cut out the last few months to make sense of the paperwork. It didn't help that after the funeral Robert had retreated into a world of his own for some time, the strain of being Sandra's mainstay and support, as well as mother and father to the children, telling at last.

'De Capistrano?' Robert ran a tired hand through his thick hair, which immediately sprang back to its previous disorder.

Georgie noticed, with a little pang in her heart, that there were several strands of grey mixed with the honey-gold these days. But then that wasn't surprising after all her big brother had been through, she thought painfully. They were all of them—David, Annie and herself—missing Sandra like mad, but Sandra had been Robert's childhood sweetheart and her brother's grief was overwhelming.

'We'd need to take on more men and hire machinery to make it viable, and the bank's screaming blue murder already. I had relied on the profit from this other job to finance de Capistrano's.'

'But we can go and see them and ask at least?' Georgie's small chin stuck out aggressively, as though she was already doing battle with the pinstriped brigade. 'They aren't stupid. They'll be able to see the potential, surely?'

'I'd have thought you were dead against the de Capistrano deal after all your "green" rallies and such at uni?' Robert remarked quietly. 'Animal rights, save the hedgerows, Greenpeace… You were into them all, weren't you?'

Georgie stared at him, her heavily lashed eyes narrowing. Robert had been sixteen years of age when she was born, their parents having long since given up hope of ever having another child. Consequently his attitude had always been paternal, even before the car crash which had taken their parents, and she had often rebelled against his staid and—Georgie considered—prosaic views about a million and one subjects dear to her heart. But now was not the time to go into all that, she reminded herself, as she looked into the blue of his worried eyes.

'That's a separate issue,' she said very definitely. 'If it's a case of the de Capistrano contract or virtual bankruptcy for you, I'll take the contract.'

'If they could hear you now…' Robert summoned up something of a grin—his first one for days—which Georgie took as a good sign.

'They can't.' It was succinct. 'So, how about approaching the bank?'

'Useless.' It was clear all Robert's normal get up and go had got up and gone. 'I've got de Capistrano himself coming in later this morning and he won't be interested in a building firm that's on the rocks.'

Georgie searched her mind frantically. 'Well, what about asking de Capistrano to finance the men and machinery on a short-term basis?' she suggested brightly. 'Once we got going we could pay him back fairly quickly, and it's common knowledge he is something of an entrepreneur and filthy rich into the bargain.'

'Exactly, and he hasn't got that way by doing anyone any favours,' Robert said cynically. 'His reputation is as formidable as the man himself, so I understand, and de Capistrano is only interested in a fast turnover with huge profits. Face it, Georgie, he can go elsewhere and have no hassle. End of story.'

Her brother stretched his long, lanky body wearily in the big leather chair behind the desk strewn with the morning's post, his blue eyes dropping to the fateful letter open in front of him. It stated that Sandersons—not Milletts—had been successful in securing the contract for the town's new leisure complex. A contract which would have provided the profit margin to finance the extra men's wages and hiring of the machinery for de Capistrano's job.

'But, Robert—'

'No buts.' Robert raised his head to take in his sister's aggressive stance. 'De Capistrano is a Sanderson type, Georgie. He knows all the right angles and the right people. Look at the deal we were going to discuss this morning; he negotiated that prime piece of land for a song some years ago and he's been holding on to it until the time was right to build housing. He'll get his outlay back a hundred times over on the sort of yuppie estate he is planning.'

'Yes, well...' Georgie wrinkled the small straight nose she'd inherited from her mother in disgust, unable to hide her real opinion any longer. 'I'm sorry, but I have to say destroying that beautiful land *is* out-and-out sacrilege! People have enjoyed that ground as a park in the summer ever since I can remember and the wildlife is tremendous. Do you recall that rare butterfly being found there the year I started uni?'

'Butterflies aren't good business.' Robert shrugged philosophically. 'Neither are wild flowers and the like, come to that, or putting family first and being less than ruthless. Maybe if I'd been a bit more like the de Capistranos of this world my kids wouldn't be in danger of losing the roof over their heads.'

'Don't say that,' said Georgie fiercely, her eyes sparking green flames. 'You're the best father and husband and brother in the world. You've already admitted you've no regrets in putting Sandra first and it was absolutely the right thing to do. You're ten times the man—a hundred times— de Capistrano will ever be and—'

'Have we met?'

Two blonde heads shot round as though connected by a single wire and a pair of horrified green eyes and amazed blue surveyed the tall dark man standing in the doorway of the small brick building that was Robert's office. The voice had been icy, and even if the slight accent hadn't informed Georgie this was de Capistrano she would have known any-way. The impeccable designer suit and silk shirt and tie sat on the tall lean body in a way that positively screamed unlimited wealth, and the beautiful svelte woman standing just behind the commanding figure was equally well dressed. And equally annoyed if the look on the lovely face was anything to go by. His secretary? Or maybe his wife?

And then Georgie's racing thoughts were focused on the man alone as he said again, 'Have we met?' and this time the voice had all the softness of a razor-sharp scalpel.

'Mr de Capistrano?' Georgie's normally clear voice was more of a weak squeak, and as she cleared her throat nervously the black head nodded slowly, the deep, steel-grey eyes piercingly intent on her face. 'I'm sorry... I didn't know...' She took a hard pull of air before continuing more coherently, 'No, Mr de Capistrano, we haven't met, and I have no excuse for my rudeness.'

'So.' The furious anger in the frosty face hadn't diminished an iota.

'Mr de Capistrano.' Robert pulled himself together and strode across the room, extending his hand as he said, 'Please understand. What you overheard was less a comment on you than an endeavour to hearten me. There was nothing personal intended. I'm Robert Millett, by the way, and this is my sister, Georgie.'

There was a pause which seemed to last for ever to Georgie's tortured senses, and then the hand was accepted. 'Matt de Capistrano.' It was pithy. 'And my secretary, Pepita Vilaseca.'

Georgie had followed her brother across to the others and as the two men shook hands she proffered her own to the immaculate figure at the side of the illustrious Mr de Capistrano. This time the pause was even longer and the lovely face was cold as the tall slim secretary extended a languid hand to Georgie, extracting it almost immediately with a haughty glance which said more clearly than any words could that she had done Georgie the most enormous favour. Pepita. Georgie looked into the beautifully made-up ebony eyes that resembled polished onyx. Sounded like an indigestion remedy to her!

And then, as Robert moved to shake the secretary's hand, Georgie was forced to raise her eyes up to the dark gaze trained on her face, and acknowledge the reality of what she had imbibed seconds earlier. This was one amazingly…handsome? No, not handsome, her brain corrected in the next moment. Male. One amazingly *male* man. Overwhelmingly, aggressively male. The sort of man who exuded such a primal masculinity that the veneer of civilisation sat frighteningly lightly on his massive frame.

The leanly muscled body, the jet-black hair cropped uncompromisingly short, the hard good looks—

'Do you always…encourage your brother by doing a character assassination on complete strangers, Miss Millett?' Matt de Capistrano asked with arctic politeness, interrupting Georgie's line of thought and forcing her to realise she had been staring unashamedly.

She turned scarlet. Help, she breathed silently. Get me out of this, someone. He had held out his hand to her and as she made herself shake his, and felt her nervously cold fingers enclosed in his firm hard grip that sent frissons of warmth down to her toes in a most peculiar way, her mouth opened and shut like a goldfish in a bowl before she was able to say breathlessly, 'No, no, I don't. Of course I don't.'

'Then why today and why me?'

His voice was very deep and of an almost gravelly texture, the slight accent turning it into pure dynamite, Georgie thought inappropriately. 'I… You weren't supposed to hear that,' she said quickly, before she realised just how stupid that sounded.

'I'd worked that one out all on my own,' he said caustically.

Oh, how could she have been so unforgivably indiscreet?

Georgie's heart sank into her shoes. Her flat shoes. Which didn't help her confidence at all with this huge six-foot avenging angel towering over her measly five foot four inches—or perhaps angel was the wrong description. 'It was just an expression,' she said weakly. 'There was absolutely nothing personal in it, as Robert said.'

'That actually makes it worse, Miss Millett.' It was cutting. 'When—or should I say if?—anyone had the temerity to insult me I would expect it to be for a well-thought-out and valid reason.'

Well, hang on just a tick and I'm sure I can come up with several, Georgie thought darkly, forcing a respectful nod of her head as she said out loud, 'All I can do is to apologise again, Mr de Capistrano.' Which is exactly what you want, isn't it? Your full pound of flesh.

'You work here?'

Georgie thought frantically. If she said yes it might be the final death knell to any faint hope Robert had of persuading this man to finance the cost of the new machinery for a short time, but if she said no and the deal did go through he'd soon know she'd been economical with the truth!

'Temporarily,' she compromised hesitantly.

'Temporarily.' The lethal eyes demanded an explanation, but Robert—tired of being virtually ignored—cleared his throat at the side of them in a way that demanded attention. Matt de Capistrano paid him no attention at all. 'Does that mean you will be here for the foreseeable future, Miss Millett?'

Without your contract there isn't a future. It was that thought which enabled Georgie to draw herself up straight and say, as she met the icy grey gaze head-on, 'Not if you feel that would be inappropriate after what I've said, Mr de Capistrano.'

He blinked. Just once, but she saw she had surprised him. And then he swung round to face Robert, his dark aura releasing her as his piercing gaze left her hot face. 'I came here today to discuss a proposed business deal,' he said coldly, 'and I am a very busy man, Mr Millett. You have the financial details ready which my secretary asked you to prepare?'

Robert gulped. 'I do, Mr de Capistrano, but—'

'Then as we have already wasted several minutes of valuable time I suggest we get down to business,' Matt de Capistrano said tightly, cutting across Robert's stumbling voice.

What an arrogant, ignorant, overbearing, high and mighty—Georgie's furious adjectives came to a sudden halt as the grey eyes flicked her way again. 'I trust you have no objection to that, Miss Millett?' he asked softly, something in his face making it quite clear to Georgie he had known exactly what she was thinking. 'I take it you are your brother's…temporary secretary?'

Somehow, and she couldn't quite put a finger on it, but somehow he made it sound insulting. 'Yes, I am,' she responded tightly.

'How…convenient,' he drawled smoothly.

'Convenient?' It was wary.

'To have a ready-made job available like this rather than having to fight your way in the big bad world and prove yourself,' was the—to Georgie—shocking answer.

How dared he? How *dared* he make assumptions about her just because she had ruffled his wealthy, powerful feathers? That last remark was just plain nasty. Georgie reared up like a small tigress, all thoughts of appeasement flying out of the window as she bit out, 'I happen to be a very good secretary, Mr de Capistrano.' She had worked her socks off as a temp all through the university holidays in order to be less of a financial burden on Robert—one of her ten GCSEs being that of Typing and Computer Literacy before her A Levels in Business Studies, English and Art and Design—and every firm the temping agency had placed her with had wanted her back.

'Really?' Her obvious annoyance seemed to diminish his. 'You did a secretarial course at college?'

'Not exactly.' She glared at him angrily.

'My sister graduated from university two years ago with a First in Art and Design,' Robert cut in swiftly, sensing Georgie was ready to explode.

'Then why waste such admirable talents working for big brother?' He was speaking to her as though Robert and his secretary didn't exist, and apart from the content of his words hadn't acknowledged Robert had spoken. 'Lack of ambition? Contentment with the status quo? Laziness? What?'

Georgie couldn't believe her ears. 'Now look here, you—'

Robert cut in again, his face very straight now and his voice holding a harsh note as he said, 'Georgie left an excellent job a few months ago, Mr de Capistrano, in advertising—a job she was successful in obtaining over a host of other applicants, I might add. She did this purely for me and there is no question of it being a free ride here, if that is what you are suggesting. My wife used to run the office here but—'

'You don't have to explain to him.' Georgie was past caring about the contract or anything else she was so mad.

'But she died six months ago. Okay?' Robert finished more calmly.

There was a screaming silence for a full ten seconds and Georgie moved closer to Robert, putting her hand on his arm. She noticed the secretary had done the same thing to

Matt de Capistrano which seemed to suggest a certain closeness if nothing else.

'I'm not sure that an apology even begins to cover such insensitivity, Mr Millett, but I would be grateful if you would accept it,' the tall dark man in front of them said quietly. 'I had no idea of your circumstances, of course.'

'There was no reason why you should have.' Robert's voice was more resigned than anything now. He had the feeling Matt de Capistrano was itching to shake the dust of this particular building firm off his feet as quickly—and finally—as possible.

'Perhaps not, but I have inadvertently added to your pain at this difficult time and that is unforgivable.' The accent made the words almost quaint, but in view of the situation—and not least the big lean figure speaking them— there was nothing cosy about the scenario being played out in the small office.

'Forget it.' Robert waved a dismissive hand. 'But it is the case that I find myself in somewhat changed circumstances. We discovered this morning we had lost some vital work, work which I had assumed would finance the extra men and hire of machinery I need for your job, Mr de Capistrano.'

'Are you saying the estimate you supplied is no longer viable?' The deep voice was now utterly businesslike, and Georgie—standing to one side of the two men—suddenly felt invisible. It was not a pleasant feeling.

'Not exactly,' Robert replied cautiously. 'I can still do the job at the price I put forward, if my bank is prepared to finance the machinery and so on, but—'

'They won't,' Matt de Capistrano finished for him coolly. 'Are you telling me your business is in financial difficulties, Mr Millett?'

'I'm virtually bankrupt.'

Georgie couldn't stop the gasp of shock at hearing it put so baldly, and as the men's heads turned her way she said quickly, without thinking about it, 'Because he dedicated himself to his wife when she and the children needed him, Mr de Capistrano, *not* because he isn't a good builder. He's a great builder, the best you could get, and he never cuts corners like some I could mention. You can look at any of the work he's done in the past and—'

'Georgie, please.' Robert was scarlet with embarrassment. 'This is between me and Mr de Capistrano.'

'But you *are* a fine builder,' Georgie returned desperately. 'You know you are but you won't say so—'

'*Georgie.*' Robert's voice was not loud but the quality of his tone told her she had gone as far as she could go.

'I think it might be better if you waited in your office, Miss Millett,' Matt de Capistrano suggested smoothly, nodding his head at the door through which her small cubbyhole of a place was situated.

Georgie longed to defy him—she had never longed for anything so much in all her life—but something in Robert's eyes forced her to comply without another word.

For the first time since childhood she found herself biting her nails as she sat at her desk piled high with paperwork, the interconnecting door to Robert's office now firmly shut. She could just hear the low murmur of voices from within, but the actual conversation was indistinguishable, and as time slipped by her apprehension grew.

How long did it take to rip up a contract and say byebye? she thought painfully. Matt de Capistrano wasn't going to twist the knife in some way to pay her back for her rudeness, was he? Those few minutes in there had made it plain he'd never been spoken to like that before in his life, and a man like him didn't take such an insult lying down. Not that she had actually *spoken* to him when she'd insulted him, just about him. She groaned softly. Her and her big mouth. Oh, why, *why* had he had to come in at that precise moment and why had she left the door to her office open so he'd heard every word? And Robert. Why hadn't he *told* her how bad things were?

The abrupt opening of the door caught her by surprise and she raised anxious green eyes to see Matt de Capistrano looking straight at her, a hard, speculative gleam in the dark grey eyes. 'Daydreaming, Miss Millett?'

The tone of his voice could have indicated he was being friendly, lightly amusing in a pleasant teasing fashion, but Georgie was looking into his face—unlike the two behind him—and she knew different. 'Of course. What else do temporary secretaries do?' she answered sweetly, her green eyes narrowing as she stared her dislike.

He smiled, moving to stand by her desk as he said, 'I intend to phone your brother tonight from Scotland after certain enquiries have been made. The call will be of vital importance so can you make sure the line is free?'

'Certainly.' She knew exactly what he was implying and now added, 'I'll let all my friends and my hairdresser and beautician know not to call me then, shall I?' in helpful, dulcet tones.

His mouth tightened; it clearly wasn't often he was answered in like vein. 'Just so.' The harsh face could have been set in stone. 'I shall be working to a tight schedule so time is of the essence.'

'Absolutely, Mr de Capistrano.'

The grey gaze held her one more moment and then he swept past her, the secretary and Robert at his heels, and as the door closed behind them Georgie sank back in her seat and let out a big whoosh of a sigh. Horrible man! Horrible, horrible man! She ignored the faint odour of expensive aftershave and the way it was making her senses quiver and concentrated her mind on loathing him instead.

She could hear the sound of voices outside the building and surmised they must all be standing in the little yard, and, after rising from her chair, she peeped cautiously through the blind at the window.

Matt de Capistrano and his secretary were just getting into a chauffeur-driven silver Mercedes, and even from this distance he was intimidating. Not that he had intimidated *her*, Georgie told herself strongly in the next moment, not a bit of it, but he was one of those men who was uncomfortably, in-your-face male. There was a sort of dark power about him, an aggressive virility that was impossible to ignore, and it was…Georgie searched for the right word and found it. Disturbing. He was disturbing. But he was leaving now and with any luck she would never set eyes on him again.

And then she suddenly realised what she was thinking and offered up a quick urgent prayer of repentance. Robert's whole business, his livelihood, *everything* hung on Matt de Capistrano giving him this contract; how could she—for one second—wish he didn't get it? But she hadn't, she hadn't wished that, she reassured herself frantically the next moment, just that she wouldn't see Matt de Capistrano again. But if Robert got the job—by some miracle—of course she'd have to see him if she continued working here. *'Oh…'* She sighed again, loudly and irritably. The man had got her in such a state she didn't know what she was thinking!

'Well!' Robert opened the door and he was smiling. 'We might, we just might be back in business again.'

'Really?' Georgie forgot all about her dislike of Matt de Capistrano as the naked hope in her brother's face touched her heart. 'He's going to help?'

'Maybe.' Robert was clearly trying to keep a hold on his optimism but he couldn't disguise his relief as he said, 'He's not dismissed it out of hand anyway. It all depends on that phone call tonight and then we'll know one way or the other. He's going to make some enquiries. I can't blame him; I'd do the same in his shoes.'

'Enquiries?' Georgie raised fine arched eyebrows. 'With whom?'

'Anyone he damn well wants,' Robert answered drily. 'I've given him a host of names and numbers—the bank manager, my accountant, firms we've dealt with recently and so on—and told him I'll ring them and tell them to let him have any information he wants. This is my last hope, Georgie. If the man tells me to jump through hoops I'll turn cartwheels as well for good measure.'

'Oh, Robert.' She didn't want him to lose everything, she didn't, but to be rescued by Matt de Capistrano! And it was only in that moment she fully acknowledged the extent of the antagonism which had leapt into immediate life the moment she had laid eyes on the darkly handsome face. She didn't know him, she'd barely exchanged more than a dozen words with him, and yet she disliked him more intensely than anyone else she had ever met. Well, almost anyone. Her thoughts touched on Glen before she closed that particular door in her mind.

'So, cross your fingers and your toes and anything else it's physically possible to cross,' Robert said more quietly now, a nervous note creeping in as they stared at each other. 'If it's no we're down the pan, Georgie; even the house is mortgaged up to the hilt so the kids won't even have a roof over their heads.'

'They will.' Georgie's voice was fierce. 'We'll make sure of that and we'll all stay together too.' But a little grotty flat somewhere wouldn't be the same as Robert's pleasant semi with its big garden and the tree-house he had built for the children a couple of years ago. They had lost their mother and all the security she had embodied; were they going to have to lose their home too?

'Maybe.' And then as Georgie eyed him determinedly Robert smiled as he said, 'Definitely! But let's hope it won't come to uprooting the kids, Georgie. Look, get the bank on the phone for me first, would you? I need to put them and everyone else in the know and explain they'll be getting a call from de Capistrano's people. I don't want anyone else to tread on his very wealthy and powerful toes.'

Georgie looked sharply at Robert at that, and was relieved to see he was grinning at her. 'I'm sorry about what I said,' she said weakly. 'I didn't know he was there. I nearly died when I saw him.'

'You and me both.' Robert shook his head slowly. 'I'd forgotten there's never a dull moment around you, little sister.'

'Oh, you.'

The rest of the day sped by in a flurry of phone-calls, faxes and hastily typed letters, and by the end of the afternoon Georgie was sick of the very sound of Matt de Capistrano's name. Yesterday her life had been difficult— juggling her new role as surrogate mum, cook and house-keeper, Robert's secretary and shoulder to cry on wasn't easy—but today a tall, obnoxious stranger had made it downright impossible, she thought crossly just before five o'clock. Robert had been like a cat on a hot tin roof all day and neither of them had been able to eat any lunch.

One thing had solidified through the hectic afternoon, though. If Matt de Capistrano bailed them out she was leaving here as soon as she could fix up a good secretary for Robert. She could get heaps more money working at temping anyway, and every little bit would help the family budget for the time being. And temping meant she could be there for the children if either of them were ill, without worrying Robert would be struggling at the office, and she could pick and choose when she worked. She might even be able to do a little freelance advertising work if she took a few days out to tote her CV and examples of her artwork designs round the area.

Her previous job, as a designer working on tight deadlines and at high speed for an independent design studio situated north of Watford had been on the other side of London—Robert's house and business being in Sevenoaks—but there were other studios and other offices.

Whatever, she would remove herself from any chance of bumping into Matt de Capistrano. Georgie nodded to the thought, her hands pausing on the keyboard of her word processor as she gazed into space, only to jump violently as the telephone on her desk rang shrilly.

She glanced at her wristwatch as she reached for the receiver. Five o'clock. Exactly. It was him! She ignored the ridiculous churning in her stomach and breathed deeply, her voice steady and cool as she said, 'Millett's Builders. How can I help you?'

'Miss Millett?' The deep voice trickled over her taut nerves gently but with enough weight to make them twang slightly. 'Matt de Capistrano. Is your brother there?'

'Yes, Mr de Capistrano, he's been waiting for your call,' Georgie said briskly.

'Thank you.'

Boy, with a voice like that he'd be dynamite on the silver screen—Sean Connery eat your heart out! Georgie thought flusteredly as she buzzed Robert and put the call through. Deep and husky with the faint accent making it heart-racingly sexy— And then she caught her errant ramblings firmly, more than a little horrified at the way her mind had gone. He was a hateful man, despicable. End of story.

She heard the telephone go down in the other office and when, a moment later, the interconnecting door opened with a flourish she knew. Even before Robert spoke his beaming face told her what the outcome of Matt de Capistrano's enquiries had been. They were in business.

CHAPTER TWO

'WE MEET again, Miss Millett.' In spite of the fact that Georgie had been steeling herself all morning for this encounter, her head snapped up so sharply she felt a muscle in her neck twang.

A full week had elapsed since that day in Robert's office when she had first seen Matt de Capistrano, and it was now the first day of May and a beautiful sunny morning outside the building. Inside Georgie felt the temperature had just dropped about ten degrees as she met the icy grey eyes watching her so intently from the doorway.

'Good morning, Mr de Capistrano.' There was no designer suit today; he was dressed casually in black denim jeans and a pale cream shirt and if anything the dark aura surrounding him was enhanced tenfold. Georgie knew he and Robert were going on site for most of the day, along with Matt de Capistrano's architects and a whole host of other people, but she hadn't bargained for what the open-necked shirt and black jeans which sat snugly on lean male hips would do to her equilibrium. She wanted to swallow nervously but she just knew the grey gaze would pick up the action, and so she said, a little throatily, 'Robert is waiting for you if you'd like to go through?' as she indicated her brother's office with a wave of her hand.

'Thank you, but I wish to have a word with you first.'

Oh, help! He was going to come down on her like a ton of bricks for her rudeness a week ago. He held all the cards and he knew it. He could make their lives hell if he wanted. Georgie raised her small chin a fraction and her voice betrayed none of her inward agitation as she looked into the dark attractive face and said quietly, 'Yes, Mr de Capistrano?'

Her little cubby-hole, which was barely big enough to hold her desk and chair and the filing cabinet, and barely warranted the grand name of an office, was covered by one male stride, and then he was standing at the side of her as he said, 'Firstly, I do not think it appropriate we stand on ceremony with the Mr de Capistrano and Miss Millett now we are working together, yes?'

In spite of his perfect English he sounded very foreign. Georgie just had to take that swallow before she could say, 'If that's what you want, Mr de Capistrano.'

'It is,' he affirmed softly. 'And the name is Matt.'

The grey eyes were so dark as to be almost black, Georgie thought inconsequentially, and surrounded by such thick black lashes it seemed a shame to waste them on a man. And he seemed even bigger than she remembered. 'Then please call me Georgie,' she managed politely.

He inclined his head briefly. 'And the second thing is that I find myself in need of your assistance today, Georgie,' he continued smoothly. 'My secretary, Pepita, has unfortunately had a slight accident this morning and twisted her ankle. Perhaps you would take her place on site and take notes for me?'

Oh, no. No, no, no. She'd never survive a day in his company without making a fool of herself or something. She couldn't, she really couldn't do this! If nothing else this confirmed she was doing absolutely the right thing in trying to find a new secretary to take her place for Robert.

Georgie called on every bit of composure she could muster and said steadily, 'Perhaps you had better ask Robert about that. It would mean closing the office here, of course, which is not ideal. His men are finishing work on a shop we've been renovating and are expected to call in some time this afternoon, and there's the phone to answer and so on.'

'You have an answering machine?' Matt enquired pleasantly.

'Yes, but—'

'And your presence will only be required during the discussions with the architect and planner. After that you may return here and perhaps type up the notes for me,' he continued silkily.

Oh, hell! It would be today his precious secretary decided to twist her ankle, Georgie thought helplessly. She doubted if Matt de Capistrano would be around much in the normal run of things; a wealthy tycoon like him had his fingers in a hundred and one pies at any one time, and within a few weeks she would hopefully be out of here anyway. This was *just* the sort of situation she'd been trying to avoid when she'd decided to find a replacement secretary for Robert. 'Well, like I said, you'd best discuss this with Robert,' she said faintly.

'And if Robert agrees? I can tell him you have no objection, yes?' he persisted.

No, no and triple no. 'Of course, Mr—Matt,' Georgie said calmly.

'Thank you, Georgie.'

His accent gave her name emphasis on the last 'e' and lifted it into something quite different from the mundane, and she was just coping with what that did to her nerves when the hard gaze narrowed as he said conversationally, 'You do not like me, Georgie.'

It was a statement, not a question, but even if it had been otherwise Georgie would have been unable to answer him immediately such was the state of her surprise.

'This is not a problem,' he continued smoothly as she

stared at him wide-eyed. His gaze rested briefly on the dark gold of her hair, which hung to her shoulders in a silky bob, before he added, 'Unless you make it one, of course.'

'I... That is—' She was spluttering, she realised suddenly, and with the knowledge came a flood of angry adrenaline that strengthened her voice as her mind became clearer. If he thought she was some pathetic little doormat who would let him walk all over her just because he was bailing them out, he'd got another think coming! She was no one's whipping boy. 'I have no intention of making it one,' she answered smartly.

'This is good.'

Georgie's soft mouth tightened further as she caught what she was sure was the hint of laughter in the dark voice, although his face was betraying no amusement whatsoever, and she struggled to keep her tone even and cool as she said, 'In fact, I don't expect to be working for Robert much longer, actually. It's far better that he has someone else working for him here so that I can divide my time between looking after the children and temping work. So I doubt our paths will cross after that.'

To her absolute horror he sat down on a corner of the desk, his body warmth reaching into her air space as he said quietly, 'Ah, yes, the children. How old are they? Are they coping?'

That same expensive and utterly delicious smell she'd caught wafting off the hard tanned body before was doing wicked things to her hormones, but Georgie was pleased to note nothing of her inward turmoil showed in her voice as she answered evenly, 'The twins are seven, coming up for eight, and they are coping pretty well on the whole. They have lots of friends and their teacher at school at the moment is actually Sandra's—their mother's—best friend, so she is being an absolute brick.'

'And your brother?' he asked quietly, his head tilting as he moved a fraction closer which made her heartbeat quicken. 'How is he doing?'

Georgie cleared her throat. There were probably a million and one men who could sit on her desk all day if they so wished without her turning a hair and without one stray thought coming into her mind. Matt de Capistrano was not one of them.

'Robert is naturally devastated,' she said even more quietly than he had spoken. 'Sandra was his world. They'd known each other since they were children and after they married they even worked together, so their lives were intrinsically linked.'

'I see.' He nodded slowly, and Georgie wondered if he was aware of just how sexy he looked when he narrowed his eyes like that. 'Such devotion is unusual, one might even say exceptional in this day and age of supermarket marriage.'

'Supermarket marriage?' she asked bewilderedly.

'One samples one brand for a while before purchasing another and then another,' he drawled in cynical explanation. 'The lawyers get fatter than anyone, of course.'

'Not all marriages are like that,' Georgie objected steadily. 'Some people fall in love and it lasts a lifetime.'

The grey eyes fastened even more piercingly on her face and now the metallic glint was mocking. 'Don't tell me you are a romantic,' he said derisively.

She had been, once. 'No, I am not a romantic.' Her voice was cool now, and dismissive. 'But I know what Sandra and Robert had was real, that's all.'

She couldn't read the expression on his face now, but as he opened his mouth to speak Robert chose that moment to open the door of his office, his face breaking into a warm smile as he said, 'I thought I heard voices out here. Come on in, Matt. There's just a couple of points I'd like to discuss before we leave.'

Whew! As the door closed behind the two men Georgie slumped in her chair for a moment, one hand smoothing a wisp of silky hair from her flushed face. Something gave her the impression this was going to be one of those days!

She had been banking on using the time the office was quiet with Robert on site to organize the arrangements for the twins' birthday party. She and Robert had suddenly realised the night before that the children's birthday was only a couple of weeks away and neither of them had given it a thought. Sandra had always made a big deal of their birthday and Georgie wanted to keep everything as normal as she could in the circumstances, so—Robert being unable to face the thought of the house being invaded by family and friends and loads of screaming infants—she had thought of booking a hall somewhere and hiring a bouncy castle and a magician and the full works.

The buzzer on her desk interrupted further musing. 'Georgie?' Robert's voice sounded strained. 'Could you organise coffee, make it three cups, would you, and bring in your notebook? I want you to sit in on this.'

What now? Georgie thought as she quickly fetched out the best mugs and a packet of the delicious chocolate caramel biscuits her brother loved. He had lost a great deal of weight in the last months and she had been trying to feed him up since she'd come home.

Once the coffee was ready she straightened her pencil-slim skirt and demure, buttoned-up-to-the-collar blouse and steeled herself for the moment she faced those piercing grey eyes again. Since her first day of working for Robert she had always dressed well, bearing in mind that she was the first impression people received when they walked through the door, but today she had taken extra care and it was only in this moment she acknowledged the fact. And it irritated her. Irritated and annoyed her. She didn't *want* to care what Matt de Capistrano thought of her. He was just a brief fleeting shadow in her life, totally unimportant. *He was*.

The brief and totally unimportant shadow was sitting with one knee over the other and muscled arms stretched along the back of the big comfy visitor's seat in Robert's office when she entered, and immediately her body's re-action to the overt male pose forced her to recognise her own awareness of him. Georgie was even more ruffled when her innate honesty emphasised that his flagrant mas-culinity was all the more overwhelming for its casual un-consciousness, and after serving the men their coffee and offering them the plate of biscuits she sat down herself, folding her hands neatly in her lap after placing her own coffee within easy reach. She was not going to fidget or gabble or react in any way to Matt de Capistrano, not if it killed her.

'So...' Robert's voice was still strained. 'To recap, you feel Mains and Jenson will have to go?' he said to Matt, referring to the two elderly bricklayers who had been with Robert since he first started the firm fourteen years ago.

'What?' Georgie forgot all about the non-reaction as she reared up in her seat. 'George and Walter?' She had known the two men even before she had come under Robert's wing and they had always treated her like a favourite grand-daughter, as had their wives. The first summer she had come to live with Robert and Sandra, when she'd been bitterly grieving for her parents, Walter and his wife had taken her away to France for two weeks to try and take her mind off her parents' untimely death and they had been utterly wonderful to her. 'You can't! You can't get rid of them.'

'Excuse me?' The steel-grey eyes had narrowed into slits of light and he was frowning.

'They're like family,' Georgie said passionately.

'Family's fine,' Matt said coolly. 'Inefficient employees are something else. Walter Jenson is well past retiring age and George Mains turned sixty-five a year ago.'

'They are excellent bricklayers!' Her green eyes were flashing sparks now.

'They are too slow,' he said dismissively, 'and this is not a charitable concern for geriatrics. Your brother must have lost thousands over the last few years by carrying men like Mains and Jenson. I've no doubt of their experience or the quality of their work, but Jenson was off sick more than he was at work over the last twelve months—severe arthritis, isn't it?' he asked in a brief aside to Robert, who nodded unhappily. 'And Mains's unfortunate stroke last year has slowed him up to the point where I believe he actually represents something of a danger to himself and others, especially when working on scaffolding. If you drop something from any sort of height you could kill or maim anyone beneath.'

'I don't believe this!' She glared at him angrily. 'They are craftsmen, the pair of them.'

'They are old craftsmen and it's time to let some young blood take over,' Matt said ruthlessly, 'however much it hurts.'

'And of course it really hurts you, doesn't it?' Georgie bit out furiously, ignoring Robert's frantic hand-signals as she jerked to her feet. 'Two dear ol—' She caught herself as the grey gaze sharpened. 'Two dear men who have been the rocks on which this business was built just thrown on to the scrap heap. What reward is that for all their faithfulness to Robert and this family? But faithfulness means nothing to men like you, does it? You've made your millions, you're sitting pretty, but you're still greedy for more and if more means men like Walter and George get sacrificed along the way then so be it.'

'Have you quite finished?' He was still sitting in the relaxed manner of earlier but the grey gaze was lethal and pointed straight at Georgie's flushed face. 'Then sit down, Miss Millett.'

'I don't think—'

'*Sit down!*'

The bark made her jump and in spite of herself Georgie felt her legs obey him.

'Firstly, your brother has made it clear just what he owes these two employees and they will be retired with a very generous package,' Matt ground out coldly. 'I think, as does Robert if he speaks the truth, that this will not come as a surprise to them; neither will it be wholly displeasing. Secondly, you talk of sacrifice when you are prepared to jeopardise the rest of your brother's employees' livelihoods for the sake of two elderly men who should have retired years ago?

'It is human nature for the rest of the men to tailor their speed to the slowest worker when there is a set wage at the end of each week. Your brother's workers have been underachieving for years and a week ago they were in danger of reaping their reward, every one of them. If Robert had gone bankrupt everyone would have been a loser. There is no place for weakness in industry; you should know that.'

'And kindness?' She continued to glare at him even though a tiny part of her brain was pressing her to recognise there was more than an element of truth in what he had said. 'What about kindness and gratitude? How do you think they'll feel at being told they're too old?'

'They know the dates on their birth certificates as well

as anyone,' he said icily, 'so I doubt it will come as the surprise you seem to foresee.'

He folded his arms over his chest, settling more comfortably in his seat as he studied her stiff body and tense face through narrowed eyes.

Georgie didn't respond immediately, more because she was biting back further hot words as the full portent of what she had yelled at him registered than because she was intimidated by his coldness. And then she said, her voice shaking slightly, 'I think what you are demanding Robert do is awful.'

'Then don't think.' He sat forward in his seat, draining his mug with one swallow and turning to Robert as he said, 'I'd suggest you take this opportunity to change the men over to piece work. With a set goal each week and good bonuses for extra achievement you'll soon sort out the wheat from the chaff, and you've limped on long enough.'

Georgie looked at her brother, willing him to stand up to this tyrant, but Robert merely nodded thoughtfully. 'I'd been thinking along the same lines myself,' he agreed quietly.

'Good, that's settled, then,' Matt said imperturbably. 'Now, if you'd like to get Georgie to note those few points that need checking on site we'll be on our way. Have you got any other shoes than those?' he added, looking at her wafer-thin high heels which she had never worn to the office before but which went perfectly with the charcoal skirt she was wearing. They also showed her legs—which Georgie considered her best feature, hating her small bust and too-slender hips—off to their best advantage, but she'd tried to excuse that thought all morning.

Georgie was still mentally reeling from the confrontation of the last few minutes, and a full ten seconds went by before she could say, her voice suitably cutting, 'I wasn't aware I was expected to go on site this morning, if you remember, so, no, I haven't any other shoes with me.'

'There's your wellies in the back of my car,' Robert put in helpfully. 'You remember we put all our boots in there when we took the kids down to the river for that walk at the weekend?'

Her brother probably had no idea why she glared at him the way she did, Georgie reflected, as she said, 'Thank you, Robert,' in a very flat voice. She was going to look just great, wasn't she? Expensive silk jade-green blouse, elegant skirt and great hefty black wellington boots. Wonderful. And that...that *swine* sitting there so complacently with his hateful grey eyes looking her up and down was to blame for this, and he was enjoying every minute of her discomfiture. She didn't have to look at him to know that; it was radiating out from the lean male figure in waves.

As it happened, by the time Georgie jumped out of Robert's old car at the site of the proposed new estate she wasn't thinking about her appearance.

Newbottle Meadow, as the site had always been called by all the children thereabouts, was old farmland and still surrounded by grazing cattle in the far distance. When Georgie had first come to live with her brother and his wife the area had been virtually country, but the swiftly encroaching urban advance had swallowed hundreds of acres and now Newbottle Meadow was on the edge of the town. But as yet it was still unspoilt and beautiful.

Georgie stood gazing at the rolling meadowland filled with pink-topped grasses and buttercups and butterflies and she wanted to cry. According to Robert, Matt de Capistrano had had the foresight to buy the land a decade ago when it had still officially been farmland. After several appeals he had managed to persuade the powers-that-be to grant his application for housing—as he had known would happen eventually—thereby guaranteeing a thousandfold profit as relatively inexpensive agricultural land became prime development ground. And then with the yuppie-style estate he was proposing to build...

Philistine! Georgie gulped in the mild May sunshine which turned the buttercups to luminescent gold and the grasses to pink feathers, and forced back the tears pricking the backs of her eyes. Badgers lived here, along with rabbits and foxes and butterflies galore. She and her friends had spent many happy hours marching out of the town to the meadow where they had camped for days on end and had a whale of a time. And now it was all going to be ripped up—mutilated—for filthy lucre. But it would be the saving of Robert's firm and ultimately her brother himself. The blow of losing his business as well as his wife would have been horrific.

Georgie bit hard on her lip as she turned to see Matt de Capistrano's red Lamborghini—obviously the Mercedes and the chauffeur were having a day off!—glide to a silky-smooth stop a few yards away. She had to think of Robert and the children in all of this, she told herself fiercely. Her ideals, the unspoilt meadow and all the wildlife, weren't as important as David and Annie and Robert.

'You could turn milk sour with that face.'

'What?' She was so startled by the softly drawled insult as Matt reached her side that she literally gaped at him.

'Forget Mains and Jenson; the decision has been made,' Matt said quietly, his eyes roaming to Robert, who had joined the other men waiting for them in the middle of the acres of meadowland.

'I wasn't thinking about George and Walter,' she returned without thinking.

'No?' He eyed her disbelievingly.

'No.''

''Then what?' he asked softly, turning to look into her heart-shaped face. 'Why the ferocious glare and wishing me six foot under?'

'I wasn't—' She stopped abruptly in the middle of the denial. Maybe she had been at that. But he would never understand in a million years, besides which she would be cutting off her nose—or Robert's nose—to spite her face if she did or said anything to stop Robert securing this contract. Matt de Capistrano would simply use another builder and the estate would become reality anyway. 'It doesn't matter,' she finished weakly.

'Georgie.' Before she could object he had turned her round, his hand lifting her chin as he looked down into the green of her eyes. 'Tell me. I'm a big boy. I can take it.'

It was the mockery that did it. He was laughing at her again and Georgie stiffened, her eyes slanting green fire as she fairly spat, 'You're going to spoil this beautiful land, desecrate it, and you just don't care, do you? You've got no soul.'

For a moment he just stared at her in amazement, and she observed—with a shred of satisfaction in all the pain and embarrassment—that she had managed to shock him. 'What?' he growled quietly.

'I used to play here as a child, camp out with my friends and have fun,' she said tightly. 'And this land is still one of the few places hereabouts which is truly wild and beautiful. People come here to *breathe*, don't you see? And you are going to destroy it, along with all the wildlife and the beauty—'

'People have been allowed to come here because I didn't stop them,' he said impatiently. 'I could have fenced it off but I didn't.'

'Because it was too much trouble,' she shot back quickly.

'For crying out loud!' He stared at her with very real incredulity. 'Is there no end to my crimes where you are concerned? Don't you want Robert to build this estate?'

'Of course I do.' She stared at him angrily. 'And I don't. Of course I don't! How could I when I look at all this and think that in a few months it will be covered with bulldozers and dirt and pretty little houses for people who think the latest designer label and a Mercedes are all that matters in life? But I don't want Robert to lose his chance of making good; I love him and he's worked so hard and been through so much. So of course I want him to have the contract.'

He shut his eyes for a moment in a way that said far more than any words could have done, and she resented him furiously for the unspoken criticism and the guilt it engendered. She was being ridiculous, illogical and totally unreasonable, but she couldn't help it. She just couldn't help it. This meadowland had healed something deep inside her in the terrible aftermath of her parents' death. The peace, the tranquillity, the overriding *continuing* of life here had meant so much. And now it was all going to be swept away.

It had welcomed her after the Glen episode in her life too, reaching out to her with comforting fingers as she had walked the childhood paths and let her fingers brush through grasses and wild flowers that had had an endless consistency about them in a world that had suddenly been turned upside down.

'I'm sorry.' Suddenly all the anger had seeped away and she felt she had shrunk down to a child again. 'This isn't your fault, not altogether.'

He said something in Spanish that she was sure was uncomplimentary, then said in English, 'Thank you, Georgie.

That makes me feel a whole lot better,' in tones of deep and biting sarcasm.

'You won't take the contract from Robert because you are angry with me?' she asked anxiously.

His mouth tightened still more and now the hand under her chin became a vice as he looked down into the emerald orbs staring up at him. 'I think I like it better when you are aware you are insulting me,' he said very softly.

Under the thin silk shirt she could see a dark shadow and guessed his chest was covered with body hair. He would probably be hairy all over. Somehow it went with the intoxicating male perfume of him, the overall *alienness* of Matt de Capistrano that was threatening and exciting at the same time. And she didn't want to be threatened or excited. She just wanted... What? She didn't know what she wanted any more.

'Georgie?'

She heard Robert calling through the buzzing in her ears as the warm hand under her chin held her for a second more, his gaze stroking over her bewildered face. And then he let her go, stepping away from her as he called in an unforgivably controlled voice, 'We are just coming, Robert. Georgie has been reminiscing about her childhood up here. It must have been fun.'

Philistine!

CHAPTER THREE

GEORGIE felt it wise to keep a very low profile during the rest of the morning, quietly taking notes on all that was said as she plodded after the men in her flapping wellington boots. She made sure she had no eye contact at all with Matt, even when he spoke directly to her as she found herself walking with him to the parked cars. 'Thank you, Georgie, that's your job here done for today,' he said easily. 'We are going to grab a spot of lunch before we finish off this afternoon. Would you care to join us?'

'I don't think so.' She looked somewhere in the middle of his tanned throat as she said quietly, 'I've things to do back at the office.' The last thing, the very last thing in all the world she wanted to do was to sit in a social atmosphere and make small talk with Matt de Capistrano.

'But surely you will have to eat?' he persisted softly.

'I've brought sandwiches which I'll eat at my desk.'

'How industrious of you.'

Sarcastic swine! 'Not really,' she answered tightly. 'I want to telephone a few places and set up the arrangements for Robert's children's birthday party. It's been pretty busy over the last few weeks and it's only just dawned on us they'll be eight in two weeks' time. We want to make their birthday as special as we can for them.'

He nodded as she forced herself to meet the grey eyes at last. 'What are you planning?' he asked, as though he were really interested.

Which she was sure he wasn't, Georgie thought cynically. Why would a multi-millionaire like Matt de

Capistrano care about two eight-year-olds' birthday party? 'A hall somewhere with a bouncy castle and so on,' she answered dismissively.

'Ah, yes, the bouncy castle.' He looked down at her, his piercing eyes glittering pewter in the sunshine. 'My nephews and nieces enjoy these things too.'

He was an uncle? Ridiculously she was absolutely amazed. Somehow she couldn't picture him as anything other than a cold business tycoon, but of course he would have a family. Robert had mentioned in passing some days ago that Matt de Capistrano was not married, but that didn't stop him being a son or a brother. She brought her racing thoughts under control and said quietly, 'Children are the same everywhere.'

'So it would seem.' He looked at her for a second more before turning to glance at Robert in the distance, who was still deep in conversation with the chief architect. 'I will take you back to the office while the others finish off here and meet them at the pub,' he said expressionlessly.

'No.' It was too quick and too instinctive and they both recognised it. Georgie felt her cheeks begin to burn and said feverishly, 'I mean, I wouldn't want to put you to any trouble and Robert won't mind. Or, better still, I could take his car and he can go with you—'

'It is no trouble, Georgie.' The words themselves were nothing; the manner in which they were said told her all too clearly she had annoyed him again and he was now determined to have his own way. As usual.

Could she refuse to ride with him? Georgie's eyes flickered to Robert's animated face and her brother's excitement was the answer. No, she couldn't. 'If you're sure you don't mind,' she said weakly, striving to act as if this was a perfectly normal conversation instead of one as potentially explosive as a loaded gun.

'Not at all.' He bent close enough for her to scent his male warmth as he said softly but perfectly seriously, 'The pleasure will be all mine.' And he allowed just a long enough pause before he added, 'As we both know.'

This time Georgie couldn't think of a single thing to say, and so she stood meekly at his side as he called to Robert and informed him he would see them all at the White Knight after he had taken Georgie back to the office. Her eyes moved to the red Lamborghini crouching at the side of the road. She had never ridden in a Lamborghini before; in fact she hadn't seen one this close up before either. Perhaps at a different time with a different driver the experience would be one to be savoured, but the car was too like its master to be anything else but acutely disturbing.

It was even more overwhelming when she found herself in the passenger seat and Matt shut the door gently behind her. She felt as though she was cocooned in leather and metal—which she supposed she was—and the car was so low she felt she was sitting on a level with the ground. However, those sensations were nothing to the ones which seized her senses once Matt slid in beside her.

The riot in her stomach was flushing her face, she just knew it was, but she couldn't do a thing about it, and when Matt turned to her and said quietly, but with a throb of amusement in his voice, 'Would you like to take those off?' as he nodded at her boots which were almost reaching her chin she stiffened tensely. How like him to point out she looked ridiculous, she told herself silently. He couldn't have made it more clear he found her totally unattractive. But that was fine; in fact it was great. *Really* great. Because that was exactly how she viewed him.

'No.' She forced herself to glance haughtily his way and then wished with all her heart she hadn't. He was much, much too close.

'I can come round and slip them off for you if it's difficult with that tight skirt?' he offered helpfully.

Georgie felt more trapped than ever. 'No, I'm fine,' she said tightly, staring resolutely out of the windscreen.

'Georgie, it is the middle of the day and I am giving you a lift back to the office,' he said evenly. 'Can't you let yourself relax in my company for just a minute or two? I promise you I have no intention of diverting to a deserted lane somewhere and having my wicked way with you, even if you do view me as a cross between the Marquis de Sade and Adolf Hitler.'

Shocked into looking at him again, she said quickly, 'I didn't think you were and of course I don't think you're like either of those two men!'

'No?' It reeked of disbelief.

'No.' This was awful, terrible. She should never have got into this car.

He raised his eyebrows at her but then to her intense relief he turned, starting the engine, which purred into life with instant obedience.

She turned back to the windscreen, but not before she had noticed the lingering amusement curling the hard mouth. He was obviously enjoying her discomfiture and, more to show him she was completely in control of herself than anything else, Georgie said primly, 'This is a very nice car.'

'Nice?' He reacted as though she had said something unforgivable. 'Georgie, family saloons are *nice*, along with sweet old maiden aunts and visits to the zoo and a whole host of other unremarkable things in this world of ours. A Lamborghini—' he paused just long enough to make his point '—is not in that category.'

She'd annoyed him. Good. It felt great to have got under that inch-thick skin. 'Well, that's how I see it,' she said sweetly. 'A car is just a car, after all, a lump of metal to get you quickly from A to B. A functional necessity.'

'I'm not even going to reply to that.'

She saw him glance down at the leather steering wheel and the beautiful dashboard as though to reassure himself that his pride and joy was still as fabulous as he thought it was, and she repressed a smile. Okay, she was probably being mean but, as he'd said earlier, he was a big boy; he could take it. 'I'm sorry if I've offended you,' she lied quietly.

'Sure you are.' The husky, smoky voice caught at her nerve-ends and she allowed herself another brief peek at the hard profile. He had rolled the sleeves of his shirt up at some point during the morning and his muscled arms, liberally covered with a dusting of black silky hair, swam into view. His shirt collar was open and several buttons undone and his shoulders were very broad. His body had an aggressive, top-heavy maleness that was impossible for any female to ignore.

The incredible car, the man driving it so effortlessly, the bright May sunshine slanting through the trees lining the road down which they were travelling—it was all the stuff dreams were made of, Georgie thought to herself a touch hysterically. He was altogether larger than life, Matt de Capistrano, and he was totally unaware of it.

'Are both the Mercedes and this car yours?' she asked carefully after a full minute had crept by in a screaming silence that had become more uncomfortable second by second.

'Would that be a further nail in my coffin?'

The very English phrase, spoken in the dark accented voice and without a glance at her, caused Georgie to stiffen slightly. 'I don't know what you mean,' she said flatly.

'I think you do,' he returned just as flatly.

'Now, look—' Whatever she had been about to say ended in a squeak as he pulled the car into the side of the road and cut the engine. 'What are you doing?' she asked nervously.

'I want to look at you while I talk to you,' he said softly, 'that is all, so do not panic, little English mouse.'

'Mouse?' He couldn't have said anything worse, and then, as she jerked to face him and saw the smile twisting the firm lips, she knew he was teasing her.

And then the smile faded as he said, 'I think we need to get a few things out into the open, Georgie.'

'Do we?' She didn't think so. She *really* didn't think so. And certainly not here, in this sumptuous car with him about an inch away and with nowhere to run to. She should never have antagonised him, she acknowledged much too late.

'You look on me as the enemy and this is not the case at all,' Matt said softly. 'If your brother fails, I fail. If he makes good, it's good news for me too.'

The hostility which had flared into life the minute she had set eyes on him, and which showed no signs of abating, was nothing to do with Robert and all to do with her, Georgie thought as she stared into the metallic grey eyes narrowed against the sunlight. But she could hardly say that, could she? So instead she managed fairly calmly, 'I think that's stretching credulity a little far. This business is everything Robert has; your interest here is just a tiny drop in the vast ocean of your business empire. It would hardly dent your coffers if this whole project went belly up.'

'I have never had a business venture go "belly up", as you so charmingly put it, and I do not intend for your brother's to be the first,' Matt returned smoothly. 'Besides which…'

He paused, and Georgie said, 'Yes?'

'Besides which, you underestimate his assets,' Matt said quietly.

'I can assure you I do not,' Georgie objected. 'Robert has no secrets from me and—'

'I wasn't talking about financial assets, Georgie.'

'Then what?' She stared at him, her clear sea-green eyes reflecting her bewilderment.

He had stretched one arm along the back of her seat as he turned to face her after switching off the engine, and she was so aware of every little inch of him that she was as tense as piano wire. It wasn't that she expected him to jump on her—Robert had told her it was common knowledge Matt de Capistrano had women, beautiful, gorgeous women, chasing after him all the time and that he could afford to pick and choose—more that she didn't trust herself around him. She seemed destined to meet him head-on and usually ended up making a fool of herself in the process. He was such an *unsettling* individual.

'What do you mean?' she repeated after a moment or two when he continued to look at her, his eyes with their strange dark-silver hue holding her own until everything else around them was lost in the intensity of his gaze.

'He has you.' It was soft and silky, and Georgie floundered.

'Me?' She tried for a laugh to lighten what had become a painfully protracted conversation but it turned into more of a squeak.

'Yes, you.' He wasn't touching her, in fact he hadn't moved a muscle, but suddenly he had taken her into an intimacy that was absorbing and Georgie found herself thinking, If he can make me feel like this, here, in the middle of the day and without any desire on his part, what on earth is he like with those women he does desire? No wonder they flock round him. As a lover he must be pure dynamite.

And that shocked her into saying, 'Sometimes I'm more of a liability than an asset, as you well know,' her voice over-bright.

'I know nothing of the sort. How can honesty and idealism be viewed in that way?' he returned quietly.

She wished he would stop looking at her. She wished he would start the car again. She wished she had never agreed to have this lift with him in the first place! 'You don't agree with me about Newbottle Meadow for a start.' She forced an aggressiveness she didn't really feel as an instinctive protection against her body's response to his closeness.

'I don't have to agree with you to admire certain qualities inherent in your make-up,' he returned softly.

'No, I suppose not,' she agreed faintly, deciding if she went along with him he would be satisfied he had made his point—whatever that was—and they could be on their way again.

He gave her a hard look. 'Don't patronise me, Georgie.'

'Patronise you?' She bristled instantly. 'I wouldn't dream of patronising you!'

The frown beetling his eyebrows faded into a quizzical ruffle. 'But you enjoy challenging me, don't you?' he murmured in a softly provoking voice that stiffened Georgie's back. 'Do you know why you like doing that?' he added in a tone that stated quite clearly he knew exactly what motivated her.

Because you are an egotistical, unfeeling, condescending—

He interrupted her thoughts, his voice silky smooth. 'Because you are sexually attracted to me and you're fighting it in a manner as old as time,' he stated with unforgivable coolness.

For a moment she couldn't believe he had actually said what she thought he had said, and then she shut her mouth, which had fallen open, before opening it again to snap, 'It might be hard for you to accept, Mr de Capistrano, but not every female you look at feels the need to swoon at your feet!' as she glared at him hotly.

'I can accept that perfectly well,' he returned easily, 'but I'm talking about you, not anyone else.' His expression was totally impassive, which made their conversation even more incredible in Georgie's eyes. The colossal *ego* of the man, she thought wildly. 'And I know I'm right because I feel the same way; I want you more than I've wanted a woman in a long time. For however long it lasted it would be good between us.'

Georgie fumbled with the door handle. 'I'm not listening to this rubbish a second longer,' she ground out through clenched teeth, more to stop her voice shaking than anything else.

'You are going to look slightly…unusual walking through town with your present attire, are you not?' Matt asked evenly as he glanced at the acres of rubber adorning her feet. 'And there is no need to be embarrassed, Georgie. You want me, I want you—it is the most natural thing in the world. There's even a rumour it's what makes it go round. It doesn't have to be complicated.'

The amusement in the dark face was the last straw. She turned on him like a small green-eyed cat, her eyes spitting sparks as she shouted, 'You are actually daring to proposition me? In cold blood?'

'Oh, is that what the matter is?' His expression was hard to read now but she thought it was cynicism twisting the ruthless mouth. 'You wanted a bouquet of red roses and promises of undying love and for everness? Sorry, but I don't believe in either.'

'I didn't want anything!'

'Then why are you so upset?' he asked reasonably. 'You could just tell me I've got it wrong without the melodrama, surely? It's not the most dreadful thing in the world to be told you are desirable by a member of the opposite sex.'

Desirable. Matt de Capistrano thought she was desirable and, if she hadn't got all this horribly wrong, he had been suggesting they have an affair. Georgie felt a churning in her stomach that wasn't all fury, and it was only in that moment she acknowledged Matt knew her better than she knew herself. But she would die before she let him know that, she added with deadly resolve.

'There are ways and ways of being told something,' she said tightly, hearing the prim-sounding words with something of a mental wince.

'I thought you appreciated honesty.'

'I do!' She glared at him, furiously angry that he was trying to make her feel bad about objecting to his stark proposal.

'Let's just test that statement, shall we?' he suggested silkily, and before she could object she found herself in his arms. The kiss was as devastating as ever she had imagined—and she *had* imagined what it would be like to be held in his arms like this, she admitted silently. It was sweet and knowing and erotic, and the feel of him, the intoxicating exhilaration which was inflaming her senses and making her head spin, was irresistible.

Matt was breathing hard, his muscled body rigid as he held her to him in the narrow confines of the car, and the gentle eroticism was a conscious assault on her senses. Georgie knew that. But somehow—and this was even more frightening than the sensations his lovemaking was calling forth—somehow she couldn't find the strength to resist him.

If he had used his superior strength and tried to force her, even slightly, she might have objected. But he was a brilliant strategist. Even that thought was without power compared to the tumultuous emotions flooding her from the top of her head to the soles of her feet.

He was holding her lightly but firmly, one hand tilting her chin to give his mouth greater access to hers, and slowly but subtly his mouth and tongue were growing more insistent. She didn't want to kiss him back and she knew she mustn't, but somehow that was exactly what she was doing. Which didn't make any sense, her struggling thoughts told her feverishly. But then what did sense have to do with Matt de Capistrano?

Everything! Now her mind was screaming the warning. Everything, and she forgot it at her peril. A man like him wouldn't be interested in a girl like her for more than two minutes. She had sparked his attention because she had stood up to him—insulted him, actually—and that was all. It would be a fleeting episode in the life of a very busy man; remembered one moment and then forgotten for ever. *But she wouldn't be able to forget it.*

When she jerked away from him he made no effort at all to restrain her, which to Georgie was further proof of the strength of his interest. He saw her as a brief dalliance, she thought wildly. Wham, bam and thank you, ma'am, while this project was on the go and he had to be around now and again, and then he would be off to pastures new without a second thought.

'I don't want to do this,' she said feverishly, straining back against the passenger door as she stared into the dark face and the piercingly grey eyes fixed on her flushed face.

He said nothing for a moment, his expression unreadable, and then he settled back in his own seat and started the engine again, drawing out on to the road before he said quietly, 'Yes, you do, but you are frightened of the consequences. You needn't be. It would simply be a case of two relative strangers getting to know each other a little better with no strings attached and no heavy commitment.'

Oh, yes, and pigs might fly. However nicely he put it, he wanted her in his bed, and whilst he might be able to engage in sex with 'no strings attached' she could not. She simply wasn't made that way. She breathed in deeply and then out again, calling on her considerable will-power to enable her voice to be calm and steady. 'I don't want to get to know anyone right at the moment, Matt,' she said firmly. 'I have more than enough on my plate with Robert and the children. I neither want nor could cope with anything else.'

'Rubbish.' It was brisk and irritatingly self-assured, and had the effect on Georgie of making her want to lean across and bop him on his arrogant nose.

'It's not rubbish,' she said tightly. 'And we don't even *like* each other, for goodness' sake!' She glanced at him as she spoke, and saw the black brows rise. 'Well, we don't,' she reiterated strongly.

'I like you, Georgie,' he said very evenly.

Okay, plain speaking time! 'You want me in your bed,' she corrected bravely. She heard him draw a quick breath, and added hurriedly, 'And that is something quite different.'

'I can assure you I would not take a woman into my bed whom I did not like,' Matt said calmly. 'All right?'

She wasn't going to win this one. Georgie forced herself not to argue with him and said instead, 'There is no question of my having a relationship with you, Matt, however free-floating.'

They had drawn well into the suburbs now, and as the Lamborghini purred down a main residential street an elegant young woman, complete with obligatory designer shopping bags, stepped straight in front of the car. Matt swore loudly as he braked violently, coming to a halt a foot or so away from the voluptuous redhead, whereupon he wound down the window and asked her, in no uncertain terms, what exactly she was playing at.

Georgie watched as the beautifully made-up face turned his way and a pair of slanted blue eyes surveyed first the car, and then Matt, and she wasn't surprised at the gushing apology which followed, or the suggestion that if there was anything, *anything* she could do to make amends for giving him such a fright he must say.

To be fair Matt didn't appear to notice either the redhead's beauty or her eagerness to make atonement, but no doubt if he had been alone in the car that would have been a different matter, Georgie told herself as they drove on. And this sort of thing would happen a hundred times over, in various forms, to someone like Matt de Capistrano. There would always be a redhead somewhere—or a blonde or brunette—who would let him know they were ready and available.

He was a wealthy, powerful and good-looking man, and the first two attributes made the third literally irresistible to some women. Not that it was just women who were drawn to members of the opposite sex who could guarantee them a life of wealth and ease… Her soft mouth tightened at the thought.

And Matt was a sensual man, dynamic and definitely dangerous. He was as much out of her league as the man in the moon.

'You haven't said a word in five minutes.' The deep cool voice at the side of her made her jump. 'I'll have to kiss you more often if it turns you into a sweet, submissive-type female.'

'I said all there was to say,' she bit back immediately, bristling instantly at the covert suggestion his lovemaking had rendered her weak and fluttery.

'You didn't say anything.' They had just reached the set of traffic lights before they turned into the street in which Robert's premises were situated, and as the lights glowed red Matt brought the car to a halt and glanced at her, his eyes narrowed and disturbingly perceptive. 'Someone has hurt you, haven't they, Georgie?'

She blinked just once, but other than that slight reaction she forced herself to remain absolutely still and keep her expression as deadpan as she could. Nevertheless it was some seconds before she trusted herself to say, with a suitably mocking note in her voice, 'You assume I've been hurt because I don't want to jump into bed with you? Now who's being melodramatic?'

And then the lights changed and the lasers drilling into her brain returned to the windscreen as he drove on. She wanted to sink back in the seat but she kept herself straight, willing herself to think about nothing but exiting from the car in as dignified a manner as possible.

Her lips were still tingling from his kiss, and now she was berating herself for not responding more vigorously to his audacity in thinking he could come on to her like that. She should have made it clear that she considered his effrontery impertinent at the very least, she told herself silently, not entered into a discussion on the pros and cons of having an affair with him! She'd handled this all wrong. But ever since she had got into this sex machine on wheels she had felt intensely vulnerable and more aware of Matt than ever.

They drew up outside Robert's small brick building after Matt had negotiated the Lamborghini carefully into the untidy yard, strewn with all manner of building materials, and before she could move he had opened his door and was walking round the sleek bonnet to hers.

'Thank you.' Emerging gracefully from a Lamborghini clad in the original seven-league boots was not an option, and Georgie was pink-cheeked by the time she was standing. 'I'll type those notes ready for you to collect later,' she said stiffly.

'I've no intention of giving up, Georgie.'

'I beg your pardon?'

He looked down at her from his vantage point of six foot plus, his eyes wandering over her small heart-shaped face and corn-coloured hair, and he brushed one silky strand from her cheek as he said, 'I want you...very much.'

'That...that doesn't mean anything. There must be a hundred and one women out there who are more than willing to jump into bed with you,' she said quickly through the sudden tightness in her chest.

'You've got some sort of fixation about me and bed, haven't you?' It was thoughtful. 'I wonder what Freud would make of that?'

'Now, look, Matt—'

'But I don't mind,' he said kindly. 'You can fantasise about it all you want, but I can assure you when it happens it will be outside all your wildest imaginings.'

'I've told you, it is *not* going to happen!'

She was talking to the air. He had already disappeared round the bonnet of the car and slid into the driver's seat, letting the growling engine have its head as he roared out of the yard with scant regard for other road users.

Georgie stood for some minutes as the dust slowly settled in the golden sunshine and the mild May breeze ruffled her hair with gentle fingers. He frightened her. The thought was there before she could reject it but immediately she rebelled. He didn't. Of course he didn't! Maybe her own reactions to him frightened her, but that was different. She could control them. *She could.* And she would. This time the affirmation in her head was even stronger. Oh, yes, she would all right. She'd had enough of love and romance to last her a lifetime. Once Robert and the children were over the worst, perhaps in a few months, she would put all her energy into the career she had begun on leaving university two years ago, and she would work until she reached every goal she set herself. Autonomous. That was how she wanted to be.

She turned sharply, entering the office and kicking off the boots as though they were the source of all her present troubles. She had the notes to type up and the children's party venue to arrange; she had to get working immediately. The thought was there but still she stood staring out of the window, the incident with Matt evoking a whole host of memories she normally kept under lock and key.

Glen Williams. If she closed her eyes she could picture him easily: tall lean frame, a shock of light brown hair that always fell over his brow in a lopsided quiff, bright blue eyes and a determined square chin. His parents had lived next door to Robert and Sandra and she had met Glen, who was two years older than her, on the first day she had come to live with them, along with his two sisters, one of whom was her age and the other a year younger.

She had immediately become great friends with the two girls, which had been just what she needed at the time, being heartsore and tearful at the loss of her parents, and for the first few years Glen had treated her in the same way he had his kid sisters—teasingly and with some disdain. And then, on her fourteenth birthday, something had changed.

She had dressed up for her birthday disco and had had her waist-length hair cut into a short sleek bob earlier in the day, and from the moment Glen had walked in with a bunch of his pals he had monopolised her. Not that she had minded—she had been consumed with a schoolgirl crush on him for ages. And from that evening they had been inseparable and very much an official 'item' in their group of friends.

Glen had not been academic but had always had a passion for motor cars. After failing every one of his A levels, he had used his considerable charm and got taken on at a local car supermarket-type garage in the town as a trainee mechanic.

That same year she had achieved mostly As in her GCSEs, and had gone on to attain two As and a B in her A levels two years later. During those years they had spent every spare moment they could together and had had some wonderful times, even though they hadn't had two pennies to rub together.

Georgie continued to stare out of the window but now she was blind and deaf to anything but the memories swamping her consciousness.

Glen had been so encouraging when she had tentatively discussed embarking on an Art and Design degree. She would come home weekends—he'd come and fetch her himself—and with him doing so well at the garage and Georgie sure to qualify well and get a great job, they'd be set up for the future. Nice house with a garden, holidays abroad and later the requisite two point four children. They'd got it all worked out—or so she had thought.

And so she had happily trotted off to university with Glen's ring on the third finger of her left hand—he had proposed the night before she had left—and for the first little while everything had seemed fine. He had arrived to collect her each weekend and they had planned a small register office wedding—all they could afford—at

Christmas. She would be nearly nineteen then and Glen had just had his twenty-first birthday. His parents had offered to convert Glen's big double bedroom into a little bedsit by adding a two-seater sofa, small fridge and microwave to the three-quarter-size bed, TV and video and wardrobe the room already contained, as their wedding present, and Robert and Sandra's gift had been a proposed two-week holiday in the sun. They would be together every weekend in their snug little nest and once she had finished her degree and got a job they would think about looking for a house. Life had been cut and dried.

It had been round about the end of November she'd really noticed the change in him. The last couple of weekends she had felt he was distant, cool even, but he had just been promoted at work and she had put his remoteness down to the added responsibility and pressure. The problem had been work all right—but the owner's daughter, not Glen's new position.

Harold Bloomsbury owned a string of garages across London and the south east and his only daughter was the original pampered darling. Julia had made up her mind she wanted Glen—Georgie had later found out she had been flirting with him for ages on and off, but when Glen had got engaged Julia's pursuit had become serious—and although she was plump and plain the Bloomsburys' lifestyle was anything but Spartan. Magnificent townhouse and a villa in Tuscany and another in Barbados, along with a yacht and fast cars and all the trimmings of wealth—Julia's husband would be guaranteed a life of comfort and ease by daddy-in-law.

Glen had weighed all that on the one side and love in a tiny bedsit in his parents' house on the other, and three weeks before they were due to get married had told her the wedding was off. He hadn't said a word about Julia;

Georgie had found out about the other girl through a friend of a friend a few days later. They were too young to settle down, he had lied, and he'd felt it was being terribly unfair to her to get married whilst she was doing her degree. They had lived in each other's pockets for five years—perhaps it was time for a break to see how they both felt? Maybe at Easter they could meet and review the situation and go from there?

She had been stunned and bewildered, Georgie remembered now as she turned abruptly from the window and gazed at her desk piled high with paperwork. She had cried and—this made her stomach curl in recollection—had begged Glen to reconsider. He'd been her life for years; she hadn't been able to imagine a world in which he didn't have pre-eminence.

For a week she had been sunk in misery and unable to eat or sleep, and then she'd found out about Bloomsbury's daughter and her ex-fiancé and strangely from that moment she had begun to claw back her sanity and self-esteem. Hating him had helped, along with the bitter contempt she'd felt for a man who could be bought. The one small comfort she'd had was that she hadn't slept with Glen, however tempted she'd felt when their petting had got heated. She'd had a romantic vision of their wedding night being special. Special! Her lip curled as she sat down. But at least it had saved her from making the mistake of giving her virginity to that undeserving rat.

He'd married Julia the following May, and it had been a relief when, six months later, Glen's parents had moved to a small bungalow on the coast, their daughters now living in the centre of London in a student flat. Glen's parents hadn't liked Julia and had frequently reported she was making their son's life a misery, but Georgie hadn't wanted to know. The Glen chapter of her life was a closed book. But

it had left deep scars, how deep she hadn't fully acknowledged until she had come face to face with Matt de
Capistrano.

He was fabulously wealthy and arrogant and ruthless—
just like Julia Bloomsbury. He thought he only had to want
something for it to happen, that everything—people, values,
morals—could be bent to his will just because he could
buy and sell the average Mr Joe Bloggs a hundred times
over. Well, he was in for a surprise. Her green eyes flashed
like glittering emeralds and the last lingering sensation induced by his kiss was burnt away.

People like Julia Bloomsbury and Matt had no conscience, no soul; they rode roughshod over people and
didn't even notice they were trampling them into the
ground. Money was their god, it bought them what they
wanted and that was all that mattered. And the meadow,
Newbottle Meadow, was a perfect example of that. She
hated him. Her chin rose and her shoulders straightened as
a little inner voice asked nastily why she was so adamant
about convincing herself of the fact.

'I do, I hate him.' She said it out loud, opening the
drawer of her desk and fishing out her wilting sandwiches
as she did so. 'And the sooner he accepts that the better
it'll be for both of us.'

And then she grimaced at the foolishness of talking to
herself, bit into her chicken and mayonnaise sandwich and
determined to put all further thoughts of Matt de Capistrano
out of her mind.

CHAPTER FOUR

AFTER eating her lunch Georgie was on the phone for more than an hour searching for a venue for the children's party. She drew a blank at all the community and church halls in the district, and the prices one or two of them wanted to charge were exorbitant anyway for someone in Robert's current position. She then decided Robert would have to allow her to hold the twins' party at home and he could disappear for the afternoon, after he had helped her set up, but trying to hire a bouncy castle for that particular day proved just as fruitless.

Eventually she put all thoughts of the party on hold and decided to type up the notes from the morning before attacking the rest of her workload.

She worked like a beaver all afternoon, clearing a vast mountain of paperwork and dealing with the men's wages when they called in later in the day. There was still no sign of Robert at four o'clock and then at ten past she heard the door open and looked up expectantly. 'Where have you been—?' She stopped abruptly. Instead of Robert's pleasant face Matt de Capistrano was looking at her, his eyes molten as they roved over her creamy skin and golden hair.

She tried to make a casual comment, to look away and busy herself with the papers on her desk, but she could not. She felt transfixed, hypnotised, and as her heart began to pound at the expression on the dark face she told herself to open her mouth, to say *anything*. 'I thought you were Robert,' she managed weakly.

'But as you see I am not,' he returned coolly.

'No…' Oh, what an inane conversation, she told herself angrily. Say something sensible, for goodness' sake! 'Do you know where he is?'

'We had a few hitches on site after lunch, potential drainage and so on, so we've been pretty tied up all afternoon,' Matt said quietly. 'He should be here in a few minutes; he was leaving just after me.'

She nodded in what she hoped was a brisk secretarial fashion. 'Your notes are all ready.' She wrenched her gaze from his and pointed at the large white envelope on one side of the desk. 'I hope I got everything down and—'

'You're incredibly lovely,' he said slowly. 'And without artifice. Most women of my acquaintance put on the war paint before they even get out of bed in the morning.'

And no doubt you speak from experience, she thought tartly. 'Really?' she managed a polite smile. 'Now, regarding the west part of the site, where the architect said—'

'Damn the architect.' He had moved to stand in front of her and now, as her surprised eyes met his, he said softly, 'Have dinner with me tonight?'

Was he mad? She stared at him, her cheeks flushing rosy pink as her eyes fell on to the V below his throat where his shirt buttons were undone to expose a tantalisingly small amount of tanned skin and the beginnings of dark body hair. She snapped her eyes upwards but it was too late; her body was already tingling. As much in answer to her own traitorous response to his maleness she said very stiffly, 'That is quite out of the question, as I thought I made perfectly clear this morning.'

'Would it help if I kissed you again?' he asked contemplatively.

Just you try it! You'll soon know what it feels like to have a word processor on top of your head. She glared at him and her face must have spoken for itself because he nodded thoughtfully. 'Perhaps not,' he acknowledged drily.

He was enjoying this! It was just a game to him, a diversion! 'I have plenty of work to do if you've quite finished,' she snapped angrily.

'Finished? I haven't even started.' And his smile was a crocodile smile.

'Wrong.' Georgie's gaze was sharp. 'I haven't got time to bandy words with you, Matt.'

'Then cut out the necessity and have dinner with me,' he responded immediately.

What did it take to get it into that thick skull of his that she would rather dine with Hannibal Lecter? 'No.' It was final. 'I like to get dinner while I listen to the children tell me about their day and then we all dine together. They need that sort of reassurance in their lives at the moment.'

'And you don't ever have an evening off?'

'No.'

'Then I will pick you up about nine, yes? Once they are in bed,' he drawled silkily, his accent very strong as he stared down at her, his hands thrust into the pockets of his jeans and a shaft of sunlight from the window turning his hair blue-black.

'For the last time, I am not going to have dinner with you!'

It was unfortunate that Robert chose that precise moment to walk into the building. Georgie saw him stop dead, his eyes flashing from her pink face to Matt's coolly undisturbed one, before he said, 'Problems?'

'Not at all,' Matt said easily. 'I asked Georgie to have dinner with me tonight but she informs me she feels the children need her at the moment and she has to stay at home.'

'Georgie, you don't have to do that—'

'I want to, Robert.' She cut off her brother's protest abruptly.

'Well if you're at a loose end tonight why don't you join *us* for dinner?' Robert asked Matt in the next moment, much to Georgie's horror. 'It's not exactly restful, so I warn you before you say yea or nay. The kids are always pretty hyper at the end of the day, but you're welcome.'

'Great, I'd love to.' It was immediate and Matt didn't look at Georgie.

'Good. Problem solved.' Robert smiled happily at them both and for the first time since Sandra's death Georgie felt the urge to kick him. It had happened fairly frequently through her growing up years, but never as strongly as now.

'But…' Matt turned to Georgie as he spoke and she just knew the tentative expression on his face wasn't genuine. 'Will there be enough for an extra mouth at such short notice?'

She would have loved to have said no, because she knew as well as he did that she had been manoeuvred into a corner, but she gritted her teeth for a second and then said brightly, 'If you like pot roast?'

'Love it.'

'Oh, good.'

And then she ducked her head to hide the acid resurgence of bitterness that had gripped her. Manipulating, cunning, Machiavellian, underhand—

'White wine or red?'

'What?'

Robert had walked through into his office but Matt had paused at the interconnecting doorway. 'I said, white wine or red?' he said easily, the gleam of amusement in the grey eyes telling Georgie all too clearly he had known exactly what she was thinking.

'Whatever,' she growled ungratefully.

'Right.' And then he had the audacity to add—purely for Robert's benefit, she was sure, 'It's been a long time since I've enjoyed a family evening round a pot roast; I really appreciate the kindness.'

Add hypocritical and two-faced to the other list, Georgie thought balefully as the door closed and she was alone, her teeth clamped together so hard they were aching.

Matt was only ensconced with Robert for some five minutes before he emerged again, stopping by her desk and picking up the envelope as he said, 'When and how do you want me?'

'What?' The ghastly sexual awareness that took her over whenever she was within six feet of this man made her voice breathless.

'Dinner?' He smiled innocently. 'What time and how do I dress? Formal or informal?'

Impossible man! She kept her voice very prim and proper as she said, 'Half-past six. I don't like the twins to eat too late as their bedtime is eight o'clock. And informal, very. The children might even be in their pyjamas if there's a programme on TV they want to watch after dinner and they've finished any homework they have.'

'Homework?' He wrinkled his aristocratic nose. 'Poor little things. Why are children not allowed to be children these days? There is enough time for the homework and other such restrictions when they are a little older.'

She agreed with him absolutely but she wasn't about to tell him that. 'They have to learn a certain amount of discipline,' she said evenly as her stomach churned at the thought of the forthcoming evening.

'How stern you sound.' His voice made it very clear he didn't rate her as an aunty and it rankled—unbearably. She hadn't been cast in the role of Wicked Witch of the West before. 'Half-past six it is, then. Robert's given me the address.'

Georgie waited until she was sure Matt's Lamborghini had left and then knocked on Robert's door before she popped her head round to say, 'There's a couple of things I need to get for dinner so I'll see you at home later, okay?'

'Georgie?' As she made to withdraw, Robert's voice called her back. 'You didn't mind me inviting him, did you? I didn't think at the time, but you're doing enough looking after me and the kids without me asking along any Tom, Dick or Harry.'

Matt de Capistrano was definitely not your average Tom, Dick or Harry, Georgie thought wryly, but as she looked into her brother's eyes—the lines of strain and grief all too evident on Robert's countenance—she said brightly, 'Of course not; it pays to keep him sweet at the moment, doesn't it? And the kids will like a guest for a change. Just don't make a habit of it, eh?'

'You're a brick, and take the car. I'll get a taxi later.'

A brick she might be, but this particular brick was going to have to vamp up a boring old pot roast into something great, and she only had a couple of hours to do that, clean the house, make the children presentable and a hundred and one other things that were *absolutely* imperative if Matt de Capistrano was going to set foot across the threshold of their home.

After buying two very extravagant desserts, flowers for the table, a packet of wildly expensive coffee and a good bottle of brandy, Georgie drove home at breakneck speed to find the children involved in building a castle of Lego with the middle-aged 'grandmother' from next door who came in to sit with them each day when they got home from school.

Five minutes later—with Mrs Jarvis happily toddling

home after her customary little chat—the house was a scene of feverish activity. Once the sitting room was cleared of every piece of Lego, Georgie organised David vaccing downstairs and Annie dusting, whilst she dressed up the pot roast with cream and wine and quickly prepared more vegetables and a pot of new potatoes to add to the roast potatoes she had peeled that morning.

That done, she marshalled the children upstairs to bath and change into their clean pyjamas, whilst she set the table in the dining room with the best crockery and cutlery and arranged the flowers she had bought earlier.

The children downstairs again, looking demure and sweet as they sat on the sofa in front of their favourite video, Georgie flew upstairs to shower and change after spraying the house with air freshener and lighting scented candles in the dining room.

She heard Robert arrive home as she stepped out of the shower, and shouted for him to check the vegetables before she dived into the bedroom she shared with Annie and pulled on a pair of casually smart trousers and a little fig-ure-hugging top in bubblegum-pink cashmere.

Too dressed up. She looked at herself in the mirror and gave a flustered groan. Definitely. The children would be sure to make some comment and then she would just die.

She whipped off the trousers and replaced them with a pair of old and well-washed jeans. Better. She stood for a moment contemplating her reflection. Yes, that was just the right note and this top *was* gorgeous; she couldn't consign it the same way as the trousers.

Her hair only took a minute or two to dry, courtesy of her hairdryer, falling in a soft silky veil about her face, and apart from her usual touch of mascara on her fair eyelashes she didn't bother with any make-up. She had just fixed her big silver hoops in her ears when she heard the doorbell ring, and her stomach turned right over.

'Calm, girl, calm.' She shut her eyes tightly before opening them and gazing into the mirror. 'This is nothing. You've had guests for dinner in the past, for goodness' sake, and that is all Matt de Capistrano is. Get it into perspective.'

The faltering perspective received a death blow when she walked into the sitting room a few moments later. The two men were standing with a glass of wine in their hands and Matt's hard profile was towards her as he listened to something Annie was telling him. He was giving the child his full attention and was not yet aware of her, but as Georgie looked at his impressively male body clothed in black trousers and an open-necked charcoal shirt her breath caught in her throat. *He was gorgeous.* It was the last thing she either needed or wanted to think. And dangerous. Infinitely dangerous.

And then he turned towards her and she was caught in the light of his eyes, and she had never felt so vulnerable or unprepared. 'Hallo, Matt.'

'Hallo, Georgie,' he murmured softly, her name a caress as his accent gave it a sensuality that made her innermost core vibrate.

'I'll…I'll just see to the dinner.' She fled into the kitchen and then stood for a moment or two just staring helplessly around her. What was she going to do? *What was she going to do?* And then the panic subsided as cold reason said, Nothing. You are going to do nothing but play the hostess. This is one night in a lifetime and once it is over you can have a quiet word with Robert and make sure he doesn't repeat the invitation. Simple.

By the time they all walked through to the dining room it was clear Annie was in love and David had a severe case of hero worship. Georgie had drunk two glasses of wine on an empty stomach, however, and her Dutch courage was high as she watched the children hang on Matt's every word.

'And you *really* have some horses in Spain and here as well?' Annie was asking as Georgie brought in the last of the dishes. Annie was horse-mad and had been having riding lessons for the last year. 'What are they like?'

'Beautiful.' Matt's eyes stroked over Georgie's face for the briefest of moments as he said the word, and then his gaze returned to the animated child. 'You could perhaps come and see them some time if your father wishes it?'

'Really?' It was said on a whoop of delight. 'You mean it?'

'I never say anything I do not mean.' And again Georgie felt the glittering gaze pass over her, although she was intent on removing the lids of the steaming dishes. 'Of course I mean the ones in England,' he added teasingly. 'Spain would be rather a long way to go to see a horse, would it not?'

'I wouldn't mind.' Annie's tone made it clear she would go to the end of the earth if Matt was there and Georgie gave a wry smile to herself. Any age and they'd go down before that dark charm like ninepins. He had a magnetism that was fascinating if you were foolish enough to forget the ruthless and cold mind behind it.

'That's very good of you, Matt.' It was obvious Robert was a little taken aback and not at all sure if this was a social pleasantry said lightly but without real intent.

And then Matt disabused him of that idea when he said, 'Why not this weekend, if you aren't doing anything? You and the children and Georgie could come for the day and have a look round the estate. It would be a distraction for the little ones.' This last was said in an undertone to Robert, and then Matt added to David, 'And bring your swimming trunks, yes? I have a pool and you can practise your breast stroke.'

So David had told him he and Annie were learning to swim at the local baths at some point when she had been busy in the kitchen? And Matt, being Matt, hadn't missed a trick. Horses and a pool—he really was the man who had everything. But not as far as she was concerned.

Georgie kept her voice light and pleasant as she said, 'Tuck in, everyone, and I'm sure the children would love a day out. Unfortunately I shan't be able to make it this weekend as I'm meeting an old university friend who is down in London for a few days, but you and the children must go, Robert.'

'Your friend is very welcome to come along too,' Matt said just as pleasantly.

'Thank you, but I think we'll leave it as it is.' Georgie offered him the dish of roast potatoes as she spoke and as their fingers touched she felt an electric shock shoot right down to her toes.

'Your friend doesn't like horses?' She'd seen the awareness in his eyes and knew the physical contact had registered on him too.

'I don't know.'

'You could ask her.'

Enough was enough. He could try his big-brother tactics on everyone else but she was not having any of it. 'Simon is the quiet type.' She saw the name connect in the dark eyes and assumed a smiling mask to cover up the apprehension his narrowed gaze was causing. 'He doesn't like crowds.'

'He would consider six a crowd?' The mocking voice carried an edge of steel which said only too plainly such a man would be an out-and-out wimp.

Georgie shrugged dismissively. She didn't trust herself to speak without telling him exactly what she thought of him, and that was not an option with the twins present; neither did she think it opportune to mention that Simon was engaged to be married to her best friend from her university days, and that he'd asked her to help in selecting a piece of jewellery to give to his bride as a surprise wedding present.

'I'm going to be eight soon.' Annie cut into the awkward moment and Georgie could have kissed her niece. 'So is David 'cos we're twins.'

'Right.' Matt nodded as he smiled into the little girl's openly admiring face.

'I think I should have been eight ages ago,' Annie continued firmly. 'Stuart Miller is nearly nine and he can't spell yet. Can he, David?'

David had his mouth full of pot roast and merely shook his head in agreement.

'And me and David know really big words.' Annie's massive blue eyes were fixed on the object of her adoration. 'Have you got any children at home?'

Georgie choked on a piece of potato. Never let it be said that Annie was backward in coming forward! However, by the end of the meal Georgie had discovered plenty about Matt de Capistrano through Annie's innocent chattering. He was the product of an English mother and Spanish father and had one sibling, a sister, who had produced a quiverful of children. His father had died several years ago and his mother continued to reside in her own home in Spain, where Matt also had business interests. He had homes in both countries and divided his time equally between them, and he liked horses and dogs and cats. This last was important to Annie, who had decided she wanted to be a vet when she grew up. And his favourite colour was green.

This last question was answered along with a glance at Georgie and the grey eyes smiled mockingly.

Oh, yes, she just bet, Georgie thought silently as she returned the smile politely without giving anything away. And with a blue-eyed blonde it would be blue, and a brown-eyed brunette brown and so on.

Once dinner was over Georgie shooed everyone into the sitting room and retired to the sanctuary of the kitchen, refusing any offers of help, where she dallied until the children's bedtime. She spent longer than normal upstairs with them and then when they were both asleep and it became impossible to delay the moment a second longer, she made her way downstairs, glancing at her watch as she did so. Half-past nine. In another half an hour or so, once she had made them all more coffee, she could gracefully retire and leave the two men to talk. This evening might not be as bad as she had feared.

She realised her mistake as soon as she entered the sitting room. 'Georgie, did you find anywhere to have the kids' party?' Robert asked before she had even shut the door behind her.

'The party?' She was desperately aware of the dark figure sitting to one side of the open French windows on the perimeter of her vision but she kept her eyes on Robert. 'No, no, I didn't, as it happens. I'll try again tomorrow and—'

'Don't worry, Matt's had the most brilliant idea,' Robert interrupted her.

'He has?' She darted one quick wary glance Matt's way and saw the dark face was totally expressionless. It was not reassuring.

'As you can't make this weekend he's offered for us all to go over the next and have the kids' party at his place.'

Robert imparted this news as though it wasn't the most horrendous thing he could have said.

For a moment Georgie was too astounded to say anything, but then reason came back in a hot flood. 'We couldn't possibly,' she protested quickly. 'It's very kind, of course, but they will want their schoolfriends to their party. It's far better we leave things as they are.'

'I meant for their friends to be invited.' Matt was sitting on the large oak chest used to store the children's huge collection of Lego and now he folded his arms over his chest, settling more comfortably on the wood as he surveyed her flushed face with an air of cool determination. 'I bought an old farm some time ago and had the place gutted and rebuilt, and there's plenty of land for the children to enjoy themselves in. The pool is indoors and heated, so they can let off some steam in there, and we can have that bouncy castle on the lawn outside the house if it's fine or in one of the old barns if the weather is inclement. And all kids love a barbecue.'

'I...I couldn't get a bouncy castle,' Georgie said weakly. 'There's not one for hire.'

'There will be if I want one,' Matt said smoothly. 'I've suggested to Robert you have a run over to my place now so you can satisfy yourself it would be okay; it's only half-an-hour's drive.'

This was going from bad to worse. 'I don't think—'

'We can make a day of it,' Matt continued evenly, 'and any parents who want to stay for the day are welcome, or if they just want to come back for the barbecue in the evening that's fine too. My staff are used to large social gatherings and there's a very good catering firm my housekeeper uses at such times.'

His *staff*?

'So it could be a morning by the pool and a buffet lunch,

followed by the bouncy castle and a magician and so on in the afternoon with an evening barbecue,' he continued seamlessly.

'Matt—'

'Do you think David and Annie would enjoy that?' he added with innocent deadly intent. It was the clincher and they both knew it.

How could she deprive David and Annie of such a treat? Georgie asked herself silently. She couldn't. And this master strategist had played her like a virtuoso playing a violin. But he was mad; he had to be. To do all this just because she had refused to have a date with him? This was megalomania at its worst.

'That's settled, then.' Robert appeared to be quite unaware of the electric undercurrents in the room as he nodded from one to the other of them. 'I'll get the coffee on, Georgie. You sit down for a while; you've not stopped all day.'

Before she could stop him Robert had bustled out of the room. Georgie, still coping with her shock, sank down on to the sofa before she realised she should have chosen the single safety of a chair, and the fact was emphasised when Matt sat down beside her in the next moment, slanting a look at her from under half-closed lids.

'I'd genuinely like to give the twins a treat after what they have been through, Georgie,' he said quietly. 'They're nice children, both of them.'

His thigh was touching hers and she had never been so aware of another human being's body in her life, and it took a moment or two before she could say, forcing sarcasm into her voice, 'And that's why you offered to accommodate hordes of screaming infants for the day? Pure magnanimity?'

'Ah, now that's a different question.' He shifted slightly

on the sofa and her senses went into overdrive. He was half turned towards her, one arm along the back of the sofa behind her, and she felt positively enclosed by his dark aura, enclosed and held. 'I've never pretended to be "pure" anything.'

He was doing it again. Laughing at her in that dark smoky voice of his, although there was no trace of amusement on the hard male face. She had made the mistake of raising her eyes to his and now she found it impossible to look away.

'Will you come with me tonight?' The words themselves were nothing, but the way he said them sent a shiver of something hot and sensual down her spine.

'I…I can't.' She gestured helplessly towards the dusky twilight outside the window. 'It's dark now, and late. And…and Robert's getting the coffee.' There was no way—*no way*—she was leaving here with Matt de Capistrano tonight, not with him looking and smelling like the best thing since sliced bread, Georgie thought feverishly. She needed time to distance herself again, get her emotions under control and let cold reason take the place of sexual attraction. But how long—the nasty little voice that was forever making itself known these days asked— how long would that take? An hour? A day? A month?

'Okay.' His voice was soft, silky soft. 'It's probably better you see it in the light anyway. Tomorrow, then. I will call in the office and drive you out there before you come home.'

'I don't need to see your home, Matt, I'm sure it's fine,' she had the presence of mind to say fairly firmly.

'I insist.' It was firmer still.

'But—'

'And then if there is anything you are not happy with— matters of safety, that sort of thing—we can sort it before the party. You'll be quite safe,' he added mockingly as he lifted her small chin and gazed down into the sea-green eyes with a cynical smile. 'My housekeeper and her husband, who oversees the gardens for me, live in, and my groom has his own purpose-built flat above the stables so there are always people about.'

His thick black lashes turned his eyes into bottomless pools, Georgie thought weakly. And then she took a hold of herself, straightening slightly as she removed her chin from his fingers with a flick of her head. 'I didn't think my safety was in question,' she said stiffly, and then was mortified when he laughed softly.

'Little liar.'

His smoky amusement made her face flame. 'No, really—'

'You were worried I would do this...' He put his mouth to hers and stroked her sealed lips lightly, the scent of him heady in her nostrils. He wasn't touching her now except by their joined mouths, but he might as well have been because Georgie was utterly unable to move.

The kiss was sweet, even chaste for a few moments, and then the hand on the back of the sofa slipped down into the small of her back and she found herself drawn into the hard steel of his body as her lips opened beneath his. And he was ready for her, plunging swiftly into the secret contours of her mouth as his tongue and his lips created such a wild rush of sensation she moaned softly, trembling slightly.

His other hand was lightly cupping one breast now through the baby-soft wool, and as he began a slow erotic rhythm on the hardening peak that caused little tremors of passion to shiver in ever-increasing waves Georgie felt drugged with passion.

He was good. He was so good at this. The acknowledgement of his expertise was on the edge of her consciousness and didn't affect the tumultuous emotions which had taken hold.

She could feel the solid pounding of his heart under the thin charcoal silk and as he pulled her even closer his body told her he was as aroused as she was. And it felt so good, *wonderful* to know she could affect him in this way, Georgie admitted fiercely.

Her hands had been curled against the solid wall of his muscled chest, but now they moved up to the powerful shoulders as she moaned softly in her throat and he answered the unspoken need with a guttural sound of his own.

He had turned her into the soft back of the sofa at some point as his body covered hers, and now, as the trembling in her body was reflected in his, he raised his head, his eyes glittering in the semi-light of the standard lamp Robert had switched on earlier. 'You see?' he murmured softly. 'You want me as much as I want you, Georgie. The chemistry is red-hot.'

She was breathing hard now his lips had left hers, and although part of her was crying out in mute protest at the declaration, she was having to fight the urge to reach up for his mouth again. And she mustn't, she mustn't. He had already stormed her defences and caused an abandonment that was only fully dawning on her now his mouth had left hers.

She stared at him, her eyes huge. 'This...this is just sex,' she whispered shakily.

'I know.' He smiled, a sexy quirk of his firm mouth. 'Great, is it not?'

'It isn't enough, not for me.' She pushed at him and he immediately released her, his hand returning to the back of the sofa as he still continued to lean over her without touching her now. His retreat gave her the courage to say more firmly, 'I mean it, Matt. I don't want this.' She drew in a deep breath and added, 'All I want is for you to leave me alone. That's not too much to ask, is it?'

'Much too much,' he said with quiet finality. 'I have tasted you twice now and I want more, much more. But I can be patient, believe it or not.'

'All the patience in the world won't alter my mind.'

'And I never back down from a challenge,' he warned softly.

So she had been right; he saw her as a challenge because she hadn't immediately fallen gratefully into his arms, Georgie thought hotly, her anger banishing the last remnants of his lovemaking and putting iron in her limbs. 'I have absolutely no intention of having a relationship with you,' she stated very coldly, 'or anyone else for that matter. Robert and the twins are my prime concern at the moment, but even if they weren't around I wouldn't sleep with you. Is that clear enough?'

'Abundantly.'

At least he wasn't smiling now, she thought a trifle hysterically, before she said, 'Good. I'm glad you've seen sense at last.'

He muttered something dark and Spanish and—Georgie was certain—uncomplimentary under his breath, and had just opened his mouth to reply when Robert called from outside the door, 'Georgie? Open the door, would you? I've a tray in my hands,' and she leapt up and fairly flew across the room.

It was another twenty minutes before Matt stood up to leave and Georgie was amazed at his acting ability. If it wasn't for the steely glint in his eyes when he glanced her way she might have been convinced she had imagined the whole episode from the way he was smiling and conversing with Robert.

'That was a wonderful dinner, Georgie.' As the three of them stood on the doorstep his voice was the epitome of a satisfied guest thanking his hostess. 'You certainly know the way to a man's heart,' he added smoothly.

Sarcastic so-and-so! Georgie smiled sweetly. 'So it has been said,' she agreed demurely.

She saw the grey eyes spark and then narrow, and reminded herself to go carefully. Matt de Capistrano was not a man it was wise to annoy, but he made her so *mad*.

The telephone had started to ring in the sitting room. Robert said, 'I'm sorry, Matt, do you mind if I get that?'

Matt was already shaking his head and saying, 'No, you go and I'll see you tomorrow.'

'Goodnight, Matt.'

The two of them were alone now, and in answer to her dismissive voice he smiled. 'Walk me to my car.'

She didn't have time to agree or disagree before he took her arm and whisked her down the shadowed drive.

'Let go of me!' Her voice was on the edge of hostility but she was desperately trying to remain calm; Matt *was* Robert's bread and butter, after all.

'I like you better when you are soft and breathless in my arms than spitting rocks,' he drawled with mocking composure.

Her face bloomed with colour and Georgie was desperately glad of the scented darkness which hid her blushes as she breathed, 'I *told* you to forget all that.'

'Have there been many?' he asked with sudden seriousness, his hand still on her arm.

'What?' She stared at him, bewildered by the abrupt change.

'Men who have complimented you on your dinners,' he said with silky innuendo.

'That's my business.' She was shocked and it showed. How *dared* he question her about her love life? Not that she had one at the moment, and the last three years hadn't been anything to write home about, either, if she was being honest. She had had the occasional date after Glen, of course, but after a time she had begun to wonder why she was bothering to make the effort when there wasn't anyone she remotely fancied. She knew she didn't want to get involved with anyone again—certainly not for a long, long time anyway, if at all—and even when she made it perfectly clear the date was on a purely friends basis, the man in question always had to try and paw her about at the end of the evening. And so she had made up her mind that unless that magical 'something' was there she was content to be single. And it hadn't been. Until now. She shuddered as the last two words hit.

'You're cold.' He enfolded her into his arms as he spoke, but loosely, his fingertips brushing her lower ribs and the palms of his hands cupping her sides. 'You should be wearing something more than that pink thing out here.'

The warm fragrance of him was all about her and the harnessed strength in the big male body caused a fluttering inside that Georgie recognised with a stab of disgust at her own weakness. 'I didn't plan to be out here, if you remember,' she said as tartly as she could, considering her legs were like jelly. 'And the "pink thing", as you call it, is a very expensive cashmere top that cost me an arm and a leg.'

'Which arm and which leg?' He drew her closer, so they were thigh to thigh and breast to breast. 'They all feel like the real thing.'

She tried to push away but it was like pushing against solid steel. 'Matt, please.'

'Yes, Georgie?' His eyes moved to the soft gold of her hair for a moment.

'I...I have to go in.' It wasn't as firm as she would have liked.

'Okay.' He didn't relax his hold an iota. 'But first you repeat after me: I will be ready and waiting when you arrive to pick me up tomorrow night, Matt.'

'But I told you I don't need to see your house; I'm sure it's quite suitable and—'

'No, that was not right. I will be ready and waiting when you arrive to pick me up tomorrow night, Matt,' he repeated softly, his dark body merging into the shadows like a creature of the night.

'Matt!' She wriggled but it was useless. 'Robert will see us.'

'Good.'

'I'll scream.'

Georgie looked at him steadily and saw he was vastly amused. Oh, this was ridiculous! What must they look like? But he wasn't going to give in; she could read it in the dark, aggressively attractive face looking down at her. Well, one quick visit to his house wouldn't hurt, would it? She could make it clear she had to be back in time to get the children's dinner and so on, she comforted herself silently. 'I will be ready and waiting when you arrive to pick me up tomorrow night, Matt.'

'That wasn't so bad, was it?' Grey eyes softened to warm charcoal. 'I'll be at the office for five, yes?'

'And I must be home to get the twins' tea.'

'Cinderella, twenty-first century,' he murmured softly. 'But first you shall go to the ball.' And he kissed her, long and hard until she was breathless, and then put her aside and slid into the Lamborghini seemingly in one fluid movement.

She was still standing exactly as he had placed her, one hand touching her tingling bruised lips, when he roared out of the drive into the street in a flash of gleaming metal. And then he was gone.

CHAPTER FIVE

GEORGIE didn't sleep much that night. She spent most of the long silent hours trying to sort out her feelings, but by the time a pale, pink-edged dawn crept stealthily over the morning sky she'd given it up as hopeless. This was disturbing and outside her understanding, or more to the point Matt de Capistrano was disturbing and outside her understanding! She corrected herself wryly. And she didn't want to feel like this; it horrified her.

For the last few years she had been in control. Once she had recovered from the caustic fall-out of Glen's rejection she had changed her mindset and her goals. She had known exactly what she was doing, where she was going and what she was aiming for. And now...now she wasn't sure about anything and it terrified her; in fact it was totally unacceptable.

For some reason Matt's dark face seemed to be printed on the screen of her mind. She didn't want it there, in fact she would give anything to have it wiped clean, but somehow there it stayed.

She was sitting in front of the bedroom window, Annie asleep in her small single bed in one corner of the room, and as the small child stirred and then settled down to sleep again Georgie's eyes remained on her. It was true what she had said to Matt, she told herself fiercely. She had more than enough to do to cope with the twins and Robert. If he couldn't understand that then it was tough.

She turned and looked outside again to where an adolescent song thrush was sitting in the copper beech outside the bedroom window. Its bright black eyes surveyed her for one moment and it seemed to hesitate before rising up into the sky in a glorious swoop of freedom, the earth and all its dangers and difficulties forgotten in the wonder of being alive. She mustn't hesitate either. She nodded to the thought as though it had been spoken out loud. Matt had made it quite clear he wanted her for one thing and one thing only, and if she didn't put him behind her and escape—like that bird into the sky—he would clip her wings in a way Glen would never have been able to do. She had recovered from Glen; she had a feeling Matt de Capistrano was the sort of man you never recovered from.

At five o'clock she was in the shower and by six she was dressed and downstairs, preparing breakfast for everyone and four packed lunches. She paused in the middle of spreading mashed egg and salad cream on to buttered bread, glancing round the small homely kitchen as she did so. What had Matt thought of this home? His lifestyle was so different as to be another world away. He had staff to cater to his wants, to serve him breakfast and anticipate his every need. And in his love life she was sure there were plenty of willing women to supply everything he needed there too! He was rich, ruthless, selfish and shallow. *He was.* She reiterated it in her mind and didn't question why she needed to convince herself of his failings. She saw it clearly now, she reassured herself as the pile of sandwiches grew. Crystal-clear.

The crystalline certainty continued until the moment she saw Matt.

He arrived prompt at five and drove her away from the office after a word or two with Robert in private, and when the Lamborghini entered a winding drive some twenty-five

minutes later, after a sign which said, 'Private. El Dorado'
She turned to him with questioning eyes.

'It means the golden land,' he answered her softly, 'a
country full of gold and gems.'

'And have you filled your El Dorado with gems?' she
asked a little cynically. No doubt the house would be a
monument to his success and full of all the trappings of
wealth. Which was fine, of course it was, if that was what
he wanted. It fitted the image.

'In a manner of speaking,' he answered somewhat cryptically.

She opened her mouth to ask him what he meant, but
the words hovering on her tongue were never voiced as in
that same moment the car turned a corner in the drive and
the sort of sprawling thatched farmhouse that belonged in
fairy stories came into view.

'Oh, wow...' It wasn't particularly articulate but the look
on her enchanted face must have satisfied Matt because he
smiled slowly after bringing the car to a halt on the end of
the horseshoe-shaped drive.

'Come and have a look round inside first,' he suggested
quietly, 'and then I'll show you where we could have the
barbecue if it is wet, and of course the bouncy castle.'

His accent lent a quaintness to the last two words that
made her heart twang slightly, and as they walked up the
massive stone steps towards the big oak door she said, aiming to keep the conversation practical and mundane, 'This
is very nice; did you have to do much work to get it to this
point?'

'The place was almost derelict when I purchased it,' he
said, taking her arm as he opened the front door to reveal
a large hall panelled in mellow oak that was golden in the
sunlight slanting in from several narrow windows above
them. 'An old lady, the unmarried daughter of the original

farmer, had lived here for years alone, getting more and more into debt as the house fell down about her ears.'

'What a shame.' As Matt closed the front door Georgie stared at the curving staircase a few yards away which was a beautiful thing all on its own. 'Why did she decide to sell in the end?'

'She became too arthritic to continue,' he said shortly.

'Poor thing,' Georgie sympathised absently, her eyes on a fine painting on the far wall. 'She must have hated leaving her home.'

'Not so much the house, more the animals she had here,' Matt said quietly. 'She needed to go into a nursing home for proper care, but she had used the house and the grounds almost as a sanctuary for the remainder of her father's farm animals and the pets she had accumulated, who had grown old with her.'

Something in his voice caused her eyes to focus on him. If the person speaking had been other than Matt de Capistrano, ruthless tycoon and entrepreneur extraordinaire, she would have sworn there was tenderness colouring his words when he'd spoken of the old lady.

'What happened to them? To the animals?' Georgie asked softly.

Now his voice was expressionless, brisk even, when he said, 'You can meet a few, if you wish.' He had been leading her down the sun-kissed hall, which had bowls of fresh flowers on several occasional tables, and as they reached the far end he opened another door which led on to a large, white-washed passageway.

The opening of this last door caused a bell to tinkle somewhere, and in the next moment a big—very big—red-cheeked woman appeared from a doorway at the end of the passage, several dogs spilling out in front of her with a medley of barks and woofs.

'You kept them?' Georgie stopped abruptly and stared into his dead-pan face before she bent to fuss the excited animals who were now jumping round their feet. 'You kept the old lady's pets?'

'Aye, that he did, lass.' The woman—Matt's house-keeper, Georgie assumed—had now reached them and began shooing the dogs back into the room they had come from, continuing to say as she did so, 'We've more geriatrics here than in the nursing home where poor Miss Barnes is, bless her.' And then she straightened, holding out her hand as she said, 'I'm Rosie, by the way, Mr de Capistrano's housekeeper, and I'm very pleased to meet you, lass.'

She must have replied in like because everything continued quite normally for the next few minutes, but as Matt led her after Rosie, who had walked back into the massive farmhouse kitchen at the back of the house, Georgie's head was spinning. She was conscious of an overwhelming desire to take to her heels and run. This was danger—this place, the man at the side of her, all of it. He wouldn't stay in the niche she had made for him in her mind and it was imperative he did so.

This feeling continued as, after a tour of the farmhouse, which Matt had turned into a fabulous place, he took her outside into the surrounding grounds.

She had met what Rosie called 'the inside pests'—five dogs and several assorted cats—but now in the fields directly behind the house and to one side of the stable block she saw there was a small flock of ten or so sheep, two donkeys and several ancient horses meandering around along with one or two bony bovines.

'They took all her savings, most of her furniture and certainly her health,' Matt said quietly at the side of her as Georgie looked across at the animals pottering about in the sunshine. 'But she loved them more passionately than most people love their children. What could I do but agree they could live out their time quietly and peacefully here?'

'I suppose to her they *were* her children.' Georgie kept her voice even and steady although inside she felt as though she were drowning.

'Come and see my other gems,' Matt said lightly, seemingly unaware of the body blow he had wrought her. 'These are the 24-carat kind.'

She followed him into the stable block, where Matt's groom was working, and the young man joined them as Matt introduced her to his two thoroughbred Arab stallions and a dappled mare and young colt.

Okay, so he was kind to old ladies and animals, Georgie told herself silently as she listened to the two men talk about the merits of a new feed on the market. But she was neither, and she forgot that at her peril. He had already made it quite clear how he viewed an affair with her. It was a thing of the body, not of the mind, and the sexual attraction he felt for her would eventually burn itself out. And in view of her inexpertise in the bed department that might be a darn sight quicker than he had bargained for!

She was not a *femme fatale*, like his secretary or the women he normally associated with socially, and his world was as alien to her as—she searched her mind for an appropriate simile—as fish and chips out of a paper bag would be to him!

She ran her fingers over the raw silk coat of one of the stallions. The advertisement for a replacement secretary for Robert should be appearing in the paper tomorrow; hopefully she would soon be out of Matt's sphere and it wouldn't take long for a man like him to forget her.

'Magnificent, isn't he?' The warmth in Matt's voice brought her eyes from the horse to his face, and he turned to glance at her in the same moment. 'Do you ride?' he asked quietly.

'No.' There hadn't been any spare cash for anything so frivolous as riding lessons when she had been younger, and even now she knew Robert was struggling to pay for Annie's lessons.

'Would you like to?'

She shrugged, turning away from the stable and the horse's velvet nose which was twitching enquiringly over the half door. 'Annie's the horsewoman,' she said lightly. 'She'll go ape over this place.'

'Ape?'

'She'll love it,' Georgie explained as Matt fell into step beside her. 'She's crazy about animals although Robert and Sandra never wanted any. Your menagerie will be heaven on earth to her.'

'So I will be a means of satisfaction to at least one Millett female?' he enquired with silky mockery.

She ignored that, turning at the entrance into the stable block and waving to the young groom as she called her goodbyes.

Once outside in the mild May air she glanced about her as she said, 'You were going to show me where we could have the barbecue and bouncy castle if it is wet?'

'So I was. Please come this way, ma'am.' He imitated her brisk, no-nonsense voice with dark amusement and Georgie wanted to kick him, hard.

From the outside the large building some fifty yards to the left of the farmhouse looked like a big barn—but as Matt opened the huge wooden doors and they stepped inside Georgie saw it had been converted into what was basically a massive hall. A row of windows ran right round three walls at first-floor level and there was a stage at the far end where she presumed a band could play. To the side of the stage was a well-equipped bar, and a host of tables with chairs piled on them stood all along the right wall.

'Would this do?' Matt asked with suspicious meekness.

She nodded stiffly, suddenly vitally aware of the height and breadth of him beside her. 'It's very nice,' she said flatly.

'And the pool met your requirements?'

The pool had been terrific, more in keeping with a leisure centre than a private home, and being joined to the main house by means of a covered way off the well-equipped games room at the back of the house it was just as consumer-friendly in the winter as the summer. 'Everything's lovely,' she said reluctantly.

'Why don't we have a dip before dinner?' he suggested softly.

'I haven't got a swimming cos—' She stopped abruptly. 'Before *dinner*?'

He shut his eyes briefly at the shrill note and said patiently, 'People do, Georgie; it is quite a civilised way to live. I have a changing room full of suitable swimwear.'

And he knew exactly where he could stick it! She glared at him, berating herself for being so foolish as to trust him. 'You promised me you would take me straight home,' she said frostily. 'I need to look after the twins.'

'No, you do not,' he stated evenly. 'Robert might be just a mere man but he is more than able to take them out for a burger and then tuck them up in bed later. He is their father when all is said and done. Besides which...'

He hesitated, and Georgie eyed him with blazing green eyes as she clipped, 'Yes?'

'They need to bond, the three of them, and you are in danger of getting in the way,' he stated with unforgivable clarity.

'What?' Georgie couldn't believe her ears.

'You're pushing Robert out and swamping the twins with an over-indulgence of love in the process,' Matt stated quietly. 'Before long you'll have two brats on your hands if you aren't careful.'

Nothing in the world could have stopped her hand connecting with the hard tanned skin of his face. The slap echoed round the barn for some moments as they both stood stock still, looking at each other, Matt with a face of stone and Georgie wide-eyed and shaking. 'How dare you, how *dare* you say that when you have only met David and Annie once?' Georgie said painfully, her face reflecting her shock and hurt. 'They are wonderful kids, the pair of them.'

'I know that; I'm talking about what could happen in the future,' he grated tightly.

She called him a name that made his eyes widen and which surprised the pair of them. 'I want to go home right now,' she bit out furiously, her anger masking the horror that was now dawning as she saw her red handprint etched on the skin of his face.

'No way.' His eyes narrowed and she knew he meant it. 'You are going to stay here and have dinner with me whether you like it or not, and if you'd just take a little time to think about what I have said you might see there is some truth in it.'

'So you're saying I'm ruining the twins and stopping my brother from seeing his children?' Georgie asked wildly.

'*I am saying—*' He paused, moderating his tone before he continued more quietly, 'I am saying you need to let the three of them have some time together now and again, that is all. When was the last time Robert took David to the swimming baths or Annie to her riding lesson? When does he put them to bed and listen to what has happened in their day? When, Georgie?'

She stared at him, stunned and silent.

'David needs his father to go and see him when he has a football match now and again.' The dark husky voice was relentless. 'It is necessary and healthy.'

'Robert has had enough to do to cope with Sandra's death,' Georgie said fiercely.

'Initially, yes.' He allowed another brief pause before he said, 'But it has been six months, Georgie, and that is a long time in the life of a child. Robert has slipped into the habit of letting you be mother *and* father to the twins and I feel his wife, Sandra, would not have wanted this.'

'You didn't know her!'

'This is true.' The grey eyes were fixed on her stricken face. 'And this is why I can speak with impartiality. Sometimes it takes an outsider to see what is happening, and I do not doubt your love for your brother and his children but you cannot be their mother, Georgie. You are their aunty—precious, no doubt. But you will burn yourself out if you continue to try to be everything to everyone.'

Where had the shallow philanderer gone? She couldn't see him in this man who spoke with quiet but determined force and it scared her to death. And it was in challenge to that thought that she flung out, her voice scathing, 'All this talk about Robert and the twins when you know full well what you really want! You don't care about them; you're using them to get your own way. You are just the same as all the others!'

He was angry. Really, really angry. A muscle had knotted in his cheek and his grey eyes were steely, but his voice was even and controlled when he said, 'I'll ignore that because it is not worthy of a reply. You are a young woman of twenty-three and yet you act like a matron several decades older. When do you ever go out and enjoy yourself, Georgie? Have fun? Let your hair down?'

'With men, you mean?' she bit out with open hostility.

'We don't all need to sleep around to think we're having a good time. I like my life, as it happens.'

'I have it on good authority you have barely left the house in six months except to escort the children to and fro and go to work,' Matt returned harshly. 'That is not a life; that is an existence. Even this Simon is not what you led me to believe.'

'Excuse me?' He could only have got all this from Robert and she couldn't believe her brother had betrayed her in this way. Only it wouldn't have been like that, she reasoned in the next milli-second. Matt knew just how to word a question to get the maximum response and Robert would have been quite unaware he was being pumped for information. 'I did not "lead" you to believe anything!' she protested with outraged dignity.

'That is a matter of opinion.' He stared into her furious face, his own as angry, and then after a moment she saw him take a deep breath and visibly relax as he raked back his hair in a gesture that carried both irritation and frustration in it. 'Damn it, I did not want it to be like this,' he growled tightly.

She could believe that! Oh, yes, she could believe that all right. She knew quite well what he had had in mind. He had made sure of that himself—no strings attached and no heavy commitment was how he had termed it. He didn't believe in love or for everness. Well, if she was absolutely truthful, she wasn't quite sure what she believed in, but one thing she did know—when she made love with a man it would have to be believing there was at least a strong chance they would have some sort of a future together. It was just the way she was made and she wasn't going to apologise for that or anything else about herself either.

She drew herself up to her full five foot four inches and glared at him before turning out of the barn, but she had only gone a few steps when he caught at her arm, turning her round to face him. 'Would it help if I said if I was the twins' age you would be my ideal as a surrogate mother?' he asked with exaggerated humbleness.

'No,' she snapped hotly.

'Or that I think Robert is the luckiest brother in the world and that you have steered the good ship Millett through turbulent waters wonderfully well?'

'No again.'

In truth she was having a job not to cry, but she would rather die than let him know that. Maybe she *had* been a touch obsessional in trying to be everything the twins needed, but she could still remember how she had felt at ten years old when she had lost her parents and her world had disintegrated about her. But...but it *was* different for David and Annie. Her innate honesty was forcing the recognition in spite of herself. They still had their father, for a start, along with each other and the security of their home and all their friends. She had been whipped out of the environment she'd always known and placed with Robert and Sandra, and although they'd been wonderful, *marvellous*, it had been a terribly tough time. She *had* been over-compensating without realising it and in the process encouraging Robert to sit and brood rather than take his share of responsibility with the twins. *Oh, hell!*

'Georgie?' As she raised stricken eyes to Matt's face she saw he was watching her very closely. 'It is not criminal to have the kind heart,' he said softly. 'Better an excess of indulgence and pampering at this time than for them to feel cast adrift.'

If he had continued with the home truths in that cool relentless voice she could have coped, even the slightly mocking teasing attitude after he had caught her arm had kept the adrenaline running hot and strong, but this last was too much.

'I...I want to go home.' Her voice wobbled alarmingly over the declaration but she continued to fight the tears until the moment he pulled her into his arms, holding her against the solid warmth of his body. And then she just bawled her eyes out, in an unladylike display of wailing and choking sobs and a runny nose that was all out of proportion to anything which had gone before.

She couldn't have explained that her tears were as much for the lost little ten-year-old she had been as for Robert and Annie and David, for Glen's cruel cavalier treatment, for the humiliation and desperation she had felt at that time, and for Sandra. Poor, poor Sandra. Everything was all mixed up together and she cried as she hadn't done in years, not since her parents' death in fact.

Matt let her cry for long, long minutes, making no effort to ask any questions as he held her pressed against his chest and made soothing noises above her blonde head. And then, as the flood reduced to hiccuping sobs, and then valiant sniffs and splutters against his damp shirt-front, Georgie was overcome with embarrassment at her ignominious tears. How could she, how *could* she have lost control like that, and in front of Matt de Capistrano of all people? What must he be thinking? And then she found out.

'At a guess I would say that has been held in for far too long.' His voice was low and soft, his hands warm and soothing as they stroked her slender back. 'Am I right?'

Georgie stiffened slightly. This was a very astute and clever man in the normal run of things, and she had just given him a heaven-sent opportunity that even the thickest of individuals would capitalise on.

'I didn't mean to make you cry,' he continued quietly. 'You know that, don't you?'

'It wasn't you.' Her face was burning now, she could feel it, but she couldn't stay pressed against his chest for ever and so she pushed away from him, only to find he wasn't ready to let her go. She rubbed her pink nose, knowing she must look like something the cat had dragged in. 'Have you a hanky I can borrow?'

'In a moment.' He continued to look down into her tear-smudged face, into the startlingly green eyes that were so incredibly beautiful. 'If it was not my clumsy remarks, then what?'

'I...I don't know. Lots of things.' She heard her shaking voice with a dart of very real irritation at herself. She had to be strong and on her guard around Matt; trembling femininity was not an option. 'It's been a stressful time for everyone.'

'And you have been very brave.'

Oh, hell; if he kept this up she was going to blub all over him again, Georgie thought feverishly, as tears pricked at the back of her eyes again. After not crying for years it now seemed she couldn't stop!

'Not really.' She shrugged, trying to move out of his arms but not quite able to break free. 'I suppose the twins' situation is so close to the one I endured as a child that it makes it difficult to separate the two in my mind. The feelings I had then tend to get in the way sometimes.'

'Explain.' He let go of her long enough to delve into his pocket for a crisp white handkerchief, but after he had handed it to her and she was mopping at her face the strong arms enclosed her again, but lightly now, a few inches between them.

Not that it made much difference, Georgie thought a trifle hysterically. The big hard body, the delicious and literally intoxicating smell of him was all around her and it made her head spin. She had never in her wildest dreams believed that sexual attraction could be so strong or so physical, but it was making her legs weak.

She drew a deep breath, the handkerchief still clutched in one hand, and began to explain about the circumstances that had placed her in Robert's home.

He listened without interrupting until she had finished. 'So tiny and so ethereal.' There was what sounded like a note of disconcertment in the deep male voice. 'You appear at first sight to be...'

'The original dumb blonde?' she finished for him with a slight edge to her voice now, the memory of their first meeting suddenly very vivid. He had thought she was the type of female who spent all her time on the phone talking to other dumb females, then!

'Delicate and breakable,' he corrected evenly. 'But in truth you are—'

'As tough as old boots?' She did it on purpose, as much to annoy him and thereby shatter the intimate mood he'd created so effortlessly as to assure herself she was *not* going to be fooled by this new side of him.

'A very strong and courageous woman.' He tilted his head. 'You still haven't told me his name, Georgie.'

'Whose?' She had tried to hide the instinctive start she'd given at his ruthless strategy, but she knew the piercingly intent gaze had registered it.

'The man who has caused you to build this shell around yourself,' he said silkily.

He was not going to have this all his own way! She stared up at him, wondering why God had given him such a sexy mouth on top of all his other attributes, and said steadily, 'I could ask you the same question, Matt. You've told me you don't believe in love and for everness; there has to be a reason for that.'

He drew back and stared into her face, not able to hide

his surprise. And then his eyes narrowed and his hands fell from around her waist, and she knew she had hit a nerve. It was disturbing that it didn't give her the satisfaction she'd expected.

'*Touché*, Miss Millett.' His voice was cool, withdrawn, and in spite of herself she felt the loss of the warmth that had been there previously with a physical ache. 'So we are both...realistic; is that what you are saying?'

It wasn't at all what she had said and he knew it. She scrubbed at her face one last time and then offered him back the handkerchief. She could probe but, as she wasn't prepared to talk about Glen, it wouldn't be wise. She had said far too much already when she thought about it, all that about her childhood and so on. She wished now she had kept quiet.

'Come.' He held out his hand, his grey eyes unfathomable as he stared down into her heart-shaped face. 'I know just the thing to relax you and make you feel better,' he added with a touch of dark amusement.

Her imagination running rampant, Georgie peered up at him suspiciously. 'What's that?' she asked flatly.

'A swim, what else?' His smile was definitely of the wicked kind. 'As I said, I have many costumes in one of the changing rooms and you will find something suitable I am sure. We can swim a little, have a cocktail or two, and then change for dinner later.'

'I told you I'm not staying for dinner.'

'And I told you you are,' he said pleasantly. 'If nothing else, Rosie would be very upset to think you do not wish to partake of the meal she has been preparing most of the day.'

Georgie flushed. He was making her feel crass and it was so *unfair*. 'That's emotional blackmail,' she said tightly.

Matt shrugged and the gesture was very Latin. 'It is the truth.' And then his attitude changed somewhat as he added, 'I want to give you an evening off duty for once, Georgie; is that really such a crime? And Robert was in full agreement when I suggested this to him. ''Very kind'' was how he termed it, I think.'

Her flush deepened, and now the grey eyes were definitely laughing when he said, 'I promise to be a good boy at all times; does that help? I will treat you as I would treat my maiden aunt.'

He was standing in front of her, tall and lithe, his arms crossed over his broad chest and his shirt open at the bronze of his neck. He looked very masculine and dark and good enough to eat. Georgie swallowed hard. Impossible man. Impossible situation! 'All right.' She heard herself say the words with a faint feeling of despair. 'But just dinner, no swim.' Clothed, she could just about cope, but half-naked?

'You cannot swim?' he asked evenly. One dark eyebrow had slanted provocatively and she just *knew* he was sure of her answer.

'Yes.' It was reluctant.

'Then this is what we will do,' he stated firmly. 'Already Rosie will have taken the cocktails out to the pool area and I have had it heated warmer than usual so it will be quite pleasant. I have a swim before dinner each evening. It is very good for the circulation.'

Maybe, but the thought of Matt in next to nothing was playing havoc with her blood pressure.

And then he stretched out his hand again, this time taking one of hers as though he had a perfect right to touch her whenever he pleased, and she found herself walking alongside him as they made their way back to the house. She was all out of arguments.

CHAPTER SIX

AN HOUR later, as Georgie lay on a thickly cushioned lounger at the side of the pool sipping an exotic pink cocktail, she had to admit to herself she was having a whale of a time.

Admittedly there had been several sticky moments. Firstly, when she had stood in the changing room used by Matt's female guests and looked at the vast row of minuscule bikinis and wraps, she had panicked big time. The tiny scraps of material all bore designer labels, and all seemed indecent to her fevered gaze, but eventually she had managed to find a one-piece among all the wisps which, although cut away at the sides and with a frighteningly plunging neckline, was a size eight and a little more decorous than the rest.

She had ignored the dozen or so diaphanous wraps, all gossamer-thin and quite beautiful in a rainbow of different colours, and regretfully reached for one of the towelling robes, which she had slipped on over the swimming costume and tied tightly round her waist.

She had glanced into the huge mirror which took up all of one wall at her reflection. The only thing showing were her feet and hands! She'd cope with the moment when she must find the nerve to disrobe later; this concealed almost every inch of her, and it had given her the courage to leave her hidey-hole with her head held high and her back straight.

Her cucumber-cool resolve had faltered somewhat when she'd emerged to find Matt climbing out of the pool, obviously having swum a few lengths while he was waiting for her.

He was wearing a pair of brief black swimming trunks which left nothing—absolutely nothing—to the imagination, and his thickly muscled torso had gleamed like oiled silk, the body hair on his chest a mass of tight black curls. She had known he would be magnificent unclothed, but the reality of the powerful male body, which didn't carry a morsel of fat and was primed to lean perfection, had been something else. Something dangerous and threatening and utterly mind-blowing.

She had forced herself to pad across towards him as he'd raised a casual hand in welcome, her mouth dry and the palms of her hands damp, but thankfully he had bent to pour out their drinks at her approach, and by the time she'd reached him she had pulled herself together.

'To the most beautiful maiden aunt anyone could wish to have,' he drawled mockingly as he placed one glass in her hand, raising his in a salute. 'And to a pleasant evening getting to know each other a little better.'

Georgie found it almost impossible to concentrate on anything else but the acres of hard tanned flesh in front of her, but somehow she found the strength to say, in a voice that could have passed for normal, 'To a nice evening,' as she raised her glass too. 'Mmm, that's gorgeous.' The cocktail tasted wonderful. 'What's in it?'

'Sloe gin, banana liqueur, crushed raspberries, white wine...and a couple of other things which are my secret,' Matt returned softly. 'I invented this cocktail a few years ago and there's many who would love to know the ingredients.'

'What's it called?' She took another gulp, needing something to distract her from the flagrant maleness in front of her, the taut belly and hard male thighs.

'Passionate Beginnings.' He was totally straight-faced.

She eyed him severely. 'You just made that up,' she accused uncertainly.

'Would I?' His voice was even softer now, and she shivered in spite of the hothouse warmth.

'You're not cold?' he asked in surprise.

'No, not cold exactly.' Her oxygen supply was in severe danger of running out and she felt weak at the knees, but just at this moment a lack of warmth was not one of her problems!

'Good.' He smiled, utterly at ease with himself in spite of practically being in the nude. 'Then finish that and come and have a swim.'

Apart from the acute discomfort she felt when she first slipped off the robe and sensed Matt's eyes on her—she didn't dare to look at him—the time that followed was full of laughter and fun. Matt was like a kid again in the water, splashing her and grabbing her ankles until she was forced to pay him back in kind, and they had a time of clowning around as well as some serious swimming.

Georgie was not a particularly strong swimmer, but even if she had been she realised quite quickly she wouldn't have been able to compete with Matt. He cut through the water with incredible speed, an automaton clothed in flesh and blood and sinew.

After half an hour or so she climbed out of the pool and sipped her drink again, lying on one of the sun loungers as she watched him cover length after length with effortless ease.

It was another ten minutes before he joined her, and Georgie's stomach muscles clenched as he pulled himself out of the water and strolled over to the lounger at the side of hers. It was one thing lying here supposedly relaxed and cool, sipping elegantly at a drink, when that powerful male body was in the water; quite another when it was a foot or so away.

She had debated whether to clothe herself from head to foot in the robe again when she had first sat down, but with the temperature in the pool area being what it was had decided that would be too ridiculous. And she was a grown woman, she told herself firmly, not some adolescent green behind the ears. Two adults in swimwear was not a prelude to an orgy, even if one of them *was* Matt de Capistrano.

And so she topped up his barely touched drink with a smile when he sat down, exchanged a little small talk and then settled herself back and shut her eyes, commenting this was the most restful evening she had had in a long, long time. She was surprised how well she lied.

She didn't know what she expected in the minutes that followed her declaration, but after a little while she dared to open her eyes enough to slant a quick glance at the side of her.

Matt was lying back on his lounger too, apparently perfectly relaxed, his eyes shut and the big body stretched out and still damp from the water. Georgie frowned. He hadn't made a move on her at all, hadn't even tried to kiss her. And then she felt her face flame at her own inconsistency. She didn't want him to! Of course she didn't. What on earth was the matter with her anyway?

'David and Annie will have the best birthday party ever here,' she said quietly as she sat up and reached for her glass.

'Good.' He didn't move or open his eyes.

'It's really very kind of you to allow your home to be invaded by a host of strangers, especially as most of them will be screaming infants.'

'My pleasure.'

What was the matter with him, for goodness' sake?

Georgie's irritation was totally unfair and she knew it, which made it all the more aggravating. Suddenly the desire to talk, to find out more about the enigmatic individual at the side of her was strong. There was a whole host of questions burning in her brain, and all of them much too personal. She brushed back a strand of silky blonde hair from her cheek and swallowed hard, before she compromised with, 'Do you manage to spend much time at your home in Spain?'

He opened his eyes then, the piercing gaze focusing on her for a moment before he sat up and reached for his own glass, draining the last of the pink liquid before he said, 'Not as much as I would like. My sister's last child is three months old and I have seen him only twice, although this last period has been a particularly difficult one business-wise, with a complicated takeover here in England. Fortunately the Spanish side of things is flowing easily at the moment, and with my brother-in-law at the helm out there I know I have someone I can trust to oversee things for me.'

'Do you have any family from your mother's side here in England?' she asked carefully.

'An uncle.' He swung his legs over the side of the lounger to face her and her senses went into hyperdrive. 'He and my father started the English side of the business with my English grandparents, who are now dead, although my uncle chooses to do less and less these days. He prefers to travel and as he never married and has no ties he is something of a free spirit.' It was wry, and Georgie got the impression not wholly acceptable.

She wanted to ask about Pepita; why he didn't have an English secretary here in England for a start. She had sensed a closeness between Matt and the beautiful Spanish woman that went beyond the bounds of a working relationship, although she could be wrong. But she didn't think so. She hesitated, not knowing how to put it. 'Is…is Pepita's ankle any better?' she asked lamely.

'Yes, I think so.'

It was dismissive and perversely made Georgie all the more determined to continue.

'Does she travel with you back and forwards to Spain?' she asked in as neutral a voice as she could manage, just as a door at the far end of the huge room opened and Rosie called out, 'Dinner in fifteen minutes, Mr de Capistrano.'

'Thank you, Rosie.' He rose as he spoke, holding out a hand to Georgie as he said quietly, 'No doubt you will want to shower before dinner; you should find all you need in the changing room.'

Had he purposely not answered her, or had the question been lost in Rosie's ill-timed interruption? Georgie wasn't sure but the moment had gone anyway. She looked up at him, but before she could take his hand he said, his voice silky smooth now, 'I do not bite, Georgie,' as he bent down and pulled her to her feet.

For a heart-stopping moment she was held against his muscled chest, her hair tousled and her cheeks pink, and she knew he was going to kiss her. So it came as a drenching shock when she was put firmly to one side and Matt's voice said coolly, 'You'll find the towels to one side of the shower cubicle.'

The *towels*? She tried with all her might to show no reaction at all when she said politely, 'Thank you,' before she scurried away, grabbing the robe as she went.

Had he known she expected him to kiss her? Probably. She groaned softly as she stood under the deliciously warm water in the shower after lathering herself with an expensive-smelling body shampoo. Very probably. He was an experienced man of the world; reading a woman's body signals was as natural to him as breathing. But he had shown her he didn't kiss a woman because she indicated she was available, only when he was ready to do so.

She groaned again before taking herself in hand. But she wasn't available, she *wasn't*. She might have suffered a momentary aberration but that was all it had been.

She lathered her hair with the shampoo quickly before rinsing down and drying herself with one of the huge fluffy bath sheets. On the wooden shelf which ran under the mirror along one wall there was every available cream and lotion known to man, along with a display unit holding a vast array of cosmetics, including nail varnish, combs and brushes in unopened packages, lipsticks and anything else a beautician might need.

Georgie ignored it all, drying her hair quickly before she slipped on her own clothes and surveyed herself in the mirror. Without even her customary touch of mascara she looked about sixteen, but that suited her! She scowled at the small slim figure staring back at her. She couldn't compete with the sort of glamorous, dazzling women he was used to and she didn't intend to try, she told herself fiercely, as a beautiful face with slanted ebony eyes flashed across the screen of her mind.

Matt was waiting outside for her when she stepped out of the changing room, looking dark and foreign against the light surroundings. His eyes roamed over her freshly scrubbed face for a moment and then he seemed to echo her previous thoughts when he said softly, 'Sweet sixteen and never been kissed. Although you have, haven't you? Been kissed. Did you respond to him like you respond to me, Georgie?'

'Who?' His previous attitude had lulled her into a false sense of security, she realised now, which was probably what this master strategist had had in mind.

'This man you will not talk about,' he answered with gross unfairness, considering he had closed up like a clam about his own past.

She stared at him for a moment, feeling out of her depth, and then tossed her head slightly as a surge of anger swept away the weakness. She opened her mouth to tell him to mind his own business but he was too quick for her, bending swiftly as his arms went about her and he started to kiss her.

'Let me go, Matt.' She struggled but only briefly, her movements accentuating the softness of her shape against the hard angles of his body, that supremely male body she had had to fight not to ogle for the last hour.

'Why?' He lifted his head but only after he had clasped her face and kissed her until she was gasping.

'Because you said you'd be good,' she managed breathlessly.

'Oh, I am good, Georgie, I promise,' he said with a wicked twist of his lips. 'If nothing else I'm good.'

'You know what I mean.' She was flushed and excited and desperately trying to hide the evidence of her own arousal.

That she'd failed miserably became obvious when he brushed a tantalising finger down the soft slope of one breast and up again. She was swollen and aching, the nipple hard and tender, and as her breath caught in her throat he smiled again. 'You're going to continue to fight me?' he murmured mockingly. 'Why, when you know this can only have one conclusion?'

The Julia Bloomsbury philosophy again. I want therefore I must have. The grating quality of the thought stiffened her back and gave her the strength to jerk away from him, her voice holding a harsh note as she said, 'Matt, there is no way—*no way*—I would sleep with a man I've only known for a few days. I'm not made that way.'

'How long would you have to know a man, my innocent?' he asked smoothly, watching her with gleaming eyes.

Oh, this was crazy; she was getting in deeper and deeper here.

'I don't know.' She shrugged, her face straight and her eyes unhappy. 'A long time.'

'Time is relative.' His mouth was tilting with amusement. And then suddenly his attitude changed, his head nodding as he said, soberly now, 'But I like this in a woman, the ability to hold herself with some value. This is good.'

'It is?' She eyed him uncertainly. She didn't trust him an inch.

'But yes.' His hand reached out and lifted a lock of her hair, allowing it to fall back into place strand by strand as it fanned her face with silky gold. 'Man is the hunter. Did you not know this?'

'Maybe long ago before we became civilised,' she agreed warily.

'I am not civilised, Georgie.'

He didn't appear to be joking and she wasn't altogether sure she disagreed with the statement anyway. The veneer of civilisation sat very lightly on Matt's dark frame; he was dangerous and alien and had more than a little of the barbarian about him.

And then he flung back his head and laughed, the first real laugh she had heard from him, before he said as he met her eyes again, 'You frown at me when I try and make love to you and you frown at me when I agree I must not. What can I do to please you?'

He was laughing at her again and the mockery enabled her to say, her voice very cool, 'Why not try to be a friend first and foremost, or is that too radical a concept for you to take on board?'

'You want friendship from me?' he asked, his eyes on her full soft lips.

'That's beyond your capabilities?' she mocked tauntingly.

'With your brother, no.' He let his gaze take in her creamy skin, the small firm breasts and slender waist, and his voice was dry when he added, 'But you are not a six-foot male, Georgie.'

'It's friendship or nothing.' She sounded much firmer than she felt, she thought with some satisfaction, considering inside she was a quivering mess. She didn't have the first idea what made Matt tick, but she did know it would be emotional suicide to have an affair with him. She would be leaving Robert's office soon but, Matt being Matt, he would still arrange things so he could see her, at least while Robert was involved businesswise with him. This way, with certain ground rules in place, she would have some protection—whether from Matt or her own desire she wasn't sure. Whatever, she needed something!

'Then I agree.' His capitulation was too quick and too easy to be believable.

'Just friends,' she reiterated distrustfully.

'If this is what you want, Georgie.' The way he said her name never failed to set the juices flowing.

Her heart squeezed a little and her voice was all the more firm when she said, 'It is.'

'Then let us go into dinner and celebrate finding each other—as friends,' he murmured silkily. 'Yes?'

She nodded doubtfully. How was it, she asked herself silently, that instead of a victory this felt more like a defeat?

* * *

The dinner was absolutely wonderful, and Georgie found in spite of her racing heart—which just wouldn't behave itself—she enjoyed every mouthful. Goat's cheese, pepper, radicchio and pine nut salad for starters, followed by ravioli of lobster with a red pimento sauce and then chocolate and pear roulade. As she finished the last mouthful of dessert she looked at Matt, seated opposite her across a table resplendent with crystal and silver cutlery in a dining room which was all wood beams and antique furniture and flowing white silk voile curtains, and said, her tone awestruck, 'Do you always eat like this?'

He grinned at her. 'If I was trying to get you into my bed— which now of course I am not,' he clarified meekly, 'I would say, yes, of course, Georgie. As it is…' He allowed a moment or two to elapse. 'You are my friend, yes? And friends do not embroider the truth. So I have to say that I asked Rosie to make something of an effort tonight, although she is an excellent cook and always feeds me well.'

Georgie was still reeling from the grin, which had mellowed the hard face and made him appear years younger, and it took her a moment or two to smile back and make a light comment. He was *dangerous* and never more so than when he was pretending not to be, like now. Or was he pretending? As the evening continued and they had coffee in the exquisitely furnished room Matt had had turned into a drawing room and which overlooked the rolling landscaped gardens at the front of the house, she wasn't sure.

He was relaxed and amusing and the perfect host, and he didn't put a foot—or a hand—wrong. When she made noises about going home just after eleven o'clock he jumped up immediately without any ploys to detain her, and the drive home was uneventful. He saw her to Robert's door, lifted her chin and kissed her fleetingly on the tip of her nose and returned to the car without demur, leaving her standing on the doorstep long after the Lamborghini had disappeared into the night.

Whether it was the wine she had imbibed alone at dinner—Matt had been drinking mineral water after the one cocktail he had allowed himself, due to the fact he intended to drive her home—or the fact that it was the end of an emotionally exhausting day, Georgie didn't know, but she suddenly felt utterly drained.

It was an effort to mount the stairs and get into bed, and she fell asleep as soon as her head touched the pillow, but after a few hours' deep sleep she awoke, knowing Matt had been in her dreams. She lay quietly in the room she shared with Annie, her mind going over all she and Matt had said and done, and she couldn't even think of going back to sleep.

He was in her mind, in her head... She stared into the shadows caused by the burgeoning morning light as her heart thudded at the thought of all that had happened in such short a time, and again the sense of danger enveloped her. And it warned her—more effectively than any spoken words could have done—that she had to be very careful not to let him into her heart too.

Georgie had cause to think, over the next few weeks, that she had grossly exaggerated everything that morning after she had first had dinner with Matt.

As the days passed—the twins' party being the sort of success that would be talked about for years afterwards by their envious friends—and May merged into a blazing hot June, Matt seemed to have inveigled himself into the position of family friend with very little effort.

In spite of there being some sort of hiccup with regard to the starting date of his contract with Robert, he had insisted on financing the hire of extra men and machinery for another job which Robert had won in the meantime and which he would have been unable to accept but for Matt's magnanimity. The two men seemed to have more in common than Georgie would have thought, and it wasn't uncommon for Matt to call round for a coffee or a meal once or twice a week now, when he was always greeted rapturously by Annie and David.

Georgie had left Robert's employ as she'd planned and was now working for a temping agency at double the money Robert could afford, with the knowledge she could take time off in the children's school holidays without feeling she was putting pressure on Robert in his office. Consequently she was not privy to the ins and outs of what was happening with his business, but Robert himself had assured her that the very tasty contract with Matt was still on but just delayed a while due to a few problems with the planners.

'Couldn't have worked out better, actually,' Robert had said when he'd first broken the news in the middle of May. 'This way, with Matt agreeing to lend me the money to finance the Portabello job, we can do that through the next two or three months and then have Matt's job round about September onwards when it's often slack. We've never been busier, Georgie.'

And that was helping him come to terms with Sandra's loss. Georgie nodded to the thought as she fixed the children's breakfasts one baking hot Saturday morning towards the end of June. Which was good, very good. And he was taking more time out to be with the twins in spite of being so busy, and that was even better. He was on an even keel again, Annie and David too, and she had to admit all this was due in no small part to Matt de Capistrano. So why, knowing all this, and accepting Matt now seemed to have done exactly what she had asked and relegated her to friend status and nothing more, was she becoming increasingly dissatisfied and on edge with the status quo?

Did he see other women? She paused for a long moment, staring blindly out of the kitchen window at the sun-scorched grass, before shaking herself mentally and going to the door, whereupon she called the twins, who had been playing in their tree-house since first light, due to the muggy heat in the bedrooms which made sleep difficult. Of course he would.

She dished up the pancakes loaded with lemon and sugar which were the twins' treat every Saturday morning when there was a little more time for a leisurely breakfast, and after going to the foot of the stairs called Robert down too.

He'd be bound to carry on with his social life as normal, she told herself, her mind functioning quite independently of her mouth as she joined in the small talk between Robert and the twins now and again. He had certainly made no attempt to seduce her! Friends she had said and friends they were—he probably viewed her as a female Robert. She glanced at her brother's big square face and sighed inwardly. Perhaps she needed a holiday?

After cooking more pancakes for the other three and serving gallons of freshly squeezed orange juice, Georgie eventually had the house to herself after Robert carted the twins off to their swimming lesson.

She glanced at the kitchen table loaded with dirty dishes and the huge bowl on the worktop which still held some pancake mixture and sighed again. Once she had cleared up in here, the house was waiting for its weekend cleaning session, and there were the beds to change and the fridge to defrost… Life seemed a never-ending cycle of work and more work these days. She grimaced at the maudlin self-pity even as she reiterated, I'm twenty-three, not eighty-three. I want to enjoy life, feel free again, have some fun!

'Oh, stop it!' Her voice was harsh and she was suddenly horrified at her selfishness. 'Think of Robert and the kids, for goodness' sake. What's the matter with you?'

'I have it on good authority that it is the first sign of madness to talk to yourself.'

Georgie jumped so violently as the deep male voice sounded from the doorway behind her that the last of her orange juice shot up in an arc over the table.

'Matt!' She spun round, her hand to her breast, to see him standing big and dark behind her. 'You scared me to death,' she accused breathlessly.

He looked good, very good, but then he always did, she thought ruefully. But today, clothed in light grey cotton trousers and an opened-necked cream shirt, he looked especially good. Or perhaps she was just especially pleased to see him? That thought was too dangerous to pursue, and so she said, forcing a cross note into her voice. 'Why do you creep up on folk like that?'

'I wasn't aware I *was* creeping,' he said with amiable good humour. 'I met Robert and the children on the drive and Robert opened the door for me. He called to you.'

'Did he?' She had been so lost in her own dismal thoughts it would have taken more than her brother's voice to rouse her. 'Well, what do you want?' she asked ungraciously, suddenly aware of how sticky and hot she had got bending over a hot hob.

They looked at each other for a second, his grey eyes pinning her as they darkened and narrowed, and Georgie found she was holding her breath without knowing why.

'A pancake?' His gaze moved to the remaining mixture in the bowl.

A pancake? She found she was staring at the dark profile

stupidly and had to swallow hard before she could say, 'I'm sure Rosie has given you breakfast.'

'As it happens she has not,' he answered almost triumphantly. 'She has gone with her husband to visit relatives in Newcastle for the weekend. I had some toast and coffee earlier but I was in the pool at five this morning and it has given me the appetite.'

It wasn't often he made a mistake in his excellent English and on the rare occasions he had Georgie hadn't liked what it had done to her heart. She didn't like it now, and to cover the flood of tenderness she said abruptly, 'Sit down, then.' He sat, and, chastened by his obedience, she added, 'I suppose the heat made you unable to sleep?'

He didn't answer immediately, and as she turned to look at him she read the look in his eyes and flushed hotly as he said, very drily, 'This...friend thing carries certain penalties, does it not?'

'I wouldn't know,' she lied firmly.

He slanted a look at her from under half-closed lids and her colour rivalled that of a tomato. 'I'll see to the pancakes,' she snapped tightly.

'Thank you, Georgie.' It was meek and most un-Mattish.

Fifteen minutes later Matt had demolished three pancakes, a further two rounds of toast and two pint mugs of black coffee, and Georgie was trying to fight the immense satisfaction she felt in seeing him sitting at her kitchen table.

'You have given me breakfast; I intend to give you lunch.' She had been washing the dishes at the sink and as he turned her round to face him she kept her wet hands stretched out at the side of her as she said, 'Matt, please, I have to finish these and then start upstairs. I've masses to do and—'

'No.' He put a reproving finger on her lips. 'You're having a break. I've already told Robert you won't be back until later tonight.'

'Excuse *me*!' She glared at him. 'You can't just muscle in and tell me what to do. I need to see to the bedrooms.'

'I could tell you exactly what you need to see to in the bedroom of one particular individual who isn't a million miles away, but we won't go into that now,' Matt said smoothly.

'Matt—'

'I know, I know...friends.'

The sexual knowledge in the dark grey eyes was in danger of stripping away all her carefully erected defences and exposing her deepest desires, and Georgie felt mesmerised as she stood before him. Why could he always *do* this? she asked herself crossly. It wasn't fair.

He was holding her lightly on the shoulders, his fingertips warm through the thin material of the old cotton top she had pulled on first thing, and, in spite of everything she had said to Matt and to herself, at this very moment in time Georgie knew she wanted him to respond to her secret need. This wanting him had got worse through the last weeks, not better. It was with her every minute she was awake and it haunted her sleep to the point where she felt exhausted every morning.

She didn't know where an affair with Matt would take her; certainly he wouldn't be content with the fumbling petting she had allowed with Glen. It would be all or nothing with Matt. The only trouble was, 'all' in his case meant full physical intimacy and little else; 'all' in her case would be a giving of her heart and her soul as well as her body.

The thought freed her locked limbs and gave her the strength to step back away from him as she said, her voice very even and controlled despite the turmoil within, 'What did you have in mind for today?'

'A drive into the country, lunch at a little pub I know and then an afternoon relaxing at home by the pool. Rosie has left dinner for us; she's decided you are far too thin and need feeding up,' he added provocatively.

'Too thin?'

'I, on the other hand, think you are just right,' he said softly. 'For me, that is.'

Yes, well, she wasn't in a fit mental state to pursue that particular avenue. 'I'll have to shower and change.'

'I can wait.' There was a hungry fullness to his mouth that stirred her senses. 'I'm getting quite good at it,' he added drily.

'I won't be long.'

'Take all the time you want, Georgie.' He was wearing a sharp lemony aftershave that turned into something incredible on his tanned skin, and her heart went into hyperdrive when he added silkily, 'You are worth waiting for.'

Oh, boy, he was one of his own! Georgie didn't know if she was annoyed or amused as she hurried up to the room she shared with Annie and stripped off her sticky clothes. She didn't linger under the shower and her hair only took a few minutes to blowdry into a silky veil to her shoulders, so it couldn't have been more than a quarter of an hour before she had dressed again in a light white top and flimsy summer skirt, applying just a touch of mascara to her thick eyelashes before she made her way downstairs again.

However, the man who was sitting waiting for her at the kitchen table looked to have aged about ten years.

'Matt?' She was horrified at the change in him. 'What's the matter?'

'I've just had a phone call.' He gestured vacantly at his mobile phone which was lying in front of him on the table. 'It's my mother.'

'Your mother?' Oh, no, no.

'My sister…my sister's with her now, at the hospital. She found her collapsed and virtually unconscious, doubled up with pain.'

'Oh, Matt.' She didn't know what to do or say. His voice had been raw, and in the last few minutes worry and anxiety had scored deep lines in his face. Appalled, she murmured, 'You must go to her of course. What can I do to help?'

'What?'

He was clearly in shock, and Georgie saw his hands were trembling. She couldn't believe how it made her feel and it was in that second—totally inappropriate in the circumstances, she thought afterwards—that she realised how much she loved him. And it was love. Deep, abiding, once-in-a-lifetime love. As different from the puppy love she had felt for Glen as chalk from cheese. But she couldn't dwell on this catastrophe now.

She watched Matt take a deep breath and straighten his shoulders, and his voice was more normal when he said, 'I had better phone the airport. And my uncle, I need to let him know, and he'll have to hold the fort here.'

'I'll come with you.' She didn't even think about it; it was the natural thing to do somehow.

'To the airport? There's no need, really—'

'To Spain,' she cut in calmly. 'You need company at a time like this and we're friends, aren't we? Friends make time for each other.'

'To Spain?' There was a moment of silence and she saw he was struggling to take in what she had said. 'But your work, the twins—'

'I'm temping, so work is not a consideration. As for the twins; they have their father.' She eyed him steadily. 'And each other.' She was repeating the words he had said to her weeks earlier but neither of them were aware of it.

'You would do this? Come to Spain with me?' he asked somewhat bewilderedly.

Spain. The ends of the earth. Planet Zog! 'Of course.'

'Why?'

Because I love you with all my heart and all my soul and all my mind and all my strength. 'Because it might make things a little easier to have a friendly face with you,' she said quietly, 'and you have been terrific to the twins, Robert too, and I've never really said thank you.'

He raked back his hair in a confused gesture that tore at her heart. 'I...I do not know what to say, Georgie.'

At another time, in different circumstances and without the awful possibility of his mother being seriously ill, Georgie would have made plenty of that. The great Matt de Capistrano, silky-smooth operator and master of the silver tongue, at a loss for words? Never!

As it was she lifted up her hand and touched his cheek, careful to keep her eyes veiled so she gave nothing away as she said softly, 'You would do the same for me, Matt, for any of your friends.' And she did believe that, she affirmed silently. He was not a mean-minded man or ungenerous, far from it, and he would go the extra mile without counting the cost. The trouble was, common sense added ruefully, the masculine, ruthless side of him would keep his feelings beautifully under control the whole time. Whereas she...

'If you want to speak to your uncle and make any necessary arrangements, I can phone the airport if you like?' Georgie's voice was brisk now, but then it faltered as he took her hand in his own, holding it against his heart for a moment as he looked down into the deep green of her eyes before he raised the delicate fingers to his lips.

For several moments, moments when the world was quite still and frozen on its axis, she held his gaze. The air itself was shivering with intimacy and the trembling in her stomach threatened to communicate itself to her voice when she murmured, 'It will be all right, Matt, I'm sure of it.'

'Thank you,' he said huskily. He cupped her face in his big hands, kissing her parted lips with a tenderness she would have thought him incapable of. It hurt. Ridiculously, when he was being so nice, it hurt terribly because she wanted it so badly—she wanted *him*. But not just for a few weeks or months, even a year or two. She wanted him for ever, and for everness was an alien concept to him. Oh, what a mess, what a gargantuan mess.

'You're beautiful, Georgie.' His voice caught on her name in the way it always did, making it poignantly sweet. 'Whoever he was, he was a fool. You know that, do you not?'

She nodded. Glen had hurt her terribly at the time, but she knew now he would have hurt her more if she had married him because sooner or later he would have let her down. And it would have been worse, much worse, after they were married, perhaps even with children. He hadn't loved her enough; maybe he wasn't capable of loving anyone enough. Perhaps Julia sensed this and that was why they weren't happy? Whatever, she knew now she hadn't loved Glen enough either. Life with Glen would have been like wearing comfortable old clothes: no highs, no lows, mundane and ordinary. Millions of people the world over settled for just that, admittedly, but she wouldn't be able to do that again. Not now. Not after Matt.

He kissed her once more, and but for the circumstances and the fact that his mother was lying in a hospital bed halfway across the world Georgie was sure she would have leapt on him and ravished him on the kitchen table. As it was she called on every ounce of resolve and carefully removed herself from his hands, her voice a little shaky as she said, 'I'd better phone Robert and let him know what's happening.'

'Wait until I have spoken to the airport. It may be quicker to take a private plane,' Matt said quickly, with a return of his normal authority and command. 'We can land at La Coruna and I will arrange to have a car waiting.'

Georgie nodded silently. She would cope with this—the knowledge that she loved him—she would. As long as he didn't know, everything would be all right. Nothing had changed, not really.

'I'll go and sort out my passport and a few clothes,' she said quietly, scurrying up to the room she shared with Annie. Once in the sunlit room, however, she sank down on the bed for a few moments, staring blankly across the room.

She was committed to being with him for the next few days now, for good or ill, and however things worked out she wasn't sorry she'd offered to go with him. She wanted to see where he had been born, understand that other part of his life and see further glimpses of his complex personality which would be bound to unravel with his family and friends. Had he taken many women to his home town?

Her soft mouth drooped unknowingly for a few seconds and then she raised her head high, narrowing her eyes as she thought, If nothing else, *if nothing else* she would make sure he remembered her a little differently from all the rest. Friendship might not be what she would have chosen, but it singled her out from the crowd!

CHAPTER SEVEN

IT WAS just three o'clock in the afternoon when the private plane Matt had hired landed at La Coruna, northern Spain, where Matt's brother-in-law was waiting for them.

Carlos Molina turned out to be a small man who was as round as he was tall, but he had soft melting eyes, a mouth which looked as though it smiled a lot—but which was strained and tight today—and a shock of unruly curly hair. Georgie liked him immediately.

Matt's influence—and no doubt his wealth—had swept them through Customs in minutes, and once the introductions were over the two men conversed swiftly in Spanish for a few moments before Matt turned to Georgie and said quietly, 'I'm sorry, but Carlos's English is not good and I need to know the details of my mother's collapse.'

'How is she?' Georgie asked softly. They had said little on the journey but when she had taken his hand shortly after departure in a gesture of comfort he had held on to it like a lifeline.

'There is talk of an operation; gall bladder, Carlos thinks.'

'Sí, sí.' Carlos had been trying to follow their conversation, nodding his black head the while. 'You come now the car, she is waiting.'

Georgie hadn't known what she was expecting to see when they left the air-conditioned building, but she supposed her mind had veered towards scorched landscapes and baking hot skies. However, as the silver-blue Mercedes

Carlos was driving ate up the miles she was breathless at the scenic beauty unfolding before her eyes.

It was hot, but only as hot as an English summer at its best, and as the car made its way south-west from the airport she had an endlessly changing view of mountains and little villages set in pine-clad hills, traditional-style white-washed villas set among orange and lemon groves, fields of almond, olive and fig trees separated by ancient mellow walls, and houses of golden stone perched on rocky outcrops.

The quality of the light and intensity of colour was totally different from England and overwhemingly beautiful, and they had just passed a village square festooned with market stalls overflowing with produce into the cobbled streets beyond, when Matt said softly at the side of her, 'You like the country of my heart?'

'Like it?' She turned to him impulsively, her face alight. 'It's wonderful, Matt. How can you ever bear to leave it and stay in England for so long every year?'

He smiled slowly. 'England, too, is beautiful,' he said quietly. 'Although I look on Spain as my home I consider myself as English as Spanish, unlike my sister, Francisca. Perhaps it is the names, eh? I was christened after my maternal grandfather Matthew, whilst Francisca took our parental grandmother's first name. Whatever, Francisca is Spanish from the top of her head to the soles of her feet. Is that not right, Carlos?' he said to the man in front of them.

'*Sí, sí.*' It was very enthusiastic and obviously approving.

Matt turned back to her, his voice dry. 'Carlos is one of the old school,' he said mockingly. 'He likes his woman barefoot and pregnant.'

The way he said the words, in his husky, smoky voice, made Georgie think it wouldn't be such a bad thing after all—if you were Matt's woman, that was—but she forced an indignant note into her voice as she said, 'I'm sure Carlos thinks nothing of the sort. How many children have you got, Carlos?'

He answered in Spanish, and when Georgie glanced enquiringly at Matt, the hard mouth was twisted in a smile as he said softly, 'Hold on to your hat, Georgie. It was eight at the last count.'

'Eight?' She was truly shocked.

'But yes.' He shifted in his seat and as his thigh briefly brushed Georgie's it took all her will-power not to react. 'Spanish men are very virile,' he murmured, straight-faced now. 'Did you not know this?'

She decided not to pursue that path. 'And Francisca wants a big family too?' she asked instead, her cheeks pink but her voice prim.

His smile this time was merely a twitch. 'Of course.'

'That's ideal, then, isn't it?' She turned from him to look out of the window. They were passing a small family, the man leading a plump little donkey which had two curly-haired tots sitting on its furry back and the woman in a long red skirt with a big straw hat on her head, and something about the scene caught at her heart. The children waved to the car and Georgie waved back. They all looked so happy, so relaxed, so *alive*. Life was simple to them, a joy.

And then she caught herself sharply. No. No thinking, no cogitating. One minute, one hour at a time—that was what she'd decided earlier and that was what would see her through the next few days. If she allowed her heart to rule her head and became one of his women it would end badly, for her. As long as she kept that to the forefront of her mind she would be all right.

A few miles further on they passed a crystalline lake,

tranquil under the turquoise sky, and within minutes the
Mercedes turned into a narrow twisting lane off the main
road on which they had been travelling. 'It is better I visit
the hospital with Carlos now,' Matt said quietly, 'and you
must rest and take some refreshments. My housekeeper will
take care of you.'

Even as he was speaking they passed through wide open,
massive iron gates and into a shadow-blotched drive, huge
evergreen oaks forming a natural arch beyond which
Georgie caught a glimpse of magnificent grounds stretching
away into the distance.

'This is your home?' she asked softly.

He nodded. 'Mi Oasis. My Oasis. It has always been
named such and I saw no reason to change it when I bought
the place ten years ago.'

The car had been climbing a slight incline, and now the
drive opened up to reveal an enormous house some hundred
yards in front of them. Unlike most of the houses she had
seen on the journey this one was not whitewashed but built
of mellow, honey-coloured stone and bedecked with ornate
balconies bursting with a profusion of purple, white and
scarlet bougainvillaea, geraniums and pink begonia, and
surrounded by more oak trees. The windows were many
and large, with small leaded squares of glass that twinkled
in the sunlight, and in the middle of the drive in front of
the house a magnificent fountain complete with cherubs
riding prancing horses cascaded into a small stone pool.

'Does this place get a wow, too?' He was smiling as he
spoke, his voice faintly mocking but warm, and Georgie
wrenched her eyes away from the beautiful old house as
she said, 'A double wow, actually.'

'Once you have eaten and bathed you must have a walk
in the gardens at the rear of the house,' Matt said quietly,
his eyes on the front door of the house which had just

opened to reveal a small uniformed maid. 'Pilar will accompany you if you wish.'

'I'd rather explore on my own, thank you,' she said quickly. His voice had been slightly distant and she sensed his mind was focused on his mother now, although his innate good manners had not revealed his impatience to get to the hospital. 'You go, Matt. I'll be fine here until you get back.'

Matt insisted on introducing her to his Spanish housekeeper, Flora, who had appeared beside Pilar within moments, and then escorting her personally to her rooms on the second floor of the three-storey building before leaving, however. 'You will be all right until I return, Georgie?' He touched her cheek as he spoke. 'I have told Flora to bring you a tray in half an hour, once you have had time to shower and change.'

'Thank you.' This wasn't the time to be reflecting on how incredibly sexy he was, and she hated herself for it, but here, in Spain, he seemed ten times more foreign and a hundred times more dangerous. 'And please don't worry about me, Matt. I'll love exploring. The whole point of my coming with you was to be a help, not a hindrance.' And then she forced herself to add, 'That's what friendship is all about, isn't it?'

His thick black lashes hid the expression in his eyes as he responded, after a pause, 'Just so, *pequeña*. Just so.' He bent and touched one flushed cheek with his lips as he spoke, and such was her rush of sexual awareness that Georgie couldn't form the words to ask him what *pequeña* meant before he smiled one last time and closed the door behind him.

'Whew…' She stood exactly where he'd left her for a full minute before she trusted her legs to carry her across the room, whereupon she opened the windows on to the balcony and stepped outside after kicking off her shoes and flexing her aching toes.

The sun-warmed tiles were smooth beneath her bare feet and the ornate iron on the balcony sides was covered in bougainvillaea and lemon-scented verbenas, but it was the scent from the wonderful gardens below, bursting with tropical trees and shrubs and flowers, that flooded her senses. Acres and acres of grounds stretched before her in a dazzling display of colour, and after soaking up the sight for more than five minutes she turned reluctantly into the room behind her. And what a room, what a *suite* of rooms, she thought dazedly.

She was standing in the sitting room, which was the size of Robert's lounge back in England, and the dull rose furnishings embodied two two-seater plump soft sofas, a pine bookcase and a small writing desk and chair, a TV and video and a cocktail cabinet which enclosed a small fridge. The floor was pine and the drapes at the window the same dull rose as the sofas, and this colour scheme was reflected in the big double bedroom which led off the sitting room, although the main colour in there was cream. The bathroom was an elaborate affair in cream marble, and again the towels were in dull rose and gold.

When she had asked, Matt had told her this suite was one of four on this floor, with another four on the floor above. The east wing was given over to the servants' quarters with garages below and an extensive stable block, and the west wing was Matt's private domain which he had promised to show her later.

On the ground floor, which she had not yet seen apart from the baronial hall and huge curving open staircase, there was apparently a drawing room, a sitting room, two other reception rooms, the dining room and breakfast room, and the kitchens.

It was palatial opulence at its best, Georgie thought faintly. Luxurious, grandiose and undeniably stunning. And with more newly built stables behind the west wing, an Olympic-size swimming pool and tennis courts in the grounds... Her mind trailed to a halt. *What was she doing here?* Her, little Georgina Millett from Sevenoaks? This was Rothschild league!

She stood still, her fists pressed to her chest as she panicked big time. The house in England was gorgeous, but this...this was something else. She hadn't realised just how wealthy and powerful Matt was.

After a minute or so of silent hysteria she took a hold of herself. Matt was still Matt. He had been Matt before she had seen this place and he was still Matt. Okay, so he was richer than she'd ever dreamed. She took a deep breath and then gulped hard. But he was the same man who had sat and laughed and joked with the kids in Robert's little dining room over the last weeks, who had taken on a menagerie of decrepit animals to please a frail old lady, who was worried sick about his mother...

And then she gave in to the storm of weeping which had been threatening for the last minutes, had a good howl and dried her eyes. She loved him. She couldn't do anything about it even if every hour that passed emphasised how hopeless it was. Matt was no ordinary man, and she wasn't talking about his wealth now. If he had been dirt-poor he would still have been different, commanding, magnetic. Matt de Capistrano was...well, Matt de Capistrano, she finished weakly. And that said it all. And she'd had to go and fall in love with him...

By the time she had stood under the warm silky water for five minutes Georgie felt refreshed and calmer.

She was still in the big towelling robe which had been hanging in the bathroom when Pilar knocked on the outside door a little while later, and after calling for the little maid to enter she walked into the sitting room and took the tray from her.

There were enough slices of cold beef, pork and ham, green salad, savoury pastries, chopped egg and tomatoes to feed a small army, and Georgie looked at the tray askance, before she raised her eyes to Pilar and said quickly, 'This is lovely but I'll never be able to eat it all.'

'*Perdón, señorita?*'

Georgie repeated herself more slowly, and the little Spanish girl's puzzled frown vanished as she smiled and said, '*Sí, sí.* Do not worry, *señorita*. Señora Flora, she always give b-i-g *raciones*, big—how you say—big snacks, *sí*? Señor de Capistrano, he have the big appetite.'

Georgie nodded thankfully. 'As long as she won't be offended if I leave quite a bit.'

After dressing quickly in a sleeveless ice-blue jersey top and white wide-legged linen trousers Georgie ate a little of the food on the vast tray, washing it down with the glass of red wine that had accompanied the food, before making her way downstairs.

She met Pilar as she reached the bottom of the massive staircase and from the look on the Spanish girl's face Georgie assumed, rightly, she had committed an unforgivable *faux pas* in bringing the tray down herself. She deposited it into Pilar's hands with a smile and told her she was going for a walk in the lovely grounds at the back of the house, and departed swiftly. Her first gaffe and she didn't doubt there would be others. Clearly she didn't know the right way to behave! Unlike Matt's other women, no doubt.

Once in the gardens she paused to look back at the house again. It was so, so beautiful, she thought wonderingly. The decorative iron fretwork, the different shades of the mellow stone, the vivid splashes of crimson, mauve and white from the balconies—she couldn't quite believe she was here!

She explored for a long time, wandering through the grounds and saying hallo to the couple of gardeners she met who had clearly been alerted to her arrival as they greeted her by name.

She was sitting on an ancient wooden seat overlooking an orchard of peach, orange, lemon and cherry trees when she heard her name called, and looked round to see Matt approaching. He hadn't been out of her thoughts for a minute and now she looked anxiously into his dark face. 'Your mother?' she called across the space separating them.

'Brighter than I had expected.' He reached her in a few strides and before she had realised what he was about to do he had pulled her into him, his strong arms slipping round her waist as he moulded her into his hard, firm body, and his chin resting on the top of her head as he nuzzled the warm silkiness of her hair. 'You smell like all the summers I have ever known,' he murmured huskily. 'So fresh, so good.'

How did she answer that? And she wasn't at all sure this embrace could qualify as one of friendship! She rested against him for a moment, simply because she couldn't resist doing so, and then moved back in his arms to say, 'What did the doctors say? Is she going to be all right, Matt?'

'*Sí, sí.*' He shook his head, his voice very smoky as he said, 'Excuse me, Georgie. I have been speaking Spanish all day. Yes, she will be all right I am sure, but she will need the operation. I'm having a specialist flown in from the States tonight and he will operate tomorrow.'

'You are?' How money talked.

'He is a friend of mine and an excellent doctor. My

mother knows and trusts him and it is important she is confident and tranquil.'

Georgie nodded. He looked impossibly handsome and darkly masculine, and the subtle, delicious smell of him was undermining her resolve.

'She would like to meet you.' He was still holding her and didn't seem to notice her attempts to break free.

'She would?' This wouldn't do, she would have to manage more than two words every time she opened her mouth. 'You told her about me then?'

'Yes, I told her about you, Georgie.' His eyes were almost black slits as they narrowed against the evening light which was still very bright. 'I told her you were Robert's sister and that we were friends. This is right, yes?'

'Of course.' And as anguish streaked through her soul she told herself sharply, This is the only way and you know it. You *know* it.

'But I think maybe she guesses it is hard for me to be friends,' Matt continued softly. He traced the outline of her mouth with one finger as he looked down into her face, and when the kiss came it was hot and potent, a raging fire that devoured with dangerous intensity. She had shifted in his arms, momentarily with protest but almost immediately succumbing, even as a little voice in her head berated her for the weakness. After all she had resolved, all she'd determined, he only had to touch her and she was his. The voice was insistent but it couldn't compete with what his mouth and hands were doing, and what she wanted. She loved him so much, so very much.

He was muttering her name and somehow they had come to be lying on the thick grass which was threaded with daisies and forget-me-nots and other bell-like wild flowers. She could feel every muscle, every male contour of his hard shape as intimately as if they were naked, and he wanted her. His body was telling her that all too blatantly.

The heady rush of sensation which had exploded within her was sending waves of pleasure into every nerve and sinew, and his hands were moving erotically and with experienced purpose as they caused her to moan softly in her throat.

Their mouths were joined in a fusion that was a kind of consummation in itself, his tongue thrusting as it invaded her body. His thighs were locked over hers, his hands lifting her buttocks forward to acknowledge his arousal and his heart slamming against his ribcage so hard she could feel it in her own body.

She was returning kiss for kiss, embrace for embrace with an uninhibitedness which would have horrified her if she'd been capable of conscious thought, but it was some minutes before she realised the restraint Matt was showing. He had made no attempt to take their lovemaking to its natural conclusion, indeed she felt he had withdrawn in some way, and this seemed to be borne out when she twisted away and looked into his face, and he let her go immediately. 'What's the matter?' she asked shakily.

'Nothing is the matter except that I cannot trust myself where you are concerned, *pequeña*,' he said ruefully. 'If I had not stopped it would have been impossible to do so in another minute. You understand me?'

'But...I thought...' She didn't know how to go on as the realisation dawned that she had offered herself on a plate to him and *he* had been the one to call a halt.

'That I would take advantage of you at the earliest opportunity?' he asked silkily, his voice losing its softness. 'You came here with me because your heart was moved with sympathy, yes?'

She nodded weakly, because it was all she was capable

of with his big lean body stretched out at the side of her and the taste of him making her head spin.

'And this same sympathy has lowered your defences and made you wish to give me comfort,' he continued quietly. 'This is good, I like this, but when we make love properly, Georgie, it will be for one reason and one reason only. Because you want me as much as I want you and it is the only thing filling your mind and your heart. Not pity or a wish to comfort, not even that the evening is soft with the scent of flowers and there is romance in the air like now.'

Was he *crazy*? Didn't he know how much she wanted him? Not through pity or anything else except good old earthy desire, made all the more powerful because she loved him.

Georgie opened her mouth to tell him of his mistake and then shut it again with a little snap. It wasn't Matt who was crazy, it was her, she told herself silently as cold reason stepped in. She knew in her heart of hearts he would eat her up and spit her out and go on his own sweet way sooner or later, so why on earth was she playing with fire?

'Come.' He rose to his feet with the sinuous grace which characterised all his movements, and held out his hand to help her up. 'We will wander back to the house and have cocktails before dinner. Then we will eat and talk and laugh, and later see the moon rise like a queen in the sky. Yes?'

She took his hand, scrambling to her feet with none of his panache. He had told her he didn't believe in true love and for everness and he was thirty-six years old, not a raw callow youth who didn't know his own mind. But what had made him that way? There had to be something, surely? People didn't just wake up one morning and decide to be that cynical. Would her experience with Glen have sent her down that path if she hadn't met Matt before she had become hardened? Well, she'd never know now, would she? Because she *had* met him.

She smoothed down her rumpled clothes, her cheeks flaming as she fumbled with the tiny mother-of-pearl buttons on her top, several of which were undone.

Matt, on the other hand, appeared perfectly cool and relaxed, as controlled and in charge as ever. There were times, Georgie told herself with silent savagery, when she hated him as much as she loved him, and this was definitely one of those times!

He drew her arm through his as they strolled back to the house through the perfumed warm air, every bird in the world—or so it seemed to Georgie's feverish senses—singing a love song. Matt was chatting easily, filling her in on everything that had happened at the hospital that afternoon and reiterating his mother was bright and cheerful. Which was great, fantastic, Georgie thought ruefully, but how he could think about anything else except what had nearly happened out there, she just didn't know! But then it was just a sexual thing with him, a hunger that required sating. You ate when you were hungry, drank when you were thirsty and bedded a woman when you wanted sexual release. Matt's philosophy on life in a nutshell.

They entered the house though the open French doors of the stately drawing room, which was clearly the way Matt had exited, although Georgie had left the house by the less exalted exit by the kitchens, and he kept hold of her as they walked through the high-ceilinged, cathedral-type splendour into the hall beyond.

'Do you use the drawing room often?' she asked a little weakly. The exquisite furnishings—most of which looked to be priceless antiques—were a little daunting.

'High days and holidays; isn't that what you English say?'

His voice had held a mocking note and now Georgie's was a touch indignant when she said, 'You're English, too.'

'Half-English,' he corrected softly. 'And this makes a difference, yes?'

Oh, yes. She almost missed her footing, although there was nothing to trip over but her own sinful thoughts.

Matt glanced at his watch. 'There's plenty of time before we need to change for dinner for you to come and see my home within my home,' he offered, adding with a mocking twist of his lips, 'And you must consider yourself highly honoured to be asked. It is only by invitation anyone passes into the inner sanctum.'

Georgie didn't return the smile and stared at him steadily. 'Is that true?' she asked quietly.

The teasing look vanished, and Matt answered just as quietly, 'Yes, it is true. And I am chary with the invitations. I value my privacy.'

She could believe that. He might entertain lavishly and have a wide group of friends and acquaintances, but she had learnt Matt de Capistrano was a man who revealed only a little of himself to anyone, and then even that little was jealously monitored.

Georgie walked with him down the hall and watched as he opened the heavy wood door leading to his separate wing. Matt waved her past him, and she found herself in what appeared to be another smaller hall complete with a beautifully worked wrought-iron spiral staircase.

'Come.' He took her hand in his. 'The downstairs first, I think.'

The downstairs first. That meant he intended to show her the upstairs next. And upstairs meant his bedroom.

The hall floor was again wood—honey-coloured oak—and the painted walls reflected this colour but in a much paler hue. Instead of the fine paintings which adorned the main hall, these walls had continuous sheets of bronze-tinted mirror from waist height, and in the last of the day's sunlight slanting in the tall narrow windows on the right-hand side of the hall the space became a place of pure golden light.

Matt opened the door on his left and again stood back for her to precede him.

'Oh, Matt.' Surprised into looking at him, she saw the dark grey eyes had been waiting for her reaction. They were standing looking out over a wonderful indoor swimming pool, beyond which, at the far end of the pool, there were huge palms and plants enclosing several big upholstered loungers and a table and chairs. The end wall consisted mostly of glass, with two large patio doors which opened out onto a walled garden full of flowers and shrubs and trees.

'My gym.' He had been leading her to a door halfway along the pool and now opened it to reveal a well-equipped gymnasium and sauna, complete with showers and toilet facilities.

'It's wonderful.' As he closed the door to the gym again Georgie glanced around her, quite overwhelmed. 'Did you have all this done?'

He nodded. 'I prefer to swim and exercise in the nude,' he stated, without appearing to notice the effect of his words on the colour of Georgie's skin, 'and this would not be…appropriate outside on certain occasions.'

Georgie nodded in what she hoped was a cool, cosmopolitan kind of way and forced the X-rated pictures flashing across the screen of her mind back under lock and key. 'It's very nice,' she said primly, 'and very private.'

'Just so.'

Was he laughing at her? As they walked back into the hall she glanced at his dark face out of the corner of her eye but his expression was deadpan. Not that that meant anything. Not with Matt de Capistrano, she thought resentfully.

'Up you go.' As she climbed the spiral staircase she was terribly aware of Matt just behind her and almost stumbled as she stepped out into the open plan bedroom. She hadn't been expecting his bedroom to be next—she'd assumed that would be at the top of the house—and she certainly hadn't expected it to be so...so— She gave up trying to find suitable adjectives and gazed warily about her.

Again the end wall was all glass, and the huge, soft, round billowy bed, which was easily two and a half metres in diameter, was only slightly raised off the wooden floor, positioned so the occupant had a scenic view across tree tops and the vast expanse of light-washed sky. The left-hand wall was mirrored like the hall had been but this time in a smoky glass to five feet high, at which point shelves holding books, magazines and tapes reached to ceiling height.

A TV was fixed on the right hand wall, next to which the doors of the walk-in wardrobe were open to reveal neatly stacked shelves and racks of suits and other masculine clothing.

A large plump three-seater sofa was standing at the opposite end of the room from the bed, by the side of which was a fridge and a low table holding a coffee machine and cups. On the other side of the sofa there looked to be a well-stocked cocktail cabinet.

The sofa and the duvet, along with the floating voile curtains at the windows, were in a light cream, but the numerous pillows and massive cushions piled on the bed, along with the stack of cushions scattered on the sofa were in unrelenting black cotton.

Altogether it was an uncompromisingly masculine room,

devoid of colour and any feminine frills, and this was reflected in the *en suite* bathroom when Matt opened the door next to the wardrobe to reveal a bathroom of black marble and silver fittings without one plant or feathery fern to soften its elegant, stark beauty.

Georgie stared inside, the subdued lights which had come on automatically when the door was opened, and which were hidden for the most part, emphasising the voyeuristic nature of the gleaming marble and inevitable mirrored wall rising up behind the black marble bath.

Georgie couldn't think of a single coherent thing to say. She was still struggling to come to terms with that incredible bed, which just had to have been built inside the room to Matt's specification, and now to be presented with such unashamed lasciviousness...

She swallowed hard, her throat dry. This was one unrepentant bachelor, she told herself fiercely, everything she had seen this far screamed it, and she ignored it at her peril.

'You do not like these rooms?' He closed the door to the bathroom as he spoke and she was forced to meet the dark piercing gaze trained on her face.

'Like them?' How did she answer that? They were beautiful, magnificent, but they carried their own warning and it was like a slap in the face. But the rooms themselves were out of this world. 'Yes, of course I like them,' she answered after a moment, her voice very even. 'They're extraordinary; the whole house is stunning.'

He surveyed her unblinkingly. 'Never play poker, *pequeña*.'

'What?' She pretended not to know what he meant, to give herself time to get her brain in gear.

He smiled, but it was just a movement of his lips and didn't reach the steel-grey eyes. 'Come and see the top floor,' he said easily, as though he wasn't in the least bothered by what he imagined she was thinking. Which he probably wasn't, Georgie affirmed miserably.

And then she flushed furiously when, instead of moving towards the staircase, he paused for a moment, brushing his lips across her forehead as he murmured, 'The top floor is safer, I promise.'

'Safer?' She tried to ignore what his closeness was doing to her hormones and injected a note of annoyed surprise into her voice. 'I don't know what you are talking about.'

'Sure you don't.' Now the hard, faintly stern mouth was wolfish.

'Matt, I'm telling you—'

And then her voice was cut off and her stomach muscles contracted when his hand followed the curve of her cheek down to her throat. He wasn't holding her, he was barely touching her, and yet his fingers were fire against her skin and she had to stiffen herself against his touch.

'This is what I'm talking about,' he said very softly, 'the chemical reaction that happens whenever we're in ten feet of each other.'

His gaze dropped to her mouth and her lips parted instinctively, as though her body had a mind of its own. She could feel warmth pulsing through her and sensed the tension that was holding his big muscled body taut, and she knew she had to break the moment. That bed, that wonderful, marvellous, voluptuous bed, was too close…

'I'm ready to see upstairs now,' she said in a staccato voice. Chemical reaction he'd said. Just chemical reaction. *What was she going to do?*

CHAPTER EIGHT

THE top floor of Matt's wing was another surprise. A large part of it was given over to a frighteningly well-equipped study, with all the latest technology in use, but behind this area, at the far end of the room, an extended enclosed balcony in the form of a small sitting room gave a bird's eye view stretching into infinity.

Beyond Matt's estate there were rolling hills and countryside and small villages, a dramatic vista which was awe-inspiring.

'Sit down. I'll fix us a drink.'

Georgie nodded her acquiescence, wandering over to the full-length semicircle of windows. 'I don't think I've ever seen a view to match this one,' she said slowly without turning to look at him.

She heard the chink of ice against glass and then was conscious of him just behind her. 'Incredible, isn't it?' he murmured softly.

'Surely all this part of the house didn't have such huge windows when you bought it?' she asked quickly, the scent of his male warmth surrounding her and telling her she had to keep talking.

There was a brief pause and then he said, 'No, it didn't. I had this wing changed to suit my requirements. I like space and light.'

It wasn't what he said but something in his voice, the merest inflexion, which sent pinpricks of awareness flickering down her spine. The almost obsessive demand for spaciousness, the mirrors, the huge windows... 'You're claustrophobic?' She turned to him but it wasn't really a question. And as his eyes narrowed, she reiterated, 'You are, aren't you?'

He shrugged. 'A little.'

A lot, she bet. 'Have you always been so?'

'No, not always.' His voice was dismissive and he made it clear he didn't intend to respond further to the curiosity in her voice when he took her arm and drew her down on to the sofa, handing her a glass of white wine as he said, 'Relax and enjoy the view, Georgie.'

Easier said than done.

She sat, her knees tightly together and her back straight, staring rigidly out across the rolling hills and countryside which merged to a dusky faint mauve on the far horizon. So he had a small chink of weakness in that formidable armour he wore—claustrophobia. And it was indicative of the inner strength of the man that she had known him for many weeks now and had never guessed. She found that thought incredibly depressing.

'Are you ready to tell me about him yet?'

'What?' She had jerked away like a skittish colt before she could collect herself.

'Did he break your heart, Georgie?' he asked gruffly.

This was so *unfair*! He revealed nothing—*nothing*—of himself and yet he expected her to spill everything. She stiffened and then raised her small chin. 'His name was Glen,' she said steadily. 'What was her name?'

'Her?' His eyes went flat and cold.

'Yes, her. There must have been a her.' She was guessing, but everything about his body language told her she'd hit gold. Or ashes, depending on how you looked at it.

'Kiss and tell?' he said harshly.

She blanched at his tone, but she wasn't going to back down now. She was tired of going round in circles, and since the first moment she had laid eyes on Matt she felt that was what she'd been doing. 'Exactly,' she challenged bravely. 'Or aren't you up for it yourself? You just expect me to tell you all, is that it?'

He stared back at her for a long moment as something worked in his hard face which she couldn't read. 'I didn't mean—' He stopped abruptly, dark colour slashing his cheekbones. 'Or maybe I did. Hell, I don't know what I mean.'

The momentary loss of composure pleased her more than words could say. It was a start. If nothing else it was a start, wasn't it?

He drew air in between his teeth in a low hiss, his glittering eyes narrowed on her pale face, and then said coldly, 'You won't like what you hear and it will serve no useful purpose.'

'I'd prefer to be the judge of that,' she said, speaking evenly, not wanting him to guess that part of her was terrified. 'I haven't lied to you, Matt, I've been totally honest since we met.' Her conscience twanged here but she brushed aside the still small voice which questioned why she hadn't told him she loved him. That was different, quite different. It was. 'I've always made it clear I'm not in the market for a casual affair; I don't live my life like that. I know you but I don't know you, and you offer nothing of yourself, not really.'

'Charming.'

'Oh, you've been great to Robert and the twins, don't get me wrong, and you're amazingly generous, but that's just money, isn't it?' she said, looking him straight in the eyes and trying not to dwell on how darkly handsome he looked sitting there, a touch away.

'Which of course is nothing,' he drawled sarcastically.

'No, it's not,' she agreed tersely, suddenly furiously an-

gry with him too. 'Money is great if you've got it and it
certainly smoothes the way, but Sandra and Robert had
something no amount of cash could buy. And, having seen
them, having seen what they had, I would never be content
with anything less.'

'It's dangerous to put a relationship on a pedestal like
that and rather arrogant to assume you know what their
marriage was really like.' It was expressionless and cold.
'You could find yourself following some sort of illusion for
the rest of your life and end up with nothing.'

'I saw their ups and downs and know how hard they
worked at their marriage to make it the success it was,'
Georgie answered tightly, 'and I didn't view it through
rose-coloured spectacles, if that's what you're insinuating.'

He stared at her, his black brows drawn together in an
angry scowl. 'How are we arguing when I meant this to
be—?' He stopped abruptly.

'Cosy and intimate?' she suggested with acid sweetness.

'Relaxing and beneficial.'

Relaxing and beneficial? Yeah, sure! She glared at him,
her green eyes stormy, and took a long gulp at the wine to
prevent herself from throwing it at him.

From rage he was suddenly grinning and it had the effect
of leaving her in no man's land, especially when he said,
his voice husky, 'You're a formidable opponent, Miss
Millett.'

'Opponent?' She wasn't ready to melt yet. 'I thought we
were supposed to be friends, and friends should be able to
have healthy disagreements.'

'Right.' He nodded, his mouth quirking at the haughty
note in her voice. 'What else are friends allowed to do?'

'Do you mean to tell me you've never had any women
friends?' she answered stiffly.

'Not ones with eyes the colour of pure jade and hair of

raw silk,' he murmured softly. 'You've bewitched me, do you know that? You fill my thoughts and you invade my dreams, and all I think about is you.'

It was an unexpected confession and Georgie couldn't quite believe it was real.

'I mean it.' As always he read her face.

He probably did. For now. But now would turn into yesterday and then what would she do? She knew, even without looking too deeply inside herself, that once she gave Matt everything she would never recover from it.

'Her name was Begonia.'

'What?'

He tilted her face towards him, his fingers gentle, and said again, 'You asked her name. It was Begonia.'

She didn't want to know her name. She didn't want to know anything about this woman he had known and cared for. And she wanted to know everything.

'I met her at university, here in Spain,' he said quietly. 'We were together for eighteen months and then it finished.'

Was she beautiful? Had he loved her with all his heart? Had Matt finished it? Where was she now?

'And Glen?' he asked without a change of tone. 'Who was Glen?'

Glen was nothing. Georgie took a deep breath. 'Glen was the original boy next door,' she said carefully. 'I grew up with him once I went to live with Robert and Sandra; his sisters were my best friends for a while. We got engaged and he broke it off a few weeks before the wedding.'

'Why?'

'He found someone else.' He was still holding her face and now she broke the hold, turning away slightly and taking another gulp of wine before she added, 'He went off with his boss's daughter; she was very wealthy or, rather, her father was. They got married a few months later.'

'He was a fool.' It was tender.

'Yes, he was.' She was trying very hard to keep any emotion out of her voice. 'But I realised later—' once I had met you and realised what love was all about '—it would have been a huge mistake.'

'Do you mean that?'

There was a note in his voice she couldn't quite place, and now she raised her eyes to meet the piercing gaze trained on her face and said quietly, 'Oh, yes, it's not bravado. I had hero-worshipped him when we were younger and he could do no wrong in my eyes, so it was an awful shock when he unceremoniously dumped me, but after a while I realised I'd built him up in my head as someone completely different to who he really was. Puppy love, I suppose; certainly blind infatuation. Marriage to Glen would have been a disaster.'

She swallowed hard. She wanted to ask more about this Begonia and now was the time, she might never have another opportunity like this, but could she bear hearing it?

And then the decision was taken out of her hands when the telephone at the side of the sofa began to ring. Matt swore softly as he picked up the receiver, his voice sharp as he said, *'Sí?'*

Georgie could hear it was a woman's voice on the other end of the line and as her senses prickled she wasn't surprised to hear him say, *'Sí,* Pepita,' followed by more Spanish. And his voice was not sharp now.

She rose to her feet, wandering across to the windows with her back towards him and looking out on to the view as her ears strained for every inflexion of his voice.

'I am sorry, Georgie.' As Matt replaced the receiver she turned round slowly, her face showing nothing but polite enquiry. 'That was Pepita. She was anxious for news of my mother.'

'She knows her, then?' She was amazed how calm and matter-of-fact her voice was when the screen of her mind was replaying a picture of the other woman's elegant, red-taloned hand resting intimately on his arm.

He nodded. 'Pepita has been with me for many years,' he said absently. 'She knew my mother well; they are great friends.'

Yes, they would be, because Pepita would have made sure of it. She wanted Matt. Georgie suddenly realised the knowledge had been there in her head from the first morning. Pepita was in love with him. Was he aware of it?

'She was phoning from her car; she is on her way here with some flowers for my mother.'

Right. She wasn't taking them to the hospital or arranging for them to be delivered. She was bringing them here, to Matt's home. 'I wasn't aware Pepita was in Spain,' Georgie said pleasantly. And now she asked the question she had asked once before in England, and never received an answer to, 'Does she travel backwards and forwards with you between England and Spain?'

'Most of the time.' There was the faintest note of mild irritation, as though he didn't want to talk about his beautiful secretary. 'My uncle in England has his own secretary, of course, and the office there is efficient, but I prefer to have Pepita with me for any confidential work.'

He preferred to have Pepita with him. Georgie put the half-full glass of wine down on a small occasional table and gestured at her clothes as she said, 'I'll think I'll go and freshen up before dinner, if that's all right?'

'Of course.'

Yes, it would be 'of course' now Pepita was on her way here. And then Georgie caught at the thought, self-disgust strong. She loathed the destructive emotion of jealousy and she had never been subject to it before. She had to get a handle on this. Matt was a free agent; he could sleep with a hundred women, including his secretary, and she had absolutely no right to object. No right at all...

Georgie hadn't known what clothes to bring with her when she had hastily packed her suitcase earlier that morning in England, but now, standing in her bra and panties in front of the open wardrobe in her room, she blessed the impulse that had made her grab two or three dressy outfits at the last moment. She would bet her life on the fact that Pepita was not going to arrive in anything less than designer perfection, and although her salary couldn't run to Versace or Armani her jade-green silk dress with an asymmetric hemline, the off-the-shoulder three-quarter length pastel cashmere dress and, lastly but not least, the viscose-crêpe minidress in soft charcoal would all hold their own with a designer label.

Her green eyes narrowed on the minidress. The wafer-thin straps on the shoulders and touch of embroidery which followed the neckline took the dress to another dimension once it was on, and her strappy sandals in dark pewter toned perfectly. It wasn't quite so dressy as the other two but that was perfect; she didn't want Pepita to think she had tried too hard. And the material and colour were misty and chimerical, bringing out the colour of her hair and eyes and accentuating the honey tone of her skin.

She had a thick braided bracelet and necklace in silver that she'd worn with the dress at the dinner dance she'd originally bought it for, and apart from two sets of earrings they were the only pieces of jewellery she had brought with her. Fate? She reached for the dress as she nodded at the reflection in the mirror.

She brushed her hair until it hung either side of her face like raw silk, but apart from darkening her thick eyelashes with mascara and applying the lightest touch of peach-coloured lipstick to her mouth she titivated no more, in spite of the picture of a beautifully made-up face and exquisitely enhanced ebony eyes which kept getting between her and the fresh-faced girl in the mirror. She wasn't used to wearing much make-up and she wasn't about to make herself feel uncomfortable. She wasn't a *femme fatale* and there was no point in trying to look like one.

Once she was ready she glanced one more time in the mirror. The three-inch heels gave her slender five feet four inches a boost, but she would never be model material, she decided resignedly. And Pepita must be five foot ten if she was an inch.

But that didn't matter. She frowned the admonition. She was here to give moral support to Matt through a difficult time by way of thanks for all he had done for Robert and the twins. That was all. *That was all.*

She picked her way carefully down the wide curving staircase once she had left her suite of rooms, vitally aware that the last thing she needed was to trip over the unaccustomed high heels and go sprawling from top to bottom. Once in the shadowy hall she came to a halt, however, uncertain of which room Matt would be in.

'*Señorita?*' A uniformed angel in the shape of Pilar appeared from the direction of the kitchens. 'You want the señor, *sí?*'

Oh, yes. Georgie nodded, her hair shimmering as she moved her head. 'I wasn't sure if he was in the drawing room or not,' she preferred tentatively.

'No, no, *señorita*. Is blue room, I think.'

Pilar led the way to one of the other reception rooms, opening the ornately carved door for Georgie and standing to one side for her to enter. And in the split second it took for Georgie to look into the room beyond she saw the couple standing by the window draw apart, Matt turning to face her as he said coolly, 'Georgie, we have been waiting for you. Come and have a cocktail.'

They had been embracing. Georgie tried to think of something to say and failed utterly, so she merely walked into the beautiful room which was furnished in shades of blue with as much aplomb as she could muster, forcing herself to smile as Pepita extended a languidly limp hand and said flatly, 'It is nice to see you again. I hope your brother is well?'

'Hallo, Pepita. Yes, Robert's fine.' Her voice was steady and even friendly, but she felt as though she had just received a heavy blow in the solar plexus. *They had been embracing*; Pepita's hands resting against the cloth of his dinner jacket and her head lifted up to meet Matt's downward bent one. Had they actually kissed? It was a pose which suggested they had but she hadn't seen that. Whatever, this wasn't your average working relationship!

Matt was pouring her a drink, and as he handed her the fluted glass his eyes roamed hungrily all over her for a few vital seconds, but his voice was contained when he said, 'You look lovely tonight, Georgie.'

'Thank you.' She smiled and took the drink as though she hadn't a care in the world, but even though she wasn't looking directly at Pepita now the image of the beautiful Spanish woman was imprinted on her mind.

As she'd suspected, Pepita was dressed to kill. The sleeveless silk dress with a deep V neck in dark scarlet was the ultimate in clingy sultriness and Pepita's figure was amazing; the high red sandals with studded ankle straps she was wearing showed her long slim legs off to perfection.

Had Pepita known she was staying with Matt? Georgie

rather suspected not. She also had a sneaking suspicion her presence was as welcome as an old flame at a wedding.

It soon became clear Matt had invited Pepita to stay for dinner and Georgie supposed—if she was being honest—he could have done little else, but it was a terrible evening as far as Georgie was concerned.

Pepita had obviously decided to sparkle, and she accomplished this with a brittle effervescence that had Georgie wanting to punch the other woman on the nose for most of the time. Pepita was never actually rude, but she managed to introduce people and situations Georgie had never heard of into the conversation, constantly emphasising Georgie was the odd one out. It was annoying, it was very annoying, but other than cause a scene Georgie could do little about it, and a scene was quite out of the question with Matt's mother lying ill in hospital with a forthcoming operation looming.

The food Flora had prepared was wonderful and the dining room was like something out of a Hollywood movie, but Georgie could have been eating cardboard for all it registered. Matt himself said little—it was difficult for anyone other than Pepita to get a word in, and Georgie could see how the other woman kept her slim figure because she never stopped talking long enough to swallow anything—and Georgie got the impression once or twice he was almost bored. Or perhaps he was regretting bringing her with him now Pepita had turned up?

This thought occupied her all through Flora's wonderful dessert of strawberry granita with a liqueur muscat chantilly. When she thought about it, Georgie reflected she had left him no choice but to let her tag along. She had *announced* she was accompanying him rather than asking him. Other than being blatantly rude, she hadn't left him with any option, had she? Her ears began to burn with embarrassment and her mouth went dry with panic.

She should never have come. This had been a huge, huge mistake and Pepita's presence confirmed it. Probably the Spanish woman spent most of her evenings with him here when they were both in Spain? And Pepita was only one of many glamorous women who would vie to be noticed by him. What on earth had she been thinking of to push herself on him the way she had? What must he be thinking?

She suddenly felt very naïve and stupid, all the confidence the lovely dress had given her evaporating away, but in the next instant she raised her chin a fraction, her eyes narrowing slightly. She was blowed if she would give Pepita the satisfaction of even an inkling of what she was thinking. Cool, calm and collected—that was her mask for the evening and she would wear it even if it killed her, and to the bitter end too. No slinking away or pleading a head-ache, even if that was in actual fact a reality. But then Pepita's chatter was enough to give a deaf man a headache! It continued all through their after-dinner coffees and brandy. By the time eleven o'clock chimed Georgie was just thinking she couldn't survive another minute without screaming, when Pepita rose to her feet, her movements slow and languid.

'Thank you so much for a lovely dinner, Matt.' She smiled and touched his arm as she spoke—he had risen with her—and Georgie reflected, with a painful squeeze of her heart how good they looked together. 'Do give your mother my love along with the flowers? And if there is anything, *anything* I can do you know you only have to ask.'

'Thank you, Pepita.' He turned to Georgie, holding out his hand and pulling her to her feet whereupon he drew her into the side of him as he said easily. 'We'll see you out.'

Georgie knew she had turned lobster-red but she couldn't help it; there had been an intimacy about both the gesture and the words she was sure Matt hadn't meant, but certainly it had hit Pepita on the raw if the stone-hard glint in the other woman's onyx eyes as she met Georgie's was anything to go by.

Matt kept hold of her as they all walked into the hall, and once he had opened the front door and they all stepped outside he didn't seem to notice her subtle attempts to disentangle herself.

Pepita was driving a bright red Porsche—which somehow seemed to sum up the evening as far as Georgie was concerned—and whether by design or accident showed a great deal of smooth tanned leg as she slid into the driver's seat. And then the car was pulling away with a flamboyant hoot of the horn and within a moment or two they were alone.

'Nice car.' Georgie had finally managed to extricate herself by pretending to fiddle with the strap of her sandal a moment before, and now she straightened, her voice cool.

'Yes, it is.' His face was in shadow and she couldn't see the expression in his eyes.

'Does she live near?' She had hoped her voice would sound polite and conversational and heard the edge to it with a feeling of despair.

'Quite near.'

'That's very convenient.' The black brows rose and she added quickly, 'For work purposes, I mean.'

'Of course,' he agreed pleasantly. There was a second's silence and then he horrified her by saying evenly, 'There is no need to be jealous, Georgie.'

'*Jealous?*' Matt was the second person she wanted to hit on the nose that evening and her response shocked her because she was normally a very non-violent person. 'I think you flatter yourself, Matt,' she bit out with caustic venom.

'Possibly.'

'And I can assure you I don't have a jealous bone in my body!'

'A very delectable body too.'

She glared at him, so angry she didn't trust herself to speak for a moment. How dared he suggest she was jealous of Pepita? she asked herself furiously, ignoring how she had felt for the last few hours. The ego of the man was colossal! No doubt he'd thoroughly enjoyed the thought he had two women panting after him all evening! Well, he could go and take a running jump, the arrogant so-and-so.

'Pepita's mother—when she was alive; she died three years ago—was my mother's closest friend,' Matt said from behind her as they turned into the house. 'I was ten years of age when Pepita was born and I have watched her grow from an infant.'

How cosy. And that explained the hungry look in Pepita's ebony eyes, did it? Who did he think he was kidding? 'You don't have to explain anything to me,' Georgie said tightly.

'I am not doing it because I have to,' he said softly, catching her arm and turning her round once he had shut the door, 'but because I want to. I do not wish any mis-understanding between us.'

She stared at him in the dimly lit hall, her green eyes huge with doubt.

'Pepita is like family,' Matt said quietly, 'that is all.'

She wanted to believe him, and the fervency of the want-ing carried its own warning. He was pure enigma; she didn't understand him at all and she never would. For the moment she was someone he wanted, a passing obsession, but he was used to women who were content to have fun with him for however long it took for the affair to burn itself out and then leave his life as gracefully as they had entered. And she didn't have it in her to be like that. She'd leave wailing her head off and clinging hold of his legs! She loved him.

'Like I said, Matt, you don't have to explain anything to me,' she said steadily, her voice quiet now. 'I came here because I thought it might help to have a friend with you at a difficult time. That's all.' Which was probably the most stupid thing she had done in her life.

'You are very good to your friends, Georgie.' He had bent and wrapped his arms around her before she realised what was happening, his lips seeking hers hungrily, possessive and devouring.

If someone had told her just two or three minutes before that she would be kissing him back she would have laughed at them, but that was exactly what she was doing as a flood of passion engulfed her. Her arms had wound round his neck and her body was pressed close to his, and she could no more have stopped her response to him than ceased breathing.

He didn't draw away until she was trembling and weak in his arms, and then his voice carried a smoky mocking note when he murmured, 'Very good.'

This was just a game to him. It gave her the strength to take a step backwards and say determinedly, 'Goodnight, Matt.'

'Goodnight, Georgie.'

She had half expected him to try and detain her but he didn't move as she walked to the staircase, and she was halfway up the stairs when his voice arrested her. 'I would like you to come with me to the hospital tomorrow and meet my mother.'

She remained perfectly still for the split second it took

to compose her face, and then she turned, one hand holding the smooth carved handrail as she said lightly, 'I'd like to meet her.'

It didn't mean anything, she warned herself firmly as she continued up the stairs. Not a thing. He obviously felt obliged to introduce her after she had come all the way from England, and no doubt his mother would think it odd if he didn't. Nevertheless the misery of the evening spent in Pepita's company was suddenly all gone and she all but floated along to her suite, walking through the sitting room and straight into the bedroom where she stood and looked at the bright-eyed girl in the mirror. 'Careful, Georgie.' She touched her lips, which were moist and swollen from his kisses, with the tip of one finger. 'He hasn't made any promises except that he doesn't believe in love or commitment.'

She stood at the mirror for a moment more, her eyes searching her flushed face as though the answer to all her confusion was there, and then sighed deeply, turning away and kicking off the sandals before making her way into the bathroom.

She would run herself a warm bath and lie and soak for half an hour at least; she was far too het-up to go to sleep yet. And she would not think of Matt at all. She wouldn't. These few days were a brief step out of time and that was the way she had to look at them. Pepita, the love affair that had gone wrong for him at university, his other women— she would go mad if she tried to sort it all out in her head tonight. He was one of those men whose dark aura engulfed everyone and everything it came into contact with, and she couldn't trust herself any more than she could trust him.

She walked back into the bedroom thoughtfully once the bath was running, taking off her clothes and donning a towelling robe before wiping off her mascara with her eye-make-up removing pads.

She must phone Robert tomorrow and assure him everything was all right; he had sounded worried when she'd said she was going to Spain with Matt although he had calmed down once she had explained about his mother. But she knew her brother had still been unhappy about the situation when she had put down the phone. Had he guessed how she felt about Matt? No, not Robert. Intuition wasn't his strong point. Perhaps he just wanted to warn her from getting involved, let her know that men like Matt de Capistrano were not the roses round the door type. Well, she knew that.

She narrowed her eyes as she padded back into the bathroom and turned off the taps. Yes, she knew that all right—in her head. So why was her heart still hoping for something different?

CHAPTER NINE

WHETHER it was the warm bath or the fact that Georgie had expelled enough nervous energy in the last twenty-four hours to exhaust ten women, she didn't know, but she awoke the next morning after a deep refreshing sleep that had—as far as she could recall—been dreamless. It was Pilar who woke her, placing a steaming cup of coffee on the bedside cabinet as she said gently, '*Señorita*, you sleep well, *sí*? You wake now.'

'What time is it?' Georgie sat up and sank back against the pillows as she watched the little maid draw back the drapes and let bright sunlight flood into the bedroom.

'Is ten o'clock, *señorita*.' And at Georgie's gasp of dismay, Pilar added, 'Is no problem. The *señor*, he have his swim an' he say for you to come to the breakfast, *sí*? In...' Pilar held up her fingers.

'Ten minutes?' Georgie suggested.

'*Sí, sí, señorita*. The ten minutes. Okay?'

'Okay.'

Once Pilar had left the room Georgie let the coffee cool a little while she had a quick shower, gulping it down as she partly blowdried her hair and then pulled it up in a loose ponytail on top of her head, although more strands fell about her face than stayed in the band.

She pulled on a pair of jeans and a skinny midnight-blue top and glanced at her watch. Ten minutes exactly. She'd better get downstairs.

She felt quite in control as she walked into the breakfast room but her aplomb was blown to pieces in the next mo-

ment. Matt was already sitting at the breakfast table casually reading a newspaper, and it was clear he had just showered, probably after his swim.

It was also clear he didn't believe in formal attire at the
breakfast table. The black silk robe was open to the waist
and the muscled hairy chest was the stuff dreams were
made of. That, and the way his damp hair curled slightly
over his forehead, softening the hard features and giving
them a touch of dynamite, robbed Georgie of the power to
respond immediately to his easy, 'Good morning.'

She lost the power to know how to walk as she tottered
across the room towards the table, almost falling over her
own feet, and by the time she sank gratefully into a chair
her cheeks were scarlet.

'Did you sleep well?' Matt asked gravely, apparently not
noticing he was sharing breakfast with a beetroot.

'Fine, thank you.' She cleared her throat twice. 'Have
you rung the hospital yet? How's your mother?'

'She had a good night and my friend is with her now.
He said they will operate first thing tomorrow, when he's
had a chance to do some necessary tests.'

Georgie nodded in what she hoped was a calm, informed
sort of way.

'Coffee?' He was already pouring her a cup as he spoke
and the movement of the big male body sent her hormones
spiralling.

'Thank you.' She took the cup from him and hurriedly
gulped at it, burning the inside of her mouth and trying to
pretend her eyes weren't watering with pain.

'Help yourself to cereal and fruit and croissants,' Matt
said nonchalantly. 'Flora will be bringing in a cooked
breakfast in a little while and she gets hurt if you don't
clear the plate.'

'Does she?' Georgie was alarmed. She had seen the

amount of food Matt seemed able to tuck away with seemingly little effort, and the loaded tray Pillar had brought to her room when she had arrived the day before was in the forefront of her mind.

'I told her just a little for you,' Matt said soothingly. 'You don't eat much, do you?'

'I eat loads.' It was indignant. 'Don't forget I'm eight or nine inches smaller than you and probably weigh half as much. Women are built differently to men.'

It probably wasn't the cleverest thing she had ever said. She watched the dark eyes turn smoky as he murmured, 'I'm aware of that, Georgie.'

She dragged her eyes away from his face and the acres of bare flesh beneath it, and concentrated on the array of cereals, fruits, toast, croissants and preserves in the middle of the table, hastily reaching for a ripe peach and beginning to slice it on her plate. If she was having a cooked breakfast she wouldn't be able to manage anything more.

Matt demolished a bowl of muesli to which he added a sliced banana and peach, followed by two croissants heaped with blackcurrant preserve, before Flora appeared wheeling in the heated trolley holding their plates.

Georgie was eternally grateful that Flora had heeded Matt's advice where her plate was concerned, but she stared fascinated at the contents of Matt's plate.

'I'm a growing boy.' He had noticed her rapt contemplation and his voice was amused. 'I have to keep my strength up in hope of...'

'In hope of what?' she asked absently, her mind still occupied with the half a pound of sausages and bacon, three eggs, mushrooms, tomatoes, fried potatoes and onions adorning Matt's plate. And then, as the silence lengthened, she raised her eyes to his face and he said gravely, 'Just in hope.'

An image of that wickedly voluptuous bed flashed across her mind and she quickly lowered her eyes to her plate. He was too sexy and flagrantly male clothed, but partly clothed... She bit into a sausage and prayed for composure. What did he have on under that robe? A piece of mushroom went down the wrong way and she coughed and spluttered, her agitation not helped at all when Matt left his seat to come and pat her back and offer her a glass of water.

'I'm fine, really,' she mumbled, sniffing loudly and trying to ignore the muscled legs at the side of her. He could at least have put on some pyjama bottoms or something after his swim if he didn't want to get dressed, she told herself self-righteously. But perhaps he didn't wear pyjamas?

'Here.' He bent down, dabbing at her wet eyes with a napkin, and she caught the full impact of the smell of expensive body shampoo on clean male skin before he strolled round the table again.

She finished her breakfast without further mishap but with every nerve and muscle in her body as taut as piano wire and conscious of the slightest movement from the big male body opposite. Matt, on the other hand, appeared supremely relaxed, enjoying a leisurely breakfast with obvious enjoyment.

As well he might, Georgie thought feverishly. *She* wasn't the one flaunting herself! Although, to be fair, Matt didn't appear to be aware he was flaunting himself, she admitted silently. He was a man who was very much at ease with his own body, as his comment the day before about his preference for swimming and exercising in the nude proved. She didn't dare dwell on that thought.

'So...'

She raised her eyes as she forked the last mouthful of

food from the plate into her mouth, and saw Matt was looking at her with unfathomable eyes. 'Yes?' she asked warily.

'We will visit the hospital this afternoon after an early lunch,' Matt said decisively. 'What would you like to do this morning?'

The aggressive sexuality that was as frightening as it was exciting made her voice slightly shaky as she said, 'Anything, I don't mind.'

'If only...' He gave a small laugh, low in his throat, at her expression. 'Well, as it is no good my suggesting a lazy morning in bed, and you did your exploring of the gardens yesterday, perhaps it would be good to show you a little of the surrounding area, yes? And we can maybe stop for something to eat close to the hospital rather than come back here.'

'Whatever you think.'

'How submissive.'

She stared at him, not sure if he was being nasty or not, and suddenly his expression cleared and he smiled ruefully. 'There is something of the spoilt brat in every man, *pequeña*, and I have found since I met you I am like every man. I do not like this; I had thought myself above such ignoble behaviour, but it would seem you bring out the worst in me. Of course, if we were lovers all this tension would be dealt with and life would be sweeter for both of us.'

'Life is quite sweet enough, thanks,' she said tartly.

'Liar.' It was slightly taunting but said with a smile which Georgie found it difficult to return. He was such a *disturbing* man, she told herself resentfully. The last weeks she had felt she was living on a knife's edge all the time, and it was exhausting. The very air seemed to crackle with electricity when Matt was about and these moments of honesty he seemed to indulge in made things worse.

'Come.' He rose from the table, holding out his hand as

he walked round to her chair. 'If you feel the need to persist in this ridiculous wish to deny us both I can only be patient until you accept the error of your ways.'

'Matt—' Her voice was cut off as he pulled her to her feet and his mouth caught hers with an urgency that was thrilling. He kissed her long and deeply, draining her of sweetness before his lips moved to her ears and throat causing convulsive shivers of ecstasy.

Her fingertips slipped under the silk at his shoulders, roaming over the leanly muscled flesh beneath the robe before they tangled in the pleasing roughness of the hair on his broad chest and then up again to his hard neck.

He was all male and unbelievable sexy, and Georgie allowed herself another moment or two of heaven before she pulled firmly away.

'I know, you are not that sort of girl,' he murmured, not quite letting go of her as he looked down with smouldering eyes.

'What sort?' she asked with a trembling attempt at lightness.

'The sort who makes love on the floor of the breakfast room.'

If he loved her as she loved him it could be the breakfast room table and she wouldn't care! 'I think Pilar might be just a little surprised,' she managed fairly blandly. 'Don't you?' She removed herself from his hold, stepping back a pace as she said evenly, 'What time do you want to leave?'

'Half an hour?' he suggested softly. 'It will give me time to take a shower.'

'I though you had showered,' she said, surprised.

'A cold shower, Georgie.'

When Georgie stepped outside into the scented warmth of a hot Spanish day half an hour later, Matt was waiting for her. He was sitting at the wheel of a Mercedes-Benz SL convertible and the beautiful silver car purred gently to life as she slid into the passenger seat. 'Another boy's toy?' she asked lightly, partly to hide what the sight of him—clothed in black shirt and trousers—had done to her equilibrium.

'Just so.' He smiled, his teeth flashing white in the tanned skin of his face.

She enjoyed seeing more of the country of his birth nearly as much as she enjoyed being with him. They ate lunch in a shadow-blotched plaza in a small cobbled town, the tall tower of a brown church in the distance with a great bell outlined against the blue sky. It was heaven. Or, rather, being with Matt was heaven. And dangerous. And perilous. And a hundred other adjectives that described jeopardy.

When they arrived at the hospital Georgie found she was nervous. Excruciatingly nervous. Matt's mother was his nearest and dearest and although he had never said so in so many words she knew he loved his mother deeply. And his mother was a friend of Pepita's.

The hospital was luxurious, and obviously not run of the mill, and Matt seemed to be something of an icon. They were practically bowed along the thickly carpeted corridor to his mother's room, although the sister in charge left them at the door at Matt's quietly polite request.

'Just be yourself.' She wasn't sure if he had sensed her agitation but his voice was distinctly soothing. 'You'll get on like a house on fire.'

No pressure! But before she could say a word he had knocked and opened the door, his voice warm as he said, 'Visitors for Señora de Capistrano?'

'Matt...' The voice was English but perfumed with a melodious sweetness that suggested years in a warm climate as it said, 'I have been waiting for you and Georgie.'

Georgie wasn't aware she had been ushered into the room; all her senses were tied up with Matt's mother.

Señora de Capistrano was one of those women whose age was immaterial compared to her beauty. She must have been over fifty—Matt was thirty-six after all—but the blonde-haired woman lying in the bed could have been any age from forty upwards. Her blonde hair was threaded with silver, which only seemed to add a luminescence to her faintly lined, creamy skin, and her blue eyes were of a deep violet shade that was truly riveting.

She was beautiful, outstandingly beautiful, and she was smiling a sweet, warm smile that took Georgie completely by surprise. She didn't know what she had been expecting—perhaps a strong reserve, even hostility in view of the fact that Pepita was a friend—but Matt's mother was either an incredible actress or genuinely pleased to see her.

'Georgie, this is my mother.' Matt's voice was tender. 'Mother, Georgie.'

'Come and sit down, dear.' One pale slim hand indicated the chair at the side of the bed, and as Matt went to draw another from across the room his mother said quickly, 'I understand the doctor, your friend Jeff Eddleston, wants a word, dear. He was most insistent you see him as soon as you arrived. I think he wants to go to his hotel and go to bed as soon as he can.' The violet gaze included Georgie as Matt's mother said, her voice indulgent now, 'My son summoned poor Mr Eddleston from halfway across the world in the middle of the night, and he came. That is true friendship, don't you think?'

Georgie was of the opinion that Matt could summon almost anyone without a refusal—he was that sort of man—but she simply smiled and left it at that.

'Now?' Matt was clearly loath to leave.

'Now.' Señora de Capistrano smiled gently. 'He's a brilliant doctor, so I understand? Everyone is in awe of him here.'

Matt's expression said very clearly that he was not. 'I won't be long.'

'Take all the time you need, dear. Georgie and I will get to know each other a little.'

When the door had closed behind her son, Señor de Capistrano turned her violet gaze on Georgie and looked at her for a long moment. 'So you are the one,' she said softly.

'I'm sorry?' Georgie stared at her bewilderly.

'Matt has spoken of his English ''friend'' more than once lately, but I did not think it would be in these surroundings that we met.' It was a touch rueful.

'You're feeling a bit better, I understand?' Georgie said carefully.

'Yes, yes.' It was impatient, and for the first time Georgie could see Matt in the beautiful woman in front of her. There was a moment's pause, and then Matt's mother said, 'My name is Julia, Georgie. I would like us to be friends.'

'So would I.' Georgie was out of her depth and it showed.

'Can I talk to you confidentially?' The lovely eyes were piercing. 'You know I am to have an operation tomorrow?' Georgie nodded. 'Then I am claiming that as my reason for putting aside all politeness and convention and coming straight to the kernel in the nut,' Julia continued urgently. 'I love my son, Georgie. I want the very best for him; he deserves it.'

It could have been unfriendly but it wasn't, neither was it inimical. Georgie sat and waited, knowing it was a time to be silent.

'When I met my husband and we fell in love there was

great opposition from his family.' It wasn't what Georgie had expected to hear and her eyes opened wide for a moment, but Julia continued, 'We weathered the storm until we came into calmer waters, and that only happened after Matthew was born. I was accepted then. I had given my husband a son so all was well, and it didn't matter I was English. As far as Matthew's father and I were concerned it hadn't mattered anyway. We loved each other, deeply. If we had been childless all our lives we would still have been together, loving each other.'

'You were very fortunate,' Georgie said softly. 'My brother and his wife were like that.'

The silver-blonde head nodded in acknowledgement. 'Matthew was brought up in a loving home,' Julia said quietly, 'but he also has the genes from his father's people in his blood. My husband was a wonderful man, kind and gentle, but not so his parents or their parents. They were very proud and hard, one could say cruel even.'

'I don't understand?' Georgie said quietly.

'They were the kind of people who never forgot an insult or a harm done to them,' Julia said softly. 'Vendettas, blood feuds, honour. This was the language they talked and lived. My son is not like his father, Georgie, but neither is he all his grandparents either. There is a little of both in my Matt, I think, and life will shape which takes pre-eminence. Life…or a woman.'

Georgie looked at the woman in front of her, her eyes wide with sudden understanding. But Julia had got it all wrong, she thought feverishly. Matt didn't love her; she had no sway over him except that he wanted her body for a brief time. But how could she say that to his mother?

'When such a person as my son is hurt or betrayed it goes deep.' Julia was no longer looking at Georgie but had turned to gaze out of the big picture window opposite the bed, where the tops of green trees could be seen beneath a cloudless blue sky. 'And it takes an equally deep feeling to cauterise the pain and bring about healing.'

'Julia?' Georgie didn't know what to say but she had to say something to stop this terrible misunderstanding. 'If you are saying what I think you're saying, that I am the one to bring about the healing from some incident in Matt's past, you've got it all wrong. He doesn't love me; he has already told me he doesn't believe in love or commitment.'

'Honour and pride.' It was said on a sigh.

She had to say it, crass though it might sound. Georgie took a deep breath and said quietly, 'He wants an affair, that's all. A brief interlude. He…he is interested because I haven't immediately fallen into bed with him.'

Julia's amazing eyes fastened on Georgie's flushed face, and they stayed there for what seemed like an endless time. And then Matt's mother said quietly, 'He needs you, Georgie, but how do you feel? Do you care for him? Really care for him?'

It took more strength than Julia was aware of for Georgie to strip off the armour and say steadily, 'Yes, I do, but I'd prefer him not to know.'

'I can understand that, and I promise you he will not learn it from me. But in return for that confidence I want to tell you something. Something very private and something I have not spoken of before, not to anyone. But you, you I want to tell.'

Georgie stared into the beautiful face and she felt a shiver run down her spine. This had been far from a cosy chat and she had the feeling it was about to get worse.

'When Matthew went to university he was a bright, strong boy with a zest for life that was unquenchable and a warmth that was very much like his father's,' Julia began slowly. 'When he graduated the brightness and strength was still there, but the zest for life had been turned into a desire to take it by the throat and the warmth was quite gone. This…' Julia hesitated, her hand moving to her throat. 'This was due to a girl.'

'Begonia.'

'He has spoken to you of Begonia?' It was sharp and Julia's face was amazed.

'No. Well, yes. At least…' Georgie tried to pull her thoughts together. 'He said he knew her for eighteen months and then it finished,' she said quickly.

Julia looked at her for another moment before nodding. 'It is not as simple as that, but then knowing my son you would not have expected it to be. He was in love with Begonia and she betrayed him,' she said flatly. 'But not in the normal sense. They were together for a year—you know?'

Georgie nodded painfully. Yes, she knew.

'And then something dreadful happened. We received a phone call from the university to say that Matt was missing and that the police were involved. Then came a ransom note. It stated Matt was being held until we delivered a certain amount of money to a designated pick-up point. We delivered. Matt was released from the tiny underground room he had been held in for five days and left in the middle of nowhere. But my son is no fool, Georgie.

'He had taken a note of sounds and driving distances, even though he was blindfolded and cuffed, and eventually the police found the street and then the actual cellar. Then it got worse. I won't bore you with the details, but suffice to say he had been held by supposed friends who needed money for their drug addiction.'

The claustrophobia. Georgie stared at Matt's mother in horror. 'Begonia was one of them?' she whispered weakly.

Julia nodded. 'Matt did not know about her drug habit;

perhaps he would have helped her if he did. Anyway, needless to say, the abduction affected him deeply. He…he was not the same afterwards. He became very cynical and cold.'

Georgie nodded. She could understand that. 'And Begonia?' she asked quietly.

'Begonia and the others received a severe prison sentence. The parents of one of the boys involved got a clever lawyer, who insisted it was just an ill-advised practical joke which had gone wrong, but in view of the sum of money involved this argument was not acceptable. It transpired Begonia had been sharing her favours with this boy as well as Matt.'

Georgie shook her head slowly, her hair brushing her cheeks in a shimmering veil. For a first love to go wrong was bad enough, but in those circumstances…

'Matt has had women companions since then, of course, but he has chosen only those who were beautiful enough and shallow enough to fit into his lifestyle. Francisca calls them dolls and she is right. Matt only smiles when his sister says this, but when he spoke of you… He did not smile. No, he did not smile.'

'Julia—' Georgie squirmed on the upholstered seat. 'He doesn't *love* me. Whatever he feels, he's made it clear it's not love.'

'Then he is a fool,' Matt's mother said very softly, her eyes gentle on the lovely face in front of her.

'That's what Matt called Glen,' Georgie said ruefully. 'My ex. He…he let me down rather badly.'

'And Matt called him a fool? Well, well.' Julia lay back against the plump pillows behind her and surveyed Georgie afresh. 'Don't give up on him, Georgie. Not yet. It takes time to climb out of the darkness into the light, especially when that darkness is the only protection you have against a giant step that makes Neil Armstrong's look easy. I know my son. I know what is of his father. My husband loved me utterly and absolutely, and that is the way Matt will love when he finds the right woman.'

And if she wasn't the right woman? Where did that leave her? Georgie's green eyes were cloudy. Matt's mother loved him and that was right and proper, but it coloured her viewpoint to look at things for Matt's good. What about *her* good?

Matt could have any woman he wanted and he couldn't fail to recognise the fact by the number which pursued him. He was handsome and wealthy and powerful, and she was an ordinary girl from a little town in England he had happened to meet, and who didn't tell him exactly what he wanted to hear. That had interested him, intrigued him even. But what happened when the chase stopped and the hunter got his quarry?

'I think you're mistaken about me,' Georgie said quietly, 'about how Matt feels, but thank you for telling me about what happened in his past anyway. It...it explains a lot.'

Julia nodded. 'It does, doesn't it?' she agreed softly. 'But as to my being mistaken... Well, time will tell, Georgie.'

Time. Would it be friend or foe? She wished she could believe for the former but cold reason told her it would be the latter.

And then the door opened and Matt was back, and in spite of all her fears Georgie's heart leapt as she looked at him.

They spent over an hour at the hospital and by the time they left Georgie knew she could love Matt's mother. Julia was so sweet, so warm; she could understand what had attracted Matt's father to his English bride after being brought up in a home which, by the sound of it, although palatial, had been devoid of much love and laughter.

'You'll come again before you leave?' As Georgie made her goodbyes, Julia's voice was insistent.

'If you want me to.'

'I do.'

It was very definite, and once outside in the corridor Matt took her arm, drawing her round to face him as he said softly, 'I told you you two would like each other.'

And it was ridiculous, really ridiculous, and probably just because her emotions had been oversensitised during the talk with Julia, but somehow Georgie got the strangest feeling he wasn't altogether pleased at how things had gone. The grey eyes looked down at her, their expression hidden behind congeniality, and then they were walking down the corridor again and the moment was lost as they enjoyed the rest of the day together.

Julia's operation went well the next morning, and after Matt had visited the hospital he returned before lunch and found Georgie in the gardens, his voice light and easy as he said, 'Grab a swimming costume and a towel, I'm taking you to a beach I know where we can swim and laze the afternoon away.'

'But lunch?'

'Flora's packing a picnic hamper,' he said smoothly. 'We'll eat on the way; I know a spot, and I prefer it to having sand in my food.'

She nodded, but her smile was faintly wary. He had been different since their visit to see his mother the day before. The rest of the afternoon and evening spent sightseeing had been lovely, and the small restaurant at which they had eaten—surrounded by fragrant almond groves—had been magical, but there had been a distance, a coolness in Matt she was sure she hadn't imagined. Or maybe she had. She didn't know where she was when she was within six feet of him!

She had had the foresight to bring her own swimming costume with her from England—a somewhat uninteresting one-piece in dark blue so after picking up a bath towel from her bathroom Georgie joined Matt on the drive outside where he was just putting the picnic basket into the car.

He surveyed her slim shape clothed in three-quarter length jeans and a figure-hugging top in bright poppy-red silently for a moment, before he said quietly, 'Youth personified.'

'Hardly.' Georgie pushed back a strand of silky hair, tucking it behind her ear, as she said, 'I am twenty-three, Matt.'

'Ancient,' he agreed drily.

She stared at him, uncertain of his mood but knowing there was something she didn't like in his tone, and then slid into the car silently. If he wanted an argument he could argue with himself; she only had a few days here with him and they were going to have to provide a lifetime of memories.

Once they were on their way, however, the brief unease was lulled by the ever-changing vista outside the car. Sugar-white houses with balconies of iron covered in morning glory, flowered walled gardens adjoining small orchards, simple granite churches and quiet lanes hedged with hibiscus and jacaranda—Georgie drank in the rich tapestry of views and scents and began to relax.

She had vowed she would live life minute by minute with Matt, expecting nothing, and she wasn't going to spoil today by thinking too much, she decided, just after the car passed two small bare-footed children. The tiny tots were leading a bewhiskered nanny goat along the dusty road by means of a piece of frayed rope tied round its furry neck.

She had to stop examining everything his mother had said, she told herself firmly, and hoping for a miracle.

'Here.' Beyond the small village they had just passed stretched green meadows, and now Matt turned the car off the road and on to an unmade track winding away into the distance. 'I know the perfect spot for a picnic.'

After some two hundred yards or so he stopped the car. 'Look over there,' he said quietly. 'My mother and father used to bring Francisca and myself here before we went on to the beach, and my sister liked it better than the sea. She was frightened of the waves, you see, but this was safe to paddle in.'

Georgie looked. The grass sloped down to a small, crystal-clear stream fringed with pebbles, the water running with gurgling purpose over smooth mounds of polished rock. It was an enchanting little dell and she could just imagine the delight of two small children eating a picnic by the side of the stream.

Had he brought other women to this idyllic haven of days gone by? Days when he had been carefree and happy? She didn't dare ask. Instead she said, her voice very even, 'Does Francisca bring her children here?'

'That tribe of monkeys?' Dark eyes crinkled as he smiled and Georgie's heart was rent with love. 'She would never round them all up again if she let them loose in the open.'

'I'm sure they're not as bad as all that?' Georgie said reprovingly.

'Worse than you could imagine,' he returned drily as he opened his car door, walking round the bonnet and helping her to alight before he reached for the picnic basket and blanket in the back of the car. 'If I ever needed anything to convince me that marriage and children and settling down is not for me, a visit to my sister's house would do it. Bedlam. All the time.'

It was too softly vehement. Georgie watched him as he carried the hamper down to the stream, but it was some moments before she moved herself. If that hadn't been a warning, or at least a reminder, of all he had said in the past she didn't know what was! How dared he? How *dared* he warn her off like that? And then a terrible thought struck—had his mother told him what she had admitted yesterday, that she loved him? But no, no, she trusted Julia. This was just Matt being Matt.

Her stomach was churning as she sat down on the blanket he had spread out on the grass, but his remark had brought her up with a jolt. Which was probably exactly what she had needed, she admitted ruefully.

The picnic was definitely a de Capistrano one, and therefore in a different league from anything masquerading under that name which Georgie had enjoyed in the past. Wine, Flora's delicious home-made lemonade, slices of ham, turkey, beef and pork, crusty bread and little pats of butter, ripe red tomatoes, crisp salad, hard-boiled eggs, pâté, little savoury pastries, tiny tubs of fondant potatoes, goat's cheese, olives; the list went on and on, and that was before they looked at the various individual portions of mouth-watering desserts Flora had included.

'How many people did Flora think were coming on this picnic?' Georgie asked after they had eaten hungrily in companionable silence for some minutes.

'Just you and I, *pequeña*.' Matt had had one glass of the fruity red wine Flora had included before refilling his glass with lemonade, but now he poured more of the rich black-currant liquid into her glass before lying back on the blanket and shutting his eyes against the glare of the sun.

Georgie looked at him at the side of her, the big lean body stretched out like a relaxed panther but with all the inherent dangerousness of the big cat merely harnessed for the moment. A small pulse was beating at the base of his tanned throat and she had an overwhelming urge to place her lips to it before she took hold of herself firmly.

Matt had perfect control of his emotions. Why couldn't she feel the same? She drank the wine in a few hasty gulps, the warmth of it comforting after the bleakness of her thoughts, and then lay back on the sunwarmed blanket herself. He could pick her up or put her down seemingly just as he pleased whereas her head, her mind, her soul were all filled with him twenty-four hours a day. But then her heart was involved, not just her body. Unlike his.

The sun was warm on her face, a gentle breeze caressing her skin idly as it wafted the scent of a hundred wild flowers against the background music of the gurgling water. She must have slept, because when she became aware of the mouth brushing her lips it seemed part of the dream she had been having. An erotic, disturbing dream.

She opened dazed green eyes and looked into Matt's face above her and for a long moment they were both immobile, drowning in each other's eyes. Then with a muffled sound which came deep from his throat he pulled her into him, turning so that she was lying across his hard chest, her racing pulse echoing the slam of his heart.

The kiss was achingly sweet, his mouth pleasuring them both as it explored hers. A deep languorous warmth was filling her, moving into every little crevice and nerve and causing her body to throb as the ache inside her slowly ripened.

And then he lifted her from him, his voice none too steady as he said, 'Time to go, I think, or we will never have that swim.'

She didn't care about that, about the beach! She just wanted to stay here for ever, in this little place away from the real world and reality. She watched him sit up, his back

tense under the black cloth of his shirt, but when he turned
to face her he was composed again, the lover of a few
moments ago gone.

'It is not far.' He offered her his hand as he rose to his
feet and she accepted it with a smile that was forced. 'And
the sea is perfect today, calm and tranquil.'

Unlike her! Georgie shut her eyes for a second as he
gathered the hamper together, and then opened them to
watch him pack the basket with expert precision. But then
he did everything perfectly, she thought with a moment's
bitterness. That was the trouble.

It was just after three o'clock and the sun was high when
Matt drove the car out of the long winding lane they had
been following for the last five minutes, and out on to the
tough springy grass beyond which stretched the sort of
beach Georgie had only seen in advertisements on the TV.

The secluded bay was set against a dramatic backdrop
of pine-clad hills and in the far distance blue-mauve mountains. The dazzling white beach was strewn with delicate
rose-pink and mother-of-pearl shells beyond which lapped
vivid turquoise-blue water.

Matt had stopped the car and Georgie was aware of him
watching her face, but it was some moments before she
could drag her eyes away from the enchantment in front of
her and say softly, 'It's the most beautiful place in the
world, Matt. Thank you for showing it to me.'

Something worked in his face as she spoke but his voice
was restrained when he said, 'My pleasure, Miss Millett.'

'Matt—' She stopped abruptly, not knowing how to continue but conscious of his pain beneath the composed mask
he wore. There had been something in his expression, almost an acceptance, that had sent a chill flickering down
her spine. His will was iron-like, the intensity of the spirit
deep inside the man frightening. She could never reach him,

never get through to the hurt individual behind the mask. She just didn't know *how*.

'Yes?'

'It doesn't matter.'

By the time Georgie had struggled into her swimming costume under the towel Matt was already in the clear blue water, and he waved to her from where he was swimming in the slight swell of the waves.

The sand was hot beneath her feet as she ran down to the water's edge, but at least she felt *herself* in her own swimming costume, she told herself bracingly.

In spite of the warmth of the sun the water was icy cold, and she gasped as she waded further and further towards Matt, although once she was swimming she didn't notice the cold any more. The water was silky, wonderful, and the small turquoise waves were totally non-threatening.

She lost sight of Matt just when she thought she was close to him, and then squealed in surprise—taking in a mouthful of salt water in the process—as he emerged just in front of her like a genie from the depths of a bottle.

'You did that on purpose!' she glared at him, but then, as he gathered her to him and kissed her thoroughly, the pair of them sinking under the clear water, she forgot to be angry. This was paradise; it was, it was paradise, and she would never feel so alive, so *aware* in the whole of her life.

They spent a crazy half-hour in the water, acting like two kids let out of school for the day, before Georgie, utterly exhausted, made for the shore. Matt had indicated he wanted to do some serious swimming before he came in, and after she had collapsed on the blanket he had brought from the car Georgie watched him for a few minutes.

The hard lean body cut through the water with military

precision, and she found herself wondering at the ruthless determination which drove him to push himself to the limit. Most people found swimming therapeutic, but she had the idea that to Matt it was just another area in which he had to prove to himself he could do it alone—beat the elements. It saddened her, taking some of the joy out of the time they had shared, and she lay back on the blanket, suddenly weary.

The air was warm and salty, the lapping of the tiny waves on the beach a soothing background music, but she couldn't really relax. After a little while she became aware the sun was too hot to ignore and sat up, wrapping the towel round her cocoon-fashion as she continued to watch Matt in the water.

And then he came out. He might just as well have been nude for all the tiny black briefs concealed.

Georgie watched, fascinated, as the lithe, tanned body strolled up the beach towards her. The hair on his powerful chest narrowed to a thin line bisecting his flat belly, and the smooth-muscled hips and long strong legs were magnificent. *He* was magnificent, every perfectly honed inch of him.

She couldn't tear her eyes away from him as he came nearer, even though she knew he must be aware she was ogling him, and it was only when he was within a few yards of her that she found the strength to lower her eyes and pretend to fiddle with the towel.

'Enjoy yourself?'

'What?' For an awful minute Georgie thought he was referring to her brazen gawping.

'The sea is so much better than even the best swimming pool, don't you think?' he said.

She forced herself to say, 'Definitely. Oh, definitely.'

'Fancy a drink?'

'What?' Oh, she had to stop saying that, she thought a trifle desperately.

'A drink?' he reiterated patiently. 'I'll bring the picnic basket down.'

'Great.'

Great, great, great! Please put some clothes on! She watched him pad towards the car and she watched him return, and she wondered if he was aware of how woefully inadequate the small piece of cloth round his hips was. But if he was, he didn't care. She shut her eyes tightly for a second as he threw himself down beside her on the blanket, and then opened them wide when he said coolly, 'Wine or lemonade?'

She didn't need anything to heat her blood further! 'Lemonade, please.'

He poured her a glass, and then himself, downing his in a few swallows before lying back on the blanket contentedly. 'This is very good.'

Speak for yourself. 'Yes, it's very nice,' she said faintly.

'Few people know of this bay; it is usually deserted.'

That wasn't actually much comfort right at this moment. She glanced at him warily. 'You must be exhausted after all that swimming,' she said carefully. 'You were in the water for more than an hour.'

'No, I am not tired, Georgie.'

She knew what was coming. She had known from the moment they had walked on to this beach what he had in mind, but as he rolled over and took her into his arms she made no attempt to push him away. She wanted him. The rights and wrongs of it suddenly didn't matter any more. She needed him in a way she had never imagined she could need anyone.

His lips were first coaxingly seductive, and then, when she met his kiss for kiss, fiercely erotic. He penetrated the softness of her mouth with his tongue, producing flickers of sensual awareness from the tips of her toes to the top of her head, his increasingly urgent caresses reflecting the fine tremors shivering across his muscled body.

'You taste and feel so good,' he murmured huskily. 'Deliciously salty-sweet and incredibly soft. Hell, Georgie, do you know what you do to me?'

The question was rhetorical, the leashed power of his arousal all too evident. It brought a fiercely primitive response from the depths of her, a wild satisfaction that his body couldn't deny his need of her. She could feel his shudders of pleasure and she exulted in them, in his strength, his maleness.

She loved him. She wanted to know what it would be like to make love with him. It was as simple as that in the end.

His hands were moving over the silky soft material of her swimsuit with slow, tantalising sureness, causing her body to spring to life beneath his fingers. Her nipples were erect and hard under their cover, her whole being gripped by quivering sexual tension.

She opened her eyes, which had been shut, so she could see his face, and his eyes looked back at her, hot and dark and glittering. But he wasn't rushing her. She was aware of this. His hands and mouth were moving with seductive insistence and creating rivulets of fire wherever they touched and teased, but this was no swift animal mating but rather one of calculated finesse. He was making her liquid with desire and he knew it; knew every single response he drew forth before she did.

She was responding to his expert mastery with instinctive passion and desire born of her love for him, and just for a moment she felt a vague sense of loss that it wasn't that way for him. He wasn't being swept along by love for her, he merely wanted her. It was just sex for him. But then he moved in a certain way, his hard chest creating a tight, exquisite pressure over her aching breasts and she forgot to think, forgot everything in the sensation after sensation washing over her body.

'Georgie, say it. Say you want me.' He was murmuring against her hot skin, his voice a low growl. 'Say you want me like I want you.'

He raised himself slightly, looking down into her dazed face as his hands cupped her cheeks.

'Say you want me to undress you, to take you here on the sands with the sky above us. Tell me.'

She stared up at him with drowning green eyes, gasping slightly as his hands moved to her breasts, shaping their full roundness through the fabric of her swimming costume. And she said the only words that were in her heart, 'I love you, so much,' as her head moved from side to side in a feverish agony of need, her eyes closing.

'No, say it as it is. No pretence, Georgie, not between us.'

For a moment she didn't understand, lost as she was in a spinning world of sensation and light, and then as his fingers traced a path into the soft hollow of her breasts before he began to peel the swimming costume away she understood what he was demanding. This had to be on his terms; he wanted her to tell him she was inviting him into her body, that she wanted and needed him, but she wasn't allowed to say love. *But she did love him.*

'I love you.' This time it wasn't said with frenzied desire but was a statement of fact, and Matt recognised it as such, his hands freezing on her body.

She lay very still, looking up at him, allowing him to see the truth in her eyes, and as she saw the shock on his face slowly being absorbed by the coldness spreading over it she knew she would remember this moment all of her life.

'No, no, you do not.'

'Yes, I do.' As his hands left her she sat up quickly, adjusting the swimming costume and drawing the towel round her shoulders. Suddenly, in spite of the heat of the sun, she felt cold. 'You might not like it,' she said with painful dignity as he sat, half turned away from her, his profile hard and stunned, 'but nevertheless that's how it is. You asked for no pretence between us, Matt, after all. And you might as well know the rest of it now. I wanted to make love with you *because* I love you, and there has never been anyone else in that way.'

'You're telling me you didn't sleep with Glen?' Although his voice was very flat she sensed the shock.

'No, I didn't. It just didn't seem right, somehow, but until I met you I hadn't realised why. But I didn't love him, not as you're supposed to love the person you want to be with for the rest of your life.' There, she'd said it. It would do no good, she knew that, but she couldn't have gone the rest of the life wondering whether if he knew it would have touched something deep inside. It was scant comfort when she looked at his rigid face, but at least he had heard it as it really was. The ball was well and truly in his court.

'I never made you any promises, Georgie.' His voice was cold now, his accent strong, and he still didn't look at her. 'You knew how it was all along, how I feel about the sort of commitment you are talking about. I am not cut out for togetherness; I do not want it.'

'Why are you so frightened to say the word?' she asked quietly. 'Because love goes hand in hand with the possibility of betrayal and loss?'

He did look at her then, his grey eyes as sharp as cut slate.

'This Begonia you told me about, the girl at university, she hurt you badly, didn't she?' His mother had said she'd never talked about it to anyone and Georgie had the feeling Matt hadn't, either. 'What happened, Matt?' she prompted softly, hoping her voice didn't betray the way she was shaking inside with the enormity of the confrontation. If he would just tell her, open up a little...

He drew in a deep hard breath. 'It will accomplish nothing to talk about it,' he said gratingly. 'The past is the past.'

'But it isn't the past for you, not really,' she countered steadily. 'And until it is you'll never be able to reach out for the future.'

'Save me the trite platitudes, Georgie!'

'You want to row with me, don't you?' she said, struggling for composure in the face of his anger. 'Attack is the best defence and all that. And it's just to cover up the fact that you are scared stiff to take a chance and trust someone!'

'You want to hear about Begonia?' he rasped bitterly. 'Then I will tell you! Every little sordid detail.' And he did. He told her it all, his voice sinisterly quiet now and very cold.

Georgie stared at him the whole time. He was right; this had accomplished nothing, she realised miserably, except to make him hate her. She had expected he would feel some relief in the telling, but instead, in revealing what he saw as his humiliation and defeat, she had made him hate her. He was a proud man, obsessively so. He would never forgive her for this.

'She was sick, Matt.' When he had finished talking and the silence became painful Georgie's voice was a whisper. 'Sick in mind and body, and someone like that can't love anything or anyone. Love is not like that—'

'And what makes you the expert?' As he swung to face her again his voice was savage.

'How I feel about you.'

He flinched visibly, but almost immediately rose to his feet, his face icy-cold. 'You are talking about sexual attraction,' he said stonily, 'although you have dressed it up to appear as something else to placate the conscience years and years of civilisation has bred. You are fooling yourself, Georgie. The emotion you are talking about does not exist in the pure form. A biological urge to mate, a wish for a nest and procreation, a need for protection or warmth, security—all those are facets of this thing you call love. It is totally unnatural to expect two people to live together for the rest of their lives. Man is not a monogamous animal.'

She had lost him. Or perhaps you had to have something in the first place to lose it, and she had never had Matt. 'I don't believe that and I don't think you do, not in your deepest heart of hearts.' Her voice *was* shaking now, she could hear it. 'There *is* a kind of love that lasts for ever, a kind that wants and needs intimacy and commitment and all that embraces. My brother and his wife had it, and I think your parents did too.'

'You know nothing about my parents,' he said cuttingly, 'so do not presume to lecture me.'

She had stood to her feet as he had been talking, and now her head jerked back as his arrogance hit a nerve. For the first time since they had been talking raw anger flooded her and she didn't try to quench it. She needed its fortifying heat to combat the agony inside. 'Lecture you?' she said with acidic mockery. 'Lecture *you*, the great Matt de Capistrano? I wouldn't dare! How could a mere mortal like me dare to disagree or venture a opinion in such exalted presence?'

'Do not be childish.'

'I might be childish but I'd rather be that than a block of stone like you,' she shot back furiously, his coldness serving to inflame her more. 'At least I'm alive, Matt! I feel, I ache, I cry—I do all the normal things that human beings do. Sure, life can make us wish we'd never been born on occasion, but real people fight back. You have let Begonia destroy you, do you realise that? They might have released you from that hole in the ground but you've dug yourself a deeper and more terrible one. You're not a man; you're a dead thing.'

'Have you quite finished?' It was thunderous.

'Oh, yes, I've finished all right. With you, with this ridiculous farce, with this country! I want to go home.' The last five words came out in a wail which wasn't at all the impression she wanted to give after he'd labelled her childish.

'I promise you you will be on the first available flight to England tomorrow,' he bit out caustically.

'Careful, Matt.' She might be devastated but he wasn't going to crush her completely! 'Promises aren't your thing.'

The drive home was the sort of nightmare Georgie wouldn't have inflicted on her worst enemy.

Matt's face could have been cut in stone and he didn't look at her or speak to her once. Georgie sat, huddled on her seat with her side pressed up against the car, as her mind reiterated all the harsh words she had thrown at him. And they had been harsh, she told herself with utter misery. She loved him, she loved him with all her heart, and all she had done was to call him names. She should have been understanding, kind, loving, showed him that true love turned the other cheek and that it didn't matter to her how he was, she still adored him.

But he was so arrogant, so infuriating, so altogether impossible! She had never even considered she'd got a temper before she'd met Matt, and then, boy, had it come to the fore! But all she'd said... She shut her eyes tightly and then opened them again, staring blankly through the windscreen without seeing a thing. She dared bet no one had ever spoken to him like that in his life. How could he make her say things like that when she loved him so much? She'd give the world to be able to heal the wounds Begonia and his so-called friends had inflicted.

When they drew up outside the house Matt left the car and opened her door—courteous to the last, Georgie thought with agonising black humour—but he didn't say a word until they were standing in the hall. 'You must be tired after such an exhausting day,' he bit out tightly, his grey eyes granite-hard as they looked down at her. 'I will see that Flora sends a tray up to your room after you have bathed and got ready for bed.'

In other words he didn't want to see her again until she left for England tomorrow. Georgie nodded stiffly, raising her small chin and calling on every scrap of tattered dignity she had left as she said, 'Thank you, but I am not hungry.'

'Nevertheless a tray will be brought to you.'

Do what you want; you always do anyway. She inclined her head before turning away and walking towards the staircase on legs that trembled. He was an unfeeling monster, that was what he was.

Once in her bedroom Georgie sat on the bed for long minutes before she could persuade her legs to carry her into the bathroom.

She wanted to cry, needed the relief of tears, but deep inside there only seemed to be dry ashes, which was making her feel worse.

After a warm bath she washed her hair and pulled on her towelling robe, wandering out into the sitting room and walking on to the balcony where the scented twilight was heavy with the last rays of the sun. She lifted her face to the sultry air, hearing the birds twittering and calling as they began to settle down for the night, and wondered how she could still walk and talk when her heart had been torn out by its roots. But this was just the beginning; she was going to have to learn to deal with this pain for the rest of her life—a life without Matt.

Flora brought her the tray ten minutes later, but although she thanked Matt's housekeeper, and smiled fairly normally, she knew she wouldn't be able to eat a thing and didn't even bother to uncover the dishes, although she took the large glass of white wine the tray held out on to the balcony with her. She sat down in the cushioned wicker chair it held, sipping the wine as her eyes wandered over the magnificent view.

She didn't regret saying everything she'd said, not really, she decided after a long while. She just wished she'd said it differently, that was all. Not in anger.

The dusk was falling rapidly now, the sky pouring flaming rivulets of scarlet, gold and orange across its wide expanse of light-washed blue. It was beautiful, magnificent, but tonight its beauty didn't touch her soul with joy and that frightened her. She felt as dead inside as she had accused Matt of being, and something of this feeling was reflected in her voice when she heard Flora behind her.

'The tray's on the little table, Flora,' she said dully without turning round. 'I'm sorry I couldn't eat anything but I think I've probably had too much sun today.'

'Forgive me, Georgie.'

She heard the voice almost without it registering for a stunned moment, and then she shot round, spilling the wine and with her hand to her throat as she saw Matt just behind her.

He looked terrible, awful. And wonderful. Her heart gave a mighty jolt and began to race like a greyhound, and she knew she wasn't dead inside after all as the pain hit. 'What...what do you want?'

'For you to keep on loving me.' He made no attempt to come any nearer.

'You don't believe in love,' she said, her face awash with the tears she'd thought she couldn't cry.

'If what I feel for you isn't love, then all the poets have got it wrong,' he said with grating pain. 'From the first moment I saw you it was there, Georgie. I tried to tell myself it was a million other things—sexual attraction, desire—but you've heard all that. I...I can't let you leave me, Georgie. I will die if you leave me. I haven't recognised myself the last few weeks and it has terrified me.'

The last was said with a kind of angry bewilderment which would have been funny in any other circumstances.

'You...you wouldn't die. What about Pepita and all the others?' She hadn't realised until she had said the name how much the other woman's presence in his life still rankled.

'Pepita?' He made an irritable, disdainful movement with his hand, and the meaning behind it almost made Georgie feel sorry for the beautiful Spanish woman. Almost. 'Pepita is like a sister to me; I have told you this. And there are no others. There will never be any others now I have met you. You have done this; you have ruined me for anyone else.'

'You said...' Georgie took a great gulp of air, trying to control her quivering bottom lip. 'You said—'

'I know what I said.' His voice was a deep hard groan. 'I said you were fooling yourself, all the time knowing it was I who was in that state of mind, not you. You challenged me that I was frightened of speaking the word love because of all it entailed, and this is true. This was true.'

'So what's changed?' she asked, seeing him through a mist of tears. 'What's changed your mind?'

'The thought of losing you, my love.'

It was the endearment she had never thought to hear from him and Georgie found she couldn't take it in. 'You wanted an affair,' she accused tremulously.

'I still do. An affair that lasts the rest of our lives and beyond, a real love affair. I want *you*, Georgie. Not just a warm body in my bed. I want us to be everything to each other; wife and husband, lovers, friends, and, yes, I admit that still terrifies me, but not as much as living life without you. When you confessed your love for me today I knew this. You know the land I bought? Where the butterflies live?' he asked suddenly.

'The butterflies?' And then she caught her thoughts. 'Oh, yes, Newbottle Meadow.'

'It will not be built on,' he said softly. 'I have already purchased new land, an old factory site that is *very* ugly, and this will be Robert's new undertaking. I have informed the authorities that I will be turning the land into a wildlife sanctuary and a place for people to walk, and will be donating an annual sum for its upkeep and so on.'

'When did you do that?' she asked dazedly.

'When I met the girl I had been waiting for all my life,' he said simply. 'Weeks ago. It will be called ''Georgie's Meadow'' from now on.'

For a moment Georgie stared blankly at him. 'Me?' she said.

'You.' And now he took her in his arms, kissing her long and hard until she was breathless. 'My love, for ever.'

'I want babies,' she warned ecstatically, wondering how a kiss could wipe away all the agony of the last hours.

'So do I, *pequeña*, hundreds.'

'They might be like Francisca's children!'

'They will be perfect. How could they be anything else when they have a perfect mother?' he said tenderly, picking her up as though she weighed nothing at all and sitting down with her in the chair, before kissing her again until she was weak and trembling in his arms.

'Matt?' When she finally managed to pull away to look at him, her eyes were bright and her mouth full and ravished.

'Yes, my love?'

'I'm not perfect,' she said with absolute seriousness.

'Yes, you are. For me, that is.'

And that was the way it continued to be.

HER SPANISH BOSS

BARBARA McMAHON

To Los Sueños, Luis, Mario, Juan, Julian and Rooney.
I loved your music, you all were the best!
Viva España!

Barbara McMahon was born and raised in the South USA, but settled in California after spending a year flying around the world for an international airline. After settling down to raise a family and work for a computer firm, she began writing when her children started school. Now, feeling fortunate in being able to realise a long-held dream of quitting her 'day job' and writing full time, she and her husband have moved to the Sierra Nevada mountains of California, where she finds her desire to write is stronger than ever. With the beauty of the mountains visible from her windows, and the pace of life slower than the hectic San Francisco Bay Area where they previously resided, she finds more time than ever to think up stories and characters and share them with others through writing. Barbara loves to hear from readers. You can reach her at PO Box 977, Pioneer, CA 95666-0977, USA. Readers can also contact Barbara at her website: www.barbaramcmahon.com

CHAPTER ONE

RACHEL GOODSON counted the Euros once more. The total hadn't changed. She was 470 Euros away from destitution. Or the use of her bank card which she refused to do. To use it would give away her location. She hadn't come all the way to this little Spanish town to be found so easily by her powerful father. She had meant her final statement. She was leaving home, leaving him and his outrageous demands and his unbelievable betrayal.

She was also leaving behind the man her father had hand picked to marry her. This was the twenty-first century, not feudal times. She would pick out her own husband, thank you very much. And it would not be someone who had more in common with her father than with her. Anger churned when she thought about recent events.

She took a deep breath, sipped her lemonade and gazed at the fishing boats bobbing along the weathered wooden dock. A couple of old men mended nets. The hot sunshine didn't seem to bother them. She would have sought shade.

Her small suitcase rested at her side. Her voluminous purse held all the important items, such as passport, money and credit cards—which she also refused to use. Her father would know as soon as he received the bills where she was if she charged a single thing. For her rebellion to be successful, she had to stay hidden from the powerful men who sought her.

Rachel's rebellion, she thought wryly. Could she pull it off? She had done her best to vanish two weeks ago. So far she had managed beautifully on her own. But her money was running out.

The white buildings behind her reflected the afternoon sun, gleaming in the brilliant light. She'd fallen in love with the little village perched on the edge of the Mediterranean Sea the moment she'd stepped off the bus a short time before. She had already been charmed by the friendly people. Now she delighted in the simple beauty of the setting. And most important, she felt safe with the isolation. This place didn't have the glamour of Madrid, nor the appeal of Majorca. The beach curving around the bay was practically desolate. Definitely not the place her father would think of for his only child.

The hills that rose behind seemed to shelter the town from the rest of the country. To the left, olive groves marched into the distance, their rows neat and symmetrical. To the right the ground was untamed, a tangle of trees, bushes and wild flowers. At the top, almost like a crown, sat a grey stone *castillo*.

She had not seen any sign indicating a *parador* nearby, which meant it was privately owned. Too bad, she'd love to spend one night in a castle in Spain.

Her financial situation, however, was more pressing. She needed to see if she could find work. It was unlikely without proper papers, but there had to be someone willing to let her earn some money without the formality of work permits. Maybe a local restaurant needed a waitress, with no questions asked. Or—Or what?

She had never held a paying job. Her experiences had been geared to planning lavish charity events or sharing hosting duties with her father at high-powered business dinners. Since graduating from college several years earlier, she had dabbled with establishing a career, only to be talked out of it again and again by her father. He needed her too much, he'd said. No one else could handle the social aspects of his business as well as she did. If her mother had lived, she could have handled all that.

Anger threatened again at the lies and deception. Her mother had lived. Two weeks ago Rachel had learned the truth. She gripped her glass tightly, wishing she had said even more to the man who had directed her every move until she'd learned of his deception.

He had the gall to expect her to marry Paul Cambrick. An alliance for business gain. No amount of arguments from Rachel had swayed him from his position. The pressure had grown intolerable.

Running away probably wasn't the smartest thing she'd ever done, but she was sure it made an impression on her father. Now she needed to find work to prove she didn't need her father or Paul to live on. She definitely was not going to marry Paul no matter what. If she never saw Paul Cambrick again, it might be too soon. Pompous ass. And threats to cut off her trust fund would be fruitless once she was earning a living.

She gazed at the sparkling water, trying to let her anger ebb. Of course independence had sounded perfect in her bedroom in Malibu. She remembered pacing back and forth, coming up with one idea after another. In retrospect, it would have been far easier to disappear in the States. She could have found work anywhere. Coming to Spain had been impulsive, giving into a long-held dream—and the determination to put as much distance between herself and her father.

"Can I get you anything else?" the young waiter asked in rapid Spanish.

"No, thank you. This is fine," she replied, a bit more slowly. He'd been more than friendly since she'd chosen the small table near the edge of the patio. And patient with her California version of Spanish. She could be understood, and understand him, but only if the pace was slow. She had to ask repeatedly for others to slow down since her arrival in Spain.

"*Americano?*" he asked with a wide grin.

"*Si.*" She wished it wasn't so obvious. Glancing around at all the dark-haired women sitting at other tables at the café, Rachel knew her blond hair stuck out like a beacon. But she could have been German or Dutch, why did he immediately peg her as American?

"Oh, are you here for Señor Alvares's job?" the young man asked excitedly. "We have been wondering when another secretary would arrive. If not soon, Maria will recover and return."

She blinked, wondering if she'd understood the rapid Spanish correctly. "Where is Señor Alvares?" Could it be this man wanted an American secretary? No way, her luck couldn't be running that good.

He pointed to the *castillo* on the hillside. The harsh grey granite seemed indomitable, rising loftily above the trees and shrubs that partially hid it from the town.

She looked at it, various scenarios flashing in her mind. Maybe she couldn't spend the night at the *castillo*, but could she spend a few days there? What kind of secretary did the man need? She didn't have a formal background in secretarial work in English, much less Spanish. And she was having a bit of trouble conversing in Spanish, but once she'd been here a little longer, she was sure she'd pick up the different nuances. Still, she had a lot of organizing experience. Could deal with difficult vendors, meet deadlines. How hard could the work be?

''How does one get to the *castillo*?'' she asked, already determined to give it a try. Answer the phone, make appointments, do some typing, she could handle it all. The worst he could say would be no. If luck was on her side, maybe she could get a temporary job to tide her over until she figured out her next step.

Twenty minutes later Rachel was flying up the mountainous road in an old cab that probably had been in service before she was born. The driver looked old enough to have invented cars. He drove with abandon, gesturing to sights as they rounded one hairpin turn after another. The view grew more spectacular the higher they went. Not that Rachel could focus on the view—she was holding on for dear life.

Luck was definitely with her on the ride, she thought, trying to keep from sliding from side to side on the worn vinyl seat. They hadn't crashed headfirst into another vehicle. There were none descending. They hadn't flown off the edge of the road, either, though it was touch and go a couple of times.

At one bad turn, the driver crossed himself, falling silent for a moment. Rachel wondered if she should be frightened—rather more frightened than taking her life in her hands by getting into this cab in the first place. But before she could decide, they rounded another turn and he began his rapid spiel again.

She caught most of what he was saying, expounding

on the beauties of the town, the wonders of Spain and old glories. Was he practicing to be a tour guide?

They rounded another bend and Rachel gasped at the magnificence of the stone castle before her. It was not huge, but large enough to be impressive. It was in excellent repair. The grounds were simple, green and lush, but without the ornamental formality she had seen in other *castillos*. There was no one in sight, nor any cars. Was anyone home? She hadn't even considered that in her impetuous decision.

The cab stopped before the steps leading to the ornately carved double front doors. The driver turned and grinned at her, holding out his hand.

She paid him, grabbed her bag and slid across the seat. Still staring at the granite edifice, she heard the cab drive away. She had debated having him wait while she asked for an interview, but decided she'd be in a stronger position to get that interview if she had no means of return readily available. Señor Alvares would have to interview her if only to fill the time until a taxi could be summoned.

If he were home.

Why hadn't she thought of that before?

What if no one was here? She'd not be able to use a phone, which would mean a long hike back to the café if that was the case.

"Positive thinking, that's the key," she murmured, mounting the steps and ringing the bell to the right of the doors.

Endless moments slipped by.

Rachel was conscious of birds twittering in nearby trees. The soft soughing of the wind through the branches was pleasant. The late afternoon heat was starting to get to her, however, despite the breeze. She turned and looked at the view of the Mediterranean spread out before her as far as she could see. Awe-inspiring. The spanking white buildings of the village contrasted with the blue at the edge of the sea. There was a quiet kind of hush around the castle. For a moment she thought of Heathcliff and the moors. A brooding silence seemed to pervade the grounds despite the bright sunshine and birdsong.

She tried the bell again.

A moment later the left door was opened.

"Si?" A woman with a kerchief over her head and a duster in one hand looked at her.

"Señor Alvares, por favor," Rachel said, glad her voice wasn't quaking like her knees. She hoped there was a job and she could get it. Bluff your way through, she told herself, raising her chin.

"Uno momento." The woman shut the door.

Astonished, Rachel stared at the dark wood. How rude!

She leaned on the bell again.

It was flung open a moment later. A tall man gazed down at her, his frown intimidating. Rachel stared back. Tall, dark and dangerous was her first thought. He was easily six inches over her own five feet seven inches. His dark hair brushed the top of his collar. His dark eyes were narrowed as he assessed her. His face was planes and angles, with not a spark of warmth anywhere. His size and demeanor would be enough to scare anyone off.

Except someone in desperate straights who needed a job.

"Señor Alvares?" she asked brightly.

"Whatever it is you are selling, we don't want it.

Leave or I'll call the *guardia*," he growled, moving to shut the door a second time.

Rachel stepped forward and pushed against it, obviously taking him by surprise. She quickly sidestepped into the entry foyer and swallowed. Tenacity was one of her strong points. Her father usually called it stubbornness.

"I've come to see Señor Alvares. If you are not he, please let him know I'm here," she said arrogantly. She had no idea who this man was, but being assertive might be the only way she could get an interview. She wanted the job more and more, if only to prove she could get it.

"Who are you?" he asked, his stance more rigid. "And what are you doing here?"

"Rachel Goodson. I'm here about the secretary's job."

"I have a secretary," he said bluntly.

She looked at him in surprise. "Señor Alvares? How do you do? I heard in the village you needed a new secretary. An American secretary. I'd be perfect for the job."

He pushed the door shut. Instantly Rachel wished he had not. She was alone with this stranger, in a remote location. Where had the maid gone? No one else really knew she was here. Would the cab driver even remember bringing her here after a day or two? Would the maid known she'd come into the house?

"Don't believe all you hear in the village. The people there tend to gossip," he said, crossing his arms across his chest and staring at her.

Heathcliff, she thought again. Dark and brooding. He wore a blue silk shirt, open at the neck, and dark trou-

sers. Maybe he should wear all black, she thought friv-
olously. Dragging her fanciful thoughts back to reality,
she frowned at his remark.

"So you are not looking for a temporary secretary?"
she said, disappointed. She had hoped to find an easy
solution to her own dilemma. She should have known
better.

"Are you really a secretary, or a reporter who heard
I needed help and pounced on the chance for an exclusive?" he asked suspiciously.

"Exclusive what?"

He raised an eyebrow as if in disbelief. "Exclusive
interview, of course."

"Are you newsworthy?" she asked.

"American?" he asked suddenly.

"From California," she said. "But I speak Spanish
as you can see, and I'm even better at reading and writing it." She hoped he didn't question her experience in
the secretarial field too closely. Though planning events
and serving on various charity boards would surely con-
stitute experience of a kind.

"How's your English grammar?" he asked in that
language.

"Perfect," she replied in the same, showing some surprise. "You speak English?"

"As you can see," he said impatiently.

She waited, hoping he'd expand on that brusque statement, but he said nothing. The few words he'd spoken,
however, had been unaccented. As if American English
was his native tongue. Rachel wondered how long the
silence would stretch out. She refused to be the first to
break it. She was tired of being pushed around by dom-
inant males in her life. From now on, she would not be

intimidated by anyone. If Señor Alvares wanted her to leave, he could call her a cab!

Reluctantly she had to admit maybe she'd been too quick to jump on a faint job possibility. If he didn't have a position, he didn't have one. Dashing up here on the say so of a young waiter had really been dumb. What about work permits, secretarial references? Just because she desperately wanted a means to earn enough to tide her over until she decided what to do didn't mean this man wanted to hire her.

He looked at her small suitcase sitting on the black-and-white tiled floor beside her.

"You came prepared to start today?" he asked.

"Yes." No good carrying on a bluff if you didn't go full out, she decided. She angled up her chin slightly. "I'm ready to start immediately."

For a moment she thought a hint of amusement showed in his dark eyes, but decided it had to be a trick of the faint light spilling in from the fanned windows over the double doors. He didn't look as if anything amused him.

She longed to look around, to see what the rest of the *castillo* looked like. It might be her only chance to be inside a castle in Spain, but she maintained eye contact. A glimmer of hope blossomed. If he asked about her staying, maybe he was seriously thinking about hiring her.

"Come with me," he said, turning abruptly and heading down the corridor.

She picked up her bag and followed, hurrying so she didn't lose sight of him as he took long strides down the dim hallway.

He entered a room to the right and Rachel quickly

followed, stopping at the door and staring in surprise. The sheer size caught her attention first, easily the size of two or three rooms at home. They were brightly lit from the floor-to-ceiling windows that overlooked the sea. A set of French doors stood open, letting in the fragrant air.

There were two large desks, both covered in papers, files and books. A computer desk sat near one, every other flat surface, including the keyboard, overflowing with papers.

"If you can read my writing and transcribe the work, maybe we'll see about your staying until Maria returns," he murmured in Spanish.

She looked at Señor Alvares and smiled brightly. "I'm sure I can manage, if you'd tell me which desk is mine."

He looked at her. "Let's get some things clear first. Everything you see or learn here is confidential, do you understand? Any hint of a breach, of betrayal, and I'll make you sorry you were born!"

Rachel blinked, swallowing hard and wondering if other secretaries got threats as part of the job interview. If so, either they were more intrepid than she had ever given them credit for, or jobs must be so tough to get they put up with anything!

"Agreed." She only hoped the position paid enough that she didn't have to stay long. She was already regretting her impulsive visit. Maybe she should return to the village and forget the entire thing. Only the thought of having to use her credit cards and alert her father stopped her.

"How did you learn of the job opening? You aren't

from the agency,'' he said, his arms crossed over his chest, feet spread.

Rachel didn't wish to tell him she'd heard about it from a waiter, yet how else? ''A friend told me,'' she replied vaguely.

''Let me see your passport.'' He held out his hand.

She rummaged in her purse. Holding it out, she watched as he studied it. Folding it shut, he slipped it into his pocket.

''Hey, I need that.''

''Not if you are working here.''

''I can't go anywhere without it in this country,'' she protested.

''The job comes with room and board. You'll get it back when I'm assured you aren't some tabloid reporter.''

''I told you I wasn't!''

''My secretary broke her arm in three places while hiking and won't be able to return to work for a few more weeks. If you suit, you can stay until she returns,'' he said in English.

Glancing at her suitcase, he continued. ''Maria has her own apartments in the left wing, but she is convalescing with her mother in Madrid. Her rooms are not available, but you can certainly find another bedroom upstairs somewhere. There are twenty-seven bedrooms and I only use one.'' He strode over to the larger of the desks and picked up a stack of yellow paper.

''This is where you start. You do know word processing, I trust?''

''Señor,'' Rachel began.

''Call me Luis. You'll have to find your own dinner today. My housekeeper, Esperanza, is on holiday and

Ana doesn't cook. In fact, she'll be leaving at four. But Esperenza returns tomorrow, *gracias a Dios* and meals will be provided. If you can't find the file Maria started, begin another. Formatting is double-spaced, one inch margins all round. Any questions?''

Rachel had a thousand, but the impatience with which he regarded her had her hold her tongue. She had a job and a place to stay. Her immediate needs had been met. How hard could it be to transcribe those pages, whatever they were?

When she shook her head to indicate she had no questions, he nodded once and turned to leave through the French doors.

Rachel remained where she was. It was the most bizarre interview she'd ever heard of. And no mention of salary.

Still, with room and board, her 470 Euros would stretch out a long time. Easily covering the respite she'd find here until Maria returned, she thought. Maybe by then she would have recovered enough from her shock of discovery to decide what to do.

In the meantime, she was in Spain! She'd had a love affair with the country since she'd first started studying Spanish in high school. Collecting posters, brochures, photographs and books for years, she was thrilled to be here.

The last two weeks had been wonderful. She'd been to the Prado, toured the royal palace in Madrid. She'd sipped café con leche at sidewalk cafés and wandered old narrow streets with venerable buildings that enchanted. She couldn't wait to explore more on her days off. There was so much history in the country, she'd forever be learning something new. There were the fabulous gardens and old cities which she couldn't wait to see. She wanted to visit Valencia, Barcelona, Seville. There were a hundred things she could do on her free days.

Work first, she admonished herself. She'd make herself so indispensable he'd have to keep her on until Maria recovered. From the looks of things, he'd need someone just to keep track of the paper. Who had time to answer phones, arrange appointments and deal with the mail?

He hadn't made any mention of routine. What did he do?

She frowned. How effective a secretary would she be without that basic knowledge?

She crossed the room and peered out onto the terrace. Luis Alvares had disappeared. It looked as if she needn't worry about him hovering over her while she stumbled through the first awkward moments of a new job.

First things first, however. Rachel took her suitcase and headed for the hallway. She retraced her way to the front foyer and climbed the wide stairs. Looking left and right when she reached the second floor, she hesitated. If Maria had quarters in the left wing, maybe she should find a room there as well. As she walked along the carpeted corridor, she studied the paintings on the walls. Dark and depressing for the most part. Were they portraits of ancestors?

She stopped by the first door on her left and knocked. Feeling silly when she knew she was virtually alone in the house, she opened it and peeped inside.

Drapes were closed. Through the dim light, she could see a huge four poster bed and heavy ornately carved furnishings. The room itself was as large as the biggest room in her father's house.

In only moments, Rachel had opened the drapes and the windows to allow sunshine and fresh air in. The view was the same as from the front door, without any shrubs or trees to block it. Near the shore the Mediterranean was a light turquoise, but farther out the water turned a deep indigo. On the horizon, she saw a huge ship.

"Señorita, Señor Alvares told me to find you. I have come to make the bed," the maid said from the doorway, a pile of sheets in her arms.

"Oh, thank you. If you leave the sheets, I can manage."

"Oh, no." The woman looked shocked.

Rachel shrugged and started to unpack while Ana made the bed.

After freshening up, Rachel headed back to the office.

Curious about her new employer, she was disappointed to see the room remained empty. Where had he gone? For someone who didn't trust she wasn't a reporter, he'd sure disappeared fast. What was to stop her from snooping into everything?

She crossed to the desk and looked at the papers, startled to find them written in English. Quickly scanning one or two, she realized she was reading a manuscript. He was a writer.

But why write in English? Why not Spanish?

She studied the page numbers, searching out from different piles, putting the sheets in numeric order, noting the lowest page she could find was page seventy-three. Where were the first seventy-two pages? Maybe on the other desk.

Rachel looked in vain for the first pages. But as she

ruffled through the pages, she noticing other papers apparently dealing with the olive industry. There were trade publications, reports and a reference to cargo containers.

"Was there something I can help you with, or shall I leave you to snoop to your heart's content?"

She spun around. Luis stood in the open doorway, watching her with an intensity that was intimidating.

"I couldn't find the first pages. It's a book, isn't it? But it starts on page seventy-three."

"Maria transcribed the first part before she injured herself. I said to start a new file if you couldn't find hers."

"Oh." Rachel felt as if she'd made a fool of herself. She was only trying to be organized.

"Then I'll look for it on the computer," she said with as much dignity as she could muster.

She tried to stack the pile of papers neatly, but fumbled as she grew more and more nervous with his steady regard. She wasn't here to steal the family silver, for heaven's sake. Couldn't he back off?

She looked up, but he hadn't moved. "Um, you didn't tell me about answering the phone or opening any mail."

"The mail can wait until you catch up on the typing. I've been taking it into the office in Benidorm. They can continue to handle it there. The phone won't often ring. If I'm here, I'll answer it. If not, take a message."

"Will you be gone often?"

His eyes narrowed at her question. "Why?"

"So I'll know how much time I'll need for the phones."

"I work in Benidorm."

"You write there?"

"I said I work there. Writing is a hobby. I do it as time allows."

She looked at the thick stack of sheets to be transcribed. He must have a lot of time.

"What do you do?" she asked.

"For someone who claims she isn't a reporter, you have a lot of questions."

"Forget it, then. I have work to do."

"It's after five. You can wait until the morning to start."

"So you don't expect me to slave night and day," she murmured.

"When you are ready for dinner, you can help yourself." He ignored her comment, but the lift of one eyebrow suggested he heard her.

"I don't know where the kitchen is."

"It's down the right corridor at the end of the main hall."

She placed the manuscript pages she had straightened on the desk by the computer. She couldn't wait to get started to see if the book was anything she'd like to read.

"How long have you been writing?" she asked.

"Another question?"

"Don't you expect a secretary to take an interest in her boss's business? Maybe if you'd give a little information, I wouldn't have to ask so much. Is your other job raising olives or something?" She held up a thick report by someone named Juan.

"Raising olives?"

Once again Rachel thought she caught a glimpse of amusement in his eyes.

"Growing olives? Whatever."

"I am in charge of the Alvares Olive Consortium. It has been in the Alvares family for four generations. And yes, I guess you could say we grow olives. We also process them, making the finest oil as well as producing a line of Spanish olives for the American market."

"So in your copious spare time you write? Isn't running a business enough?"

He inclined his head slightly. "I enjoy writing."

"English Literature was my major in college. I'm surprised to find you writing in English, however. I would have thought you'd write in your native language." While not another question, she sure wished he would explain.

"English is my native language, as well as Spanish. My mother is an American."

"She is?" She couldn't think of anything else to say without asking another question. How had his parents met? Were they still living? Did he have books published in the United States? Should she recognize his name? Vainly she tried to recall any books by a Luis Alvares. Nothing came to mind. Not that she knew the name of every author published in the U.S.

Finally she moved toward the door. She'd see what she could get for dinner. It was early, but she'd been traveling most of the day and was tired. Leaving felt like escape. She wanted some time to herself. Dealing with this man was difficult enough. Tomorrow she'd be rested and raring to go.

Passing Luis, she could smell the faint tang of his aftershave, feel some of the warmth from his body. She'd noticed Spaniards didn't require the same amount of personal space she was used to. They stood closer,

almost touching, while talking with friends. Stepping
away, she hoped she didn't look like she felt intimidated.

He surprised her by leading the way down the hall
and into the kitchen. It was huge. Rachel could imagine
it staffed with a dozen people, all scurrying to fix a meal
for the imperial master of the castle. Though modern
equipment was in place, the huge room reflected its early
days. Had the castle ever defended its land against in-
vaders? Or fallen to enemy hands?

She wished she felt comfortable enough to ask. The
building was old enough to have been through the two
world wars, and a lot more.

"Do you cook?" Luis asked.

"Yes. Shall I make dinner?"

"Take anything from the cupboards and refrigerator
you wish. Esperanza left me several meals to heat in the
microwave. If you wish to have one of them, help yourself." Without another word, he left.

Was Luis Alvares always so abrupt? She wasn't a
guest, she reminded herself. Maybe that was his tech-
nique with employees.

Or with young women who might make a play for the
lord of the manor, she thought. He seemed highly suspicious—yet had left her alone in the study. She didn't
know what to think about the man, but speculation was
better than dwelling on her father and his perfidy. Or
Paul and his outrageous plans that never included her
input.

Not that Luis Alvares was in any danger from her
developing a crush. The last thing she wanted was to get
involved with anyone. She had to make plans first to
convince Paul she was serious in calling off their sup-

posed alliance. He and his father seemed deaf when she'd denied there was an engagement.

Then she had to decide what to do about her mother. Would she search for her or not? How else would she discover what had really happened twenty-four years ago? Was there someone who had known her parents then who would tell her? None of her father's friends, of that she was sure. Someone else?

She was fed up with domineering men. If she ever let herself fall in love some day in the future, it would be with a man who was kind and gentle and who cherished her for herself, not one who saw her as a dynastic means to build his empire. A man to whom money wasn't important, or power. Only the happiness from living with her and a family they might start.

"But that's ages away," she said aloud. "After I find the mother I never knew was alive."

CHAPTER TWO

LUIS HEADED BACK to the study. He wasn't certain he'd done the right thing by impetuously hiring a stranger. But the fact was he needed to get the manuscript transcribed. He had a deadline looming and would rather have it typed where he could keep an eye on the progress than ship it off to New York and have someone transcribe it there.

He ought to check references. Make sure she wasn't some tabloid reporter worming herself into his household. But it was time his luck turned. He hoped she was just as she looked—a tourist who wanted to stay longer so applied for a temporary job. An American would be familiar with the slang and spelling of the words. He'd hoped she would be able to decipher his handwriting. Maria was used to it, though she complained mightily some days when he was in a hurry and rushed through the writing, or the car ride had been bumpy. If he didn't have his car and driver, he would never get as much done as he did.

He looked at the desk Rachel had been searching when he entered the office and hoped the need for secretarial support hadn't outweighed his good sense. He should find out more about the woman who had invaded his home. At least with her passport in hand, he could keep some control.

Transcription was getting too far behind to ignore. If she could handle the task, it would suffice until Maria returned. It was that or get someone in from the office. While one or two of the staff members spoke English, their mastery wasn't enough to make sure he'd used correct tense, or to catch spelling errors.

He'd talk to Esperenza when she returned in the morning, to make sure she kept an eye on Rachel. No sneaking around the place. And he'd make sure all the work-related documents were returned to Benidorm.

He'd also warn his housekeeper to refrain from talking out of turn. Having known him since he was a baby, she thought of herself more like a mother than a housekeeper. She often regaled visitors with boyhood exploits best forgotten. Of the summers he'd spent at the *castillo,* and the letters he'd so often written her when he was with his mother in America.

She was proud of him. Had been even before his literary success. His expression softened for an instant when he thought about the older woman. He loved her. She was one of only a few people on the planet he could say that about.

With Maria's accident, he was behind schedule. Maybe with Rachel he could get caught up. If not, he'd have to ship it as it was to his editor and have him get it typed. He doubted his editor would complain. The last book had been five weeks on the New York Times bestseller list, and was already in its fifth reprinting cycle. But Luis would rather have the control over the manuscript until he'd reread every page and knew it was as he wanted it.

He had other business to attend to. He often thought he would write full time if he could, but he had responsibilities for the Alvares Olive Consortium. Tomorrow, he had a meeting with a company interested in becoming a new outlet for their extra vigin oil.

He hoped Rachel would make a dent on the hand-written manuscript pages while he was gone, and not end up spending the day searching his private records.

For the first time in three years, his curiosity rose. How had she really heard of his need for a secretary? She had said only a friend. Who? Why was she looking for a job in a remote village like this one? Vacationing and running out of funds before she was ready to return home, he suspected. If her story was true and she wasn't a reporter.

Luis's interest was piqued. He liked a good mystery—whether one he devised or one that fell into his lap. Who was Rachel Goodson and why was she here?

If she were a reporter, she was doing a great job of hiding the fact. Unless she was too clever to show her hand the first day. Yet, he'd swear she had been genu-inely perplexed when he'd accused her of seeking a story. Was it possible there were people on the earth who didn't know of the great love of Luis and Bonita? And the tragic end?

Cynically, he doubted it. More likely she was playing some deep game. He'd watch her. If there was any sign of betrayal, he'd make sure she rued the day. He'd learned his lesson with women. A healthy dose of cyn-icism kept things on an even keel. One mistake could be excused to anyone. A second would be downright foolish.

Rachel made herself an omelet and ate at the large kitchen table. Fresh fruit finished her makeshift meal and once she was done, she washed the dishes. No sense in his housekeeper arriving to a messy kitchen when she had nothing else to do to while away the evening.

Next she'd take a walk around the *castillo* and then retire. Though what she'd do for the hours after that until bedtime, she hadn't a clue. The book she'd bought at the bus depot yesterday was almost as boring as reading a telephone directory. Maybe Luis had a book lying around that he'd written. Might as well learn a bit more about her elusive employer.

She returned to the study. Luis was sitting at the desk near the doors, his chair turned, staring out into the early evening. He looked over his shoulder when he heard her. His dark eyes watchful.

Rachel glanced at the stack of papers on the desk. Were they the manuscript pages she'd put in order? Had he been checking them? Probably in order to gauge how much she got done tomorrow.

For some reason, she was uneasy about entering the study with him there. If felt almost as if she were trespassing.

"Did you want something?" he asked, turning and standing.

"I thought if you had already published a book, I could read that this evening," she said. His gaze unnerved her, as if he were trying to see down to her very soul. His watchfulness annoyed her. If he couldn't trust her, he shouldn't have hired her.

No, he thought she was a reporter. Why would a reporter try to infiltrate her way into this man's house? She'd seen nothing out of the ordinary today. Except Luis Alvares himself. He was definitely not an ordinary man.

"I have published several as it happens." He crossed

to a cabinet on the side wall. The wooden doors were shut. When he opened them, they revealed several shelves of books. He selected one and handed it to Rachel.

She looked at it, and then at him.

"You're J. L. Allan?"

He waited.

"I've read your books. All of them, I think. I love mysteries." She studied a familiar cover, a smile breaking out. "Wow, I'm going to see the next one before it gets published!"

Still he waited.

She looked up, puzzlement causing her smile to fade. "This is what you meant by confidential, isn't it? So no one knows about the new book before it hits the bookstores? I would never tell a soul. You can trust me."

She didn't like his skeptical expression, but ignored it. She couldn't believe she was going to have a hand in the next book by bestseller J. L. Allan. "I didn't know you were Spanish. I mean that J. L. Allan was Spanish."

"My mother is American. That market is larger than Spain, though the books have been translated into Spanish." He turned back to his desk. "I don't usually write here, so the place will be yours during the day. Maria started at ten and worked until six. Will those hours suit you?"

"I'm a morning person, could I start earlier?"

"Whatever works. There's a lot to catch up on. The completed manuscript is due in another month. I've finished the first draft, but need the transcriptions before I can edit the work. I'll take what you finish each day, make notations and return it to you. If I could have them done by the next day, it would help."

"Sure." She hoped she could figure out the computer, the printer and read his handwriting, but she let none of her doubts show. She was almost giddy with excitement. Wait until her friends heard who she was working for!

The reality returned. Not that she could tell anyone—at least not now. News like that would spread like wildfire and her dad was sure to hear. It wouldn't take him two seconds to have someone track down J. L. Allan and find her.

Would working for J. L. Allan give her some pointers in unraveling the mystery in her own life? She wondered if she dare share her quest with him. Would he be scornful, or helpful? It was too early to tell. Time enough to ask for help once she decided if she really wanted to proceed in locating her mother or not. There were dangers in revealing the past. Would she like what she found?

As Rachel approached the kitchen early the next morning, she heard the murmur of voices. The housekeeper was obviously back. Esperenza, was that the name Luis had said?

She slowed, not wanting to interrupt without knowing if the conversation was private. She could hear Luis quite clearly as he told Esperenza to keep quiet about everything.

The woman sounded comfortable in arguing with the man.

"What is there to hide? It is all in the newspapers."

"Just don't tell her anything. And if she questions you, let me know immediately."

"Curiosity is natural in women," she replied.

"About the job, maybe. But not me."

"Oh, Luis. It is time to put the sadness behind and move on. Go to America and celebrate the new book. Visit friends and family. Forget the past and find a new woman."

"Esperenza, your kindness does you credit. I'm satisfied with my life the way it is. I do not wish it disrupted. Understand? No answering questions."

"*Si,* I understand."

Rachel heard his step a moment before the door swung open. She had enough time to take a step back and then look as if she'd been walking forward all along. She paused and smiled innocently at Luis. "Good morning."

He looked at her for a moment then nodded curtly, striding past her.

Rachel continued into the kitchen, feeling as if she'd fallen down the rabbit hole. What kind of secret might the housekeeper tell a perfect stranger?

"*Buenos Dias, señorita,*" the older woman called to Rachel upon spotting her. "I am Esperenza. Señor Alvares said you are Señorita Rachel Goodson. Welcome. Are you ready for breakfast?"

"Yes, thank you. I'm happy to meet you."

"Ah, Americano, like la Señora. You will want a big breakfast, not just bread and coffee. Where will you eat? On the patio? Or the dining room?"

"Here is fine," Rachel said. The thought of sitting alone in the vast dining room she'd seen from the doorway in the hall was not appealing. It looked large enough to hold state dinners.

"Has Señor Alvares already eaten?" she asked.

"*Si.* He rises before dawn most days. He works in

Benidorm and always wishes to arrive early. Come, sit. I will prepare breakfast. Do you start with coffee?''

''That would be great.'' Rachel's curiosity was running rampant. So her new boss had something to hide. Mysteries abounded everywhere. What was his? And if he went to the Consortium's offices in Benidorm, why hadn't he taken his writing in for the secretaries there to transcribe?

Writers were eccentric. It was the only answer.

She'd been up late. It had been several years since she'd read *Night into Day*. She'd enjoyed it almost as much last night as when she'd first read it, even though she'd remembered partway through who the killer was. It was fun to know the ending and see the clever way Luis had led the reader on. The clues were subtle. Only by searching for them could she find how he wove the plot so skillfully to fool the reader until the very end.

''Where are you from in America?'' Esperanza asked as she began preparing an omelet. Rachel remembered her own meal the night before. Never could get too many omelets, she thought.

''California.''

''Ah, I know it. I have been to Hollywood.''

''You have? Did you star in a movie?'' Rachel asked, smiling.

''No, no, I went with Señora Bonita before her death.'' She crossed herself, her expression turning sad for a moment. ''California is—extravagant.''

''Yes, it is. That and more. Who was Señora Bonita? Was she Luis's mother?'' Rachel frowned. That couldn't be right. Luis talked as if his mother were still alive when he mentioned her. Another thought took hold.

Would Esperanza dash to Luis to tell him Rachel had asked a question?

"Ah no. La Señora is still living. She and her second husband are in Cannes. She loves the beach. After the tragedy, she remarried and moved away. She is from Iowa. Do you know that state?"

"I know of it, of course. But I've never been there," Rachel said, growing confused. What tragedy?

"Luis, he went to school in the United States. But not Iowa. His mother lived in California when she left here. Is there something wrong with Iowa?"

Rachel shook her head. "No, but it is not extravagant like California. Very quiet lifestyle. Maybe she wanted more for her son."

Esperanza looked pensive. "Maybe he should have gone there to study, to stay with his grandparents. Maybe everything would have turned out differently. Ah, who is to know." She placed an artfully arranged plate before Rachel. In addition to the fresh fruit and fluffy omelet, there was lightly buttered toast. Rachel looked at the plate. There was enough food to feed a family of three.

"Such a tragedy," Rachel murmured, giving her attention to her meal, but hoping the lack of questions would open flood gates. At least Esperanza couldn't complain to her employer that Rachel had questioned her.

"Ah, it was. After Señora Bonita's death, I thought he would go mad with grief. He raged, and refused to have anything to do with old friends. He has shut himself away from all the old routines. Three years have passed, but still the silence encases this house. Still he mourns. It is not right. He needs to move on to life and happiness. Find another wife. Have children."

Luis? Somehow Rachel couldn't envision her new employer full of happiness. The brooding intensity suited his dark looks. She tried to picture the man in love, and failed. Still, how awful to lose his wife. She couldn't have been very old. What had the woman been like? Something very special if Luis mourned her death three years later.

"He swears he will never again marry. But how will he ever have children? Who will fill this house with laughter if not young children?" She shook her head and refilled Rachel's cup with fragrant coffee.

Careful, Rachel admonished herself. She wanted more information, but refused to ask the questions that bubbled. Hadn't she heard Esperanza mention newspaper accounts? Maybe she could learn more from that source, if she could find a library in this small village.

At least speculating about Luis took her mind off her father for a while, Rachel thought as she headed for the study after eating as much of the breakfast as she could manage.

Entering, she went to her desk, surprised to recognize the software program Maria used for word processing. It was the same one Rachel used at home. In California, she corrected herself. She no longer considered her father's house her home.

Luis's handwriting wasn't the best in the world, but she could read it easily enough. Soon she was engrossed in the story and typed as fast as she was able to keep up with the reading. She was coming in after the beginning and wished she could read the opening pages to get the background she was missing. Even so, the story was captivating.

"I'm going, now," Luis said from the doorway.

Rachel broke her concentration and looked at him. She thought he'd already left. "To Benidorm, right?"

He nodded. Slipping a piece of paper on her desk, he said, "That's the number of the office. Call if you run into problems. I need you to concentrate on the manuscript."

"Got it." She could make some inroads if that was all she had to do today, though her typing wasn't that fast. Still, whatever she could do was more than had been done yesterday.

Time was suspended as she was drawn further into the twists and turns of the plot. The man was brilliant. No wonder his books were so enjoyed. She couldn't wait to see what happened next.

"It is bad enough to have to chase after Luis when he is home during the day, but I expected you to be at lunch on time," Esperanza said from the doorway.

Rachel looked up, blinked. She glanced at her watch. It was after one! Where had the morning gone? She looked at the small stack of turned over pages. That's where. She'd taken a short break around ten, but beyond that, she'd been at the computer nonstop. She wasn't a very fast typist, but did her best to be accurate. More uniformity and clarity in Luis's handwriting might have helped.

Stretching, she tried to loosen her neck and shoulder muscles. She felt so stiff. No wonder. Hours without a break would do that.

"Sorry, Esperanza. I didn't realize it was so late."

"Tsk, tsk, do not get like Luis. I don't have the energy these days to chase after you both!" the older woman grumbled as she walked back down the hall.

"I have served lunch on the terrace. Take a walk, maybe siesta, then work." Grumbling even more about people not eating, she disappeared into the kitchen.

"What terrace?" Rachel asked, looking over her shoulder at the patio outside the French doors. There was nothing but the flagstone.

Good grief, she'd either have to get Esperenza to take her there, or find it on her own. The *castillo* was bigger than she'd first thought. Not only were there the twenty-seven bedrooms Luis had mentioned, but at least two formal sitting rooms, the huge state dining room that would easily seat fifty guests, and numerous other rooms and corridors she hadn't explored.

All for one man?

A huge family wouldn't fill up the place, but at least every kid could have friends over without infringing on anyone's space.

She peered into the dining room. Through the opened doors she spotted the fluttering of a tablecloth on the terrazzo terrace beyond. Hurrying through the room, she stepped into the shaded area. A round table had been set for one. Rachel sat down and began to eat. The chicken salad was delicious, as were the warm rolls. Esperenza had even made iced tea.

Rachel was glad for the break, and in such a lovely setting. Did Luis ever entertain? Fill the lower floor with laughter, discussions and music? Not recently, according to his housekeeper. But she whiled away the time thinking of elegant Spanish couples being entertained on a grand scale.

All too soon, she'd finished and returned to the study. She could have taken a longer break, but Rachel wanted to see what came next in the book. She was not even a tenth of the way through the stack of yellow papers. It would be days before she was caught up. But she was being entertained every moment.

At the end of the day, Rachel's shoulders ached and she had a slight headache. Hoping to clear her head, she went for another walk around the grounds, pausing to study the rows of olive trees that stretched to the horizon. It was quiet. Did the atmosphere change when olives were being harvested? Was it done by hand, or did huge machines crawl over the land, plucking olives from the limbs? She had a better picture of joyful workers swarming over the trees as they did in California, laughing and shouting as they worked the fields. When were olives harvested? She'd probably be long gone by then.

After freshening up for dinner, Rachel was directed by Esperanza back to the terrace where she'd had lunch.

Luis was seated, reading a newspaper. He rose when he saw her and inclined his head gravely, indicating the second chair.

Slipping into it, Rachel rushed into speech. ''I'm sorry if I kept you waiting. Esperanza said dinner was at seven and it's just seven now.'' She wasn't sure she liked the idea of sharing a meal with her boss. Whatever would they talk about?

''I have not been waiting.'' He folded the paper and put it on an adjacent chair.

''The story is fantastic. I was so caught up in it, the entire day flew by. Where can I find the opening pages? I want to read it all,'' Rachel said. She had not been able to figure out which file Maria had saved the opening chapters to. She would search every one if necessary, but if he discovered her searching through the computer, he'd believe her to be searching for incriminating evidence of something. If he just told her which file, it would save time and effort and misunderstanding.

"So it starts," he murmured.

"So what starts?" Rachel asked, placing her napkin in her lap and looking at the array of food on the table. Rice was piled high. Fresh fruit salad in a strawberry sauce tantalized. The roast looked cooked to perfection.

"I don't care for flattery. I'm not in the market for a romance. I have everything I want in my life as it is right now. Do the work and when Maria returns, leave," he said.

Rachel looked him, stunned by his rudeness and assumptions.

"Now wait a minute! I'm not flattering you. The book is darn good. You must know it from how well the others were received. And if you think I have the slightest interest in romance, guess again. Why you think any woman would want to deal with you is beyond me. That brooding Heathcliff demeanor might appeal to some, but not me. I want laughter and fun, not gloom and doom. Maybe I had better eat in the kitchen with the rest of the help." She threw her napkin on the table and made to rise.

His hand gripped her wrist. "No. Please sit."

For a moment Rachel resisted. His clasp wasn't unbreakable, just firm. Would he release her if she yanked away?

"I refuse to sit here and be insulted," she said haughtily.

"I...apologize." He released her arm. "I believe I jumped to an erroneous conclusion."

"Well, for a hotshot writer of detection, your own powers don't seem so great. I'm not out to flirt with you, or do some kind of expose. I'm not some groupie flattering you for some attention. I only want a job. A temporary job.''

''For which you have no papers.''

She swallowed and tried to keep her gaze locked firmly with his as if it wasn't the major problem it could become.

''Papers?'' As a dissembler, Rachel feared she was inept.

His look turned speculative. ''The story has a lot of work ahead before it's ready for the publisher. Even when the first draft is transcribed, there'll be revisions, editing. Check the list of files Maria has on the computer, there should be one called City. That's the working title of the book, *City Nights*. Would you care for rice?''

Rachel was startled at the abrupt change of topic. She expected to be on her way out by now. Insulting her was one thing. Ignoring her lack of work papers was another. Did he need secretarial help that badly? She didn't think so. He'd managed without for several weeks, he could have done so for longer. Or made use of someone in his business office.

She took the bowl, her fingers trembling slightly. Desperately hoping he wouldn't notice, she served herself and then began to eat. The food almost caught in her throat, but she hoped her demeanor appeared as calm and controlled as his.

Gradually the awkwardness evaporated. She looked around, searching for something to spark a normal, calm conversation. They were at the side of the house and from this angle could not see the Mediterranean Sea. Instead, banks of flowers bordered the patio with colorful red and pink blossoms. There were a few small white buds on one bush. The air felt warm, even though they sat beneath a trellis which would have shaded them completely from the late afternoon sun had the *castillo* not already done so.

It was a lovely setting. One she would have enjoyed a lot more without the brooding presence of her boss. Maybe tomorrow she'd see about eating her meals on her own or with Esperenza.

That reminded her of breakfast and the limited revelations she'd been given. Would Esperenza open up after knowing Rachel better? She wasn't a reporter. She wasn't planning to sell some story and make a fabulous amount of money. But she was curious as to why Luis thought she could do so. Unless he'd murdered his wife. Which was highly unlikely. Otherwise, what dark secrets did he hold?

"Tell me about yourself," Luis said a few moments later. "Are you vacationing in Spain?"

"Yes." Sort of.

He waited patiently, his eyes never leaving hers.

"I've always wanted to visit Spain. I studied Spanish for years in California. So I thought I would be ready when I arrived, but it's a bit daunting. I've been to Segovia, and to Toledo. And of course, Granada and the Alhambra. I could have lived there, I think."

"It is lovely to look at, but think of the inconveniences—no indoor plumbing, no microwaves."

She looked at him. Was he actually conversing with her? Amazing.

"Of course I never think about that. I imagine only the glorious times. With my luck, I'd have been the scullery maid or something, not the pampered daughter of the palace. But it's so lovely and impressive. Imagine what it must have been like in its prime."

"A romantic," he scoffed gently.

"Better than being a cynic," she returned, thinking of her father and Paul.

"You find me cynical?" he asked.

Rachel shrugged. "I don't know you, señor. We have hardly had time to exchange philosophies. But I'd bet you are. Aren't most men?"

"Only those who have seen the world as it is," he replied easily.

"Where did you go to school?" she asked.

He raised an eyebrow at the question.

"Esperenza mentioned at breakfast that your mother is from Iowa, and that you went to school in the States. That's why your English is so good, isn't it? Otherwise how could you write novels in the language?"

"What else did Esperenza mention at breakfast?" he asked silkily.

"Not much," she was suddenly aware of the trap. Why couldn't she learn to think before she spoke?

"If you wish to know something about me, ask me, not my housekeeper." His voice was cold as stone.

"I didn't ask her anything, she volunteered the information." She didn't want to get the other woman in trouble.

"You expect me to believe she didn't mention our great tragedy? How my wife was killed in a horrible car accident? How I grieve and mourn her passing?" The mocking tone in his voice was pronounced. Rachel suspected it wasn't the first time Esperenza had expounded on the event.

He rose and leaned so close Rachel drew back a few

inches. The anger pouring from his eyes was enough to drown her.

"If you value working where papers are not required, stay out of my life," he said very slowly, very clearly.

"Or?" she challenged recklessly.

"There are many ways to end things, remember that." His gaze held hers without wavering.

Rachel watched, shivering in the warm spring air. She felt helpless to look away. The strength of his will was formidable. He had obviously loved his wife a great deal to protect her memory at all costs.

For an instant, Rachel envied a dead woman. What would it be like to be loved so much? To be the happy recipient of all that intensity. To know a man would do anything to keep her happy.

She cleared her throat. "I apologize, Señor, if I stepped out of line. I didn't question Esperanza about your personal life and in future will refrain from listening if she begins to talk."

The tension that was thick enough to cut with a knife gradually eased. He nodded abruptly once and resumed his seat as if nothing had happened.

Rachel wondered how long it would be until she could leave without it appearing as if she were running away. Too long. Every second seemed like an eternity.

She tried to eat, but the food clogged in her throat. She took a sip of iced tea. It helped ease the tightness but not enough. Toying with her food, she hoped Luis would not notice. She had enough with her own family matters to deal with. She was not trying to pry into his. Could she continue to work with him? Not unless they came to an understanding. If he continued to think she was a spy, she couldn't remain no matter how much she needed the money. But how to convince him she wasn't a threat to him or the memory of his wife?

CHAPTER THREE

THE MEAL BLESSEDLY came to an end a short time later when Esperanza came to tell Luis he had a phone call. Without a word to Rachel, he rose and went inside. She exhaled as if she'd been holding her breath.

"The food is not to your liking?" Esperanza asked, noting the amount remaining on Rachel's plate.

"It's delicious. We, er, were talking and I just haven't had a chance to eat," Rachel said, loathed to have Esperanza guess the topic of conversation.

The housekeeper nodded and returned inside, leaving Rachel alone with her own thoughts.

"Great, I've managed to tick off possibly the only employer between here and Madrid who wouldn't ask for a working visa. Must be a knack," she murmured, taking another bite of the delicious roast. With her disturbing boss gone, she was able to enjoy the meal.

His chastisement didn't erase her curiosity, however. She wondered what his wife had been like. What their life together had been like. Obviously a great love story. Unlike the planned marriage her father had insisted upon. If she had given in, would she ever have grown to love Paul? Or would theirs have been a marriage that grew cold and distant over time?

And what of her father's own marriage? What had caused that ending? How could he have lied to her all her life?

The disquieting thought of her mother ignoring her

for more than twenty years would not be quelled. She knew where Rachel lived, why hadn't she tried to get in touch with her only daughter? Maybe not immediately after she left, but later, when Rachel had been a teenager?

Or *was* she her mother's only child? Had she married again, raised a family with someone else?

Rachel wished she knew more—more of her own family, and more about her mysterious employer. Her father had refused to say anything about her mother except Rachel was better off not knowing her. She had so many questions, and he hadn't answered a single one. Instead he'd been furious she'd even brought up the subject once she'd discovered their divorce papers, railing at her for meddling into things that were not her concern.

As if longing for her mother had nothing to do with her. She could understand bitterness between partners after a divorce, but to deny her very existence to her own daughter was not something Rachel could fathom, much less condone.

Luis's edict not withstanding, she planned to see what she could find from local papers at her first chance. Maybe she'd get some answers at least to one mystery.

Rachel headed for the study the next morning with some trepidation. She felt awkward after their confrontation at dinner. Luis was on the phone when she slipped into her chair and pulled up the transcription she'd been doing yesterday. The stack of yellow paper had barely diminished. There was still a huge stack of pages to go before she caught up. More than she could do in several weeks at the rate she was going. Maybe practice would accelerate her typing, though she strove for accuracy more than speed at this point.

Much as she tried to focus on the work at hand, she was distracted by her employer. She could see him from the corner of her eye. He leaned back in his chair, his speech rapid and colloquial. She had some difficulty understanding it, not that she was eavesdropping, but it was hard to ignore his strong voice when they were separated by only a few feet of space.

He seemed to be arguing with someone about appearing at an event, she gathered. Trying to concentrate on the transcription, she wasn't drawn into the story like she had been yesterday. The sound of his voice took precedence.

Finally he hung up. With a short expletive, he rose and paced the room. Warily Rachel watched him.

He turned and looked right at her.

"I've been pressured to speak at fiesta next week," he said angrily, as if it were her fault. "A friend of mine is mayor of the town. He insists."

Luis spun around and stalked across the room to the opened French doors, gazing out. "I have refused the last three times he's asked. This time he says he won't take no for an answer."

Rachel was surprised anyone could stand up to Luis if he said no. She waited. Was he just thinking aloud, or did he need some secretarial assistance? He was a writer, so probably didn't need help with a speech. She wished she had a true background in office work, maybe then she'd know where he was leading, why he was telling her all this.

He turned and walked to her desk.

"I want you to accompany me to the fiesta."

That was the last thing she expected. "If you need me to, of course." Was she to take notes? Carry his appointment book?

He nodded, letting his gaze drift over her hair, his perusal going down to where the desk cut off his view. "I do not wish to be the target of every matchmaker and groupie in attendance. If I arrive with a date, they will leave me alone. At least, I hope so." He shrugged. "Time will tell. It will be next Thursday night. We'll leave here shortly before seven. I do not plan to stay late."

"Fine." Did all secretarial jobs include this kind of work? How many groupies could the village hold? It wasn't a large place to begin with. As to matchmakers, she wasn't sure her presence would stop anyone.

"Uh, how dressy is this?" She had packed light when she'd left home. She had no dress fancy enough for a party. She'd have to use some of her precious Euros to buy something suitable for the event if needed.

"Not dressy. It's fiesta, a parade, eating from food stands in the streets, crowds, loud music, fireworks."

"Why do you need to go?" she asked. "It doesn't sound as if it's your favorite activity."

"The olive groves are mine. There are a lot of workers who live in the village. The mayor wants an appearance for a pep talk, essentially a lord of the manor type thing. 'Thank you for your hard work. This year will be the best ever.' I'm sure you know the drill."

She suspected his wife's death had kept him from going in years past. Each person grieved in his or her own way and time. But after three years, maybe he should venture forth a bit. Life did, after all, move on.

Even when someone hadn't died, she thought wryly.

The pang hit again, the anguish and disbelief. She still hadn't thought of how to proceed. Maybe instead of unraveling the mystery of her boss and his past, she should concentrate on her own.

Luis snapped the briefcase shut and lifted it. "If Juan or Julian call, tell them I'm on my way into the office."

After a solitary dinner that evening, Rachel was at loose ends. She had her wish to dine alone, but not because of anything she'd said. Luis had not returned when Esperenza served the meal. He'd been delayed, the housekeeper explained.

Rachel's neck and shoulders ached from the long day at the computer. She was quite a few more pages along, and enjoying the story more and more. She'd found the file Maria had started and printed out the first several chapters to read later tonight. Tomorrow she'd be up to speed on the story line. It would help in transcribing the rest. And in satisfying her curiosity.

Once again, Rachel sought relaxation after dinner by wandering around the grounds, enjoying the early evening. The setting sun painted the sky a brilliant rose and pink. The gentle breeze carried sweet fragrances from the blossoms surrounding her. The grounds were private—the perfect place for someone in hiding. She frowned. She preferred to think of it as retrenching.

Soon she'd go into the village, or to Benidorm to contact her friend Caroline. She had checked the computer she was using, but there was no e-mail connection. While she was angry at her father, she didn't wish him to worry needlessly. She'd contacted her best friend via e-mail when she'd first arrived in Spain to ask her to call her father to let him know she was safe.

She knew it placed Caroline in an awkward position, but it gave her a crucial buffer. When she thought about it, she and Luis had something in common—both requiring a buffer against the situations they were in.

Exploring the grounds more fully tonight, she rounded a hedge and found an old stone wall. The flat stones had been matched and placed so close together no mortar had been needed. It looked old, but substantial. Who had built it? In the distance she could see where flowers grew near the base.

Sitting on the top, she lifted her legs over until they dangled on the far side where the ground slopped away. The stones were still warm from the sun. She could easily see the sea from this position and the spread of olive trees extending to the horizon. Gradually dusk fell.

The lights in the village came on. She imagined families eating together, laughing, sharing the day's events. Wistfully she wished for such an end to the day. But even when she'd been a child, her father rarely ate dinner at home. Business was all-consuming for him. Late nights working, or entertaining clients. When she grew old enough, she began to attend such functions with him. But in thinking back, she couldn't remember a time when just she and her dad had gone somewhere for fun. Never once had they done anything not connected to growing the business. It paid off; he was a wealthy man. But what had he lost along the way?

"I wondered where you were," Luis said coming out of the darkness.

"It's so peaceful and serene here," she said, gazing at the village below. The lights sparkled, some reflecting off the pier onto the water.

"It's even more beautiful during fiesta. Lights are

strung around doors and windows, across the streets and outlining businesses. The fireworks are brilliant."

"Do you watch them from here?" she asked.

"I used to." He fell silent. Gazing off into the past, she suspected.

"But we will see them from the village next week, won't we?" she said practically.

"Unless we can get away before they start." He rested a hip against the stone wall. Rachel glanced at him, not seeing much as the night grew darker. He wore black again. Was it because he was in mourning, or did he like the color?

"Tell me about Rachel Goodson," he said.

She grew instantly alert. Why was he asking? She thought he'd been satisfied with her answers before.

"There's not much to tell. I grew up in California. Came to Spain."

"And now you're working without permits, right?"

"I don't have any, it's true. But I don't know of any reason I couldn't get the permits given enough time. I didn't apply."

"Planning on vacationing only?"

"And fell in love with Spain, so I want to stay as long as possible."

He was silent a moment then spoke softly, "Why do I feel there is more?"

Because there is, and you are very astute, she wanted to say, but dared not. Men stuck together. He'd probably insist she call her father, or phone him directly himself. Despite his own love match, would he see merit in her father's idea of a dynastic marriage? In the old days, Spanish nobility had married for wealth, land and position. It was entrenched in their history.

"Perhaps you see mysteries where none exist," she said. "How do you come up with your stories?"

"I do not murder people to get authenticity," he said wryly.

She laughed. "I never thought you did. Why would I?"

"Someone suggested it once."

"You're kidding."

"An American, actually, at a book signing tour my publisher talked me into. I guess he couldn't figure out how else I could come up with such realism."

"I don't see you being talked into anything," she mused.

She felt his gaze.

"It happens. Like fiesta."

"That sounds like a favor for a friend."

"I wanted to stay on the good side of my publisher, back then, too."

"So it must have been an early book. I would expect any publisher in the free world would love to have you as an author these days, on whatever terms you dictate. Your books sell terrifically well."

He said nothing.

"Oops, was that groupie mentality?" Rachel wanted to laugh. Couldn't he take some things as they were meant, without looking for hidden meanings behind everything?

"Did you mean it as flattery?"

"No, I meant it as fact. I understand a lot about the bottom line and what contributes to it."

"Business background?"

"Sort of. I learned a lot from my father," she said reluctantly.

"What does your father do?"

Warning bells sounded. "He's in business."

"What business?"

Someone born and raised in Spain would likely not have heard of the conglomerate her father headed. But someone who had spent his educational years in the States probably would have. Would knowing that raise even more questions?

"A word of advice," he said, amusement sounding in his tone. "If you don't wish to make a mystery of things, have a ready answer to questions. Even if it's wrong, it'll put people off the scent. My curiosity is piqued by your reluctance to talk about your father. Are you two estranged?"

"You could say that."

"Does he know you are here?"

"Here in your home, or here in Spain?"

"Either?"

She hesitated another moment. "It's really not any concern of yours, señor, is it?" She swung her legs over the wall and jumped down. He rose and stood beside her, a dark shadow in the darker night.

"When a young woman is living in my household, all her concerns are mine."

"I'm your secretary—your temporary secretary. That doesn't give you any special responsibility toward me or what I'm doing. And if staying here makes a difference, I'll find a room in the village. Good night." She started for the house hoping he wouldn't follow. So what if his interest was piqued. Let him stew in his own curiosity. She had a quest to pursue and it was not his business nor that of her father how she accomplished her ends.

Being in Spain was delaying the implementation of

her plans. She should have begun the search for her mother immediately upon learning she had not died. But she wasn't sure she wanted to find her. Once Maria returned, Rachel would go back to the U.S. and begin her search in earnest. If she located her mother, she didn't have to meet her. Was there a way to find out more about the entire situation before blundering into the midst of it? Who could she trust to tell her the truth?

Luis watched as Rachel walked to the house without looking back. When she rounded the hedge and was lost from view, he sat again on the wall and glanced toward the village. She was right, she was not his concern. But for the first time in many years, he felt interest in another person.

Her blond hair was sunshine in the night. Her blue eyes fascinated him. She was a mixture of enticing femininity and baffling standoffishness. American bravado and appealing fascination with Spain.

It was as if he'd been in a cave for three years, unwilling to walk into the light of day. But Rachel cracked the walls. He wasn't sure why, but he wanted to talk with her. Learn more about her. Listen to her fractured Spanish. He recognized the Mexican influence in her speech and found it charming. Maybe he should speak English to make her feel more at home, but she never asked, and he liked her accent.

He liked her honest way of looking at him. Not sexy and flirtatious like Bonita. Not flattering and oozing with false sincerity like the groupies he'd met at parties and book tours when he and Bonita went to the States the first few years of his writing success.

Since her death, he'd done all he could to avoid everyone, man and woman alike. Maybe as Esperenza was fond of saying, it was time to move on.

Not that he planned anything more than a work relationship with his unexpected secretary. But trying to piece together the various components of her life was proving interesting. Rachel Goodson was hiding something. And he suddenly realized he wanted to discover what it was.

He knew she was not a reporter—at least not like any he'd ever met. And she didn't play the part of groupie. She said flattering things, but he was beginning to suspect she meant them. Which meant she was a genuine fan. He should watch himself around her, no use alienating a reader.

He almost smiled, as if he'd cared who he'd alienated lately.

He looked over where he knew the olive grove began. The land had been in his family for generations. His father had wanted more children, but he and his mother had only had the two of them, he and his sister Sophia. And he'd lost his father far too young. Not before the man had instilled the love and responsibility of the family estates in his only son, however. Still, the man should have lived another thirty years or more. Would he have advice to give today?

When had the responsibility become such a burden? Was it Bonita's death and all that involved? Before? Or only since, when he wished he could leave Spain never to return?

Rising, he wondered where in California his mysterious guest lived. And speculated with a dozen scenarios as to why she was reticent about her father.

Her eyes flashed fire sometimes. He found himself

planning some outrageous thing to say next to spark that fire. Would the flash be there if he kissed her?

The thought struck him like a hammer. Maybe Esperenza's wish was about to come true. Maybe, to a limited degree, he could move forward.

As far as taking the delectable Miss Goodson to bed?

He was out of practice at flirting with a beautiful woman. But like riding a bike, it was not something totally forgotten. Would she agree to an affair? It would be safe, no lasting tangles, no devotion, no love. He wouldn't open himself up to that again. Rachel would be gone as soon as Maria returned. A clean break.

His idea to use her as a buffer from those who might try to get close at fiesta was a start. He'd do his best to make the evening enjoyable and see where things went.

No danger in her heart becoming involved. She was on vacation. A romantic fling with a Spaniard would probably give her endless stories to tell her friends when she returned to California.

He considered the various aspects as he headed back to the castle. In the morning, he'd implement stage one to see if he could find out if Rachel would be at all receptive to the idea.

At breakfast the next morning, Rachel was careful to keep the conversation with Esperenza neutral. She was not going to get into hot water with her employer today! Sipping the thick hot chocolate, she nibbled on the fresh baked bread. It was Friday. Would she have a chance to get to the village tomorrow?

"Is there a library in town?" she asked the house-keeper.

"No. There is a fine bookstore near the café. It carries

some books for tourists, and newspapers. They are all in Spanish, but there is an English store in Benidorm.''

No library? That could be a setback. "How about an Internet café somewhere nearby?"

"*Si,* in Benidorm. There is a big library there, too. It is required to be a resident to borrow books, however.''

Books weren't what she was interested in. Would the library have past issues of the local paper? Or would she have to visit the newspaper office directly to research the incident she had in mind?

Three years ago. Sort of vague. Was it exactly three years ago so she could start with the same month, or would she have to review all twelve months? She wished she had just a scrap more to go on.

"Is there a bus to Benidorm?" she asked. "I expect to have tomorrow free. I thought I'd go sightseeing.''

"There is a bus. It leaves early. You don't need to ride the bus. Ask Señor Luis for a car. There are three in the garage.''

"Three cars?''

"One is his, the other's his mother's. I use the third.''

Did she dare ask to borrow a car? Would he think her out of her mind?

"Maria has her own car, I take it.''

"*Si.* It is in the village until she returns. La Señora won't be visiting any time soon. Her car just sits idle between her visits.''

"Maybe I will ask then," she said. When pigs fly. Or when I get enough courage to beard the lion.

Entering the office a short time later, Rachel greeted Luis, surprised to see him sitting behind his desk. Books were scattered across the wooden surface, many lying open.

Taking her seat, Rachel looked at the stack of yellow pages. Surely it had diminished from yesterday morning, hadn't it?

Glancing at her boss, she saw he was engrossed in his reading. Wasn't he going into Benidorm today? ''Research?'' she guessed.

''Various poisons,'' he murmured absently.

Rachel sat behind the terminal and began transcribing his words onto the computer. She was more and more fascinated with the man as she typed the words he'd written. What a complex mixture of astute businessman and hardcore mystery writer.

The morning passed swiftly and to her surprise—pleasantly. She glanced up once in a while to study Luis. His concentration seemed total. He jotted notes, exchanged books, and read without seeming to notice his surroundings.

The third time she looked up, his gaze met hers.

''Do you have a question?'' he asked.

''No, just taking a break.'' She rose and stretched, rolling her head round, trying to ease the kinks. ''You don't have to go to Benidorm today?''

''No.''

''So you don't go every day?''

''No.'' He closed the book he was reading, tossed the pen down. ''Perhaps a short walk to clear your mind,'' he suggested.

''That sounds nice.'' She headed for the French doors. He rose as she neared.

''I'll join you. Researching obscure poisons and then trying to figure out how it would be obtained by the villain is hard work.''

"Not as hard as the writing, I'd think," she said. "Where do you write?"

"I have a car and driver to get to and from work. When business needs aren't pressing, I write as Marcos drives. Sometimes I take a day off to work here. There's a place nearby where I compose my books when the weather is suitable. The rewrites and polishing I do at the desk, and usually hand off the pages to Maria as soon as I've marked them up. But to think, to conceptualize and write down the ideas, I don't want interruptions."

"How close is the place nearby?"

He hesitated a moment, then nodded toward a path that meandered away from the terrace. "Come, I'll show you."

Rachel walked beside him as they started up the incline behind the castle. The path narrowed as they steadily climbed. She glanced at the man beside her, wondering if he'd been cloned. This was not the terse, suspicious man of the last couple of days. He was almost friendly.

When they reached the summit, Rachel stopped and looked around in pleasure. The view was terrific. Behind her was the sea, ahead of her more olive groves, and in the far distance, mountains rising. From left to right, she could see the entire horizon.

"Spectacular," she said reverently.

"The gazebo is where I write," he said pointing to a small structure a few yards away. He led the way and when she stepped inside, she was delighted. There were a couple of chairs, tables with pencils and pads of paper and a large chaise lounge. The view was magnificent. She was amazed he could compose the convoluted stories he wrote from here. Any time he paused, he had only to look up and gaze into forever.

How did he come up with such dark stories of murder and intrigue? She'd only want to write epics to encompass the vast expanse before her.

"How do you get any work done? I'd stare at the view all day," she said, moving around the gazebo, checking out the scene from each archway.

"It is new to you. Sad to say, if you lived here much of your life you would take it for granted. It has always been there. It will always be there. I can ignore it."

"I guess," she said, gazing at the beauty surrounding her. It would take her a long time to take such a vista for granted.

"Come whenever you wish. Just follow the path."

She turned. "Really?" It sounded very generous—not something she'd expect him to offer. "Thank you. I may do that."

"Mi casa es tu casa," he said softly.

She took a breath and boldly asked, "May I also borrow a car to drive to Benidorm tomorrow? I assume I get weekends off and I thought I'd like to see some more of Spain."

His hesitation was slight. Rachel wasn't sure if she'd imagined it. "It would be fine to borrow the car when you wish. I will show you where we keep the keys. However, as it happens, I'm going to Benidorm myself in the morning. To check up on things I missed staying home today. I can drive you there, show you the way, so next time you will know it."

"I couldn't impose," she said, suddenly wary about being in his company longer than she needed to be. There was something about the man that was creeping beneath her defenses. She needed to keep a professional distance.

"No imposition. I planned to leave at eight. Is that too early?"

"No, that's fine. And if you can show me the bus terminal, I can find my way back."

"Nonsense. I will bring you back."

"But—"

"I insist." The steely tone squelched any resistance. Even when being kind, he came across as autocratic. She thought about arguing the point, but it wasn't worth it. She would appreciate the ride, why not admit it?

Would he want to know what she planned to do in the city, or simply drop her at some plaza and arrange to pick her up at some mutually convenient time? How did someone explain her father had lied to her all her life and now she was going to take the first steps to find her mother?

"Thank you. I appreciate that." She smiled politely, her smile fading at the intensity of his gaze. His dark eyes seemed to see straight into her. Her heart rate increased slightly and she felt a warmth invade her. They were in the shade of the gazebo's roof. It wasn't sunshine warming her blood.

"I better get back," she said. Was that breathless tone hers? He'd offered her a ride, not a marriage proposal. What was the matter with her?

"Esperanza will have lunch ready before long," he said, stepping aside to let her lead the way.

Descending the path was even easier than the gentle climb had been. Before long they were at the terrace and entering the study.

"Thank you for showing me the gazebo," she said.

He stopped beside her, reaching out to brush a strand of blond hair from her cheek. Her heart skipped a beat at the unexpected touch. Was it her imagination, or had his fingers lingered? It seemed a very personal gesture. If she didn't watch it, she'd become the groupie he sometimes thought her.

"I'll wash up before lunch," she said, to escape before her foolish thoughts morphed into something more.

Promptly at eight the next morning Rachel descended the stairs. Luis was waiting in the foyer.

"Good morning," she said feeling a flutter of anticipation at his dark looks when his eyes looked at her.

"Did you sleep well?"

"Like a baby." Once she fell asleep. Of course that wasn't easy with all the thoughts of yesterday cramming for first place in her mind last night.

"And you?"

"As always. I don't require a great deal of sleep," he said opening the front door. "The car is ready. Esperanza said you had not eaten. Do you wish something before we go?"

"No, I'll find something there."

"Do you have any place special you'd like me to drop you?"

"Center of town would be great. I'll look for a café to have a *café con leche* and some rolls." Hopefully a café with Internet connection. She could eat if she had to wait, or log on immediately if there was a terminal available.

Stepping outside, she spotted the black convertible. She smiled. The weather was perfect. Her hair would get blown, but it didn't matter. She would relish the feel of the warm wind against her face, and the freedom of riding in an open car.

He drove down the winding mountain road with ease. Rachel couldn't help contrasting the wild ride up in the taxicab with the control with which Luis handled the car. She didn't feel a bit afraid with him at the wheel. Instead she settled back to enjoy herself.

She did her best to ignore her companion. Which wasn't easy with him only inches away. He seemed to fill most of the space in the car and she was acutely aware of his presence. The musky scent of his aftershave blew by in the wind. The smooth movement of his hands as he shifted the gears drew her attention. His strong jaw, dark hair, the black clothes, completed him. She couldn't see his eyes because of the dark glasses he wore, but she knew what they would be like, slightly mocking, turning to angry intensity if something displeased him.

''I can still get a ride back on the bus if your business will take all day,'' she said as they swept through the village and took the highway toward Benidorm.

''I said I'd drive you back. How long do you plan to be?'' he said with a hint of edge to his tone.

''I don't know. I thought I'd just wander around and see the sights.''

''There are some beautiful spots in the city. And the beach is renowned.''

''I didn't bring a bathing suit. Walking suits me.''

He said nothing more and Rachel gazed at the scenery. It wouldn't be hard to drive from the village to Benidorm. So far the road ran straight along the sea. Anyone could manage.

It was more than a thirty-minute drive. Rachel couldn't stand the silence for that long.

"Tell me about growing olives," she said, hoping the topic would take the remainder of the car trip.

"What exactly do you wish to know?"

"All about the business. Do you sell olives, or press them for the oil? Are the olives harvested in fall? How is that done, by machine or by hand? Do you have your own refinery or do you just grow olives and sell? Why do it at all if you like writing?"

He glanced at her. "Growing olives has been the family business for generations. My father was actively involved, as were his father and grandfather. Now I run the business."

"Do you like that?"

"Not as much as writing."

"Then why do it?"

"It's the family concern. I was the only son, it is my duty to take charge. My sister has other interests."

"Obviously you still find time to write."

"As you say."

"So what do you do with the olives?"

For the rest of the ride, the discussion centered on how old some of the trees were, how they were harvested, what he looked for in the pressing process.

As Luis finished one reply, Rachel came up with another question. Some were quite basic, but he never commented on the fact, patiently answering each one. He never once made her feel foolish. Which was in direct contrast to Paul. The man thrived on pointing out his superior knowledge on everything he could think of.

Once they reached the large resort town of Benidorm,

the traffic grew exponentially heavier. Luis dropped her near one of the main plazas, the old stone buildings a solid bulwark against time. She would be charmed if she had nothing better to do than wander around. But she wanted to find the library and get to business. Her tentative decision to begin groundwork to locate her mother had firmed into a strong resolve. Now she was impatient to get started.

She watched Luis drive away before she approached one of the *guardi* near the plaza's center to inquire after an Internet café. He directed her to one nearby and in only a few short moments, she was in line to use a computer. She sipped a *café con leche* while she waited, watching as others played games, or looked up information. Before too long, she was logged on and checking her own e-mail.

A letter waiting on her account from Caroline told Rachel of her father's attempts to locate her. Rachel responded, asking Caroline to assure her father she was fine, still angry and not ready yet to contact him herself. She couldn't help bragging to her friend about her job with writer J. L. Allen, swearing her to secrecy. She knew Caroline had read his books as well. She'd have to ask Luis if he'd autograph one for her friend.

Next she tried the name she was searching for, Loretta Goodson. Few results. She clicked on each one, but they didn't prove to be the woman she sought. If she couldn't turn up anything herself, eventually she'd try a private detective, someone who specialized in finding lost persons. She was determined to locate her mother if only to find out where she lived, what she was doing. The question of why she had not contacted her daughter in more than twenty years was something Rachel wasn't sure she wanted answered.

About to sign off, she hesitated. On impulse, she typed Luis's pseudonym into the search engine. A long list appeared. She clicked on the top one, reading about his last U.S. release, how the reviewers had loved it, how well sales had done.

Scanning the topics of the other articles on the list she stopped when she saw Bonita's name. Clicking on that article she found an American newspaper account of the tragedy. She didn't need the library after all. She'd be able to get all the information she wanted right here.

Quickly she skimmed the article. Luis was famous enough that anything surrounding him seemed news-worthy—especially the tragic death of his beloved wife.

The fateful night had been rainy. Bonita had been driving to visit someone and failed to negotiate one of the sharp curves on the road to the castle. She had plunged over the side, dying instantly. As had their un-born child.

Rachel stared at the article, unable to imagine the dev-astation and anguish Luis must have felt. Her heart ached for him. No wonder he mourned so many years later, he'd not only lost his beloved wife but the family they had started.

Esperenza was wrong. This just might be something he would never get over.

She clicked on another article, this one in Spanish. Reading the events, she was shocked further when it was suggested Luis had a hand in Bonita's death. Quickly she began reading closely from the beginning.

According to the article, he was never home, he neglected his duties in Spain, and denied his wife the attention she deserved. Instead of a grieving husband, this article painted a picture that almost accused him of murder!

CHAPTER FOUR

LUIS ADJUSTED HIS DARK glasses and leaned against the stone building. Readjusting the newspaper prop, he felt conspicuous and foolish. Hadn't he had his heros follow someone in more than one book? Never having actually tried it before, he didn't realize the many pitfalls—the most notable being what excuse would he give if Rachel saw him?

So far the surveillance had been boring. She'd gone to the *guardi*, asked a question, and been directed to a small café on a side street. She'd been inside for more than an hour. How much breakfast could she eat? What else was she doing in there? Had he missed the mark when he concluded she was not a reporter sent to get a story? Was she talking with a contact? Or had she arranged to meet someone to spend the day with? He was getting hot, but this corner was the best spot to watch the door without getting in anyone's way.

Impatiently he glanced at his watch. If she didn't show in another ten minutes, he'd move into the café himself and find out what she was doing.

Just then Rachel came out into the sunshine. She blinked at the brightness and quickly donned sunglasses. It made it more difficult to judge where she was looking, but he guessed he'd know immediately if she spotted him.

She sauntered down the street, gazing into store windows, studying displays. At the intersection, she waited for the traffic signal then crossed. Luis debated darting after her, but feared it would call attention. She didn't seem to be in a hurry, he could catch up after the next signal.

With no apparent destination in mind, Rachel wandered around the town. Luis grew impatient again. Was she just going to walk all day? She could have done that at home. The hills around the *castillo* had trails offering hikes of different degrees of difficulty. Or she could have explored the village. As to spending so much time in a café, Esperenza could have made her a dozen cups of coffee in the same length of time.

Close to noon, Rachel began to stop at restaurants and cafés, reading the posted menus.

"Enough," he said softly, moving to intercept.

"Rachel?" He hoped the surprise wasn't overdone. He'd never thought himself a very good actor. Though these last three years had proved that he could hide his feelings from family and friends.

"Luis? Are your offices nearby?"

"I thought I dropped you in another part of town." He didn't want to go into how far away the offices actually were. What excuse would he give if she pressed the issue?

"I've been walking around, seeing everything. The buildings are so old and intriguing. I wish I had a write-up of some. I bet they have fascinating histories."

"Have you had lunch?" he asked, not in the mood for a tour.

"Not yet."

"Join me," he said, slipping his hand around her elbow and guiding her toward the cross street. "There is a favorite restaurant of mine just a few blocks away."

"There's no need," she began, but he ignored her protest.

"I think you will like it. We'll have paella. Have you tried it?"

"Yes, when I first arrived in Andalucia. It's quite delicious."

"Carlos makes the best. Have you just been walking since I dropped you off?"

She shook her head. "I went first to an Internet café, to write to friends." Her expression was difficult to read. Was that guilt? Had she just been writing to friends, or filing a report?

"There is Internet access on my computer," he said, "No need to come to Benidorm."

"I checked, but didn't see a connection."

"Not the computer Maria uses. My laptop can be plugged into an outlet near the desk."

"Would it be all right if I use it sometimes?"

"Of course. In fact, I often use it for research." Had he not been holding her arm, he might not have noticed the slight tension radiating from her. Curious.

Had she been filing a report to some tabloid newspaper? If she used his computer, he could check the history log afterward to see if she was telling the truth. He wanted to trust her, beguiled by those eyes, no doubt. But he was an old hand at the games women played.

The restaurant was small and crowded. Luis spotted a table on the side and quickly headed for it. When they sat, their knees almost touched. He put his sunglasses on the table, and looked at Rachel. Her expression always seemed to be on the surface. Now she gazed around as if fascinated by the commotion and activity, but he suspected it was to avoid looking at him.

The tempting aromas from the kitchen focused their attention on food. Since he'd planned on paella, he didn't need the menu. Before long, they had cool glasses of wine before them, and the order placed.

She looked at him, a hint of wariness in her gaze. "Do you come here often?"

"Yes."

"Is it near your offices?"

"No. I had…something else to do. Tell me how Spain compares with your home in California."

She shrugged. "There is no comparison. Here the buildings are old, made of stone and built to last. There's history in every inch. Where I live in California, Malibu, it's trendy, flashy and built to suit those who just moved in. People buy houses to tear them down and build new ones on the lots. I like Spain better."

"So you came to vacation here?"

"I've wanted to for ages. The Romans, the Moors, even the Inquisition make it fascinating. And the architecture is so different as I said. Some of the cathedrals are wondrous to behold, even if they do need some dusting at the higher levels. The people are warm and friendly and not consumed with earning the almighty dollar."

"And people you know at home are consumed with earning the almighty dollar?"

She seemed to freeze. Then she slowly shook her head. "No, just a general statement."

"So what do you do when you are in California?"

"I work on charity events for the most part." She looked at him warily once again. "I really have done work as a secretary before, but never been paid."

He shrugged, trying to get a picture of her life before

he met her. It sounded as if she came from money. But then, why the need of a job to stay in Spain? Couldn't she wire home for more funds?

Unless she was running away from something and couldn't access her own source of money.

Now that was something one of his heros would deduce. Was he seeing conspiracies where none existed? He'd have done better to pay attention to clues three years ago. He wouldn't make the same mistake twice.

"I'd rather hear how you got started writing thrillers for an American market when you live here, than talk about my boring life in California," she said.

"Before my father's death eight years ago, I spent a lot of time in the U.S. My parents separated when I was young. There was no divorce, but I spent most of the school year with my mother. Summers I spent here in Spain. I wrote my first book in the U.S., actually. After my father died and I inherited his estates, I moved here."

"But you come to the U.S. to do book tours and all, don't you?"

"I did for the earlier ones."

The paella arrived and they were silent for a while as they began to eat. He remembered the book tours with loathing. He did not like being friendly to total strangers who lined up to buy the books, then asked the most insane questions. He didn't like the way the men had ogled Bonita when she accompanied him. He hadn't liked her constant need for attention, and her urging him to do more with the media.

It all seemed so long ago. He had not been back to the States in the last three years. He didn't miss it.

Rachel wondered if Luis was thinking of his wife. How could that one article have suggested he had anything to do with her death? It was chilling to read the innuendoes of the Spanish newspaper. Nothing like it had been in the American versions. Had he seen those papers? Maybe he didn't even know the speculation that had run rampant.

She'd never met anyone connected with a violent death, much less a possible suspect for wrongdoing. Her curiosity level was off the charts, but she could not come up with a single way to find out the truth without asking him. And that she couldn't do.

She tried to imagine how she'd feel if she ever were so deeply in love and the person died. She'd be crushed. Life afterward must seem so much like just going through the motions. How tragic. Or was he not grieving, but hiding?

To take her mind off of the questions she might never get answered, she plunged into talk about California, surfing at the beach, skiing in the mountains and some of the excesses of its inhabitants. He seemed to listen, but she wondered once or twice if she were talking to herself.

"Did you enjoy the meal?" he asked when she put her fork down in completion.

The paella had been delicious and the wine just fruity and sweet enough to appeal to her. Rachel was full long before the paella pan was empty. Luis ate more than she, but even so there was enough left to feed another person or two.

"I enjoyed it very much. Thank you." Especially since her host had been most charming. Nothing like the taciturn man who had first opened his door to her a few days ago. Nothing like a man who might have wished harm to his beautiful wife.

Learning what she had about her employer from the Internet articles, she felt she had known him much longer. It came from discovering some of the most intimate parts of his life. In a normal growth of friendship, such information might be a long time being shared.

Yet he knew very little about her. Not that her life was the open book she had once thought it.

"The pleasure was mine, Rachel. I enjoyed learning more about California," he said.

"Did you ever visit?"

"San Francisco and Los Angeles on one book tour. It rained in San Francisco and was hot even in November in Los Angeles. I think I'd prefer the southern California climate."

"It's nice. Temperate like here."

"If you are finished, may I escort you to your next stop?"

"Actually I've pretty much done all I needed to do. Have you finished your business?"

"Yes." He paid the bill and rose, gesturing for her to lead the way. Reaching the sidewalk, he once again donned his dark glasses. Rachel wished she could still see his eyes. The lighting in the restaurant had been a bit dim, and now it was too bright to be without sunglasses.

She put her own on and looked around. "Is your car nearby?"

"No, it's in a lot a few blocks away. We'll get a taxi."

"Or walk, if it's not too far. I love ambling along and looking at everything. Unless you're in a hurry?"

"I'm in no hurry."

As they strolled along the wide sidewalks, Rachel peered into the various display windows trying to decide if Luis could have done something so horrendous as was hinted at in that article.

Drat, she wished she'd never read the thing. Now she couldn't forget it. Every step she was conscious of Luis beside her. He'd been more attentive today than ever. Was he looking for friendship? Had he just been in a bad mood earlier and this was more like his normal personality?

She wondered if she could resist this new personality. He had made her aware of him and her own feelings before. Now she was afraid she wouldn't find the determination to resist.

The next several days flew by. Rachel faithfully continued transcribing the manuscript pages. She'd read the opening and found herself torn between trying to guess what was coming next, and trying to figure out if Luis had had something to do with his wife's accident.

According to Esperanza, he had been heartbroken at his wife's death. Was that report in the newspaper merely one man's attempt to sell more papers?

When she had finished working each day, she'd used the Internet access he'd given to comb the Web for information on Loretta Goodson. Inevitably she would end up each day reading more about Luis Alvares, or J. L. Allan as he was known in the press. She had not found anything new about the tragedy with Bonita, but she'd learned a lot about the woman from articles of happier times. Her pictures showed a sultry brunette who liked expensive clothes and bright colors. Her smile was provocative, sexy. Her exploits were notorious. She obviously liked fast living. How had she liked the *castillo* and its relative isolation?

Rachel grew depressed reading about her. She seemed to have it all. Including Luis's devotion. What had really happened that rainy night three years ago?

"If you wish information concerning my private life, you should have asked me," Luis said from behind her. Anger laced his tone as he reached over and disconnected the Internet connection.

Rachel froze, her eyes still on another article about Bonita's death. She had not heard him. He was home early. And, of course, if he'd used the door from the hall instead of the French doors, she'd have had enough warning to clear the screen.

There was no denying what she was reading. She turned slightly and looked up at him. "I was curious."

"And that gives you the right to pry into my affairs?"

"Hardly prying if it's on the Internet for the entire world to see. But I can see your point." She pushed back her chair and stood, putting some distance between them. "Um, if I had asked you any questions, wouldn't you have thought me some kind of reporter? I distinctly remember you thinking that the first day."

"Are you?"

"Oh, for goodness' sakes, no! You can't tell? I'm reading articles to find out more about you. Not to write about you."

"You could be doing background research so you don't cover the same ground in your own articles."

"Or I could be just who I am, someone who is low on money and needed a job to tide me over."

"Why not wire home for more money?" he asked.

Rachel's mind went blank. What had she already told him about her family? Had she mentioned her father?

"I want to stand on my own two feet."

"And how is it you planned this vacation and didn't allow for the money you'd need. When do you return to the States?"

"Things turned out to be more expensive. And I'll leave when I'm ready. But not before Maria returns. You need me."

"I have managed all this time without you," he said.

"What about the fiesta tonight?" she countered triumphantly. He wouldn't fire her for being curious, would he?

"Point to you. But in future, I would appreciate your asking me if you have questions, not researching other people's ideas of what happened."

"Did you sue?" she asked suddenly.

"What?"

"There is one terrible article that suggests you might have had something to do with the accident. Did you sue them for slander?"

"Actually it would have been libel, had they been more blunt. But, no, I did not sue. They are entitled to their slant on the news."

"You didn't have anything to do with it, did you?"

"What do you think?"

Rachel let her instincts guide her. "No."

"A vote of confidence I didn't expect. As it happens, you are only partly right. I did not tamper with her car, but we had a flaming row and she left in a temper. I've always wondered if that had anything to do with her driving skills that night."

"That's awful. How horrible for you, remembering

that. But I thought it was raining. It was stormy, surely that contributed to the accident.''

He shocked her when he said, ''It's not as horrible as you might imagine. Of course, that was because of the topic of the fight.''

''What was it?''

''That, Miss Nosy, is none of your business, nor anyone else's. And you won't find it in any newspaper account, either.''

''I'm sorry for your loss, nonetheless,'' she said.

''She was a beautiful woman,'' he said slowly, staring at the small photo on the computer screen. ''She died too young.'' He looked at Rachel again. ''This is how you use the Internet?''

''No, actually, I'm searching for my mother.''

''Your mother?'' He looked startled. ''Is she lost?''

''Apparently. To me anyway. I recently discovered she was not dead as I'd always thought, but had been driven from home when I was a small child.'' Actually she had no knowledge of why her mother had left. But being forced to leave her child sounded better to Rachel than to think the woman had just left with no problem or regrets.

''Driven from home? By whom?''

''My father, I think,'' she replied flatly.

She could almost see the connection clicking in his mind.

''Recently discovered as in just prior to this trip?''

She nodded.

''So you don't send home for more money because it would mean taking it from your father?''

''I don't send home for money because I don't want him to know where I am.''

''Ah. That explains a great deal.''

She stared at him, wondering if he planned to use that information in a way she wouldn't appreciate. But he still didn't know who her father was, or how to contact him. Her hiding place was safe a little longer.

Or was it? He had her passport with her address. Would he use it to contact her father?

''Where do we go from here?'' she asked.

He stepped closer, crowding her space. ''I won't pursue your father if you drop the research on my private life,'' Luis said.

''Deal,'' she said quickly, holding out her hand. His story was in the past, but she was living hers now. And she needed more time to gather her defenses against her father and Paul.

He took her hand in his. Rachel wasn't expecting the heat that seemed to engulf her with his touch. She stared at him, wondering if he was casting some kind of spell.

But he didn't seem to notice anything amiss and after a brief shake, released her.

Rachel would have agreed to anything to save him notifying her father of where she was. But the commitment didn't end her curiosity. She just wished she'd found out a bit more about him before agreeing to stop her own research into his past.

''Tonight is the fiesta. The village is already filling up with tourists and family members who have come to celebrate. There will be plenty to eat there, so I gave Esperanza the evening off. We'll leave at five, instead of seven as I originally said.''

That explained why he was home early.

''I'll be ready.'' She wished now that she hadn't committed to going.

"We'll circulate a little, I'll give my this-is-a-good-year speech and we'll leave."

"I'll do my best to keep the groupies away."

"That should prove interesting."

When they arrived in the village for the fiesta, Rachel was amazed at how it had been transformed from the last time she'd seen it. The crowds were surprising, even though Luis had warned her. The colorful lights strung everywhere would be especially delightful after dark. Flowers bedecked every surface, and there were vendor booths at every corner, selling flowers, trinkets and food.

The mood was festive. People laughed and danced in the street.

Not, of course, Luis.

He grew more grim and taciturn the closer they drew to the village. By the time he'd parked the car several blocks from the center of town, he was scowling.

"Let's get this over with," he muttered, gesturing her to precede him along the crowded sidewalk. "The speaker's stand will be in the square."

The party mood was contagious. Rachel smiled at the friendly greetings, feeling the excitement and happiness from everyone. Luis remained silent, walking steadily toward the center as if his life depended upon reaching it without speaking a word.

"Luis!" An exuberant young woman stopped in front of him, forcing him to a halt. She flung her arms around his neck and kissed him on the mouth.

Rachel looked on, startled. Obviously a good friend. Why hadn't he invited her to the fiesta?

Luis pulled her arms down and held her away from him. "Rosalie," he said.

"I didn't expect you. Juan didn't say you were coming. How are you, *querido*? You never return my calls. You can't be that busy!"

"Things have been hectic since Maria was injured."

"I would be happy to help out, you know that."

Her dark eyes were beautiful, as was the rest of her, Rachel thought. Her own blond coloring looked faint and insipid beside the lush beauty.

Luis looked at her. Rachel wondered if he was reading her mind.

"Rachel, may I present Rosalie Fontana. Rosalie, this is Rachel Goodson. A...a friend."

Rachel smiled politely, which was more than Rosalie did. She glanced at Rachel, then back to Luis, suspicion in every inch.

"A friend? I have not met her before."

"Rachel's visiting from America," he replied, reaching out to take Rachel's arm and draw her close.

So the games begin, she thought, trying to figure out what he wanted. Were they to pretend she and Luis had embarked on a passionate love affair to keep away the matchmakers? She leaned slightly against him and smiled. "It's so nice to meet a friend of Luis," she said.

Rosalie made no effort to even be polite.

"When did you arrive?"

"A week or so ago," Rachel replied.

Rosalie frowned. "I heard nothing of a guest arriving from Sophia."

"And she would need to inform you because why?" Luis asked.

Rachel wondered who Sophia was, but didn't ask. If she was someone close to Luis, Rachel should probably already know that. The best way to succeed in this charade was to say as little as possible. And snuggle up to her stern boss with all evidence of enjoyment.

"Of course she would not need to inform me, but I saw her for lunch last week and she made no mention of your having a guest."

"My sister does not know everything. Is she here today?"

"She's coming later." Rosalie put her hand on Luis's arm. "I'm delighted to see you. Maybe later you will dance with me."

Luis inclined his head, but made no further commitment.

"You will excuse us, I need to find Juan," he said, drawing Rachel away as if she wanted to linger and he had no time.

"See you again," Rachel called over her shoulder, just to provoke the woman.

Her glare was what Rachel expected.

"Sophia is your sister?" Rachel asked quietly when they were half a block along.

"*Si*. She lives in Benidorm. She and Rosalie have been close friends for years."

"And which one wants Rosalie for you?" she asked.

He glanced at her. "Picked up on that, did you?"

"It was too obvious. Why not call her to accompany you tonight?"

"I do not wish to give rise to false hopes. I have no interest in Rosalie."

"So tell your sister."

"I have done so on more than one occasion. But she sees no evidence of my interest in any other direction, so believes persistence will pay off."

"So I'm to fool your sister as well?"

"A minor diversion to get her off my back. She is the worst of the matchmakers."

"Somehow I don't see you putting up with anything like a pesky sister," Rachel said dryly.

"We all have our crosses to bear. Ah, there is Juan."

They had reached the town square. At the center was a raised platform with two rows of chairs. A podium and microphone were already in place. A colorful canopy sheltered the platform from the late afternoon sun. Sprays of flowers surrounded the base so it appeared to be floating on blossoms.

Luis introduced her to Juan. The two men discussed the program and the crowd. They would not start the speeches until after seven.

Luis didn't look happy, but he said nothing except that they would return in time. Rachel wondered what they would do for the next couple of hours.

He looked around the crowded square acknowledging several people who called greetings. Though they looked curiously at Rachel, he didn't stop to talk with them or introduce her.

"If we have two hours, let's wander around and see the booths. I've never seen a fiesta before. What is this celebrating?" Rachel asked.

"It's in honor of our patron saint. The village likes any excuse to have fiesta. There are several during the year."

"Don't you like them?" Rachel asked. How could anyone keep such a somber face in such delightful surroundings?

"Not anymore. Come, there is someone I wish to speak to."

In only a moment, Luis had introduced her to Pablo

and Maria Sanchez. Pablo was a foreman overseeing the olive groves Luis owned. It was obvious the two men were friends as well.

"So you come to the fiesta at last," Pablo said after introductions were made. "I hope you enjoy the evening," he said to Rachel.

"I'm having a great time so far," she murmured. She liked both him and his wife.

Luis had not had a single person visit in the nine days she'd been in residence. Except for the maids, Esperanza and the gardener she'd glimpsed at a distance, there was no one at the *castillo* but Luis and herself.

Had he cut himself off entirely from friends after Bonita's death? Or had they believed the innuendoes published in those articles and stayed away for fear he had had a hand in the accident? How awful if his friends had not stood by him.

"Luis!" A petite young woman quickly crossed the road and hurried over to the small group. "Luis, I didn't know you were planning to attend." She gave him a quick hug and then smiled at Pablo and Maria. "Hello. I might have known Luis would be with you two if he showed up." She turned back to Luis. "Why didn't you tell me you were coming? Julian and the baby are over there saving me a seat. We would have saved you one as well."

"We're sitting on the dias, as it happens," he said.

"We?" She looked at Pablo.

"Rachel and I. Sophia, may I present Rachel Goodson, a friend visiting from America."

Rachel was surprised he wanted to maintain the charade with his family, but saw it as necessary to keep

Rosalie at bay. She had never had a sibling. Did they all interfere with each other's lives?

"Hello." She wished she could say more, but the stunned look on Sophia's face stopped her.

"You are visiting Luis?" Sophia asked.

Rachel nodded.

She looked at her brother. "A friend from America?"

Luis reached for Rachel's hand and kissed the back briefly. "A very dear friend, come to stay for a few weeks."

"How surprising." She smiled politely at Rachel. "Forgive me, this has caught me by surprise. I didn't know Luis was expecting a visitor. He made no mention of it the last time I saw him."

"My arrival was unexpected," Rachel said.

"You two will have to come to dinner tomorrow night. I want to get to know you better. But for now, come meet my husband. I know Julian will want to meet you as well. And you can see my baby. Mario is the perfect infant."

"So speaks a doting mother," Luis said.

She threw him a look, and continued, "The fiesta is not the place to sit and chat. Tomorrow we can get to know each other better."

"We have plans for tomorrow," Luis said quickly.

"Oh? Then the next evening," Sophia said, not to be stopped.

"I'll call you when we get home tonight."

"You are staying at the *castillo*?" Sophia asked Rachel.

She nodded, glancing at Luis. He probably planned to explain everything when he spoke with his sister later.

It was hard to explain his strategy with Pablo and Marie standing by.

"I for one am happy her visit coincided with fiesta. I think Luis might not have come otherwise, eh, friend?" Pablo said.

"Showing Rachel around was certainly one incentive to come."

"Oh, no, you're not doing the man of the castle speech, are you?" Sophia said. She looked at Rachel. "Did he tell you? Our father always gave the speech, almost verbatim every year. It was part of the tradition of the fiesta, but we used to hate to attend. We could have quoted him perfectly."

"I plan to do so tonight," Luis said. The amusement lurking in his eyes clued Rachel in to his joke. Sophia didn't look amused. "You better find close seats when we gather on the dias so you don't miss a word," he added. "Pablo, I'll call you next week."

Rachel's hand was still clasped in his as they walked away to meet Sophia's husband and baby. As soon as was polite, Luis made an excuse and they left, strolling through the crowd.

"Doing it a bit thick, don't you think?" She held up their linked hands. "Don't you plan to clue in your sister at all?" Rachel asked when they were far enough away to not be overheard.

"And have her tell Rosalie? Not on your life. A couple of pertinent demonstrations will go a long way to making my life less complicated."

"Well, that's sure my goal, make your life less complicated," she murmured.

"Good." Ignoring the curious glances of others, he leaned over to kiss her on the mouth.

CHAPTER FIVE

IT WAS A BRIEF BRUSH of lips, but it shocked Rachel. She blinked. "What was that for?"

"To mark my claim?" he said. "Let Sophia, Rosalie and anyone else interested know I'm not on the market."

"Oh."

They continued to wander the streets. Luis bought her food from one stand, a drink from another. At a third, he bought her a bright fan, which she promptly opened and used. Peering at him over the edge, she smiled. "The Southerners used to use fans to great advantage when flirting," she said.

He looked at her. "And are you flirting with me?"

"Shouldn't I? If we want to fool anyone who was looking," she said, batting her eyes at him.

"I can see why it's so effective. Only your expressive eyes are showing."

Expressive eyes? She blinked. It almost sounded like a compliment.

Luis laughed, reaching out to lower the fan.

"Don't ever play poker, you'll lose your shirt."

Luis insisted Rachel accompany him on the platform when it was time. She was conscious of hundreds of eyes watching her every move. In for a penny, she thought and turned to smile at Luis. "I'm having such a wonderful time," she said, letting her fingers walk up his arm. "Can I put this on my résumé?"

He leaned closer, bringing his lips close to her ear.

"You are playing the part so well. I'm not sure where it falls on a résumé, but I'll give a glowing recommendation. Shall we stay for the dance?"

"I would love to, will that be before or after the fireworks?" More pretense?

"Dancing starts before the fireworks, but goes on until the last person drops—usually just before dawn."

She gazed at him, their faces so close they almost touched. To anyone watching, it would look like an intimate lovers' discussion. Her heart caught, then began to beat more rapidly. It was only make-believe. But for an instant, she wondered what it would be like to have him genuinely interested in her. She expected it would be like nothing she'd ever known before.

The spell was broken when Juan began to fiddle with the microphone. The loud squeals and static caught people's attention instantly.

Rachel had been behind the scenes on many events such as this, and knew how it would likely unfold. The speeches were short and entertaining. When Luis spoke, however, if she had closed her eyes, she would not have known it was him. He held the crowd spellbound. He made them laugh, had them cheering. He was obviously held in high regard, and his neighbors had missed him at recent fiestas.

When the official program ended, people swarmed the stairs to greet Luis. He spoke to each, introducing Rachel again and again. She smiled until her cheeks ached, knowing she would never remember most of the names, but hoping she was playing the role of devoted *friend*.

Darkness fell as they were talking and the string of lights came on everywhere, making the village appear like a fairyland.

When the music started, Luis swept her onto the dance floor and held her close.

"I didn't see any groupies," she mentioned. She felt like an enchanted princess waiting for the stroke of twelve. This was all fantasy, but she was savoring every moment.

"Ah, your presence worked."

"Most of the people seem to associate you with the olive groves, not writing. They do know you're an author, don't they?"

"Some do. The books are not as popular here as in the United States. I don't make a big deal of it and the name is unfamiliar, of course." He shrugged. "Here, I'm just the son of Juan Baptist Alvares. It suits me."

When the music ended, Rosalie popped up beside them. "Our dance, Luis?"

He looked at her and shook his head. "Tonight is for Rachel. Another time." He drew Rachel closer, his arm around her waist.

Rosalie obviously disliked his response, but tossed her head and looked around for someone else.

The next song was a slow one. Luis drew Rachel into his arms and moved with the dreamy rhythm.

Every cell in her body knew she was pressed against him. Her blood heated in her veins. Her heart rate tripled, and she had trouble breathing.

When his lips brushed against her temple, she almost stumbled. Anyone watching, and she didn't doubt a lot of people were watching, would suspect they were lovers. That was his intent, wasn't it?

"So, you have moved on." A harsh male voice interrupted her thoughts. Luis stopped dancing, dropped his arms and turned to face the man.

"Jose."

"So quickly you forget Bonita." He glanced at Rachel and dismissed her.

"I have not forgotten Bonita," Luis said quietly. "She will always be with me."

"She loved fiesta."

Luis nodded, his eyes hooded, his expression impassive.

"This one will never bring you the passion Bonita had."

"It's the blond hair," Rachel said, tired of the dirty looks.

"What?" Jose looked startled.

"A lot of people think blondes are cool and collected. But we have just as much passion as anyone. Right, Luis?"

"I have no complaints," he said softly, his amused gaze on her.

"Then maybe we should return home," she said as provocatively as she could manage. Let Jose think on that!

"Do you really wish to leave? The fireworks will be starting soon."

"We can watch them from our special place."

"*A dios*, Jose." Luis led the way back to the car without another word.

Once inside, he looked at her. "Our special place?"

She grinned. "Sounded good, don't you think? I meant on the old wall, where you said you used to watch the fireworks. Unless you and Bonita watched them there and they'd hold sad memories.

"No, usually Bonita and I attended the fiesta together.

It was when I was younger that I watched fireworks from the wall. I thought you'd want to stay longer."

"Why? To fight with Rosalie? Be interrupted by irrate men. What's the story with Jose, anyway? An admirer of your wife?"

"Maybe." He started the car and began the drive to the castle.

"Maybe? What does that mean?"

"Drop the subject. I told you, no more questions about my past."

So much for the feeling of camaraderie she had begun to feel around him. Firmly put in her place, she refused to speak again until they reached the castle.

Once there, she quickly got out of the car and looked at him over the roof. "Thank you for taking me, I hope I provided services as required," she said stiffly.

"Services rendered were more than satisfactory."

"Good." She slammed the car door and headed for the castle. She'd get her flashlight and head for the wall to see the fireworks. Alone.

"Where are you going?"

"To get a flashlight."

"We don't need a flashlight, I know the way perfectly well."

She hesitated. "No need to continue the charade. I'll watch them, you can go brood in your lair."

"My lair?"

She wisely kept quiet.

"Come watch the fireworks with me—from our special place," he said softly.

She headed back. "You know that was for show. If you have something else you'd rather do—"

"I don't." He took her hand as they walked away

from the castle. "To keep you from getting off the path," he explained.

She didn't need any explanation. What she needed was some distance from the disturbing man. But he held her hand firmly and led the way to the wall.

Rachel sat gingerly on the still-warm stones, swinging her legs over and studying the pretty scene laid out before them. They had hardly settled before the first burst of color lit up the night.

"Ohhh," she said in delight.

"I imagine I'll hear *ooh* and *ahh* all through the display," he murmured dryly. "I remember that from the one Independence Day Celebration we spent in the States. Usually Sophia and I spent the summers here, but one year my American grandparents insisted we spend the early part of July with them."

"Only one?"

"Summers were the only time I had to spend with my father until I was out of school."

She nodded, watching as another burst of color filled the night sky. "These are worth exclaiming over. I love fireworks."

She gazed in delight as the festive display continued for several minutes. The big finale was dazzling. When it ended, she sighed happily.

"I'm surprised such a small village could afford such a lavish display," she commented, swiveling around to stand on the ground again.

Luis was beside her. Too close. She looked up, but couldn't see him clearly, only his silhouette against the star-studded sky.

"The village has a fund people contribute to all year. Our company makes up any shortfall."

"Oh." She couldn't think. He was too close.

"Rachel." He said her name softly, his hand coming to brush against her hair. "Like silk," he said softly. "Tell me. Do you think a man should mourn the loss of his wife forever?"

"N-no. Life goes on." She cleared her throat, nerves taut with anticipation.

"For some it seems to move slowly." He leaned closer, blotting out the stars.

His lips covered hers in a warm kiss.

Rachel closed her eyes to better savor the sensations that began to fill her. His mouth moved gently, coaxing a response she could no more deny than she could fly.

When his arms drew her close against his body, she put her arms around his neck and returned his kiss with enthusiasm.

The fireworks she'd just seen were nothing in comparison to the splash of wild color behind her eyelids. She felt more alive than ever in her life. Yet there was more, she just knew it.

When Luis ended the kiss, she wanted to cry out. It was too soon.

He rested his head against her forehead. "Is there a man back in California awaiting your return from vacation?" he asked.

"There is no one," she whispered, moving closer, wanting another kiss.

He must have read her mind because he kissed her again, his lips opening her. His tongue touched hers lightly, then danced against hers, as if enticing her into further intimacies.

The sensations that grew threatened to overwhelm

Rachel, but she wouldn't exchange one moment in time for this one. She only wished they could go on forever.

"I want you, Rachel," he said, moving to kiss her cheeks, trailing little kisses to her throat. He settled his mouth on the pounding pulse point and lingered.

His words were like a glass of cold water thrown into her face. She stopped responding, and pulled away.

"Let's not let this charade get out of control. We're pretending involvement to keep the groupies away, remember?"

"Ah, was that the reason for your passionate kiss? I was under the impression it was to make sure I knew your assertion to Jose was accurate."

"Why did you kiss me to begin with?"

"I just told you, I want you."

Her heart pounding, she stared at him, wishing she could see him in the darkness.

"This is just make-believe," she repeated, to convince him or for herself, she wasn't sure.

"What if we want to change the rules, for as long as you are here?"

"What do you mean?" she whispered.

"A summer affair?"

Her heart pounded. No one had ever suggested she have an affair with them. Two men had wanted to marry her—for closer connections with her father. And Paul, of course. But even he had never pretended a passion that wasn't there.

This was outside her realm of experience. Was Luis serious? She wasn't the kind of woman with whom men had passionate affairs.

"I need time to think about it," she said. What was there to think about? She had left California to escape overbearing men. She had no reason to think Luis was any different. And she certainly had not fled one problem to become entangled with another.

Yet—the undeniable appeal was there. The man was fascinating. His kisses set her aflame. She wanted to know more about him, and about where such kisses led. Spend time with him and erase the sadness of loss. Explore the joy of involvement.

"Do not take too long," he said, and turned to walk away.

Rachel watched until she could no longer make him out in the darkness. Fortunately her eyes had adjusted to the lack of light so she could make her way back to the castle without straying from the path. She concentrated on walking, refusing to think about her feelings at the moment. A total jumble of conflicting thoughts best described her mind at the moment.

But once she reached her room, Luis's words echoed again and again. She fell into bed thinking about what it would be like to spend time with him. Share kisses, caresses. She opened her eyes wide in startled awareness. It wouldn't only be kisses. He actually wanted to make love to her.

"Oh, wow," she said softly.

"Oh, no," she said in dismay.

Rachel entered the study the next morning expecting to see Luis. He had not been in the kitchen, having eaten much earlier according to Esperanza. He wasn't in the room. As late as it was, he had probably long left for Benidorm. She bet he was bright-eyed and ready to tackle any problem that came along.

She had tossed and turned all night, alternating with

finding his comments wildly romantic, and being suspicious of why he'd picked her out. Rosalie would have been more than willing, she knew. There were several lovely women he'd introduced her to last night. Why her?

After a nonproductive morning, Rachel ate a quick lunch and then headed up the path to the gazebo. She needed some clear thinking. Feeling the pull of attraction to Luis in the castle even with him gone, she hoped expanding her horizons, if only visually, would help her sort her jumbled thoughts.

The view was wondrous. But did nothing to aid her decision.

Fact one—she was majorly attracted to Luis Alvares. There was no denying that. And she couldn't see it going anywhere.

Fact two—he was as dynamic as her father, Paul and a dozen other men she knew. Extremely successful business types tended to be driven and hard and focused.

Fact three—there was no meeting of the minds. She was still learning about him. Most of the days she'd been here, he'd been suspicious. That had eased—or had it? Was this some convoluted ploy on his part in hopes she'd confess?

Fact four—she'd never had an affair. This was probably the largest stumbling block. What would it be like? Was he only after her compliance in bed, or would it mean spending their free time together? Exploring more about each other, sharing thoughts and feelings?

Somehow she didn't see Luis as the touchy-feely kind of guy interested in sharing any *feelings*. She saw him more as the full-speed-ahead kind of man, going after what he wanted with determination. He had to have enormous willpower and control to be able to run a huge company and find time to write books that sold so well.

Did she want that focus on her?

Being romanced by a dashing Spaniard, wined and dined in fancy restaurants, romantic dancing until dawn sounded great in theory. She just wasn't sure this was the time or place to so indulge.

She was attracted to the man. Could she keep her emotions firmly in check and explore all an affair would offer? Or would she end up falling for him, even knowing going in that there was no future.

"So have you decided?"

He stood in the arch of the gazebo, dressed in black slacks and a white shirt. The collar was opened at the throat, revealing a strong brown neck. She studied him for several moments, letting the awareness build, testing her own strength against the yearning that built.

"Yes," she replied.

The sudden flare in his eyes surprised her.

"No."

"What?" he asked, crossing to stand in front of her. Rachel could feel the heat from his body as it radiated outward and engulfed her.

"I mean, yes I've decided, and I have to say no. Thank you," she added.

For an instant she thought he looked disappointed, but that was ridiculous. Nothing would faze Luis.

He raised his hand slowly and softly touched her hair, letting the strands wrap around his fingers. "Is it you don't feel the same attraction I feel?"

Her heart rate tripled. Had the air vanished? She was having trouble breathing.

"Don't you want more than just some sexual attraction?"

"Like what?" He leaned closer, lowering his head, his mouth coming closer.

"I don't know…"

She trailed off as he brushed his lips against her once, twice. Then he wrapped his arms around her and pulled her against him as he kissed her.

His lips moved over hers, teasing, coaxing. When she parted her lips, he didn't take advantage instantly, but continued the sweet coaxing until she relaxed and returned his pressure. When his tongue swept against her lips, she tentatively reacted with her own, to touch and taste. Every inch of her was alive as she'd never been before. She could kiss and be kissed by Luis forever.

He didn't push for more, seemingly content with their kiss. Others had always gone faster than she had wanted at this stage and so often Rachel had ended up fighting off unwelcomed advances. Had he pursued it, Rachel doubted she'd resist.

When he ended the kiss, she slowly opened her eyes to find him staring down at her.

"Reconsider," he said softly.

"I'd think you'd want more than just sex," she said with some asperity as she disentangled herself from him and put several feet of much needed space between them. How was she supposed to even think with her mind still numb from his kisses?

"Like what?"

"Like what you had with your wife," she snapped. Her mood was fast deteriorating. She had thought things through and decided to refuse. Now after one kiss, she was reconsidering just as he'd probably known she would.

He looked as if she'd slapped him.

''Don't be confusing yourself with my wife,'' he said.

''I'm not. I just mean if sex is all you want, find it elsewhere. If I make love with someone, I want it to mean more than just a romp between the sheets. I want caring and respect and…''

She stopped abruptly. She was not looking for love from Luis Alvares. If she said it, he'd immediately think she was after more than what he offered.

''And?'' he asked dangerously.

''And, and…something in common. We have none of that. You suspect I'm some kind of spy. I don't know you except as the man who hired me to type a manuscript.''

''You've read my books. Surely you have some kind of feeling about what kind of man I am.''

''Dutiful, honorable, focused, and successful,'' she said after a moment. ''Those are traits. I still don't know you.''

''I don't know you well, either, but I'm willing to take a chance. You could still be a tabloid reporter, biding her time. Or someone who wants marriage and is being very clever.''

''What if I'm just who I say I am. Someone on vacation in Spain?''

''Who doesn't call home for money when she runs out. Who claims she has no man waiting for her, but I find that hard to believe.''

''Why?''

He stepped closer. Rachel held her ground, watching him warily.

"You have the passion you told Jose about. You are beautiful. I know American men are not blind."

He was crowding her space. She longed to turn and flee, but she was held in place by the intensity of his gaze, by the melodious sound of his voice, the words that flattered beyond any she'd ever heard before. He thought she was beautiful? Passionate?

"Well, maybe," she temporized.

"Maybe there is a man?" he asked.

"No, maybe I'll consider an affair. But only after I get to know you better. And you me."

He cupped her chin in his hand and tilted up her face. "How long?"

"Well for goodness' sakes, Luis, I don't know. There isn't a timetable. When it's right, I guess."

"And until then?"

She licked her lips when his gaze moved to watch her tongue. The desire was so strong she could almost touch it.

"We get to know each other?" she asked softly.

"We'll try it your way for a few days. I'm not a patient man." He lowered his head and kissed her.

"Señor?" A voice came from a small speaker in the gazebo that Rachel had not even noticed.

Luis broke the kiss and hurried to the post, pressing a small button. *"Si?"*

"Your sister is most insistent she talk to you," Esperanza said.

"I'll be there in a moment." He looked at Rachel. "Until later." Quickly he strode from the structure.

Rachel watched him, bemused. Until later? What did that mean? It almost sounded like an ultimatum. He planned to try it her way for a few days. At the end, what? Would they reevaluate the situation, or was he expecting her compliance at the end of a few days?

Would she be able to resist? If he applied himself to seducing her, she had a feeling she would be more than willing to go along with whatever he planned.

So much for clearing her head by coming up to the gazebo, she thought wryly. She was more muddled after those fabulous kisses than she'd ever been.

Rachel didn't see Luis again that evening. When she arrived at the patio for dinner, Esperanza was the only one there, placing the platter of pork in the center of the table.

"Señor Alvares had to go back to Benidorm for business. He sends his apologies," she said as she surveyed the table with satisfaction.

"Nothing crucial, I hope," Rachel murmured as she sat.

Esperanza shrugged.

"Will you join me?" Rachel asked, not wishing to eat in solitary splendor.

"I have already eaten," the older woman replied.

"It looks delicious."

"Señor Luis had a call from his sister. She phoned earlier, before the business matter. She asked about you."

Rachel was tempted to tell her she'd known about Sophia's call, but didn't wish to have to explain how. Merely nodding, she began to eat. The evening hadn't turned out like she'd hoped. Had Luis gone to his sister's? Or had work demanded his attention?

Luis drove home rapidly. He had been needed at the

consortium's office to deal with a problem. The timing, in his opinion, couldn't have been worse. He had made definite strides in persuading Rachel to indulge in an affair with him. Had he lost ground by being absent this evening? Would she still be awake, wanting to learn more about him, to justify her compliance?

Women played strange games. He wanted her, she wanted him, what was the difference if they waited until they knew each other's school grades or grandparents' names? He wasn't looking for a lifelong commitment. He'd tried that once and look where it had gotten him.

Rachel wasn't moving to Spain, only visiting. It was perfect. With the added bonus of keeping others at bay. Most noticeably Rosalie. Not that invitations had been lacking in the last three years. Women especially seemed to think a man alone, a widower, needed a woman in his life.

As he rounded one of the bends in the road and saw the castle, he acknowledged someday he would probably feel the need to find another wife in order to have a child to inherit the family home. Or, maybe he'd settle for Sophia's children inheriting. They weren't a dynasty from ancient times. Luis wasn't sure he'd ever again trust a woman enough to marry her.

The castle appeared in darkness when he drew into the courtyard. No lights shone from the windows. Esperenza had left the carriage lights on, but nothing else. In other words, Rachel's window was dark. Damn.

Unless she hadn't yet gone up. Maybe she was in the lounge or the study. He'd check both before retiring.

She was in neither. But her scent seemed to linger in the air of the study, even with the French doors opened to the evening's breeze. Imagination or reality? He was growing fanciful as he aged, he mocked himself. The night air was redolent with scents from nearby blossoms. That was what he smelled, not Rachel's perfume.

He refused to admit disappointment she hadn't waited for him. If he took her at her word, he'd believe she wasn't as interested as he.

Saturday morning Luis awoke early. Day one in his new campaign.

By the time he reached the kitchen, he'd formulated his strategy.

Rachel was talking with Esperenza as the housekeeper prepared coffee. They both looked at him when he entered, surprise and speculation in Esperenza's gaze, wariness in Rachel's.

"Good morning, Señor. I shall have breakfast ready soon."

"No rush. I'll join you both in here if I may," he said, taking a chair opposite to Rachel. "Sleep well?" he asked Rachel.

"Yes."

"Today we can go to the beach," Luis said, ignoring the wariness in her eyes. "It seems a shame to come all the way to the Mediterranean and not take advantage of all it offers."

Her smile lit up her face. Luis felt it as if he'd been punched. He wanted to sweep her upstairs into his room, close the door and stay in bed all day. She was not a sultry beauty like Bonita had been. Her blondness belied the passion she'd bragged about to Jose, and he was determined to tap into it as soon as possible.

"I would love to get to the beach. If you could drop

me there, that would be terrific. I was thinking that very thing earlier.''

"I told her to ask you for your mother's car," Esperenza interjected.

Luis frowned. It was not his intention to make things easier for Rachel to do things without him. "The car needs to be serviced first." He'd see it stayed in the shop for several days.

Esperenza merely raised an eyebrow in disbelief, but said nothing.

"I meant we'd go together. I like to swim," Luis said smoothly.

"That would be great," Rachel said, color staining her cheeks.

He wished he could read her mind. Her enthusiasm had dipped when he said he'd accompany her. But her eyes held hidden promise.

Whatever her true feelings, he looked forward to the excursion. It would provide her with the chance to grow more comfortable around him, and give him a chance to push for more. Timing was everything, as he'd learned in the past. Now to turn it to his advantage.

CHAPTER SIX

RACHEL STUDIED HERSELF in the mirror, hoping the bikini she wore wasn't too blatant. It was the only suit she'd brought. And she hadn't used it once since she arrived in Spain. She tried to imagine how Luis would like it.

Not that it mattered, she told herself, but she suspected he would like it a lot. Smiling, she turned to don the coverup and slip into sandals. She didn't want to keep him waiting. Nor keep herself in suspense as to the reason for his invitation. Was it to get to know her better, or try an inquisition? Weren't the Spanish famous for that?

She laughed with happiness. Whatever happened today, it was for the two of them. She could forget her quest for a while, forget about her father. And hope Luis would forget about his beloved wife.

When Luis and Rachel arrived at the sandy stretch that was south of the town, well away from the influence of the fishing boats, Rachel wondered if she'd misread things. Luis had been as cordial as a good host should be. Yet there had been nothing of what she expected.

Marcos, Luis's driver, drove them. He unloaded a beach umbrella and two folding chairs which he promptly delivered to a wide vacant spot near the water's edge. Rachel marched across the sand, delighted she wouldn't have to lie on a towel, trying to wiggle until she found a comfortable spot. When Marcos returned carrying a cooler, she glanced at Luis. He seemed to think of everything.

The towels Marcos deposited across the back of the chairs were fluffy and large, a colorful rainbow of hues. She would be able to spot their location even if she swam out quite a way.

"Nice," she said, sitting on the edge of her chaise and looking around her.

The water lapped at the shore. The pristine white sand reflected the sun so brightly it almost hurt. Glad for her sunglasses, she studied the others on the beach. Mostly families with small children, she watched as they cavorted in the water, ran up and down the beach, or solemnly built castles of sand.

Rachel couldn't remember going to the beach often when she was a child. Her father had been too busy with work, and the succession of housekeepers hadn't wanted to bother.

If she ever married…

She shook her head at the thought. She didn't want to get married. Look at the pitfalls that awaited the unwary.

Sadly, being an only child, she didn't even have the prospect of nieces and nephews to look forward to.

"Not to your liking?" Luis asked.

"What?" She looked at him.

"By your expression, I take it this doesn't suit?"

"Oh, no, I was thinking of something else. This is lovely. With the umbrella I could stay here all day and not worry about burning."

"There's enough reflected rays from the sand and water to take precautions."

She rummaged in her carryall and pulled out a bottle of sunscreen. "Ta da! I came prepared."

Lathering the scented lotion over her legs, Rachel was reminded of afternoons in high school when she and her friends lounged by a pool. With her fair skin she had always needed to take care not to get burned. And she never tanned as darkly as her friend Caroline, try as she might.

"Shall I do your back?" Luis asked.

Rachel froze, her hand stopping on her calf, as she glanced over to him. She did need help where she couldn't reach. But Luis? She swallowed.

"Fine." She could do this. It was only sunscreen.

But the moment his warm fingertips began soothing the lotion over her already heated skin, she wondered if she could hold together. His touch was seductive. The long strokes mesmerizing. His hands felt strong, masculine. She wanted to turn and throw herself into his arms and demand he kiss her as he had before.

Was time moving slowly, or was he taking longer than necessary? It seemed as if the world stood still, only Luis's hands on her back moved. Slowly Rachel let her eyes close. It was heaven.

"Covered," he said, patting her lightly on her shoulder. "Do my back?"

"Sure." She hoped that one word, almost croaked out, sounded normal to him. She did not want to give him any idea of the turmoil that roiled around inside.

His shoulders were wide and muscular. Wearing dress shirts hid his amazing physique. How was he so toned when he worked so many hours in an office, she wondered as her hands traced the defined musculature. His skin was warm, from the sun, or his own internal heat? She poured more lotion on her hand, spreading it evenly, letting her fingertips learn the feel of his skin. She longed to have him turn around.

Almost as if he read her mind, he did. Her hands trailed across his chest. Desire spiraled up inside. Slowly she rubbed the lotion over the chest hair, feeling the rougher texture.

''I can manage,'' Luis said. His voice sounded low, husky.

Rachel looked up to his eyes, seeing the heat.

''Unless you want me to reciprocate,'' he suggested, trailing one finger across the top of her bathing suit.

''Uh, no, I already put lotion there.'' She stumbled back. ''I think I'm ready for a swim.'' She tossed him the bottle and almost ran to the water's edge. Taking a deep breath, she tried to control her wayward thoughts. She hoped the water was cold, she needed something to shock her back to normal.

She plunged in, wading out until it reached the tops of her thighs then dove in. It wasn't cold, but refreshingly cool. She headed for deeper water, swimming for pure joy. She loved the water. And the Mediterranean was especially buoyant. She could swim all day!

''No need to ask if you can swim,'' Luis said, coming up beside her.

Rachel trod water and shook her hair, water drops flying. ''I've been swimming since I was little. But not often at the beach. This is terrific.''

''The best part of spending my summers in Spain was the beach.''

''Was it hard, splitting your life like that—going first to one parent and then another?''

''Not an ideal childhood. But there were some advantages. If my parents had not separated, I would have spent all my time here and missed out on all I know of America. You spend all of yours in one place, I take it?''

She didn't want to talk about her situation, yet he'd been open with her.

''I lived with my father.''

''What happened to your mother?''

She turned and headed back toward land. ''If you really want to hear the full story, let's go back.''

Dried and enjoying the comfort of the chaise lounge chairs Marcos had brought, Rachel hated to bring up the subject. But she had wondered before if Luis might have some suggestions for searching for her mother. Now was as good a time as any to find out.

''When I was little and asked about my mother, my father always told me she had died. After a while I stopped asking. Then when I was thirteen or so, I asked a lot more questions. Why didn't we have any photos of her? How had she died? Where was she from? You know, the usual things someone would normally learn growing up—almost by osmosis, I guess. I know so little.''

''Did your father answer the questions?''

''Not really. He just said it was so far in the past what did it matter?''

''How did you learn she did not die?''

''Serendipity, I think. Marcella, who is our housekeeper, and I were clearing out some of the stuff in a storage room. There were several boxes of old papers of my father's. We looked through them to see what they were, so we could ask him later if we could toss. In one was a folder concerning my parents' divorce. She didn't die, he divorced her and apparently sent her away.''

"Why did he say she died?"

"To cut me off from her, I guess. I asked him."

"Ah, confrontation."

"It wasn't easy, but I was so upset I demanded he tell me about her." Rachel remembered the scene. Her father so impervious to her rampant curiosity. Unaware of the blow he'd delivered. So cold!

"And?"

"And I still don't know much more than I did when I found the divorce decree. But I do know now that my father lied to me for more than twenty years. And robbed me of the chance to know my mother."

Luis was silent for a moment. "So you ran away?"

She glared at him. "No, I did not run away. I left. Different thing."

He frowned. "I'm not sure I see the difference."

"I left to regroup. To decide what I want to do. I'm not going to live meekly beneath my father's thumb for the rest of my life."

"And your mother? Have you tried to contact her? Maybe find out why she didn't contact you in over twenty years?"

Rachel took a deep breath. "That's the one fact I can't get by. Why didn't she contact me at some point? If not when I was little, then when I was a teenager? Or when I turned twenty-one." She sighed softly and looked at him. "Or did she just not care enough?"

"That is something you should ask her."

"I don't know where she is. She could have died in the meantime for all I know."

"Not likely. She'd be what, in her forties now?"

"I guess."

"Your father gave no explanation?"

"No. He simply said it was his business, not mine. And so long ago what did it matter? I couldn't get anything out of him." Not even a reaction when she said she was leaving. Did he not care for her, either? Had he been stuck with raising her for some reason and was just as happy to have her off his hands one way or the other?

He certainly had been pushing for her engagement to Paul. Marriage would ensure she was taken care of and he'd be totally free for the first time in more than twenty-seven years.

Rachel's mood took a nosedive. Thinking about her life wasn't really awe-inspiring at the moment. But she wasn't going to wallow in self-pity.

"So what are you going to do?"

She raised her chin. "I'm going to find my mother and ask her what happened," she said firmly. "Can you help?"

"Me?" Luis looked surprised. "What can I do?"

"Give me some pointers. I'm sure you know how to find a person who wants to hide. Didn't one of your characters search out someone in book two or three? You must have had to research how to do that."

"Do you think your mother wanted to hide?"

"No. So it should be even easier to find her, don't you think? I've done an Internet search, but came up with nothing."

"She's probably remarried and has a new last name," he said.

She nodded. And a new family which she probably adored. How would she feel to have her long-gone daughter show up out of the blue?

"I did think about hiring a private detective, but

thought I should find out all I could by myself first,''
she said. ''Will you really help?''

''I think it could be arranged.''

''For a price.''

''What?''

''Isn't that how the phrase goes—it can be arranged
for a price.''

''Cynical?''

''Realistic. What's your price?''

Luis felt a surge of triumph. She was asking what he
wanted in exchange for helping her research her
mother's location. Should he tell her a night in his bed?

Rachel was a curious mixture of sophistication and
innocence. Her confusion when he'd suggested they
have an affair was endearing. She was not hardened as
Rosalie was. Nor did he any longer believe she was here
on some surreptitious newspaper assignment.

She wasn't immune to his touch, or kisses. She'd been
responsive as anyone he'd ever held. Which only whet-
ted his appetite for even more.

But finesse would win the day.

''Continue as we've been doing,'' he said. ''When I
have a social engagement, you can be my very dear
friend from America.''

She frowned. He was surprised to find he waited impatiently for her response. He wanted an affirmative.

''Just that, pretend to be friends?''

''What else?'' He shrugged.

''What about…'' She hesitated a moment and Luis
knew what she was thinking about. But he was not making this easy.

"I thought you wanted something more," she said in a rush.

"Ah, our affair?"

She nodded slowly, warily watching him. Did she think he would pounce on her at a beach full of families? The idea irritated him. Didn't she know him better than that? Surely she had some instincts that came into play, even if he hadn't told her his life's story.

"After fiesta, I suspect the entire village thinks we are having an affair, so it changes nothing. We pretend, or we don't. End result is the same." Not quite. He wanted her in his bed, not hers. Vast difference.

"Groupie buster."

"What?"

"You said you wanted me to pretend to be involved to keep groupies away. Groupie buster."

"So Miss Groupie Buster, we still have a deal?"

"We do."

He extended his hand, not to seal the deal so much as to touch her again. Her skin had been like the softest silk when he'd spread the lotion on her back. Her hands had wreaked havoc with his control when she spread the sunscreen on his back. And when he'd turned and she had touched his chest, it was all he'd been able to do to keep from sweeping her into an embrace that would have shocked the families frolicking nearby.

Her handshake was firm. He didn't release her when she thought he should, but tugged gently. She came forward easily, until he could lower his head slightly and brush her lips with his.

It wasn't enough, but would do for now.

Luis settled back, released her hand and tried to look

as at ease as he could. "Tell me how you came to be in Spain."

As she spoke he closed his eyes, enjoying listening to her. What had her father been thinking not to tell her the truth long ago? It might not have mattered as much to a young child, but he heard the undertones of hurt in her voice. Discovering the situation at this age had to be shattering.

He'd been sincere when he said he'd try to help. And an affair wasn't the price. He was determined to get her into his bed, but not as payment for his help. He wanted her as involved as he.

As the day progressed, Luis found himself enjoying every aspect. The picnic lunch Esperenza had prepared was delicious. The wine fruity and refreshing. Rachel had been bemused by the spread, declaring the picnics she usually went on weren't so elaborate.

He'd felt a twinge of jealousy when she talked of other picnics, wondering who had shared them with her. Not that it mattered. But for some reason, he wanted today's picnic to remain in her mind for a long time.

Having relieved herself of the burden of her past, Rachel seemed to throw herself wholeheartedly into the day. They swam, lay in the sun for a short time, returning to the shade of the umbrella. Talk was desultory. He learned more about her and knew he was sharing a portion of himself beyond what he normally did with relative strangers.

But while he talked of the past, he never mentioned Bonita, and neither did Rachel.

Marcos returned at four to pick them up. When they reached the *castillo*, Esperenza met them at the door.

"Sophia and Julian will be coming to dinner," she said.

"She invited herself?" he asked, annoyed. "Because I wouldn't commit to going to her place."

"This is still her family home, isn't it?" Esperenza said with a sniff.

"Indeed. I hope it won't inconvenience you to prepare extra for our guests." His sister obviously couldn't wait until he responded to her numerous invitations to dinner. Sophia never had any patience.

When the housekeeper left, Luis stopped Rachel before she reached the stairs.

"We continue what we started at fiesta,"

"For your sister?"

"She is friends with Rosalie."

"But she's your sister. Surely she would side with you."

"If she thinks her actions are for my best interest, she will do whatever she wants." Luis looked forward to playing the enamored suitor for his sister. Let her attend to her own problems and leave him to deal with his as he saw fit.

Rachel wasn't sure she had anything suitable for dinner with Luis's sister and brother-in-law. She showered and then donned a pale pink top matched with one of the skirts she'd brought. Not fancy by any means, but a step up from shorts. She liked the color she'd gotten at the beach, a slight glow always enhanced anyone's looks.

Satisfied she looked the best she was going to given what she had to wear, she descended to the main floor.

Hearing voices, she headed for the formal room near the front door. Sophia and Julian were talking with Luis.

She paused a moment in the doorway before they saw her.

Luis had chosen cream pants and a white blouse, opened at the throat. She was surprised to see him in anything other than the black he favored. He looked like casual elegance personified. She wished for a moment it would be just the two of them for dinner. They could continue the pleasant time they'd had at the beach. And who knew, he might kiss her again.

"Ah, Rachel," he said, spotting her at the door.

"Hello Sophia, Julian." She greeted the guests and took the small aperitif Luis handed her. Taking a sip she was pleased with the tangy taste.

He led her to the sofa and sat beside her. Too close, she thought, feeling his thigh press against hers. For a moment she lost the thread of the conversation, conscious of the awareness that exploded at his touch.

"I'm sorry, what did you ask?" she said, looking at Sophia, doing her best to ignore Luis. He made it even more difficult by laying his arm across the back of the sofa and toying with her hair.

"How long have you known Luis? Where did you meet? I'm so curious. Mama is, too."

Rachel felt Luis start beside her.

"You've talked to Mother about Rachel?" he asked.

"Of course. She's thrilled you are moving on. It's been three years, Luis. We all loved Bonita, but she's gone. She would not have wanted you to mourn her forever."

"She would not have wanted him to mourn her at all. She didn't expect to die so young," Julian murmured.

"Rachel is a guest in my home. Let's not talk of the past."

"So how did you two meet?" Sophia asked again.

Rachel looked at Luis. He was the storyteller in the group, let him answer the question.

His eyes grew amused. Had he read her mind?

"Rachel is an avid fan of my novels. She approached me."

"When you were in America?" Sophia frowned. "You haven't been to the States in three years."

"Ever hear of mail, sister dear?"

"I thought you didn't answer fan mail."

"Where did you get that idea?"

Sophia shrugged, studying the couple on the sofa. "So you invited her here to visit and she came."

"I was in Spain and thought I'd, um, drop by," Rachel said. "Meeting him in person was all I could have hoped for," she said, smiling sweetly at Luis.

He nipped her on her neck, beneath her hair.

"As for me, once I saw her, I knew I wanted her."

Rachel's gaze locked with his. He had told her the same thing, but in private. Now he was proclaiming his desire to the world. Her heart fluttered. No one had ever claimed such a thing before. She looked away, meeting Sophia's knowing eyes.

"Here's to getting to know you better," she said, raising her glass slightly.

Rachel nodded, feeling a total fraud. Sophia was a nice woman, she didn't deserve to be deceived by her brother. How was what they were doing any different from what her father had done all her life?

It wasn't quite the same thing, but deceit was deceit. Rachel looked at Sophia.

"It's not quite that way."

Luis put his glass down and reached for Rachel's

hand, standing and pulling her up beside him. "Let's go to the patio, Esperanza has set the table there for dinner."

Sophia and Julian rose and led the way.

Luis held Rachel back until they were along.

"What were you about to say?"

"We should tell them the truth. I told you about my father, how he lied to me all my life. I don't want to be doing that to your sister. She deserves the truth."

"This is not the same thing as with your father. We are only leading her to believe something that cannot hurt her in any way."

"It's not right."

"Only if it is totally false. We can make sure we don't lead her astray."

"By having an affair?"

He smiled. Rachel didn't trust him, but that smile almost melted her bones.

Luis leaned over to kiss her and she was lost. Maybe a small white lie wouldn't hurt Sophia. And if Luis had his way, they would have a full-blown affair to make everything aboveboard.

"Hurry up, you two, I'm hungry." Sophia's voice sounded amused more than impatient.

When Luis and Rachel joined the other couple on the patio, Rachel knew her face was pink with embarrassment.

Despite the rocky start, the evening turned out to be more fun than Rachel expected. Once Sophia stopped questioning her about Luis, the conversation turned to Luis's secondary career as a writer, then to Sophia's adoration of her baby son, Mario. Julian did not speak much, nor did Rachel.

They enjoyed the meal Esperenza prepared, had coffee with dessert and moved to more comfortable chairs placed on the terrace overlooking the village, which seemed to spread like a sparkling colorful tapestry before them. In the distance a faint glow lit the sky from the lights of Benidorm. The soft night air was redolent with the sweet fragrances of the nearby blossoms.

It was as idyllic a setting as Rachel had ever experienced. For a moment she wished their charade could be true. That she and Luis were falling in love. That it was possible that one day she'd actually live in a castle in Spain.

But reality crashed down. She was not here to fall in love with her temporary employer. In fact, if he would help as he'd suggested at the beach, she might be on her way home before long. Knowing where to find her mother. But still wondering what to do about her father.

Not until she finished transcribing the manuscript, though. She wanted to find out how he wrapped everything up and exposed the killer at the end. She would never again get the chance to type Luis's books and see how he developed the storyline, weaving in clues and red herrings.

One thing at a time. First she had to get through the evening.

Rachel truly felt like one half of a couple by the time Sophia and Julian left. Luis had held her hand while they all conversed easily. He'd been attentive in many ways, making her feel cherished and desired. His touch, a look, a comment made it sound as if they were already intimate friends. The whole thing had her on edge all evening.

Watching Sophia and Julian, Rachel wished she'd

found her perfect match. She would love to have the easy, loving relationship they seemed to enjoy. Wistfully she wondered if she'd ever find love.

Shutting the door firmly behind his sister and brother-in-law some time later, Luis turned to Rachel. "Thank you for this evening. It went a long way to convincing Sophia I do not need the services of a matchmaker."

She smiled. "I can't see you needing one even if we didn't pretend that we were more involved than we are."

"Ah, but maybe we are only anticipating things."

"Or not." She stepped away, afraid to become overwhelmed with her own needs to stay close to him. "Good night, Luis." Almost running for her room, Rachel wanted to gain some time alone to regroup. It seemed to become a pattern for her. When overwhelmed, run away. Wasn't that what Luis had suggested, that she was running away?

No more. In the morning, she'd face him. And try to come up with a final answer. She ought to say no. She was already attracted to him. Could easily imagine his ardent words were true, and if she fell in love, where would she be. In a pickle for sure.

Best to say no.

Are you sure? A voice in her mind whispered. She knew the situation going into it. She could guard her heart. And think of the fabulous times she'd have with such a romantic figure of a man. She sighed, once again unsure what she wanted to do. For someone who had always thought herself focused and confident, she was doing a lot of vacillating. Just say yes or no.

The next morning when Rachel went down to the kitchen, Esperenza was not there. A cold breakfast had been left on a tray. A small note told her Esperenza had gone to church, and Luis was out in the olive grove.

Taking the tray, Rachel walked to the stone wall. The panorama was as awesome as always and she sat on the top, balancing her tray beside her. In the distance, she saw two men on horseback, riding up and down the rows of olive trees. She recognized one as Luis and settled back to watch him. Once again he wore black.

He and the dark horse seemed as one. The man with him might be Pablo whom she'd met at fiesta. She wasn't sure. Not wasting time on trying to figure it out, she let herself feast on Luis. She could almost see the play of muscles beneath his loose shirt. Imagine the heat in the sun wearing dark colors. What were they looking for as they rode up and down the endless rows of trees?

A man of many talents and accomplishments. Why would such a man pretend an interest in a stranger like her?

The only answer would be because she was safe, of course. Once she finished the book, or Maria returned, she'd be gone. No long-term commitment. No strings. No need to forget Bonita. An affair would imply to the world he had moved on. And if it didn't work out, there would be others. The well-meant urging of friends would end. He could live life on his own terms, as he was used to doing.

It was Sunday, a day of rest, but Rachel was restless. She wanted to do something beside think, so when she finished eating, and Luis had moved beyond where she could easily watch him, she headed for the study. She'd work on the book to while away the time. Her days were limited and the writing was so compelling she was anxious to find out what happened next.

CHAPTER SEVEN

LUIS RETURNED TO THE HOME sometime later, moving from room to room until he found Rachel in the study, diligently typing. He almost swept into the room and picked her up to carry her upstairs. He didn't remember feeling this sudden spurt of desire with anyone else. Not even his sultry and tempting wife. There was something about Rachel that called to him on a primordial level. She had to feel it. He couldn't be in this alone.

"Have you eaten?" he asked from the doorway. He needed to shower, change. But he needed to see her even more.

She looked up in surprise, a smile breaking out. His heart caught with the sight. She was beautiful.

"Not since earlier. What were you doing in the olive grove?"

"Checking on things. There's a *restaurante* on the edge of town which makes fantastic lamb. Join me?"

"I'd love to. Do I need to change?" She rose and indicated her shorts.

He looked at her legs, then away before he did something foolish. They were lightly tanned, and shapely. He had touched her intimately yesterday, spreading on the sunscreen and when they brushed in the water yesterday. Remembering did nothing for his equilibrium.

"You might wish to wear a skirt. I'd like to leave soon to get there ahead of the after-church crowd. I won't take long to shower."

"I'll be ready," she promised.

He took the stairs two at a time, wishing he'd invited her to join him in the shower—if only to see the shock that he was certain would be her reaction. Rachel seemed too innocent for words sometimes. Was it a ploy? Or was she genuine?

Antonio's was crowded, though there were still two or three tables vacant when they arrived. It was one of Luis's favorite places. Bonita hadn't liked it particularly. Did that influence his feelings?

Touching Rachel lightly on the back, he guided her toward a table near the edge of the shaded area. The arbor was draped in thick grape vines, their wide leaves sheltering the small green fruit. When the grapes were ripe, customers could reach up and pull down a cluster to enjoy with their meal.

The boisterous camaraderie among the people already enjoying lunch was familiar. He knew most of the people if only by sight. Nodding in greeting, he didn't stop to talk. He was here to be with Rachel, not to mingle.

Soon after they sat at the table, a waiter came over to place their wine down and arrange utensils. He smiled and walked away.

"No menu?" Rachel asked.

"Sunday is lamb."

"That's all?"

"Do you not like it?"

"I do, it's just odd that a *restaurante* this large only serves one dish."

"On Tuesdays, it's fish. Wednesdays is paella."

She laughed. "So you know which day serves what and come accordingly?"

He nodded, watching her as she looked around, taking in everything. No playacting, he'd swear it. She was enchanted with Antonio's.

She looked at him and tilted her head slightly. "So, tell me what you were doing riding all over hill and dale. Checking the olives for what?"

"It is almost time to harvest. Pablo and I were combining a morning ride with checking on the readiness."

"They're still green."

"We don't harvest for table olives, but the oil."

"You explained that before, but I guess I still thought they had to be black and ripe to make oil. After harvest, do you have another fiesta?"

He shook his head. "No. Our fiestas are usually devoted to saints. In years past we had a celebration after the harvest, but not recently."

"Since Bonita's death?" Rachel asked.

He inclined his head once.

Rachel thought it was a shame the people who worked at harvest were denied their celebration because of Luis's wife's death. Maybe one day he would reinstate the tradition.

But she wasn't here to think about his dead wife. He'd invited her to lunch, and she wanted to enjoy every moment. The patio dining was delightful. She loved the grapes growing right above her head, and the view of the sylvan countryside. Spain met every expectation, and then some.

She commented on the setting and soon they were discussing the different regions of Spain—the ones she'd seen and the ones yet to explore. It was heady to have a man focus his intensity on her. She knew she was flirting, but she couldn't help herself. When had she ever had anyone interested in her for herself, not for her father's wealth?

In this case, she knew Luis only wanted a short-term affair. It didn't matter. To have his undivided attention was amazing.

And thrilling.

And sexy.

If he asked her right this moment, she'd say yes.

Lunch was delicious. The lamb so tender she could easily cut it with a fork. The vegetables had been steamed to perfection. The flan afterward melted in her mouth. Feeling replete and a bit sleepy from the fruity wine they'd shared, Rachel wanted nothing more than to relax the rest of her life with Luis.

"Ready to leave?" he asked.

"I hate to go. This has been such a lovely time," she replied with a smile. "Thank you."

"It was my pleasure."

Rachel believed him. He wasn't just saying the words, he'd enjoyed the lunch as much as she had.

Settling back in the convertible a short time later, she was glad he'd driven and not had Marcos chauffeur them. This way she had Luis all to herself. Fantasies began to play in her mind. What if instead of an affair, he asked her to stay? Could she compete with the dead Bonita? Would he tire of her quickly and move on to another?

Not if his devotion to his wife continued. Would anyone ever replace her in his heart?

"Shall we get started on searching for your mother?" he asked when they reached the house.

Rachel felt disappointed. She wasn't sure what she expected after lunch, but searching for her mother wasn't it. She didn't know what she would do with the information if she did locate her. Show up one day and knock on the door? Write? Call?

"That would be fine," she said. At least she'd still spend the rest of the afternoon with Luis.

In only a short time he had the computer hooked up and dialed the access line to get them onto the World Wide Web. Rising, he indicated the chair.

"You need to do this, so you'll remember how."

For the next several minutes, they listed everything Rachel knew about her mother. Then Luis gave her some Web site to try. Nothing turned up.

"Try this one," he said, leaning over and reaching around her to type the address in.

His cheek was scant inches from hers. If she turned her face she could touch him with her lips. Heat enveloped her as she tried to garner enough courage to do just that. One kiss, what could it hurt?

He turned slightly to look at her. "You are not paying attention."

His breath fanned across her cheeks. His dark eyes were all she could see. Almost without volition, she leaned forward and kissed him.

She felt his surprise give way immediately to desire. His mouth moved against hers, opening her lips and teasing her. She replied, feeling on fire. It was the most erotic kiss she'd ever had and only their mouths touched. Their tongues danced, brushed, moved against one another. Yearnings and desire built as the kiss continued.

When he pulled back and gazed into her eyes, she knew he'd see what she was feeling.

"Rachel?"

"Yes," she said.

"Yes?"

She nodded, afraid to break the spell. It might be a reckless move, but it was for her alone to decide. And for once she wanted to feel the passion a man would bring to someone he truly wanted. To experience all the joy of love. To know she was wanted for herself alone.

He cupped her neck gently, tilting her head for another kiss before he stepped back and offered his hand. She rose, placed her hand in his and they walked toward the stairs.

Her heart pounded like a jackhammer, yet she wasn't sure she felt the floor beneath her. She looked at him, dark and dangerous as ever, but so dear to her heart.

No, no, no, she silently admonished herself. *Don't go falling for this man. He would crush your hopes in an instant. This in only for the present.*

But a small part of her acknowledged the futility of her denial. She was already halfway in love with Luis Alvares and going to bed with him was probably the worst thing she could do. And the best thing.

He pushed open the door and led her into the large bedroom. Stopping to kiss her again, he slowly pushed the door closed behind her.

Rachel couldn't help being nervous. She'd never done anything like this before. Would he expect more than she could manage? Or was passion and love something that came naturally? She felt as if she'd known him for a long time at some points. Yet he remained an enigma. Someone she could spend the rest of her life getting to know and understand. Sadly that was not going to happen.

He tangled his fingers in her hair and tilted her head back, sipping at her mouth, trailing kisses down her cheeks, along her jaw. When he moved down her throat, Rachel wondered if her knees would continue to hold her. She gripped his wrists, feeling the pounding of his own blood. It sent her heart rate skyrocketing.

Softly she moaned in delighted pleasure. His mouth returned to hers and she gave herself up to the kiss.

The sunshine streamed in through the tall windows, blazing a path of light across the wide bed. The ornately carved headboard reflected the heavy Spanish style. The dark coverlet emphasized the masculine decor of the room.

Luis moved them closer to the bed, never breaking the kiss. When his hand slipped beneath the cotton top she wore and touched her heated skin, Rachel caught her breath. His fingers touched her like she was precious, skimming lightly against her.

She opened her eyes and leaned back a bit, wishing to savor these new sensations. Her eyes half closed as she let her gaze drift—to come to rest on a large portrait of Bonita Alvares sitting on the dresser, angled to be seen from the bed.

It was as if someone had doused her with cold water. She pulled away.

"I can't do this," she said, resettling her top, taking another step. She couldn't stop staring at the picture of Luis's wife. He could see it first thing every morning, last thing every night. This was their room. The room the two of them had shared throughout their marriage. Oh, she was going to be sick.

"What?" Luis looked at her, noticed she was staring and looked behind him. Quickly he moved to the dresser and slammed the photo facedown. "It's not what you think."

"What I think is this is your room, yours and Bonita's. I don't want to be here." She moved to the door, but he was quicker. His hand held it shut.

"Let me out," she said, refusing to look at him. She'd almost made a total idiot of herself. All for a man who still loved his dead wife. How totally *stupid* her fantasies had been.

"Not until you hear me out."

"I don't care to hear anything you have to say."

"I keep her picture there to remind me."

"Oh, well, duh. Why else would someone keep a photo of a loved one?"

"Not for love."

That caught her attention. She risked a quick glance in his direction. He was closer than she'd realized. His gaze was steady. With a sigh, he moved away from the door, rubbing the back of his neck with the hand that had held the door shut.

She turned and leaned against the wooden panels. "What do you mean, not for love? Not for love of who—Bonita? Everyone says you two had the most perfect marriage. The tragedy of her death was more than you could deal with."

"Yeah, well, everyone is wrong. The tragedy is a bloody farce. She was on her way to her lover that night."

Rachel opened her mouth, then promptly shut it. She was dumbfounded. Bonita of the famous loving couple was on her way to a *lover?*

"Unbelievable," she said slowly. "Who could top you?"

He spun around, his expression sardonic. "Is that a compliment? You find it unbelievable she could want someone else?"

"Yes, I do," she said. "Are you saying your beloved wife cheated on you?"

"The proof was in her womb."

Rachel stared at him. "The baby wasn't yours?" she whispered. "Everyone thought— The newspapers said—" She couldn't formulate a coherent thought.

"Yeah, everyone thought the baby was mine. It wasn't and it would have been clearly obvious to anyone who had taken time to find out how far along she was. I'd been in America for three months. Two weeks after I returned home she was dead. Less than six weeks pregnant, I might add."

"That's what you fought about."

He nodded. "I was throwing her out. Divorce isn't something easily obtained in Spain, but separation is. My own parents were separated from shortly after my sister was born until my father died eight years ago. I might have had to stay married to Bonita, but I wasn't going to live with her anymore."

"Everyone thought you two were so happy." Rachel was stunned with the revelation.

"No one knows what goes on in the privacy of people's homes. As long as we jetted here and there, partied long into the night, bought her jewels and fabulous designer clothes, Bonita was happy. Which made our union easier to take. But I was growing tired of all the vapidity we dealt with. I wanted to start a family, settle down. I have enough of a burden running the olive business, and trying to write. I didn't need the rest."

"But she did?"

He shrugged. "So she said."

Rachel couldn't imagine wanting to go elsewhere to meet with strangers and drink away the night when she could stay with Luis—on the patio, or at the gazebo, or their special place on the stone wall.

What a joke, their special place. She was getting in over her head.

"Why didn't you tell anyone?"

"To what end? Her parents live nearby, why hurt them? She was dead, it was enough."

For an instant she remembered the tabloid article suggesting Luis had something to do with his wife's death. If the writer had known the full truth, he would have had a field day with his theory. For that, she was glad Luis had kept quiet.

"I don't understand, why shut yourself away from everyone? Your sister thinks you are still in mourning, Esperenza does. Everyone does, I guess."

"I didn't shut myself away. I continue to run the business, write. What I no longer do is go to parties or fiestas."

"What would it hurt?"

"I don't know her lover's name."

She frowned. "What does that have to do with it?"

"It was someone from the village. That I do know. But who? I have ideas, but nothing concrete. Do you think the man would come and tell me? So when I go there, I look and I wonder—are you the one? Is it a friend who betrayed me? Or an enemy? Or a stranger?"

"Does it matter now, Luis? It's been three years. I know it must have been a horrible shock. But Bonita is dead. The man has to live with the guilt. You have nothing to hide from."

"I'm not hiding. I have no reason to go to those kinds of events. Don't forget, my sister is always hoping to fix me up with another woman. As if I'd ever trust anyone again."

"Wait a minute. Just because Bonita cheated on you, doesn't mean the next woman you get involved with would ever do such a thing."

"Since you are the next woman I'm becoming involved with, does that mean you?" The skepticism in his gaze was more than Rachel could stand.

"Yes, dammit, it does. If we have some kind of affair, I'd never look at another man."

"I'm not talking about an affair. They are quickly over. But what if it were marriage? How long could you or any woman stay loyal? A year, two? My mother lasted seven. Bonita three."

His mother had left his father. His wife had left him—in a sense. His experience hadn't been all that positive, but that was not the way of every woman in the world. It didn't look as if she was going to convince Luis of that any time soon.

Her bright dreams shattered as she realized he would never look beyond a brief affair with her or any other woman. She'd never admitted to the hope that something wonderful would come of being with him, but it had been there.

She looked around the room, memorizing every piece of furniture, every painting on the wall, the change on the dresser. Even the picture he kept nearby to remind him of his wife's betrayal. This was Luis's bedroom, his most intimate place.

It was probably the only time she'd ever see it.

Rachel fumbled for the doorknob and when found, she turned it. Pulling the door open, she turned and left.

"Rachel."

She had to ignore his call. There was nothing for her with a man who would never trust.

CHAPTER EIGHT

RACHEL FLED TO HER ROOM and closed the door. She wished there was a lock. Surely Luis wouldn't follow her.

Lunch would have to be enough to tide her over until morning. She didn't want to run any risk of seeing Luis again until she had better control over her emotions.

His cynicism dashed any hopes she had of a continuing relationship with him.

His desire for an affair was merely sexual in nature. He didn't want to get to know the real her. He didn't look for anything beyond the next couple of weeks until Maria returned. Any seductive talk had been made with one goal in mind—get her into his bed. And she'd almost gone.

She paced. Anger and unhappiness warring for top spot in her emotions. What she should do is pack her bags and head out. She could find—

What, another job? There were still only 470 Euros in her bag. Less since she'd bought Internet time and breakfast at the café in Benidorm.

Still, it would be better than living in the same house with Luis.

She remembered every kiss, every caress. Closing her eyes against the longing that burned deep inside, she tried to will the images away. But they wouldn't budge. She could almost see them entwined, feel his mouth on her skin, the skim of his fingertips over her most sensitive places.

"Argh!" She stormed over to the windows and opened them. What she should do and what she was going to do were two different things. She'd done nothing wrong. If he wanted to tie himself up in warped thinking that all women were cheats, that was his misfortune. Once she finished typing the book, she'd get paid and leave.

In the meantime, she'd use the resources he'd suggested to see if she could get a line on her mother. Maybe Caroline could help from her end. Her parents knew some of the same people Rachel's father knew. Maybe Caroline could find out what had happened.

But she'd have to wait until tomorrow to contact her friend. She had no intention of leaving her room today!

Early the next morning, Rachel heard Marcos bring the car to the front. She slipped out of bed. It was pointless to remain, she had been awake since dawn. Standing to one side, hoping no one could see her, she watched. Just like a high school girl longing for a glimpse of some boy she had a crush on, Rachel waited to see Luis.

He emerged from the house dressed in a black suit, silver-grey shirt and dark tie. His briefcase was in his left hand. She'd always think of black as his trademark color.

He spoke to Marcos and climbed into the back of the car without once looking anywhere else.

Business as usual for the man, she thought sadly. His wife betrayed him. Maybe even a friend betrayed him. But instead of letting others know it, he went on alone.

Was he always alone? Couldn't he even confide in Sophia?

Rachel watched the car as it turned and headed down the long road to the village. Sadness swept through at the thought of Luis spending all his days merely going to work and then escaping in the world of fiction. He should have a family, learn to laugh, to love.

But she wasn't the one to accomplish that miracle. She had her own problems to deal with and falling in love with some cynical Spaniard wasn't in the cards.

She gripped the drapery. No, she had not fallen in love with the man. She was merely concerned, as any good employee would be, when her boss was upset.

Liar, a voice inside chided.

She turned away from the window and went to get dressed. She'd apply herself to the typing and check the Internet sites they'd found. She would not dwell on anything foolish like imagining herself in love with Luis!

Instead of transcribing the book, however, Rachel became caught up in the search for her mother. She tried the addresses Luis had suggested, getting new ideas and leads from some of them. But nothing pointed her to Loretta Goodson. She wished her father would have just talked to her!

She was in the midst of a long note to Caroline, outlining what she wanted her to do and who she thought the best sources of information might be when Sophia breezed into the study.

"*Hola,* Rachel. I have come to have lunch with you. I understand Luis is off to work. What kind of hospitality is that when you are visiting?"

Rachel looked up in surprise. "Hi, Sophia. I, uh, Luis has work to do. I can entertain myself."

Sophia took in the stack of manuscript pages and looked at Rachel. "You're typing his book?" Her tone suggested Rachel had lost her senses.

"Not right now, I'm sending a message to a friend at home." She looked at the pages, remembering the role she was supposed to be playing. "I've been typing some of it here and there to while away the time when he has to work."

"He's so consumed with business, he believes everyone else should be as well. Come, we'll eat and then go lie on the beach. It's not often I get an afternoon away from the baby. I want to indulge myself."

"Let me finish this and I'd love to indulge myself as well!"

"Who is your friend?" Sophia made no bones about looking over Rachel's shoulder at the message.

"Caroline. She and I have been friends forever." Her fingers flew on the keyboard and then she pressed the send key. Since typing the manuscript her speed had increased tremendously. Would she be able to find a job as a real secretary when she returned to the States?

"Let's find Esperenza and have her prepare us one of her delicious salads and then we'll go soak up the sun," Sophia said. "I haven't had a day at the beach in a long time."

From the deep tan that Sophia sported, Rachel was sure Sophia had more time to indulge herself than maybe she realized. Still, an afternoon away from the castle would be a good thing. At least she wouldn't be thinking about Luis, or her mother.

They took Sophia's car to the beach. Rachel missed Marcos's attentiveness to detail. They had to carry their own things, and the umbrella. No lounge chairs today. No cooler with drinks, only two they had in the totes. Back to normal, she thought wryly.

Once settled near the water, Sophia donned her sunglasses, lay back partially in shade from the umbrella and said, "So tell me how you came to fall in love with my brother."

Rachel carefully put on her own sunglasses. "We're just friends," she said, hoping any color that had stolen into her cheeks would be put down to the sun.

"Come on, I'm family. I've seen the way you look at Luis. It's amazing to me he'd fall in love again. Bonita wasn't the easiest woman in the world to live with."

"Oh?"

"She ran Luis ragged. She was so demanding, wanting this and that. Always on the go. I think Luis actually prefers a quiet life. You fit perfectly. He's lucky he found you."

Rachel stared at the sea. Was that Sophia's way of saying she was quiet and dull?

"Of course, you will have to stand up to him from time to time." Sophia lowered her glasses and looked at Rachel. "You can do that, right?"

"Oh, yes, I've had my fill of overbearing men dictating what I should do in life."

"Ah, so, tell me all about yourself. Censor nothing!"

Rachel laughed and lay back on her towel, relishing the warmth of the sun, the fresh salt scent from the sea. She'd missed Caroline. No one to confide in over the last few weeks. Not that Sophia would replace Caroline, but girl talk would be a welcomed change!

"I first ran away from home when I was twenty-seven," Rachel began.

Sophia sat up and looked at her. "Are you another storyteller like Luis?"

"No, just giving you my autobiography."

"How old are you?"

"Twenty-seven."

"Ah." Sophia lay back down, a grin on her face.

"Do tell all."

Rachel told of discovering her mother was still alive, of her mixed feelings about finding her, and her burning anger at her father for lying to her most of her life. She was careful to mention nothing about Luis. Sophia put her own spin on it.

"So, you needed a bolt hole and immediately thought about Luis. Wow. And now that you are here, you two are more caught up in each other than worrying about your quest to find your mother."

"Um, right." If Sophia wanted to view everything through romantic glasses, Rachel would let her. She'd know the truth soon enough. And while Rachel felt badly deceiving her, she wouldn't betray Luis for anything. Even in such a small way. It was time he knew he could depend on some people!

Sophia discussed locating missing people, offering suggestions and adding her opinion that Caroline was in a prime position to assist. "Maybe I should fly over to America and see what I can find out."

"I think we'll manage. I'm curious, however, both you and Luis seemed to have spent much longer in the U.S. than here in Spain, yet you both settled here as adults."

"Umm. Luis was older when our parents separated. He was eight or nine. I was just a toddler, so I don't remember much about living at the *castillo* when I was a child—except for summer vacations. Our father was insistent upon that. And we even had tutors if you can believe it, to make sure we didn't forget Spanish. Of course, he also insisted Luis learn the olive business. I think the separation hit him harder than it did me, because he was leaving the home he'd known all his life, and our Papa. We loved our father. I've never understood quite why our mother couldn't have stayed in love with him. But she seems satisfied now with her new husband. They live in France.''

"Do you see her from time to time?"

"Oh, yes, she comes to visit two or three times a year and Julian and I have been up there several times. Luis went once.''

Sophia fell silent. "He changed a lot after Bonita's death. Not entirely because of grief, I think.''

Probably came from being betrayed by the one person he should have been able to count on above all others, Rachel thought. She and Luis were in the same boat. That should have drawn them closer. Only, after yesterday, there was an impenetrable wall between them.

"Anyway, I came one summer for my visit, fell in love with Julian and so here I live. Luis, of course, once he finished college, was called back to assume his role in the family business.''

"Did he wish to do other things?"

"Write, I suppose. His books are wildly popular in the States.''

"I know," Rachel said.

"Of course, that's how you two met, you said.''

"Tell me a favorite memory of Luis. A time when he laughed, before he became so cynical," Rachel said in a rush, hoping to avoid any inquisition into her meeting Luis.

"That doesn't bother you?" Sophia asked.

"What?"

"His cynicism. His hermit tendencies. His less than sterling opinions of women."

"That's the only way I've ever known him."

"When he was younger, he loved to tease me. I remember one time when I was about eight, I guess. He was still a teenager. He and Pablo—did you meet Pablo?—they dressed up as sea monsters. They worked on the costumes for a week, scales and fangs and all. I can still see them rising out of the water—and they scared us to death one day when I came to the beach with some friends. They laughed so hard I thought they might drown. He and Pablo were inseparable when we'd come to visit our father."

She was silent for a moment. "It's too bad we had to grow up. I do remember all the fun we had as children." She rolled on her side and propped her head on her hand. "I remember their wedding. I was an attendant. My mother didn't like Bonita, but my father thought she was the perfect foil for my brother. I wonder if he pushed because the marriage would anchored Luis to Spain. I think Papa was always afraid we'd settle in America and he'd not see us after we were grown."

Rachel kept quiet, though she longed to ask a hundred questions. What had Bonita really been like. Gorgeous, she knew from the newspaper photos. Fiery and temperamental. And dishonest.

"She wasn't very nice," Sophia said slowly.

"Who?" But Rachel knew she meant Bonita.

"Luis's wife." Sophia hesitated, then spoke, as if very

carefully choosing her words. "There were rumors in the village about her. I never told Luis. But I often wondered if he knew."

"You should have talked to him about it. He knew," Rachel said.

"What?" Sophia sat up. "Luis knew about the rumors? He never said a word. I thought he was truly grieving all this time."

Rachel nodded. "He wanted to protect her name after her death. Because of her parents."

"Wow. Oh, wow! This changes everything." She gazed at the sea, her thoughts obviously processing this new slant.

Turning to Rachel, she took off her glasses. "I meant she was seeing someone else on the side. Maybe more than one man."

Rachel sat up and nodded. "He knew, but only at the end. How long had it been going on? Do you know who it was?"

"As far as the rumors are concerned, they started almost as soon as the marriage. You know how a village likes to gossip."

Rachel didn't know firsthand, but she could imagine. "Someone should have clued him in earlier," she said.

"You think?"

"Wouldn't you rather know than remain in the dark? No matter how hard the truth is to deal with, it's better to know it." Hearing her words, she knew when she discovered her mother, she would go and meet her. No matter what, she wanted to know the truth.

Sophia returned to the *castillo* with Rachel to take a quick shower and then change in the room that had been hers as a child. She told Rachel she wanted to see her brother before heading for home.

"He may be late," Rachel said before going up to change herself. And, she hadn't a clue how he felt. Would he want to continue where they'd left off as if nothing had changed? Or would he put as much distance between them as possible? Should she finish working on the book, or leave?

She didn't want to leave.

"Not if you're here," Sophia said.

Rachel only wished it were true.

To her surprise, Luis was waiting for them in the salon when they had dressed. His dark suit seemed so formal after the weekend. It helped keep their distance. Catching her breath at his look, she felt as if he'd reached out and touched her.

Sophia accepted a small sherry. He handed one to Rachel, his fingers brushing against hers as she reached for the glass. Which almost caused her to drop it. Was she the only one to feel the tension rise in the room?

"Luis, why didn't you tell me about Bonita?" Sophia asked straight away.

He turned. "What about her?"

"That she was a cheat and a deceiver. That you knew she was seeing someone else, maybe more than one someone."

"And you know this how?" He looked at Rachel, his angry gaze promising retribution.

"Don't look at Rachel. It was common knowledge in the village. She wasn't exactly discreet. My money was on Carlos Valdiz, but she also seemed to flirt a lot with Pedro Martinez, and Jose Gonzales."

"You knew, yet you never told me?"

She hesitated. "I guess I thought maybe you knew and didn't care as long as she was not blatant about it. Or, if you didn't know, you would have been appalled to learn the truth."

"But you tell me now."

"I told Rachel, she said you already knew."

"The baby was not mine," he said.

"Oh, Luis!" Sophia reached out to hug her older brother tightly. "I'm so sorry," she whispered, tears in her eyes.

Rachel felt her own throat tighten. What she wouldn't give to have a sibling to share her own dilemma with. Someone who would be there for support, if nothing else.

She turned away and walked into the hallway. She was the outsider, let them have some privacy.

Esperenza set the table on the patio. She looked up when Rachel stepped out of the French doors. "Is Sophia staying for dinner?" she asked.

"I don't think so. She just wanted a word with her brother."

Esperenza nodded and returned to her task.

On impulse, Rachel asked her, "Do you know of any place in the village where I might stay?"

The older woman straightened and looked at her in puzzlement. "You are staying here."

"I know, but it's only temporary. When Maria returns, I won't be needed."

"My cousin's friend has rooms she rents out. It is on the street where the fountain is. If you wish, I will provide you the information."

"Thank you," Rachel said.

Luis stepped out onto the patio.

"Sophia will not be joining us for dinner."

"The meal is almost ready," Esperanza said as she headed for the house.

Rachel felt as nervous as could be. She took a deep breath, hoping to calm her nerves, but filled her lungs with Luis's unique scent. It set her heart to beating.

"I would think you would wish to discuss yesterday," he said softly, his eyes on her.

She shrugged. "What's there to discuss? Things...changed. I decided I didn't want the same thing you wanted."

"Nothing changed. Especially the feelings I have for you."

"Lust. Take a cold shower."

"Lust certainly. But more."

She rounded on him, hands on her hips. "Just how much more?"

"Do you want to hear about Bonita?"

"Not particularly. Actually I want to eat, and then go to bed."

"Funny, I have the same goal."

"Alone."

"Ah, we diverge there."

"Luis, stop flirting with me!" She felt surrounded by him, his tantalizing voice, his dark good looks, his intensity.

"And if I don't?"

She swallowed. Staring at him, she tried to read the enigmatic man before her. What game was he playing now?

"I still want you, Rachel." He stepped closer, combing his fingers through her hair. Holding her head gently as he tipped it up to his. "I still want you."

His mouth covered hers in a kiss that spiked her heart rate and sent a spiral of pure sensation through every cell in her body. Rachel found it impossible to keep a coherent thought in her mind. She was too focused on the feelings that swept through. And the one constant, *he still wanted her.*

He didn't push. He didn't force. He merely kissed her until every ounce of sense fled.

She pulled away, putting several feet between them. "It doesn't mean anything," she cried, clenching her hands into fists.

"What do you want it to mean?"

"More than just two people getting together. I...I'm starting to fall for you, Luis. Where would that leave us when Maria returns?"

"Don't confuse this with romance. We are two adults who are attracted to each other. If the exotic setting has you seeing things that aren't there, don't blame me."

"I don't. I think I've come to understand your views of relationships very clearly. Which is why I don't want to proceed any further with where this is heading."

He stepped forward. She retreated a step, watching him warily.

"Dammit, Rachel, I'm not going to pounce on you."

"You don't have to. Just being around you drives me crazy."

He stopped and looked at her. For a moment she thought he would smile. But it had to be a trick of the light, for the next instant she saw those eyes narrow as if considering the next plan of attack.

"You can tell your sister the truth, that you hired me to type your book and we were pretending at fiesta," she said desperately.

"And have her think I'm a liar."

"You are. We are. I feel badly about that."

"So let's make it reality and we don't have to tell anyone anything."

She was so tempted. What could it hurt? He was right, they were two free, willing adults. And she'd have the most fabulous memories to take with her when she left. Who would ever have expected her to catch the interest of such a sexy, dynamic man? He didn't even know how wealthy her father was. This was only about her. Her and Luis.

"What if I fall in love with you," she whispered, revealing her worst fear.

"Ah, *querido,* I can make no promises for the future. Can we not see where our paths lead us?" He stepped closer and held out his hand.

Rachel felt her resistance crumble. She didn't have to fear falling in love if he took her to bed. She'd already tumbled.

Admitting that, could she turn her back on spending time with him? On learning all she could for however long they had together? He'd been burned by Bonita's actions. Could he ever have an open mind about women again? Was it hopeless, or was there a possibility he'd come to care for her?

Dare she pass up the opportunity to try?

She laid her hand in his and went willingly into his arms when he pulled her close.

"I will do my best to make sure you do not fall in love with me," he said solemnly.

She smiled sadly and nodded. "It may be too late."

"And maybe I can find new beliefs to replace old ones," he said as he brought his mouth down on hers.

*   *   *

Luis didn't wish to end the kiss yet, but he heard Esperenza in the hallway. Stepping back from Rachel was one of the hardest things he'd done recently. He enjoyed seeing her flustered when she realized Esperenza was almost upon them. She ran her fingers over her hair in an attempt to smooth it. Her lips were damp and rosy from his mouth. The sight sent a shaft of desire straight through him. He hoped he could contain himself until after dinner.

He seated her at the table as Esperenza placed the bowls and platters in the center. She poured the wine, looking around the meal with satisfaction. Without a word to either of them she returned to the house.

"Do you think she knows?" Rachel whispered.

Luis almost laughed. "Most assuredly. She knows everything." He hesitated a moment, for the first time wondering if that were true. Had she known about Bonita—and not told him? It was likely. She had cousins and friends in the village. If Sophia's pronouncement was true, Esperenza had to have heard the rumors. For a moment anger flared. She had known him all his life, had her loyalties been so divided she kept Bonita's secrets?

Rachel reached out and touched his hand. "What's wrong?"

He cocked an eyebrow at her perception. "Nothing."

She snatched back her hand and began to serve her place from the assortment before them. "If you don't wish to talk about whatever is bothering you, fine. But don't tell me nothing when there is something," she said. Her voice was devoid of expression. Moments before she'd revealed her feelings. Now he'd cut her off.

"I wondered if Esperenza knew about Bonita."

"I doubt it," Rachel said, buttering one of the hot, fragrant rolls.

"Why?"

She looked at him. Would he ever tire of seeing those blue eyes focused on him? Ever get enough of touching her silken skin, the softness of her hair? He was getting aroused sitting at the dinner table.

"From the way she talks about you, she's known you all her life. And adores you. If she had known such a secret, I'm sure she would have told you. Her loyalties did not lie with Bonita."

"How could she not, she knows most of the people in the village."

"Who might have been very circumspect in speaking about the mistress of the *castillo* in the presence of any of her staff."

"You think?"

"Good grief, no wonder you don't socialize in the village if you suspect everyone. Ask her if you want to know. And if she didn't know, you can tell her."

"To what end? I've spent the last three years not talking about it."

"Why? To protect Bonita, or yourself?"

Her question stopped him. Had it been to protect Bonita? Or had he been angry and embarrassed his wife had turned to someone else? Had he wanted to hide that fact from the world? Bonita had known the possible consequences of an extramarital affair. She was gone—protecting her name didn't matter.

Protecting his pride had. Had his not mentioning it changed anything? His wife had still betrayed him. He had still been talked about in the village. And he'd shut himself away from normal activities for years.

Until a blonde on the run opened his eyes. Time to stop playing the outraged husband and begin to live again. With Rachel?

She was watching him warily. She did that a lot. Was he so ferocious?

"Pass the meat, *por favor,*" he said.

She handed him the platter and resumed eating. To defuse the tension, he asked her if Sophia had shown her any pictures of Mario.

Rachel laughed softly and nodded. He could listen to her laughter all day long. Or all night. Her eyes sparkled and her face became even more animated when she laughed.

"About a million. Good thing we were going to the beach instead of her house. If she carries that many with her, how many do they have at home?"

"About ten million. I do believe she takes a roll a day."

"Not really!"

"No, but it sometimes seems like it. He's a cute baby, but I don't need to relive his every living moment."

"Doting parents," she said fondly.

He nodded. At least one couple was doing things right.

"Which it sounds as if neither of us had," she said.

"You don't feel your father was a doting parent?"

"No. Attentive when convenient. Absent when work took precedence. And we know my mother wasn't even in the picture. Were your parents?"

"My father was too busy teaching me duty and responsibility, and hoping my mother's flighty nature had not shown up in my personality. My mother was too busy having a good time to want to do more than annoy my father when the mood struck her. They should never have married.''

''Why did they, do you ever wonder?''

''She said she fell in love with Spain. He fell in love with her, I think. But she isn't an easy person to live with.''

''Do you ever wonder, what if?''

''What if what?''

''Just what if? What if my mother hadn't left? Would I have a brother or sister, or both? Would my life have been totally different, or similar to what it is? Would I have felt more comfortable in high school with a mother's guidance? Would my father have spent more time with me and any siblings? What if they had not split?''

''Stupid to dwell on the past and things you can't change.''

''Still, it's interesting to speculate. What if your parents had stayed together?''

He had thought about it often as a teenager. He hadn't thought about it in years, accepting the way things were. But what if they had not separated?

''For one thing, had they stayed together, I wouldn't have been educated in America, never have written my books.''

''Ooh, then it's a good thing they didn't. You have given many the gift of entertainment.''

He was growing used to her compliments. Every time she offered one, he wanted to sweep her into his arms and get confirmation she meant it. That she wasn't just trying to build his ego. Though from the way she resisted any advances, he had had to rethink her plans some time ago. He no longer believed she was a reporter, a groupie, or a woman on the make. She was just who she said she was—a young woman suddenly confronted with a situation she needed time and distance to handle.

She would be leaving once Maria returned. She had her life and he had his. The two could never mix. But for as long as she stayed in Spain, he wanted her here, with him.

He refused to think about when she left.

"Now you tell me a what if?" she instructed.

"What if Bonita hadn't cheated?"

"Oh, then you two would be living happily ever after."

"I doubt that. We didn't live very harmoniously together at the best of times." He had never admitted that before, either. What was she, a witch who could get him to speak of things best left unsaid?

"So what if you didn't write books, what would you do?"

"Work."

"What if you had an exciting hobby?"

He thought of a hobby he'd enjoy—taking her to bed regularly.

"Such as?"

"Skydiving?" She laughed. Had he looked stunned?

"It's not an option."

"Okay, one more. What if you could have anything you wanted, or do anything you wanted, what would it be?"

Luis considered the question. What if he could have anything, do anything? Would he leave the responsibilities of the olive groves, turn his back on his duty and write full-time? He already lived in one of the most beautiful places on earth, he had no desire to change that. But the freedom to do exactly as he pleased?

Or would he rather have something he wanted. Something he thought he'd never want again—a family. A wife who genuinely loved him. Children.

He tossed his napkin on the table and rose. "I don't think I like your game. Life is how it is. What ifs won't change it."

"But what ifs can make you think."

"I think I've had enough." He didn't like where his thoughts were going. He'd tried family life. Maybe one day he'd try again, or maybe just leave the entire family enterprise to his nephew, Mario.

"Are you finished eating?" She still had half a plate left. He looked at his own, it was also half-full.

"I had a big lunch, I'm not hungry."

"Well, I am. Nothing like sunshine and fresh air to give me an appetite."

He wanted her to leave the table and come with him. Where? He couldn't hustle her from the table to bed, much as he'd like to. He glanced at his watch. How long would be a suitable interval? How could she eat so slowly?

He sat back down and watched her.

"I'm not the evening's entertainment. Look at something else," she muttered.

But she was this evening's entertainment. And the next few nights until she left as well. Maybe he'd take a day or two off from work and show her parts of Spain she hadn't yet seen. Watch her eyes light up with happiness. See his own country through the adoring eyes of a visitor. Spend enough time with her that he found her flaws and weaknesses and could end the enchantment.

CHAPTER NINE

RACHEL PUT DOWN her fork. "I'm finished. Now what?"

"Shall we take a walk?" he suggested.

"Sure." It would put off the moment she was both anticipating and dreading.

Luis switched on the pathway lighting on the way to the hilltop. They walked side by side where they could, his hand brushing hers. Rachel felt a shiver of delight. The breeze was stronger than earlier. Hearing the leaves rustle in the wind gave rise to fanciful imagining on Rachel's part. Were there wild animals hidden in the darkness?

The lights softly illuminated the gazebo at the summit. But once they stepped inside, Luis turned them off.

"The view is better without lights," he said easily. The village sparkled in the night. Out near the horizon flashes of light appeared.

"What's that?" she asked, pointing.

He stepped closer, more so than really needed to see where she was pointing. She caught her breath. His scent mingled with that of the fragrance of the flowers wafting on the breeze.

"Lightning, I think. There's a storm coming, can't you feel it?"

"Is that why the wind is up?"

"Yes. I expect it will hit here within the hour."

"The rain will be good for the olives, right?"

"For the most part. When they are ready to harvest, we don't want them wet. That would hasten the decay and alter the makeup of the oil."

"Luis?"

"*Si?*"

She turned to face him. It was too dark to see much of anything, but she thought she was looking up where his face would be.

"I'm ready."

"For what?"

"Whatever comes," she said, reaching out to rub her fingers down the sleeve of his shirt. He'd discarded the suit jacket before dinner.

He seemed to have no difficulty finding her in the dark. His arms swept around her and drew her snug against him.

"Something that comes along like this?" he murmured and covered her mouth with his.

Exactly like this, she thought before she stopped thinking entirely and gave herself up to the exquisite sensations his kiss evoked.

Rachel felt as if she floated on the night wind. The touch of his hands on her skin, the feel of his muscles beneath the cotton shirt, the wonderful magic of his mouth and tongue all combined to make her lose all track of time and place. She could only feel. There was no past or future, only the present. There were no problems facing either of them at this moment, only the sheer enjoyment of being with someone special and making it exceptional.

Lost as she was in delight, she was surprised when a loud clap of thunder shook the gazebo. She looked up, clutching Luis's shoulder.

"That was close." She looked out, the wind was still blowing, and she could smell the rain on the air. In only a moment a torrent poured down.

"Guess we won't be going back to the *castillo* in that," she murmured, snuggling even closer. There was no problem. She could stay in Luis's arms all night.

"Unless we wish to be soaked, it would be better to remain here. We have shelter. It's not too cool."

She laughed softly, tracing his jaw. "I'm so hot, I could explode. It's not too cool at all!"

"Hot, huh?" He captured her fingertips and kissed each one sweetly.

"Mmm."

"Maybe we should do something about that?"

"Like dare me to run into the cold rain?"

"No, like remove some layers of clothing which might be contributing to heat buildup."

Dropping her hands to his shirt front, she toyed with his tie. "Am I the only one who has too much on?" she asked whimsically.

"No." He snatched the tie from his neck and tossed it away.

She unbuttoned the first button feeling the heat that radiated from his body. Excitement raced through her at the thought of touching his chest, learning more about the man who had captured her heart.

She leaned closer and kissed the skin revealed beneath the opening.

"Ah, *querido,* that could prove dangerous."

"I'm forewarned," she murmured.

His hands tangled in her hair and pulled her face up to his for another searing kiss. Soon she was frantic with need. Desire threatened to swamp her. She wanted so much more. To touch and be touched. To kiss and be kissed. To love and be loved.

For an instant she almost faltered. Luis had never said a word about love.

"Let me," he said, easing her shirt over her head. In a flash of lightning she glimpsed him as he caressed her shoulder, watching her in the brief moment of illumination. She loved this man. She wanted to share everything with him.

"Luis, is this a mistake? We hardly know each other."

"You know my darkest secrets, what more do you want? I know yours, right?"

She nodded, stepping closer to close the gap. "I love you," she said inside. And for that love, she would risk anything.

The lightning flashed and the thunder roared, but Rachel didn't notice. She was in a world of two, and for them, it was a wondrous place.

The rain was a steady drizzle now. The fury of the storm had passed long ago. The air was cleaner, scented with the sea. Rachel stirred on the chaise mattress and made an effort to remain awake. She had been drifting toward sleep, lying against Luis, totally and wonderfully satiated. There was something intoxicating about making love in the outdoors. Or maybe it was making love with Luis that elated her.

"Cold?" he asked, his hand sweeping down her back, back up to her shoulder, and hugging her a little closer.

"Just a little."

"We should get to a bed. A mattress from a chaise isn't precisely commodious."

"Complaining already?" she teased.

"Wishing for a bed next time."

She held her breath. Next time. It sounded wonderful. Then she thought of his room. She didn't wish to go there. He could come to her room. There would be no lingering memories of Bonita there.

She was jealous of a dead woman. At one time Luis had thought he loved her. Rachel wished he loved her instead.

She sat up, some of the joy of the night fading. "I'll get dressed."

"No need on my account," he murmured.

"I have no intension of traipsing down the path in my birthday suit. Who knows who might be up at this time of night."

"We won't turn on the lights. I know the path. I can get us safely to the house."

"You expect us to walk together, in the rain? With nothing on?" She tried to see him but the rain had obscured any light from the stars and the *castillo* was in darkness so no source from there. This didn't sound like the duty-bound man she was coming to know.

"Think of it as taking a shower together."

She blinked. She had never thought that far ahead. Suddenly the absurdity of it hit her and she laughed. "Okay, if you're game, I am, too. Is this what you learned in Iowa?"

"Hey, don't malign my upbringing. Skinny-dipping is part of the summer-in-Iowa ritual."

"Amazing." He was acting totally different. Was this the real man, the one who had hidden the ache of betrayal behind a facade? Was being with her changing things? Her hopes rose. Maybe they could have something special after all.

They laughed and slid along the pathway. She had her clothes bundled in front of her, Luis had slung his over his shoulder, to keep his hands free to help her. The way they roamed over her back convinced her he wouldn't be much help.

Reaching the house, she held her breath.

"I have to tell you," she whispered as they stepped into the study. "If Esperanza sees us like this, I will die instantly."

"She is long asleep. Come." A moment later he uttered an expletive.

"What?"

"Stubbed my toe. Dammit, I haven't done something like this since I was a teenager."

"I've never done anything like this," she said.

In less than five minutes, they were in Rachel's room.

"Never done anything like this, huh?" he said, taking the clothes from her hands and dropping them on the floor. He pulled her against him, molding her along the long length of his body, he kissed her.

Their trip through the rain had cooled their skin, but his kiss soon had her warm as toast. Damp and hungry for each other, they made it to her bed before the last vestiges of rational thought fled. Luis had a way of making the world disappear.

The sunshine flooding in on her face awoke Rachel the next morning. She frowned, turning away from it, and saw the indentation on the pillow next to her. Luis had stayed the night, but some time ago had left. She vaguely remembered a kiss, and a promise. But she'd been half asleep.

Sitting up, she looked at the clock. It was after eleven! Good heavens, what would Esperenza think?

She showered and dressed in record time. Making her way to the lower floor a short time later, she saw one of the maids vacuuming in the drawing room. Esperenza might be in the kitchen, though it was too early to be preparing lunch and breakfast certainly was long over.

Rachel could do without food for a while. Maybe she could just pretend everything was normal and expect lunch at one like most days.

She sat behind the computer, staring at the stack of paper to be typed. She was more than halfway through. A few diligent days of effort and she might finish before Maria returned.

"There you are. I have a message for you," Esperenza said from the doorway.

Rachel smiled, feeling heat flood her cheeks. "Good morning, what message?"

"Luis said to take the car and meet him at the café by the marina in Calpe. And to wear walking shoes and cool clothes."

"Calpe? Where is that?"

"If you take the road to the village, when you reach main street, turn to the left and follow the coast until you see the signs for Calpe. There is a sidewalk café near the marina. You can drive the car, right?"

Drive Luis's convertible? "Of course." She jumped up, the typing forgotten. "I'll get my shoes and head out. Did he say what time?"

"No, but for lunch. So I would leave soon. Pay attention to your driving. This is not California."

"If I can drive in Los Angeles, I can drive any-where!" She almost hugged Esperenza in her exuber-ance. Luis wanted her to meet him for lunch at a seaside café. It sounded like the perfect romantic place. She wasn't sure about the walking shoes, but put on her most comfortable pair.

She shook her head as she drove down the winding road, enjoying the feel of the wind. This car was a dream and she savored every moment. Who would have thought a few weeks ago she would be dashing to meet the man she loved. She thought of her father, and Paul. She'd have to do something before long. Let her father know where she was. She knew he'd be worried about her. He had to realize, however, how things had altered between them.

Not that anything had changed about Paul. But maybe her father would talk to the man and make sure he knew Rachel wouldn't consider marrying him in a million years. Especially after meeting Luis. Not that she planned to share that information with her father just yet.

Traffic was light on the coast road and she enjoyed the drive, darting glances at the Mediterranean Sea as often as she dared. The play of colors from pale tur-quoise to indigo continued to fascinate her.

She found the place without any difficulty. Hurrying from the car, she saw Luis. He was watching her. Rachel swallowed, hoping she didn't make a total fool of her-self. She was so happy she could skip.

He rose when she approached the table.

"Thank you for letting me drive that car," she said breathlessly, stopping beside him.

He brushed his mouth against hers and then held a chair for her. The large umbrellas sheltered the tables from the sun. The road passed between the café and the sea, but except for the occasional car, their view was unimpeded.

She smiled at him. "This is terrific."

"I'm glad you came."

He'd changed from his suit into more casual attire. She looked around, but no one was paying them any attention. Had he chosen this place for privacy?

"So what's up that I needed walking shoes?" she asked once their lunch order had been placed.

"I thought we could climb El Pēnon de Ifach after lunch." He indicated a mammoth rock formation jutting into the sea. It towered over the town.

"You can climb that?"

"There is a path on the back side. The view from the top is worth the trek."

Walking on the back side of the moon would be worth the trek if Luis were with her, she thought. "Sounds like fun. Shouldn't you be working?"

"I took the afternoon off. Marcos dropped me here. We'll take the car back together."

She looked around.

"Something wrong?"

"I'm looking for Luis Alvares. You look like him, but certainly don't act like him."

His eyes lit in amusement. "I think you have freed me from the shackles of the past."

"Wow, that's the most romantic thing anyone has ever told me," she said, stunned. Did he really mean it?

He took her hand in his. "Seriously, Rachel, I want to show you some of Spain. You love my country. Let me share my favorite spots with you."

Seriously. He had been joking. But she didn't care. To joke was enough of a change to suspect something more had happened. And to have him show her his special places was more than she ever expected. Who knew, if they were together long enough, maybe he would fall in love with her. Wasn't love contagious?

Treasuring every moment of the afternoon, Rachel knew it would be a special memory for many years. They ate and then headed for El Pěnon. Luis made sure they had water bottles and sunscreen.

It didn't take long before the pathway steepened and walking became more than a saunter. But every time Rachel paused for breath, she had a better view. They passed tourists on the trail and nodded. When they reached the summit, Luis casually put his arm around her shoulders, drawing her closer as he pointed out places of interest. Their luncheon café looked like a miniature diorama from this viewpoint.

She dutifully looked but was too conscious of his closeness, of his touch, to pay attention. When he paused, she turned her head and looked at him. He was gazing down at her.

"Did last night really happen?" she said.

His kiss blotted out the view, the sun, the memory. A new one was in the making.

When they heard the voices of another couple nearing the summit, they broke apart.

"Not as private as the *castillo*," Luis said, brushing back her hair from her cheek. The tendrils were as soft as down. He wished he could wrap the tendrils around his fingers and let them drift through. Then he'd like to kiss her again, feeling the passion she displayed last night.

The other couple reached the wide cleared space at the top and exclaimed over the view. Luis wished they had timed their arrival for later—like next week. But he nodded cordially when they called greetings.

"Have you seen enough?" he asked.

Rachel sighed. "I don't think I could ever see enough. This is different from the view at the *castillo*, but both are sensational. I could stay here all my life."

"It gets cold when the wind picks up and there aren't a lot of amenities," he said, resting his hand on her shoulder. She was fine-boned. He longed to slip beneath her shirt and feel the silky texture of her skin. Kiss her again and taste her unique sweetness.

He was growing hot and aroused just thinking about what he wanted to do. Now was not the time nor the place. They still had to return down the steep path and get to the car. And then home. Suddenly Luis was impatient. He had denied himself for far too long because of Bonita.

Was he trying to make up for lost time?

No, he'd had opportunities over the last three years. But no one had appealed to him like Rachel. If he was in a hurry, it was because Maria was returning soon and Rachel would leave. Make hay while the sun shines, had been a favorite saying of his Iowa grandfather.

"But I'll leave if I can come again," she said, leaning against him just a little, in a cozy, companionable way. He liked it. He liked most things about his surprise secretary. He knew he'd miss her when she left.

"You can come again whenever you wish. I'll try to come with you, if you like."

"Definitely!" She smiled up at him and Luis felt his desire spike. She was beautiful when she smiled. Her entire face seemed to light up. Her blue eyes shone with happiness. Pride puffed up when he knew being with him enhanced that happiness.

They had an easier time going down the path and it didn't take long before they were back at the car.

"Home?" he asked as he closed the passenger door behind her.

"Can we drive along the coast for a little longer? I loved the stretch between here and the village. What's ahead?"

He slid behind the wheel and adjusted the mirrors. "It's the same for the next fifty miles."

In only moments they were flying along. The sea was to their right as they headed north, the sun overhead. Ahead, the road was virtually deserted. He glanced at her and saw her delight. She wasn't a woman to hide her thoughts. Was she too good to be true? He settled in and began to enjoy the drive as well. It had been too many years since he'd traveled this stretch of road for anything but business.

"Thank you for a wonderful afternoon," Rachel said as he pulled in front of the house and stopped. He killed the engine and turned slightly to look at her. "My pleasure."

"Mine, too. I'll remember today forever!"

"Tomorrow, join me for dinner in Benidorm?" The least little thing seemed to please her. How would dinner and dancing at one of the supper clubs be? He could hold her in his arms and move with the music. And later, hold her in his arms again and move to the music the two of them would make.

"Not dressy?" she asked.

"A bit. Come in to town early and shop."

"I guess."

He could have hoped for a more enthusiastic response, but he'd take what he'd get. "I'll have Marcos pick you up after lunch. He can bring us back after dinner."

"Is there some reason you asked me now rather than later?" she asked.

"No." He just wanted to make sure he had tomorrow lined up.

When it came time to retire for the night, Luis didn't give Rachel any choice. He went up with her and into her room. When she looked in surprise, he swept her into a kiss before she could say anything. He knew how she responded to his kisses and was using that to make sure he stayed. The ticking clock sounded louder in his mind. She'd be gone soon.

Before drifting to sleep some time later, he gathered her close. "I spoke with Esperenza," he said softly.

"About what?" Rachel's body was warm and soft. He could hold her forever.

"About Bonita. You were right—she never knew. But she does now. Never underestimate the gossip network in a small village. Carlos Valdiz was Bonita's lover."

Rachel sat up and looked at him in the dark. "How did she find out?"

"Once she learned of Bonita's deception, she called her cousins and brother and aunt. In no time they'd found someone who had seen Bonita more than once leaving Carlos's flat late at night. So now I know who."

"And does it help?"

He shrugged, more intent on Rachel than lost loves of the past. "He and I were never friends. I can avoid him in the future and let the past rest. Lie back down, I like feeling you against me."

She snuggled closer, as if trying to ease the pain of discovery. Luis was intrigued to find he really didn't care after all these years. Bonita was in the past. Rachel was his present. And maybe his future?

Rachel sat in the back of the car the next afternoon feeling like a princess. Marcos hadn't responded to her attempts to be friendly, so she assumed he liked silence when he drove. She held her bag, gazing out the window. She'd love to buy the most fabulous dress she could find to knock Luis's eyes out, but she was very conscious of her dwindling Euros. She hoped she could find something suitable which didn't cost the earth. She'd brought her pumps. They weren't the sexy strappy shoes she had at home—in California she corrected herself. But they would go with almost anything and look presentable.

She looked forward to shopping, though wished Caroline was going with her. She could hardly wait to tell Luis her news. Her dear friend had come through for her in spades!

Despite her concerns, Rachel found a dress she thought would be perfect and didn't cost too much. A deep maroon, the little slip dress faithfully followed her curves and valleys. It was the sexiest thing she'd ever worn. She couldn't wait for Luis's reaction.

It was all she could have wished for—he stopped for a moment when he crossed the lobby of the building. She'd slipped out of the car and gone to meet him, hoping for just such a reaction. Much more satisfying than having him slide into the back seat with her and not get the full effect at once.

He continued across the expanse, the heat in his eyes all she could have wished for. Her heart leaped in response.

"You are beautiful," he said softly. When he drew close enough, he kissed her. Right there in the lobby of the building in which his offices were located. Rachel was stunned he claimed her so openly.

"It's a little early for dinner, I thought we could visit one of the bars on the beach and listen to the music for a while."

"On the beach?" Her shoes weren't exactly the best for walking in the sand.

"At the beach perhaps is more accurate. We don't have to traipse through the sand."

Great, now he was starting to read her mind.

He walked beside her to the car, and ushered her into the back seat. Giving Marcos the directions, he settled in, and took one of her hands in his.

"Tell me what you did today?" he said.

"Typed on your book, of course."

"That's all? There's an air of excitement here, and I don't think it's from chapter eleven."

"I'm on chapter fifteen, thank you very much. You must be falling behind on reading the transcription. And I do have news, but I'll wait until we're at the table."

"Good news, I take it?"

"The best." She smiled at him, glad she could share it with him. But she didn't want to be interrupted if they arrived before she finished telling him all the details. It would wait a few more minutes.

The bar was charming. Definitely casual—they were the most overdressed couple there. Parents had brought children ranging from babies to pseudo-bored teenagers. Everyone was enjoying themselves as evidenced from the laughter and boisterous conversations. There were no walls, just supports to hold the roof. Beyond was the wide expanse of beach and the sparkling sea.

They found a table near the edge of the sand. Once their waiter had taken their order for white wine, Rachel leaned forward.

"I found my mother!"

"What?"

She nodded, her heart tripping. "Caroline asked around for me, questioning people who have known my father long enough to remember my mother as well. She ended up speaking with Harvey McMichels—whose mother is an avid genealogist. So Harvey put Caroline in touch with his mother who gave her even more ways to track someone down than you gave me. I found out her high school, went to a Web site for the school and got in contact with someone who knew my mother as a girl. And still keeps in touch! But the best part was Harvey's mother actually remembered the divorce. She told Caroline all about it."

"What happened?" Luis asked.

"My father was just as devoted to work in those days as he is now. My mother felt neglected. She began to drink rather heavily. One day she was in a solo car accident, due to being intoxicated. That was all my father needed to get her to agree to a divorce, and to leave me behind. He was worried about my safety."

"And she agreed?"

"Must have, I haven't heard from her in all these years."

Luis leaned back in his chair and gazed off at the sea lost in thought for a moment.

"There must have been more for her to stay out of your life all this time," he said finally.

"Well I don't know what it was. Maybe he did have good reasons for lying all these years. Maybe she really didn't care about me."

"Have you contacted the woman who knew her from high school?"

"Yes, I sent an e-mail and she already responded."

"You told her who you were?" he asked.

"No. I just said I was trying to find her. I know where she lives, San Antonio, Texas. She did remarry. I have three half-siblings, two brothers and a sister."

It still seemed surreal to Rachel. One moment she wondered if she'd ever find her mother, or discover what happened between her and her father, and the next, she had it all. Her feeling toward her father had changed slightly. She tried to look at the situation from his point of view twenty years ago. A wife who couldn't be trusted with their child. She still didn't know what had kept her mother quiet all these years, but no matter what, she wanted to know.

Luis lifted her hand to his lips, kissing the palm. "This calls for celebration. We should be drinking champagne, not mere wine."

"Being with you is celebration enough." She was giddy with sensations. His kiss had her wishing they could forgo dinner and return home. Her elation over locating her mother had her high as a kite. And being with Luis was celebration enough for everything.

She wasn't sure what caused the change, but he was definitely as interested in her as she was in him. She cherished every moment, amazed she could interest a man like him. And knowing it was she he was interested in, not her father's daughter. Who would have thought fleeing California would have ended up with more happiness than she could hold?

He questioned every step, congratulating her on her methodology, speculating with her on the best way to approach the woman. He offered some suggestions about finding out more about the situation before flying to Texas where her mother now lived. Rachel was grateful for all the advice. She wished she were brave enough to ask him to accompany her.

Dinner was romantic. She watched him order over the candles that graced their tables. The dinner club was the epitome of elegance. The starchy white tablecloths, the heavy silver, the fine crystal gave a festive air to their meal.

When the dancing began, Rachel knew she was in heaven. Luis was the perfect partner. She could have danced all night except for the awareness that rose every time she touched him, every instant when they turned in time to the music. Just being with Luis had her hungering for more. Wrapped in a rosy, romantic glow, she enjoyed the evening, but yearned for what she knew would follow. The last two days had been the happiest in her life.

Maybe discovering her father's lie had been fate. Otherwise she would never have met Luis. Or fallen in love.

He looked content to be with her. His gaze never wandered to others on the dance floor. He wasn't looking to see who was around he might also wish to dance with. He was focused solely on her.

Excitement licked in her veins. People were supposed to pair up, and offer love and support all their lives. She didn't know why some marriages didn't turn out that way, but if she married she'd do all in her power to make sure it lasted until death.

Would he ask her to share his life with him? Could she live in Spain? Of course they would make trips to the States. She'd miss Caroline and some of her other friends, but they could come to visit. She wouldn't mind, as long as she had Luis.

"It is late. We should be heading home," he said as a slow song ended.

Still wrapped in his arms, Rachel nodded. She hated to see the evening end, but there would be others.

As Marcos whisked them along the coast road, Luis leaned back. "This weekend, would you like to go to Madrid? I have a small apartment there. We could visit the museum, stroll La Plaza d'Espana, make sure you see as much of the city as we have time for."

"I'd love to." A vague feeling of uncertainty pricked. It sounded if they didn't have forever to explore Spain's capital city. She shook it off. It was just the way he said it. They'd have time again to visit.

"Then I will take off work early on Friday and we'll fly up that evening. That will give us two entire days."

"Sounds wonderful." Of course, picking olives at harvest time sounded wonderful if she could do it with him.

Rachel spent the days until Friday transcribing manuscript pages and searching the Internet for more information on her mother. She had a home address, a phone number, information about her husband, who was a tax consultant, and the three younger siblings she didn't know she had. Two were in college, one in high school.

She debated calling. But was afraid her mother would hang up on her. What if she hadn't told her new family about Rachel? What if contacting her would result in rejection?

She discussed it with Luis each night. They had had dinner at the terrace, telling Esperenza not to pick up the dishes until the morning. Rachel knew Esperenza must suspect more was going on than dinner, but the older woman never gave a clue as to her feelings about it.

Sophia came for lunch one day and commented on how well Rachel looked.

Of course, she was a woman in love.

Friday Luis arrived home in time for lunch on the patio. As they were finishing, Esperenza arrived in the doorway, an odd look on her face. She looked at Rachel.

"There is someone here to see you."

Rachel rose. "Sophia?"

"No, darling, it's me." Paul Cambrick stepped into the doorway.

CHAPTER TEN

RACHEL SAT DOWN HARD. The last person she had expected to see was Paul. "What are you doing here?" she asked.

Luis rose to face the man. "Who are you?"

"Paul Cambrick." He came forward, his hand extended.

Luis looked down his nose. Rachel admired his aristocratic gesture. Not many people put Paul off. What was he doing here? How had he found her? She looked beyond him. Had her father come as well?

"Are you a friend of Rachel's?" Luis asked, ignoring the extended hand.

"Fiancé, actually."

"No!" Rachel surged to her feet once more, coming around the table. "That's not so."

"Lover's quarrel," Paul said to Luis, man to man. He turned to Rachel as she stormed around the table. "Your father would have come, but I told him I could handle this. Time you got over your snit, sweetheart, and came home."

"I'm not in a snit. And I'm not your sweetheart!" She turned to Luis, her heart sinking. She was familiar with that closed-off look.

"Luis, I'm not engaged to him."

"Rachel, shame on you. Have you been leading this man on? You have my ring. How much more do you need?"

"We'd need to care about one another for one thing. And I care nothing for you." The ring had sat on her dresser in her room in California. Paul had urged her to keep it while she thought over her answer, not accepting her refusal all those weeks ago. She'd told her father to give it back to Paul.

Luis withdrew, she could feel him do it, though he didn't move a muscle.

"Perhaps you need time to get your life in order," he said to Rachel. "I should have known better. But do you know, for a while—" He stopped abruptly and with a slight nod, left them on the patio and entered the house.

Rachel rounded on Paul.

"I don't know how you found me, or why you went to all the trouble of coming here, but in case you aren't getting the picture, I'll make it clear as glass. Get away from me and leave me alone!"

"Your father sent me. I'm here to take you home and we are getting married. Once we are married, I don't expect to have to go chasing halfway around the world for you, either."

"Paul, read my lips, I will never marry you."

Anger flashed in his eyes. "You will. Your father supports the idea. We've already discussed partnerships. How will you manage without someone to support you?" He glanced around the patio, taking in the back side of the *castillo*. "It looks like you are trying for even bigger stakes."

"You're delusional if you think I plan to go home and dutifully marry you. Whatever deal you and my father work out is between the two of you. Do not use me as part of the deal. I told my father to return your ring. Do with it whatever you two wish, but leave me alone!"

"Your father misses you, Rachel. Come home. We'll discuss this later, when you are not so emotional."

"What part of 'go away' do you not understand?"

She needed to find Luis, to explain. She couldn't forget the shuttered look when Paul told him she was his fiancée. He probably thought she had cheated even as Bonita had. She had to find him. Walking toward the house, she stopped when Paul caught her arm.

"I've gone to a lot of trouble to track you down and find you. Leaving without you is not an option," he growled.

"How did you find me?"

His smug smile made her want to knock it off his face. Where was Luis? He couldn't believe she would have led him on while she really had a fiancé in her life. He had to know her better than that!

"Caroline bragged to Marty Henson. Marty was showing off at some tennis party a couple of weeks ago, and telling one and all how her friend Rachel had a job with a famous author. From there, it was just a matter of time."

She remembered that early e-mail to Caroline. Why hadn't she kept quiet? Or why had Caroline told Marty? Water over the dam now. But that didn't mean she planned to meekly leave with Paul and return to her father's house. She had more important things to do— like find Luis.

"Just go, Paul."

"I'm not going without you," he repeated.

"Then I guess you are planning to live in Spain, because I'm not leaving."

Esperanza came to the door, her face troubled. "Señor

Alvares has asked me to help you pack, Señorita.'' She threw an angry look at Paul.

"There, you see, you can no longer stay here. I've booked us both on a flight from Madrid tomorrow."

She shook off his hand. Head held high, she swept past him and Esperenza. So Luis wanted her to leave, did he? Was he too cowardly to tell her himself? To listen to her explanation?

Esperenza followed Rachel to her room.

"I really need to talk to Luis," she said, turning as she reached her door.

"He left. He will be back later, but asked to make sure you were gone before he returns. I'm sorry," Esperenza said.

Rachel reeled as if she'd been struck. He wouldn't even listen to her? Granted there was a smidgen of a correlation to the experiences he'd had with Bonita, but he needed to hear the truth. How could he ignore her and leave like that? What if she needed—

The truth hit her. He didn't care. These last few days had not been courtship, but the affair he'd originally asked for. To him it just ended earlier. The only difference was in her mind, not his. He'd never promised her anything.

Stunned, she entered the room. She'd pack and leave the *castillo*. But if he or Paul thought she would go meekly back to California, both of them were in for a surprise.

"I'm not leaving until I speak with Luis," she vowed.

"Señorita, he won't be back until you are gone."

"So I'll go to the village. Your cousin's friend still has a room I could use, right?"

"*Si.*" Esperenza smiled at this. "*Si,* she'll give you a break in the rate, if I tell her."

"Thank you." Now Rachel just had to figure out how to get rid of Paul. If Luis didn't want her, there was no need to remain. But she was not going meekly back to her father. Not until she'd met her mother. Then she'd make up her mind what she would do in the future.

Packing, she tried to ignore the knot in her chest, the tears that threatened. Folding the maroon slip dress, she remembered their dances. Placing her swimsuit in the case, she remembered their day at the beach, spreading the sunscreen on Luis's back. Memories of El Pēnon in Calpe, of the fiesta, of Sophia and Julian all crowded in her mind as she looked one more time around the room to make sure she'd forgotten nothing.

She was leaving with all she'd arrived with. Except her heart. That would remain with Luis. Maybe forever.

"Esperenza, do not tell anyone where I've gone," Rachel said as she lifted the small case. "I'll lose Paul when we get to the village and stay out of the way until he gets fed up and leaves."

She doubted Luis would even ask. Her heart broke a little more when she realized she wouldn't see him again if he had anything to do with it. All she wanted was to feel his arms around her, hear his voice reassuring her. Offering support for her choices.

Taking a deep breath, she tried to smile. So be it. "Thanks for everything, Esperenza. Maria will have to finish the book. I was so close, too."

Esperenza led the way to the large foyer where Rachel had first made her pitch for a job.

Paul paced there.

She tilted her head. Time the men in her life knew she wasn't a pawn in their games.

"Let's go, Paul," she said. In only a short time, she'd disappear again. Let him find her after that!

Luis climbed to the gazebo and walked to the railing. Here he'd first made love to Rachel. He tightened his grip on the wood and gazed out across the olive grove. He had been played for a fool a second time. Those wide blue eyes had not been guileless. What was her game? Did she enjoy pitting one man against another? Had she grown tired of life in California and was looking for more excitement, more variety? Nothing like being aligned with a famous author to get vicarious fame. He knew that from Bonita.

Rachel wouldn't be here for the harvest. He knew their time together had been limited. Maria would be returning soon. It had only been a summer fling. He never intended for it to go any further.

They'd had some fun. It was over.

So why did it feel as if there was an aching hole in his chest? Why did he wonder where she was? Why torment himself with images of her and Paul in some hotel room?

"Dammit!" He turned away. The fading light muted the colors of the sea, but he gazed over the water, remembering her delight at the café in Calpe. And her constant wonder at the view from the *castillo*. Would he ever stop thinking about her? Not want her?

He had let her off too easily. Bonita had run when he'd discovered her cheating. He'd sent Rachel away. He should have told her first what he thought of women like her. Told Paul all that had transpired. Would the man still want her for a wife after that?

Thinking about it a moment, it struck Luis there hadn't been much of a loverlike attitude from the man. And Rachel had denied their engagement. Of course, what else would he expect? She certainly wouldn't brazen it out by confessing.

It would be a long time before he let himself get involved with another woman. Twice burnt was lesson enough for any man. It was a long time before he left the gazebo.

Rachel had found it easy to escape Paul. He never expected her to even try it, she was sure. Esperenza's cousin's friend welcomed her into her home and gave her a lovely room which overlooked the small garden. Beyond, rising above the town, the grey *castillo* loomed. Rachel had spent most of the afternoon staring at the castle and wondering what Luis was doing. He had not given her a chance to talk to him. He had sent her away thinking she'd betrayed Paul in the same manner Bonita had betrayed him.

But it wasn't the same at all. And she wanted him to see he was wrong. She was not like his wife!

In the end, did it matter? He had wanted a summer affair. Maybe it would be easier to make the break this way. For him, Paul's arrival had just ended their affair a bit earlier than Luis's schedule.

Tears welled, but she brushed them aside. She wasn't so sad as angry! She would not leave until he'd heard her out. If nothing else, she wanted him to remember her favorably. She refused to leave until she knew he didn't believe she would have cheated on a man as his wife had done. She possessed more honor than that.

In the meanwhile, it was past time to contact her father.

The next morning Rachel braved the local taxi driver again and headed up to the *castillo*. Ringing the bell, she rehearsed what she would say.

To her dismay, when Esperenza opened the door, she shook her head. "He is gone, Rachel. He left early this morning. He said not to expect him back for some time."

"Oh. I came to explain about Paul." Disappointment filled her. She had counted on making him understand. "You don't have any idea when he might be back?"

Esperenza shook her head, sympathy in her eyes.

"I guess I'll check back in a few days, then."

She turned. Once again she'd sent the driver away. Now what was she going to do?

"I'll need to call for a cab," she said.

"If you can wait a while, I plan to visit a friend this afternoon. I can give you a ride to the village then," Esperenza offered.

"Thanks, I'd appreciate that. It's not as if I have anything else to do. Maybe I could transcribe some more of the manuscript while I wait."

When Esperenza hesitated, Rachel shrugged. "It's no big deal. I've seen most of the book. I'm not rushing somewhere to give it away. But if you are uncomfortable with me in the house—"

"Of course not, Señorita, come." She opened the door wide. "I'll prepare lunch at one and we can leave after that."

"You don't need to feed me."

"Come in and don't argue."

Rachel smiled sadly, wishing she'd gotten to know this kind woman better.

Settled behind the computer moments later, she began to type. Maybe while Luis was away, she could catch up and finish the book.

Maybe he could pay her for the work, too. He'd never discussed compensation the first day. Living in his home had meant she'd had to spend very few of her Euros, but still, he owed her for her time and the pages she'd done.

A thought struck her. Her father now knew where she was. She needn't hide any longer. She could use her credit cards and her bank card!

She stopped for lunch, and then resumed typing while Esperanza cleaned up and got ready to visit her friend. Lost in the book's convoluted plot, knowing she was approaching the end, she hoped she could figure out who the murderer was before Luis revealed it. She jumped when a blue square landed on the desk. It was her passport.

"It's hard to leave the country without it," Luis said.

She looked up, her heart leaping at the sight of him. His demeanor wasn't very approachable, but just to see him warmed her heart. "I forgot you had it."

"You would have remembered if you had tried to get a flight from Madrid. I went to the international counter, but you weren't there."

"You went to Madrid? Just to give me my passport?"

"No, not to give it to you. But to talk you into returning here."

"I wasn't leaving."

"Oh?"

"Paul left, I think."

"You don't know?"

"I ditched him."

"What?"

"Ditched him. Escaped. Left him on his own."

"I know what ditched means. Why?"

"I told you yesterday, I am not nor have ever been engaged to Paul Cambrick. He wishes I were, but not for me. He and my father could make lots of money if they merged operations. Actually, Paul would make more than he has now, and my father always likes opportunities like that, so it would be beneficial to both of them—"

He leaned over and put his fingers over her mouth. "You are talking about a man I don't care if I ever hear about again."

She blinked. The touch of his fingers sent her heart skyrocketing.

"Okay, I won't speak of him again. What shall we talk about? Tell me again why you went to Madrid."

"To bring you back. What you are doing here?"

"Typing your book. I'm almost finished. I have to know before I go who did it. If you don't want me to finish transcribing it, then I need to read to the end really quick."

"I thought you had left," Luis said.

"Well, I hadn't made you understand, so I couldn't leave."

"Understand what?"

"That I had not acted like Bonita. That I had not cheated on anyone. And that I would never have hurt you or anyone else in such a manner. I must say I was surprised you thought so little of me that you'd believe it even for a moment.'' And hurt. But she need not reveal that tidbit.

''All I could think of was you were just like Bonita. That no woman could be trusted.''

''That much was obvious.''

''Then I began to remember the time we spent together. How outraged you were when you learned about Bonita. The determination you showed in defying your father and his wishes so you could learn the truth. Someone who is that focused on the truth, no matter if learning the full story hurts her or not, is not someone who would bend the truth for her own ends.''

''So you know Paul was exaggerating when he said that.''

''Or indulging in wishful thinking.''

''You think?''

''I indulge in the same wishful thinking.''

She caught her breath. ''I don't understand.''

He stood and walked to the French doors, looking over the garden. ''I feel as nervous as a kid on a first date.'' Turning, he looked at her. She'd swivelled around on the office chair, not taking her eyes from him.

''I wish you were my fiancée, and then my wife,'' he said.

Rachel jumped to her feet and flew to him, wrapping her arms around his neck. ''That can be arranged. Oh, Luis, I thought you were never going to listen to me. That I would never see you again.''

He caught her tightly. ''Will you marry me, Rachel? Stay here in Spain and fill my nights with love and my days with delight—as you've done this past week?''

''Yes, yes. Of course.'' She kissed him, delighting in the feel of his arms around her, of his mouth on hers in the familiar dance of passion. Her blood rushed through her like a tidal wave. He wanted her to marry him. They would not make the mistakes of their parents. She had to tell him about her father and his long ago wish to keep her safe. She would never agree with his method of handling things, but they had taken that first step toward reconciliation. Would he rejoice in her newfound happiness? She believed he would.

"I love you, *querido*. Never leave me," Luis mumbled as he kissed her cheeks, her jaw, her ear.

"I love you. I have forever it seems. I was so happy last week and so devastated when you ordered me away. I thought you only wanted an affair, then I thought maybe you were growing to like me more, and then to have you tell me to leave—"

"I started out wanting an affair. But somewhere along the way, it changed. I want more, now. I want it all. I won't ever tell you to leave again," he said, kissing her.

"I am going now to the village," Esperenza said from the doorway. "But I think you no longer need a ride."

They broke apart to look at Esperenza.

"Congratulations are in order, Esperenza. Rachel has agreed to become my wife," Luis said proudly.

The older woman smiled warmly. "To be sure, I wondered if you'd come to your senses in time, Luis. *Gracias a Dios* you have. I am happy for you, Señor. And for you, Señorita. He's waited a long time for the right person to complete his life."

"She is the right person. For now and for all time," Luis affirmed, kissing her palm.

Rachel basked in the glow of love that filled her. Despite the past, Luis reached out to her, coming for her even before he'd known the truth. She reached up for his kiss as she vowed in her heart to love and honor this man forever.

EPILOGUE

"I'M SO NERVOUS," Rachel said as Luis stopped the car near the curb. The sprawling ranch-style house was situated in a nice suburb of Dallas. The lawn was freshly cut, the edges trimmed. Three cars crowded the driveway.

"If you want to postpone it, we can call and reschedule," he said.

"No. It's all been arranged. How awful to turn back at this juncture." She reached for his hand. "You'll be there with me, right? No matter what she says?"

"*Querido,* we made this appointment over the phone. She is expecting you and is anxious to meet you. It's not like you are going into this cold. Or that she will reject you. You know how much she's longed to see you. Only her commitment to honor the agreement she and your father made so long ago kept her away."

"But she's never seen me. What if she doesn't like me?"

"She will love you. Almost as much as I love you." He raised their linked hands and kissed hers gently.

She squeezed his hand, his words a balm. It really didn't matter if her mother wanted her in her life. She had Luis. It was more than enough.

"Okay." She took a deep breath. "I'm ready."

They walked up to the front door hand-in-hand. She reached out tentatively to ring the bell. For a moment she remembered the bell at the *castillo* she'd rung so many weeks ago. Look how that had turned out. She smiled at her husband of one week, and took another breath. Not many men would spend their honeymoon making an initial visit to strangers. She heard footsteps inside.

The door opened.

A mother's radiant love enveloped her as the woman who looked like an older version of Rachel reached out.

"Oh, my baby, my precious, precious baby. I have missed you so much," she said, drawing Rachel into her arms and hugging her tightly. Tears ran down her cheeks, and she clung as if she'd never let go.

Rachel let the love wash through her. It would all turn out right. They had all the time now for explanations, for meeting her brothers and sister, and for them to meet

Luis. The first step had been the hardest, and it was over.

Her mother pulled back and began to dab her eyes with a tissue, "Come in, come in. My husband and family are so anxious to meet you. And I want to hear every detail of your life since I left. I have missed you every single day."

Rachel smiled at Luis as they stepped into the house.

"I have it all, now, don't I?" she said for him alone. "Love beyond what I ever dreamed."

"*Si, mi tresor.*" He reached out to link her hand with his. Together they shared all the love they needed until the end of time.

* * *

Don't miss Barbara McMahon's heart-warming story
Adopted: Family in a Million.
Available in May 2009 from Mills & Boon® Romance.

THE GREEK BOSS'S DEMAND

TRISH MOREY

For Gavin, who always believed.
And for Jane, who helped make it possible.
Thanks, guys.

Trish Morey is an Australian who's also spent time living and working in New Zealand and England. Now she's settled with her husband and four young daughters in a special part of South Australia, surrounded by orchards and bushland, and visited by the occasional koala and kangaroo. With a life-long love of reading, she penned her first book at age eleven, after which life, career and a growing family kept her busy, until once again she could indulge her desire to create characters and stories – this time in romance. Having her work published is a dream come true. Visit Trish at her website, www.trishmorey.com

CHAPTER ONE

A PROPERTY company!

What was Nick Santos supposed to do with a half-share in a property company all the way over here in Australia? Especially one that by rights should have gone in its entirety to his cousin Sofia.

Taking note of the flashing light over his head, Nick duly fastened his seat belt for the descent into Sydney.

He'd never thought of his uncle Aristos as having a sense of humour, but he had to have been joking to come up with this scheme.

Half the company on condition that he stay and head up the business for six months, teaching Sofia whatever she needed to know to run the business herself.

It was crystal-clear what his late uncle had intended by his strange bequest. Nick was no stranger to the practice of arranged marriages, and he wasn't about to have one foisted on him.

As soon as he'd paid his respects to Sofia he'd gift her the balance of the company by leaving Australia and forfeiting his share of the inheritance. He didn't need the hassle when there were more important issues to consider at home—even if he had left the business in the safe hands of Dimitri, his second in charge.

He settled back into his seat, taking in the view as the plane came in for landing.

So this was Sydney. He caught a glimpse of the Sydney Harbour Bridge, with the Opera House nestled alongside—architectural icons of the busy harbour—before city buildings swallowed up the view and he had to content himself with watching the endless procession of red roofs and blue backyard pools skating under the plane as it descended steadily towards the airport.

In spite of the disruption to his schedules he could almost thank Aristos for finally getting him here. He'd grown up hearing tales of fortunes to be made in the new world. His mother's brother had made a success of it, that much was sure.

And he'd met a few Australians in his time. One in particular stuck in his mind—a girl he'd met on the island of Crete. Years ago now.

She'd been all pale skin and freckles, with long blonde hair and smiling blue eyes that infected you with laughter. Together they'd explored the crumbling ruins that dotted the island, and her fascination and boundless enthusiasm over the remnants of a civilisation so ancient had been contagious. She'd made him feel guilty that even as a student of archaeology he tended to take his country's rich history for granted. Yet at the same time she'd also made him feel proud to be Greek. She had been beautiful, vibrant and spirited—and, as it turned out, fickle.

He exhaled a long breath he hadn't realised he'd been holding and stretched back travel-weary shoulders into the wide first-class seat.

The plane touched down and taxied to the terminal, finally pulling to a halt. Everyone around him was stirring, impatient from the long flight and eager to clear Customs in the least amount of time. A smiling flight attendant appeared at his arm with his jacket.

He nodded his thanks and forced his mind back to the present.

That spring was a long time ago, and right now he had more pressing problems to think about. His place was not here. He belonged back in Greece. And as soon as he had sorted out this unusual bequest that was exactly where he was headed.

CHAPTER TWO

ALEX opened the office door and slammed into her past.

Nick Santos!

She had to be dreaming. Nick was back home in Athens, running the family engineering empire. He had no business here in Sydney, standing in the foyer of the Xenophon Property Group.

Especially not today, with the office reopening after Aristos's heart attack and funeral, when she was already days behind in getting out the monthly rental invoices, and with the new boss—some far-flung relative—expected at any time.

Not today? Who was she kidding? Not ever.

But it couldn't be Nick.

She blinked, but when she opened her eyes he was still there.

And it was still Nick.

Strange how there was no way she could mistake him—how she could be so absolutely positive, even after all this time. Even though he was standing there with his back to her, talking to Sofia, still she knew it was him—sensed it was him—with just a glimpse of profile and the wave of thick, dark hair licking at the collar of his oh-so-white shirt. Knew it from his stance, manly and confident. Knew it in the message her heart was suddenly beating.

Adrenalin danced with her pulse, readying her for fight or flight. *No contest.* There was no way her feet would move forward. Not even the welcoming scent of the coffee machine's fresh brew could beckon her inside. She would back out right now, quickly, and he would never see her. Maybe by the time she came back he'd be gone, back out of her life, back into her past where he belonged.

She let her arm go slack on the door, letting it fall back towards her. Maybe, if she was quiet…

'There you are,' Sofia called, stepping out from behind his shoulder, looking every part the grieving daughter in her black silk skirt suit, her dark hair tied back into a sleek, high ponytail. And before she'd had a chance to respond he'd spun around, arresting her retreat with the sheer impact of his features so that the only movement she was capable of was the involuntary quiver that descended her spine. His dark eyes narrowed, his gaze sweeping her from top to toe before settling on her face. Then his nostrils flared as his lips curved ever so slightly.

'So it is you,' he stated, his chin kicking up a notch.

She swallowed hard. In the eight-plus years since she'd seen Nick she'd often imagined what their first words would be and how he would say them if ever they met again. Not once had she imagined Nick would coldly and dispassionately come out with something like, *'So it is you.'*

'Who were you expecting?' she said, finally convincing her muscles there was no way out of it but to push open the door and enter the lobby. 'Kylie Minogue?'

She winced inwardly at the harshness of her words. *Damn, but how were you supposed to think in situations like this?*

'Alex?' Sofia turned from one to the other, confusion apparent on her face. 'I want to introduce you to my cousin, Nick Santos, who arrived yesterday. But...am I missing something here?'

She couldn't talk. Her throat too tight, her mouth ashen. And all the while Nick just kept on watching her intently, until she felt pinned down in the accusing gaze of his bottomless dark eyes. He had a score to settle with her; that much his hard-edged glare made clear. Aside from that, he was obviously as unimpressed at seeing her as she was stunned at seeing him.

It was Nick who finally broke the impasse.

'Alexandra and I have met before. Haven't we?'

Under his continuing scrutiny the laptop in her hand suddenly felt unbearably heavy, threatening to slip from her damp palm. She screwed her fingers tighter around the handle till her fingernails dug painfully but reassuringly into her skin. That was her laptop taken care of. Now she just had to focus on making sure her knees held up.

'I guess so,' she managed at last. 'At least I'm pretty sure we have. It was such a long time ago.'

A muscle twitched in Nick's cheek.

'Am I so hard to remember?'

Not as hard as you are to forget. The thought sprang from nowhere and, as much as Alex hated the truth of it, it was undeniable. Long nights alone, remembering their shared time back on Crete and wishing things could have turned out differently, were testament to that.

He hadn't forgotten either. But the way he looked at her now told her he was remembering different things—like the way she'd turned her back on him. The way she'd left him cold.

She took a deep breath, but Sofia was too impatient to wait for her response in a conversation that was obviously far too personal for her liking.

'Spill the beans, you two. So how do you know each other?'

Nick's eyes bored into Alex. The cold heat of them was like a kick in the gut.

'How about it? Or are you having trouble remembering that too?'

She raised her chin a fraction and shifted her gaze to Sofia. Her brain was still in shock at seeing Nick after all this time, and it was much easier trying to think while she wasn't looking directly at him. Where the damning questions in his eyes couldn't reach her.

And she had to think. Had to calm down. Sofia was still raw from the shocking death of her father. Even under the mask of her professionally applied make-up the shadows and puffiness around her eyes were all too evident. Sofia certainly didn't need Alex's baggage on top of her own.

'Crete. About—' She stopped and licked her lips. *No need to be too specific.* 'Some years ago. I was on holiday with my family. Nick was working in his university break on an archaeological dig. We met at the palace of Minos.'

'Cool,' said Sofia, although Alex noted the word she'd used mirrored her tone. Sofia was obviously less than impressed. 'So, did you know he was related to Aristos?'

'No, I had no ide—'

A cold ooze of dread rolled over her. *God, no!* Not *that* relative of Aristos? Not the one who was taking over the company?

'Way cool! Then I hardly have to introduce you to each other. That's going to make it easier, with you guys working together.'

Alex couldn't think of anything less cool as her world tilted and spun. When the direct line in her office rang, it was all she could do not to run and answer it.

'Excuse me,' she said instead, adding, 'I'm expecting this call. We'll have to catch up later.' Then she moved as quickly as she could while desperately trying to keep her balance on a planet that was shifting further off axis with every step.

She shut the door, plonked her laptop on the desk

and somehow dealt with the phone call while all the time her brain was registering only two words. Nick—*here*!

One hour later, Alex was still staring at the walls, the screensaver on her laptop the only sign of life in the room. How long she could stay secreted away in her office, she didn't know—but she'd do whatever it took to have as little to do with Nick Santos as possible, and until she had some sort of plan she didn't want to go anywhere near him.

It was weird, seeing him after so many years. Strange how they'd both thought themselves so grown up back then. He had seemed so strong and so much a man. At twenty-one he'd been more worldly and experienced than her. Yet now she could see how young they'd been. For it was obvious that the boy had become a man.

He looked every part the professional businessman. Gone was the long fringe that he'd used to flick out of his eyes with the toss of his head, replaced by a short, slick style. His dark features, even back then resonant with hidden depths, now seemed to sit more comfortably in a more mature face. Even his shoulders seemed broader.

He was a different person, clearly, from that boy she'd met so long ago.

Well, she'd changed too.

She was older, wiser, a mother.

The mother of his son!

Something like a garbled cry escaped from her lips.
Jason!

How in heaven's name was she going to prevent
him from finding out about Jason?

CHAPTER THREE

A BRIEF knock on her door made her look up, only to find Nick filling the space where the door had been.

She swallowed.

'What do you want?'

Nick took a step into her office, eyebrows raised.

'Is that any way to greet an old friend? It's not as if we're strangers after all.'

'It was a long time ago. You almost feel like a stranger.'

He hesitated. Tilted his head to one side.

'You have no idea how I feel, Alexandra.'

His words, and the flat way in which he delivered them, made her swallow. But that was nothing to how she felt when he moved closer to the desk. Panic pooled in her every cell.

Then he suddenly turned. For just a second Alex felt relief, but only for a second. She heard Nick mutter, 'Just wait—I'll be with you soon,' before closing the door. Alex caught a flash of black as Sofia, looking indignant, rushed by, then it swung shut and Nick wheeled and moved back across the office until he was standing just across the desk from her.

And then he was looking down at her—dark,

threatening and dangerous—and all Alex could think about was the pressure bearing down on top of her.

The pressure of being confronted by this man, her first love—*her first lover*—the pressure of knowing he was part of Aristos's world and had never been a real part of hers—the pressure of knowing the secret that lay between them like a chasm.

The chair-back pressed into her as she attempted, however fractionally, to increase the distance between them.

'Alexandra—'

She squeezed her eyes shut. The way he still said her name, just as he had back then, squeezing out the syllables till they seemed to curl in his rich, Mediterranean accent. Nobody had ever said her name like Nick had those weeks in Crete. It had made her feel sexy back then.

Only now she couldn't let it affect her. She was all grown up and things like that were the stuff of teenagers and holidays and holding hands. She was over it.

'Alexandra.'

She sucked in a breath, opened her eyes and forced what she hoped would pass as a businesslike expression onto her face.

'I guess you'll need to check the accounts, find out how the company is going. Our tax position—all that stuff.'

He blinked slowly. 'There's time for that later.'

'Good,' Alex said, a little too fast. 'I'm kind of

busy at the moment...' She shuffled a few papers on her desk for effect. 'Maybe I could drop the accounts into you later? I imagine you want to get things sorted out here and head back to Greece as soon as you can.'

Nick's eyes narrowed as he propped himself down on the edge of her desk and leaned dangerously close to her.

'I can see you're in the middle of something very important,' he whispered conspiratorially, nodding towards the computer. She followed his gesture and felt her cheeks heat till she was sure they matched the colour of the rosy-coloured pipe powering a cubic path around her computer screen.

Her hand reached out on impulse, but she snatched it back short of the keyboard. Better the screensaver right now than her desktop. Not with a photograph of Jason beaming out from it.

She looked up at him and grabbed a breath, anxious to steer the conversation to safe territory—wherever that might be.

'I was thinking...'

Both his eyebrows went up this time and he leaned over to swipe a pen from right in front of her, getting so close as to fill her senses with the subtle scent of his cologne overlaying the unmistakable essence of man. For a second it took her breath away, her line of thought erased, and she had no choice but to sit and watch as he began to tap the pen against the fingers of his other hand.

'Very reassuring to hear my uncle employed people

who can think.' He looked around, assessing the pale honey-coloured walls, the bookshelves and filing cabinets, as if taking an inventory. 'But what do you actually do in this spacious office of yours?'

His jibe focused her attention once more, and she straightened her spine, forced her head up higher. 'I imagine you've already discussed the staff and our responsibilities with Sofia.'

The pen kept tapping.

'I want to hear it from you.'

It was impossible not to feel intimidated by the man. From the edge of her desk he dominated the space before her, looming large and much too close. She looked up at him, feeling her eyes narrow as she tried to work out where he was coming from. No doubt he already had plans in mind for the company. Where did she fit in with those plans?

She needed this job. With a brand-new mortgage to her name, the first chance she'd had to find a real home for her and Jason, now she needed it more than ever. Aristos hadn't been the easiest boss, but the chance to get out of their poky flat and into a real house with a real backyard was worth anything her former boss had been able to dish out. Now that Nick was the boss, what would he dish out?

'All right. I'm Financial Administrator for the Xenophon Group. I've been here for almost two years, though I haven't been doing this job all that time.'

The pen stopped tapping. 'No. That's what Sofia said. You started out on Reception—is that right?'

Before she could answer she noticed the beat of the pen start up again and felt herself frown. If he was trying to get on her nerves he was doing an excellent job.

'But then the previous two accountants left...?' The query was apparent in his eyes. 'They were no good?'

She shook her head. 'I'm sorry, but your uncle wasn't the easiest person to get on with. He was a demanding boss.'

'My uncle started out with nothing and built a fortune in property worth millions. Of course he would expect a lot from his employees.'

'Of course he did. And he got that—and more. But he was difficult as a boss. Impossible at times. If he was in the office he was shouting. In both cases they were good accountants, but Aristos was always shouting at them for one thing or another—I don't think he trusted them to look after his affairs—and they just got sick of it. In the end they walked out, one after the other. The second one only lasted three months. Someone had to fill the gap immediately, and Sofia offered to look after Reception if I would do it. I'd been helping both of them out and it really wasn't such a big deal.'

'And Aristos didn't employ another accountant? Why would he keep a receptionist in such a position of responsibility?'

Alex bristled. 'Maybe because I do the job well.'

He didn't look convinced.

'If it's any consolation, I think Aristos was surprised too. He was intending to advertise, but the employment agency didn't seem too confident they could find the right person for this job—word had got back to them, obviously—and things here were going well. I was already studying for a business diploma at night—so he was relieved not to have to find someone else.'

And pay them accountant's wages. If there was one thing Aristos loved more than bellowing his commands it had been a bargain, and with her he'd got a cheap accountant—even with the extra he'd reluctantly agreed to pay over her former receptionist's salary.

'Funny, but I don't remember the young Alexandra looking forward to spending her life as some beancounter.'

Alex went rigid. She'd relaxed a little, talking about her job, thinking about things present. He'd just transported her slap-bang into the past. A past she'd rather steer clear of now.

'Funny, but I don't think of myself as a "beancounter".' She ploughed on, ignoring the black look he threw her. 'Besides, I don't think I knew what I wanted back then.'

She certainly hadn't known what she'd *need* back then. Had had no idea she'd have a son to support with no chance of finishing school for years. Had never realised how hard it would be to try and manage time with her son when she had a full-time job and night school study. Hadn't known how hard it would be to earn enough money to put a deposit on an ageing two-bedroom bungalow in the suburbs.

He tapped the pen loudly once more, this time on her desk, snapping her out of her thoughts. 'And Aristos didn't shout at you?'

She laughed a little, relieved he was talking about the more recent past once more. 'Sure, he shouted. He shouted at everyone—including Sofia. But as a property investor, he wrote the book. I learned a lot working for him.'

It was true. It might have been unbearable, just as it had proved for the former employees, except she'd needed the money and the experience more. A few years in this job and she'd be finished with her diploma and could get a decent job with better pay. Aristos had given her a chance and she'd grasped it. For all his faults, he'd at least given her this opportunity, and she owed him for that.

But Aristos was gone, and it was his nephew now sitting in front of her. And yet still she hadn't even offered the merest of condolences.

'The news about your uncle must have come as quite a shock. I'm sorry...'

He watched her for a second, but it was as if his eyes were shuttered. Then he slammed the pen down on the desk in the same instant as he heaved himself away. He took a few steps, one hand rubbing his nape.

'It was a shock—but nothing compared to what Sofia is contending with. To have lost her mother to cancer a decade ago, and now to lose her father so suddenly...' He sighed, and for a moment looked so lost in his own thoughts that she sensed there was more to his statement than just compassion for his cousin.

He turned suddenly to face her, his eyes dark and fathomless. 'My mother, Helena, was step-sister to Aristos. She died some six years back herself. Aristos and my father were as close as brothers while they were both alive, even though I didn't know him that well.'

Alex swallowed. She'd never met Nick's parents—but she'd heard enough about his father way back then to scare her socks off. It came as no surprise that he was related, even by marriage, to Aristos.

Even so, they had been Nick's parents. *Jason's grandparents.* And now he would never have the opportunity to meet them. Guilt stabbed deeper inside her.

When would she stop paying for the decision she'd made so long ago? The decision she knew was the right one.

'Your parents...I didn't know...' She shook her head. 'What happened to your father?'

'Why should you know?' he asked sharply, as if she had no right. Then his voice softened. 'About two years ago now he drove off a bridge. Drowned before he could be rescued.'

'That's awful,' said Alex. When they'd been on Crete both Nick's and her own parents had been alive. It had been less than nine years ago and now Nick's parents had gone. How long before hers too were no longer here?

She'd see them at Christmas, when they were planning to travel across the country from Perth to visit. But that was still weeks away. She'd call them tonight. The thought that they wouldn't be there for ever...it was unimaginable.

To be so alone... She sucked in a breath. As she had countless times before, she thanked her lucky stars her sister Tilly had also chosen to make her home in Sydney, to pursue her growing wedding planner career. At least she had some family close by. For all that she was struggling to make ends meet, at least she had someone to turn to, someone to give her moral support when things got too bad. Sofia had no one. And nor, it seemed, did Nick.

'I really am sorry. I had no idea.'

Nick stopped pacing and stood, propping his arms on the back of the visitor's chair. His exhale came out like a sigh. 'In a way it was a release for my father. I think he'd stopped living years before, when Stavros died.' His eyes bore the pain of loss and tragedy, and as they sought and found hers something connected between them.

He remembered. She could tell.

It was the last time they'd spoken. She'd rung, flushed with excitement at her news. After months of hiding the truth she'd finally held her baby—*their baby*—and known that in spite of all the powerful reasons why she shouldn't tell him she simply had to. He had a right to know he was a father. That he had a son.

Only when she'd finally made the connection to Nick's house it had been to find the family in mourning for the eldest son.

How did you say, *I'm sorry your brother is dead and congratulations—today you became a father* in the same sentence? How did you drop a bombshell like that into a grieving family and expect them to embrace a new branch of the family they didn't know existed and wouldn't want to know? Not after what had happened to Stavros.

Realising that no one in his family would ever believe her, let alone welcome her news, Alex had hung up the phone, keeping her secret and knowing she'd never speak to Nick again.

Stavros had been killed, Nick had become the new heir to the family fortune, and it had been obvious there could never be a future with Nick—neither for her nor their newborn child.

Alex rubbed her arms. It was cold in here. She'd have to check the wall thermostat. But not now. Not until Nick had left her office and there was no chance of getting anywhere near him.

His eyes narrowed until they glinted and he straightened behind the chair.

'Something frightened you away. Is that it? Is that why you never returned my calls after that?' His words speared through her consciousness to places she'd rather not go. It was one thing to know she'd done the right thing. It was another thing entirely to have to explain it.

'Nick, I don't think we need to rehash all that. It's in the past. Let it stay there.'

'No. I think the least you can do is offer me an explanation.'

Alex stiffened in her chair. What relationship they'd had had been over for the better part of nine years, and here he was, larger than life, insisting on the whys and wherefores. Talk about inflated male ego! As if it mattered now.

'Let it go—'

'Was it another man?' He threw a glance to her left hand. 'You're not married, but was there someone back then?'

'Look, it's not important—'

'So it *was* another man. Why else would you just stop communicating? I tried to call you. I wrote to you.'

'We moved—'

'*I* didn't. You knew where to find me.' Accusation was layered thickly in his eyes. 'So why else would you never return my calls? Why never answer my letters unless you were too busy in someone else's bed?'

Enough! Incensed, Alex pushed herself up from her chair. She'd had enough of looking up to him. And she was sick of putting up with his slurs.

'Drop it, Nick.'

'I demand to know what happened!'

Alex glared at him, at that moment totally wondering how she'd ever held the notion that she'd loved this guy. 'I grew up.' *The hard way.* 'End of story.'

'It's no wonder you've never married, if that's the way you treat men. If you want my advice—'

Alex's hands curled into tight fists.

'As a matter of fact,' she cut in, 'I don't want your advice. I don't need your advice. And, given that you don't appear to be married either, are you completely sure you're in any position to give advice?'

In that moment Nick's face might have been cast from concrete. It seemed all harsh angles and rigid planes, and she could tell he was battling to keep the fury he was obviously feeling under control.

Well, bully for him. She was furious too. How dared the brute think he could waltz back into her life and start criticising?

A muscle in his cheek twitched. 'You've changed, Alexandra. You are still as beautiful as you were then, maybe even more so, but you've changed on the inside.'

I've had to! Her mind told her to remain strong and

resolute. It shouldn't matter what he said about her looks. And it wouldn't. *She wouldn't let it.*

She sucked in one unsteady breath, battled to get her speech back to something resembling normality. 'Please leave. I have work to do.'

When he remained there motionless it was obvious that he had no intention of complying with her request. If she wanted him out of her office she was going to have to make him leave herself.

She stepped around the desk. 'I'll see you to the door.'

There was at least four feet between them and she'd mentally assessed the risk. There was no chance of them coming close to each other. In a moment she'd be safely behind the open door, ushering him out, and some sort of peace could again reign in her office.

Halfway there his hand seized her arm, halting her in her tracks. His grip burned, his hand looking so large on her forearm that her heart tripped. She'd known that touch before, known the strength of it, and yet the tenderness that could accompany it. Only there was none of that tenderness now. Now she sensed anger, and her heart raced fast and loud as adrenalin kicked in once again.

'Alexandra,' he said, half demanding, yet half imploring. She closed her eyes briefly and willed herself not to be affected by the mere sound of her name.

'Let me go.' Her voice sounded amazingly calm and level and she took strength from that.

But he didn't let go. His grip changed. Instead of

just holding her, it was tugging her, forcing her closer
to him. They were close enough now that she could
catch the tang of his subtle cologne, the faint remnants of his coffee, all infused with the scent of
man—angry man.

'Alexandra?'

Her elbow was still locked, her arm held firm, as
she looked up into his eyes. Breath caught in her
throat as anger was replaced by something else.
Something darker and far more dangerous.

In that instant he relaxed his hold, and with the
pressure off she immediately lost balance, swaying on
her heels, only to be pulled unceremoniously back
into him in the next moment.

Impacting against his chest was like colliding with
solid rock—only warm and smooth and, oh, so familiar. She sucked in a deep breath, her senses reeling
from so much male so close. Something in the back
of her mind registered that Nick hadn't changed that
much. Somehow this was just the way she remembered he'd felt back then. Maybe just a little broader
and more developed, but just the way she'd imagined,
late at night when she couldn't sleep, thinking how
he'd feel now.

Only this was all wrong!

'Let me go!' she urged, trying to push him away.
But his arms snaked around her, holding her tight.

She pulled her head back to look up at him. 'What
the hell do you think you're doing? This is harassment. You can't try these caveman tactics here.'

'Harassment?' His tone mocked and his eyes held a teasing glint.

An unkind, teasing glint she registered. Life had apparently left Nick bitter.

Then she realised he was moving, swaying ever so gently, the fingers of his hands stroking her back while his arms still kept their vice-like grip. The motion was disarming, gently soothing and strangely sensual.

'Hardly harassment,' he went on. 'Don't you remember how it was between us? We're simply sharing an embrace, and perhaps a kiss for old times' sake.'

Alarm bells went off in her head. *No way.* No way would she kiss him. He couldn't be serious.

Firmly she pressed her hands against Nick's chest and pushed for all she was worth. 'I have no intention of sharing *anything* with you.'

He must have seen something in her face because he looked down at her strangely, stopped swaying and abruptly let her go. Alex wheeled away before he had a chance to change his mind, her breath coming thick and fast. She grabbed hold of the door handle and screwed it round, yanking open the door for him.

He stood for a moment, taking a couple of deep breaths. He strode to the door, came so close to her she was afraid he might just kiss her anyway. 'There was once a time you would beg me to kiss you, again and again.'

She pushed back her shoulders, tried as best as she

could to look him in the eye—even though he had a head start of six inches on her.

'Times have changed.'

He reached out a hand and she flinched, but his fingers moved to the side of her face to tuck behind her ear a strand that had come loose from her twisted up hair. She swallowed, otherwise motionless, as they traced a path down her cheek before he gently but firmly pinched her chin between his thumb and forefinger.

'Not for the better, it seems.'

He flicked off his fingers and she fumbled for something to say.

'I...I'll get some financial statements ready for you. I guess you'll want to get things organised quickly, to allow you to get back to Greece as soon as you can.'

She could swear he almost smiled then. A smile that didn't touch anywhere near his eyes.

'Who said anything about going home to Greece? I may just decide to stay the full six months Aristos's will requires.'

Then he was finally gone. Alex shut the door and let herself collapse against it. It was barely eleven in the morning and she felt as if she'd just run a marathon.

How in the world would she survive six months?

CHAPTER FOUR

ALEX stood on the sidelines, clutching her thirty-eight-millimetre camera and waiting while the coach said a few final words to the team, grateful that Sofia had chosen this particular afternoon to show Nick around some of their properties, allowing her to slip off half an hour early unnoticed.

After an emotionally draining day Alex was more anxious than ever to be with her son. This was *their* night—hers and Jason's—with no study or classes to intrude. Just for now she'd rather not have to explain that to Nick.

She took a couple of deep breaths and rolled her shoulders, easing away some of the strain of the day, before putting the cap back on the camera lens. She'd taken enough shots today to fill another page in the album she was keeping—the albums and video recordings she was using to record every event and growth phase in Jason's life.

The albums and videos she was one day intending to show his father.

Only his father was here. *Now.*

How the hell was she supposed to deal with that? Somehow she had to work out a way of coping with Nick's presence in the office. It was only day one, but from the tension evident between them today it was difficult to believe they could ever work together comfortably as colleagues. It certainly wasn't going to happen with this huge secret hanging over them.

If he was ever going to see these pictures and videos, eventually—inevitably—she'd have to tell him the truth. Only things were so complicated. Now she couldn't just tell him about their son. Now she'd also have to explain why she had never told him at the start. Never told him she was pregnant with his child. Never told him he was a father.

And there was no easy way to do it.

Yet the longer Nick stayed, the more inevitable it would become that he would find out she had a son. Once he knew she had a son...how long would it take before he worked out the rest and know she had kept the truth from him?

Her heart kicked up a beat. Just maybe there was a chance Nick wouldn't see the resemblance. Close relatives didn't always notice such things, did they? After all, people were always telling her that in spite of Jason's dark hair and eyes he was still unmistakably hers, even though she couldn't see it herself. Maybe Nick would be the same?

She looked closer at the huddle of players. Jason had his head cocked to one side, listening intently to the coach's words, concentrating hard, his eyes dark and intense, and as she looked at him a chill whipped up her spine.

Her son stood there focused and determined—

every part a miniature version of Nick. Alex took a deep breath and tried to steady her heartbeat back into a normal rhythm.

She'd been kidding herself. There was no way Nick could deny the resemblance. She sighed. That left only one course of action. It wasn't going to be easy, but she'd have to do it—and the sooner the better.

The team huddle broke up and Jason turned and waved, smiling as he ran towards her until he collided at force into her chest, swinging her with his momentum. She breathed in the happy, warm smell of him, mingled with grass and earth, and caught his laughter as he clutched on tightly around her neck and they spun each other round.

'Pizza!' he squealed.

She laughed and stood up, catching his hand in hers as she turned to the car. 'I hope you spent some time out there thinking about soccer, and not just what you wanted for dinner.'

'Yeah,' he said, tugging her along. 'A bit.'

Four pieces of pizza later, Jason started to slow down between bites. After a brief hesitation he reached for his cola and took a long drink. 'Can you fish, Mum?'

Alex blinked and put her piece down. It was noisy in the pizza bar and she wasn't sure she'd heard correctly. 'You mean with a rod and reel?'

Jason nodded and studied the remaining pieces before reaching for the one with the most olives, despite it being the furthest away.

'I've been known to catch the odd fish, sure.'

Jason focused on his next mouthful before continuing. 'I thought so. I told them you could do anything, but they still said I couldn't come.'

'You told who? And couldn't come where?' she asked, secretly pleased that Jason still had such faith in her.

'Matt and Jack. They're going fishing one weekend with their dads. They said I could have come but you were a girl and you wouldn't know how to fish.'

'That's a shame,' she said, feeling more than slightly put out. 'Did you want to go?'

'Sort of. The camping out sounded the best bit, though.'

'Ah,' she said, getting some idea of the real reason why they might be uncomfortable with a woman along. 'I know why they didn't want us to go.'

'Why?'

She smiled. 'Well, how would they feel when we caught all the fish?'

'I knew it.' Jason leaned back in his chair and surveyed with only half interest the few remnants left in the pizza box. 'I told them it wouldn't make any difference even if I had a dad, because we'd still catch the most too.' Then he burped loudly, clapped his hand over his mouth and collapsed into a fit of giggles.

Alex laughed too, but inside felt his words as a boot to her heart. Hot tears stung her eyes.

It's the shock, she tried to tell herself as she

brushed away the evidence with the back of her hand, pretending they were laughter induced. Naturally she would be feeling more sensitive than usual after Aristos's sudden death and the arrival of Nick on the scene. Why else would she be crying into her pizza at dinnertime?

But, despite what she wanted to believe, part of her knew there was more to her tears than that. Once again she was reminded that no matter how she tried to be both mother and father to Jason, to provide him with the balance his young life required, there would be times when she just couldn't be both.

Jet lag, Nick decided. It had to be jet lag.

Why else would his legs be so unresponsive and his body so stressed and lethargic? Three kilometres into his run along the foreshore, it was obvious he wasn't going to make his usual ten. The rhythm wasn't there, his breathing was forced, and the power just wasn't happening.

And he needed to run. Needed to clear the fog that was clouding his brain, the fog that sprang from changing time zones and hemispheres—and from a girl he should have forgotten long ago.

Who was he trying to kid? She was hardly a girl any more. One touch had confirmed that. His breath caught in his throat, he coughed and shot his rhythm to hell again. In rebellion, he cursed, kicking out one foot at the sand, spraying the heavy salt-encrusted grains far and wide, scattering seagulls up into the ever lightening sky.

Breath rasped and scratched his throat. He needed sleep. Long, uninterrupted sleep. Instead last night he'd been plagued with visions of a leggy teenager, sitting cross-legged and smiling up at him from the midst of a field of yellow wild flowers, her long blonde hair almost liquid in the gentle spring breeze.

She'd been nervous. But she'd come to meet him willingly, knowing that this was the day—their last together—and her shyness had faded under his touch and they'd taken each other to a place they'd always share.

Or so he'd thought.

Maybe he'd got it wrong back then. From the way Alexandra acted now, it was clear she wasn't interested in sharing the time of day with him. He smiled to himself.

The way she'd reacted when he'd suggested staying in Australia! She obviously couldn't wait for him to get out of her life. He didn't even know why he'd said that; he had no intention of staying here. Although it was more than obvious that Sofia was keen he should hang around a while.

Maybe he should.

So far Dimitri was insisting that all was well with the business in Athens, and it was clear that Sofia needed his support here. Maybe that wouldn't be as onerous as he'd first expected. Somewhere along the line Sofia had transformed herself from a pestering child into a dark-haired beauty. Perhaps it wouldn't hurt him to stick around a while—at least until she'd had time to come to terms with her loss.

A thin smile found its way to his lips as another reason to stay crystallised. For there was something infinitely satisfying about making Alexandra think she was not going to be rid of him too easily.

But then, that was foolish thinking. He wasn't here to settle scores. He was here to make sure the business functioned well and prospered long into the future. He should be thinking instead whether there was even a place for her in the operation.

If he was going to leave the business in sound hands it was clear there'd have to be someone pretty damned capable in the financial area. Would a receptionist-cum-bookkeeper make the grade? He doubted it. It might be better to get someone better qualified in and just let her go. Although the employment agencies had had no success so far.

Maybe it would be better getting Dimitri to come out from Greece. He would know what the job required, so they could employ the right person.

Gulls wheeled overhead and a lonely swimmer hauled himself from the water nearby, shaking jewelled droplets from his body as he surged out of the shallows.

A swim. Maybe that was what Nick needed to clear his head of this infernal jet lag. Lord knows, the run didn't seem to be helping. He turned back the way he had come and headed along the beach.

*   *   *

'He's cute, don't you think?'

Alex looked up from her computer screen, in the middle of typing her letter. 'Who's cute?' she asked innocently, keeping her face deliberately schooled as she minimised her computer screen. But Sofia was too busy closing the door to notice anything. She grabbed one of the visitor's chairs by the arm and pulled it up close to the desk, hunkering down conspiratorially, her elbows on the desk, cupping her chin. She was grinning from ear to ear.

'Nick, silly. Who else around here could I mean?'

Alex smiled indulgently. While 'cute' wasn't exactly the word that sprang to mind whenever she thought about Nick, it was obvious who Sofia was referring to. Apart from the two of them, the office only employed a part-time woman for the phones, for whenever Sofia had had enough of playing receptionist, and an ageing property manager who looked after maintenance issues.

Still, she feigned surprise. 'Oh, him. Sure, he's not bad.'

It was easy to play along. Sofia was the happiest she'd seen her since her father had died. If having Nick here did that for her, then at least something good would come from his visit. With no one else to turn to, Sofia deserved it.

'I think he likes me.'

Alex's breath snagged in her throat. *Oh, please, I don't want to hear this!*

She somehow forced a bare smile to her face. 'Of course he likes you. You're his cousin. You're a nice girl. Why wouldn't he like you?'

She shook her head. 'No, you don't get what I mean. I mean he *likes* me. You know—like, seriously likes me.'

'That's...nice.' Alex wondered what else she was expected to say. She looked at the girl sitting opposite, her dark eyes shining with hope in her impeccably made-up face, her insanely long acrylic fingernails painted the exact shade of her crimson lips.

Sofia had never had the greatest history with boyfriends, and little wonder, given her domineering father and his ability to drive away potential suitors with a single bellow. If only his interest had been motivated by his daughter's welfare. Instead, Alex suspected, he'd always had the future of the Xenophon Group foremost in his mind. Whoever married his daughter and sole heir would end up with the fruits of Aristos's labour. How could any mere male qualify for such bountiful reward?

And then along came Nick, apparently with Daddy's blessing, and for the first time in her life Sofia thought she was onto a winner.

Sofia and Nick. Why did that seem such an unlikely pairing? And why should she even care? It wasn't as if she had any claim on the man, after all.

'I was wondering,' Sofia said, 'if you could help me—while he's out for a little while, talking to some of the tenants?' She tilted her head to one side, making her large gold double-hoop earrings jangle. 'Seeing you know Nick much better than me, what with being old friends and all.'

Alex shook her head. 'You've got the wrong idea. That was a long time ago.'

'But I haven't seen him since I was six, and he hardly took any notice of me. Even though way back then I thought he was gorgeous. I just thought you might have some idea of what he likes, you know. You must have talked about something when you were in Crete together. What did you guys get up to anyway?'

The breath left Alex's lungs so fast it made her cough. What on earth would Sofia think if she told her the truth? *I gave him my virginity and he took me to heaven.* No, definitely more information than Sofia needed to know. And much more information than Alex needed to be reminded of. Besides, they had done other things on Crete—it was just hard to focus on them now. Now that Nick was here. She licked her lips, buying time.

'You know—the usual things one does over there. We visited ruins and museums. Remember, Nick was studying an archaeology unit back then. No doubt he's still interested in the subject. Why don't you ask him about it?'

Sofia screwed up her nose. 'I guess. But that's not really what I had in mind.' She fidgeted with her bangles, then checked her nails. 'I don't know—does he have a favourite colour or something?'

Alex smiled to herself, instantly transported back to Crete.

Nick was holding her face in his hands, his lips close to hers, and the breeze was floating tendrils of her unbound hair around them both.

'The colour of the ocean, deep and clear. The colour of the sky, bright and endless. The colour of your eyes...'

She shook her head before she could think too much about the kiss that had followed.

'Blue.'

'Cool!' Sofia flicked her glance to her watch. 'I have to go shopping. He's taking me out to dinner tonight, and I just feel I need to get into something a little less—black.' She paused and pressed her lips together tightly, her eyes filmed with tears. 'It's just so hard being reminded all the time.'

'It's bound to be. A shopping trip is probably just what you need—but can I get you anything now?'

Sofia sniffed, and dabbed at her eyes with a tissue. 'No. I'll be fine. I have to get going. Nick and I have a lot of things to organise with the company and everything. You know how it is.' She rose and headed for the door, but halfway through stopped and turned around. 'He asked if you were coming, but I told him you probably wouldn't be able to get a babysitter at such short notice. He didn't seem to know you had a kid. You haven't told him?'

He knows!

Ice formed in her veins, yet somehow she managed to force her jaw to work.

'Ah. No, not yet. We haven't had much chance so far to catch up, that's all.'

Another sniff and a shrug later Sofia was gone. Alex sat stunned, her breathing shallow and fast, her mind racing.

He knows.

But how much did he know? How much had Sofia told him? She'd never shown much interest in children in general or in Jason in particular. What could she have given away? Maybe there was still time.

In a flash she maximised her computer screen and finished typing the letter before printing it off. She read it through once more and nodded. Perfect. All it needed was her signature.

She was doing the right thing; she was sure of it.

In a moment it was signed and sealed and ready to be dropped off on Nick's desk before he was back from seeing the tenants.

She took a deep breath and, suddenly parched, reached for her glass of water. It was empty. She stopped by the small office kitchenette to fill it, popping the envelope on the adjacent benchtop while she poured the cool spring water. She was standing at the dispenser, with her back to the door, when she felt it.

Something wasn't right.

Hairs prickled on the back of her neck and her heart belted out an erratic beat that reverberated in her head, spelling out exactly how she felt. *Scared.*

Quickly she turned, feeling his presence before there was so much as a sound.

Water sloshed over the glass's rim, but she hardly noticed or cared. 'Nick! You startled me.'

He was leaning against the doorway, hands in pockets. Strange how even in such a casual stance Nick could look all man. Relaxed, comfortable—*predatory.*

Slowly he peeled himself away from the doorway and moved closer.

There was no telling what he was thinking. His dark eyes were unfathomable. He stopped a couple of feet in front of her, filling all the remaining space in the tiny kitchenette. She swallowed. Until Nick moved she was stuck here, with a brimming glass of water the only thing between them. As defences went, it wasn't much, but somehow just holding it there made her feel better. If only she could hold her hand steady.

'Sofia took me for a tour of the properties yesterday.'

'Yes, I heard.'

'It's a large portfolio. I was impressed by the quality of the holdings.'

'That's good.'

Alex winced at her lame responses, but how was she supposed to concentrate with him in the room? It was all she could do to keep her hand from shaking and spilling some more water.

'I imagine it takes quite a bit of accounting skill to keep up with it all.'

'Not really,' she said, studying the glass and using all her powers of concentration to will it to stay level. 'Once the systems are in place—' *What am I thinking?* If he wanted to imply that she couldn't do the job, it would be in her interests to agree with him. She jerked her eyes up to meet his.

'Actually, you're right. It's very complic—'

Nick jumped back before the wave of spring water could collect him fair in the chest, and Alex realised she hadn't just kicked up her chin when she'd changed her response.

Even with his quick evasive action the water landed at his feet, beading droplets over the sculpted black leather of his Italian shoes. In a flash he relieved her of the glass, and its remaining contents, and deposited it on the benchtop alongside the letter—*his letter* while she stood there dumbfounded.

'You're jumpy, Alexandra.'

She looked up at him, preparing to apologise, but he took her shoulders in his large hands. Instantly every cell in her body seemed to contract and freeze.

'Do I make you so nervous?'

She sucked in a necessary breath—only to find the oxygen she so desperately required infused with the scent of this man. Heat replaced the coldness she'd been feeling, warming sensations and desires she'd thought long buried. Under her discount designer jacket and tailored shirt her breasts felt swollen and firm, aware of even the slightest brush of fabric over the points of her bra. And now that feeling coiled downwards, stirring feelings long since forgotten.

She sighed. There seemed little point in denying it. 'Yes, I guess you do.'

He laughed, softly and openly, his breath curling warm against her face as his thumbs gently traced the line of her collarbone, almost hypnotising her. The flesh tingled under his touch. Alex felt her eyelids flutter. Oh, God! He hadn't forgotten how to make her feel good, just as her body hadn't forgotten how to respond to his.

'But why, Alexandra, should I make you nervous? I am just a man. A man who, after all, you know—intimately.'

Something about the way he spoke made her look at him—really look at him. Why was he doing this to her? She willed her body not to be carried away by his touch, but that same body seemed intent on ignoring her. After all, this was just what she'd dreamed of, night after lonely night—being with Nick, enjoying his touch. Now her dreams had become reality, at least in part, and it was so hard to deny herself that for which she'd yearned so long.

Only she had to. Her lips felt desperate for moisture as she finally spoke.

'That was a long time ago. It's ancient history now.'

'Maybe. But sometimes the past can pave the way for the future. We were once good together. Is there any reason why we shouldn't be again—at least until I leave?'

'What?'

She dropped a shoulder and twisted out of his reach before he could react.

For just one moment his words had brought her an unexpected pleasure. For just one moment it had seemed he might still harbour some feelings for her.

In the next moment he'd shattered the illusion. 'Just what are you suggesting?'

He shrugged and leaned himself back against the cupboards, crossing his ankles, his hands resting on the bench behind. The relaxed position belied the expression on his face. His jaw was set and his eyes looked more calculating than ever.

'Simply that we fit together well—you know that. Why shouldn't we seek pleasure in each other? There's little enough to be found elsewhere in this world.'

'You expect me to sleep with you while you're here?'

He looked over at her, his lips tilted at one corner, his dark eyes resolute as he pushed himself away from the bench and took two paces towards her.

Instinctively her feet edged back.

'No, Alexandra. You have the wrong idea entirely. I don't expect you to sleep with me. I want you awake, very much awake. I don't expect we should get very much sleep at all.'

Alex could only swallow as he moved a step closer,

and then another, forcing her back against the small under-counter refrigerator. Only then did he stop— right in front of her.

'After all,' he continued, 'it's not as if you are a virgin, as I can attest. You're not married, and you've obviously had other partners. Sofia told me of your child. You expect me to believe that was the result of immaculate conception?'

Hot, angry tears pricked her eyes. Even if he didn't know that the child he referred to was his, there was no excuse for speaking to her that way. 'And that makes it okay, then, does it? I should be only too willing to fall into your bed?'

His eyes held hers as he curled one hand around one hip and then the other. Alex flinched, surprised by the move, and grabbed his forearms, trying to push them away. But his arms were like steel and couldn't be budged.

'I know the way I feel when I touch you. I know the way you respond to that touch. Can you deny that you would like me to touch you even more?'

He pulled her closer, making a mockery of her resistance.

'Can you deny that you want me in your bed?'

Alex felt his arms slide up behind her, pulling them even closer together.

He was right, in so many ways. His touch now was so much like it had been years before—firm, warm, *hot*. Back then one touch hadn't been enough. One touch had never been enough. Not when it had sparked desire and want and need. She couldn't deny that she would like him in her bed—hadn't she dreamed of just that over the last years?—but their lovemaking had never been callous then, and she wouldn't let it be reduced to that now.

Not when there was so much at stake.

Her face close to his, she delivered her answer in the steadiest voice she could muster. 'You're wrong. I don't want you in my bed.'

'Liar,' he said, smiling. 'Your body gives me a different answer.'

Before he'd finished talking he'd slipped one hand below her jacket, sliding it across the silk of her shirt and up to capture her breast. Her breath hissed in as his thumb almost casually stroked the peak of one hardened nipple. With his other hand he pulled her even closer to him, pressing her against his obvious hardness.

'Now tell me you don't want me.'

Alex's tongue met parched, dry lips as she battled to find strength she didn't feel. 'I don't want you— not like this.'

Her voice trembled, and without slackening his hold he stared down at her, disbelieving.

'Never like this,' she added, stronger this time.

A second later his hands slid out from under her jacket and he shrugged.

He'd let her go. But there was no time to congratulate herself—not before Nick was on the attack once more.

'So you might feel like this now. But have you realised just how hard it is going to be for you to keep denying this attraction between us as we work together, day after day?'

He smiled, looking entirely like a man sure he had just delivered his trump card. Alex gulped in air, trying to replace the oxygen he had scorched with just his touch.

'I don't see why that should be a problem,' she said in barely a whisper as she reached around him to retrieve the envelope. She held it up to him. 'Maybe you should read this.'

He looked at the blank envelope suspiciously. 'What's this?'

For the first time since his arrival Alex felt she had Nick at a disadvantage. It was a pleasant change, and one that brought a bittersweet smile to her face.

'My resignation,' she said. 'I'm leaving, Nick.'

CHAPTER FIVE

HE HELD the envelope, not opening it, all the while just glaring at her. Alex waited, the initial rush of adrenalin at delivering what should have been the killer punch evaporating as time strung out between them. When he finally spoke his words were barely more than an order.

'You can't.'

'Open it,' she urged. 'Read it.'

'You can't resign.'

'You don't want me here. You've made it plain you don't think I'm qualified to do the job. Well, you're right. You'd be much better off finding someone else.'

His head tilted to one side, his eyes sceptical. 'You don't believe that.'

Her shoulders lifted in a shrug, but that didn't mean she was ready to give in to him.

'What does it matter what I believe? I'm making it easy for you. I'm resigning. Now you're free to get in someone who you're sure can do the job.'

His eyes narrowed, calculating, *dangerous*, and then, without breaking eye contact, he ripped the envelope in two.

'What are you doing?' she cried in disbelief as he

tore it through again and scattered the pieces with a flick of his wrist in the general direction of the bin.

'Simple. I'm not accepting your resignation. You're staying.'

'I'm going. I'll print another copy, and another, if that's what it takes.'

'Don't bother. I'll do the same with them.'

'You can't make me stay.'

'I don't need to. You've done that yourself.'

'What do you mean?'

'Simple. You have a contract, Alexandra. A contract for two years, with more than eighteen months to run. And I'm holding you to it.'

Alex sucked in a sharp breath.

'I have no contract with you.'

'Your contract is with the Xenophon Group, and right now that means me.'

'But you don't want me here. Why are you doing this?'

'Because you know the company, Alexandra. Even when we get a qualified accountant to take over you will no doubt be useful for secretarial and...' his eyes took on a vicious gleam '...any other duties I may require.'

Alex felt as if the breath had been sucked from her, her pulse beating a storm through her veins as the meaning behind his words struck home.

'You can't be serious,' she whispered in a voice that sounded so flat and empty it mirrored her soul.

'Alexandra,' he said simply, as one might speak to

a child who couldn't comprehend something basic, 'you should know I'm *always* serious.'

Watching the lines of his face harden and set, she knew better than to doubt him. His intent was clear in the flare of his nostrils and the arrogant tilt of his jaw.

But he needn't think he had a monopoly on being serious! She gulped in air, fortifying herself for the battle she knew she had on her hands.

'Don't assume that just because I have to stay here I'll be doing anything other than my work. Because I won't.'

He smiled, then leaned back against the bench and twisted the wristband of his watch with his free hand, as if he was bored. That he looked partly amused only served to fuel her anger. She'd do anything to wipe that smile off his face.

'Really?' he said finally. 'And how can you be so sure of yourself?'

'Because, if you haven't already realised,' she replied, lifting her own chin a notch, 'I'm not the naïve seventeen-year-old you met on Crete.'

His smile deepened, his eyes raking over her.

He didn't have to do that. Look at her as if he was assessing just how much the intervening years had changed her, mentally comparing his memories of her then with the reality of her now.

'Just looking at you, I never thought for one moment that you were. But, in any event, I look forward to the challenge.' His eyes glittered, as if he'd won a major battle rather than just readied himself for the skirmish to come.

No doubt he thought it was only a matter of time before she fell into his bed. His arrogance alone was enough to ensure she wouldn't give in to his expectations.

'There's no challenge, Nick. It's a statement of fact. I'm not sleeping with you.'

Without waiting for his response, she willed herself to push past him and exit—only to almost crash into Sofia, laden with shopping bags, returning from her shopping expedition.

'Wait till you see what I've bought,' Sofia said, her smile wide and her cheeks flushed.

Normally Alex wouldn't have had the time or the inclination to be interested, but today was different. Today she could do with the diversion—and a reason for Nick not to follow her.

She smiled with a warmth she didn't feel as she ushered the girl into her office. 'Show me,' she invited, closing the door firmly after them.

'You have to tell him.' Tilly positioned the three sets of knives and forks around the small dining room table as she spoke, and only then looked up at her sister, as if impatient for a response. 'You *will* tell him?'

Alex tried to ignore her sister's glare and busied herself with the plates and salad. She'd made it through a whole week of putting up with Nick's constant presence in the office. A whole week of Nick's needling barbs. A whole week of Nick's dark eyes following her every movement.

One whole week! She wanted to congratulate herself. If she could make it through one week then maybe she could make it through two, or four, or however many weeks it took till he finally went home to Greece.

Couldn't Tilly see that? She was beginning to regret telling her sister anything. Only she'd been bursting to confide in someone. It was simply too much information to keep to herself. She opened the fridge, extracted the salad dressing from the door, and popped it down on the table.

'Alex!' repeated Tilly, sounding more agitated by the minute. 'You are going to tell him. He has a right to know. They *both* have a right to know.'

'Okay, I hear you.' She stole a glance out of the window. 'Is Jason still outside? He needs to wash up.'

'So you'll tell him, then? And Jason?'

Alex sighed and licked a trace of avocado from her fingers. 'You know, Tilly, Nick's going back to Greece. It could be in two months; it could be in two weeks. Is it really fair to tell either of them when Nick could just turn around and walk out of Jason's life?'

'You don't know that. He could decide to stay— and who knows? Maybe he'll even take you both back to Greece with him. I remember he was crazy about you when we were in Crete. You seemed to have the hots for him pretty bad too.'

Alex laughed—a low, brittle laugh. *Take them both back to Greece?* It didn't sound like the action of a man who had offered her casual sex for the duration of his visit. It didn't sound as if she figured in any long-term plans, with or without a child. 'I don't think so. Nick's changed. He seems—bitter—somehow.' She tried to remember the words he'd used—something about there being little pleasure in the world.

Nick had a hard edge that hadn't been there all those years ago. A hard edge no doubt caused by watching his family disappear around him—first his brother, then his mother and father. Aristos's death must have brought it all back in sharp relief.

And was her own hasty departure from their relationship also partly to blame? Nick had needed her and she'd abandoned him, not wanting to cause the family more pain than it already had to deal with. Was he trying to punish her now? To get back at her for that?

It wouldn't be fair if he was. She'd needed him more than ever back then. By denying that need she'd saved them more grief—only how was he to understand that?

'Anyway,' Tilly continued, 'whatever Nick chooses to do after he finds out he has a son—that's irrelevant as far as your decision is concerned. Despite whatever you think his reaction will be, he still has a right to know—and I think you know it.'

'But I have Jason to think of too. He's my first priority now.'

'So think of him! How will he feel if he finds out that his father spent time in Sydney, in close proximity to him, and yet you never told him he was here, let alone introduced him? Don't you think he'll feel just a tiny bit cheated?'

Alex opened her mouth, preparing to defend herself, but it was no good. She snapped it shut. Her sister was right. And when she thought about it that was exactly why she'd told her sister in the first place. Because she knew that Tilly would be impartial. That Tilly, in her naturally analytical way, would assess all the information and come up with what was the most fair, the most moral result. Even if it didn't seem like much of a solution for Alex.

But her sister was spot on. Alex would have to introduce Jason to his father and Nick to his son. Only how the heck was she supposed to do it? Especially with Nick appearing to bear such a grudge against her.

Not that Tilly would be much help there. She'd no doubt say that any interest or uninterest shown in her by Nick was irrelevant too. That Nick and Jason still had to know of each other's existence regardless. And she'd still be right.

Alex sighed. In a way Nick's resentment towards her should make it easier to break the news. He already thought little enough of her. What did she have to lose?

'Yeah, you're right. I'll have to tell them both.'

Tilly stopped, her glass of wine poised halfway to her lips.

'You'll tell them, then—when?'

Alex drew in a deep breath. 'I don't know. I can't just come out with it.'

'Can I make a suggestion, then? It's Jason's birthday in two weeks. Maybe it would be nice if Nick could be here for his party. Then you could all be together, just like a real family.'

Just like a real family! That was a joke. The three of them had never been any sort of family, let alone a real one. Alex nibbled at her lip.

'I don't know. What if Jason doesn't like him? What if Nick hates kids?'

Tilly reached out an arm and squeezed her sister's shoulder. 'So introduce them first. Go for a picnic or something. Anything. Of course you can't make them like each other, but Nick must have some redeeming features, surely?' She gazed at her sister pointedly. 'You certainly used to think so.'

Alex thought back to Crete and to the young man she'd fallen in love with—with his dark hair and dark eyes and a smile that had promised for ever. He'd been generous, kind and patient, and in no way flaunting his obvious wealth. She'd been in awe of his sheer magnetism, acutely aware even then of how her body responded to his, whether at a touch or a mere glance.

And Nick now? He seemed a world away from that young man—harder, more cynical—and yet still able to set her body alight with one look. Did pure sexual magnetism qualify as a redeeming feature?

No. It just made him all the more dangerous. But for Jason's sake she really hoped Nick still retained some of that generosity of spirit he'd displayed all those years ago. They were all going to need it.

The back door slammed and the tornado that was her son bowled into the house. 'What's for dinner, Mum? I'm starving.'

Alex smiled and stepped into the kitchen, relieved at the change of subject. 'Lasagne,' she said, opening the oven door, 'and it's ready, so go wash up.' She watched his rapidly departing back and shook her head.

How the hell was she going to tell him?

Tilly followed her into the kitchen, picked up the pile of plates and hesitated, as if sensing her sister's mood.

'You can do this,' she said.

Alex gently smoothed out the folds in the old papers with the flat of her hand, wishing she could iron out the creases in her own life just as easily. Her mouth twitched into a smile. *Some hope.* If anything, her life was about to get a whole lot rougher.

She looked down at the collection of letters and the pile of envelopes lying alongside the mussed ribbon and the old chocolate box she'd found after Tilly had gone home—when she was supposed to be putting away the laundry.

Letters from Nick. *Love letters.*

She looked at the stack of towels and sheets, still sunshine-fresh, sitting neglected on the floor nearby. She'd put them away in a moment—just as soon as she'd read one or two. She'd shoved the box in the back of the cupboard when she'd moved in, refusing to think about its contents. Now it seemed impossible to ignore.

Casting an eye through the nearby French doors, and satisfying herself that Jason, freshly bathed, was still happily attending to his weekend homework, Alex started to read.

The ink was faded in parts, and the words were sometimes difficult to make out in the folds, but the meaning and intent of the letters were crystal-clear, and as she began to read the years faded away.

She smiled when she looked over his earliest letters, written soon after their shared holiday. They were full of optimistic talk about how the archaeological dig he'd been working on in Crete had finished, what he was doing at university, how he missed her and when next they would have the chance to be together again.

In the months that followed the letters contained more family talk. He was increasingly worried about his brother, and the rift between him and his father over his unhappy marriage, and his anger at the woman who had forced him into it. He still missed Alex madly, he said, and worried that her letters seemed more distant, less personal.

Alex sighed as a single tear squeezed its entry into the world. He'd been right. She'd known about the baby coming by then, and known she couldn't tell him. Towards the end of the pregnancy she'd found it hard to write at all. It had been too hard to write small talk when she was keeping the biggest secret she'd ever had from the one who had a right to know but wouldn't want to.

Alex sighed again and turned up one untidily scrawled letter. She looked at the date. He'd sent it after Stavros's funeral. He must have been crying when he wrote it, and his tears had smudged the ink where they fell. It was such a pained letter. He was mourning for his brother, and at the same time mourning for what they'd lost. He seemed to sense that their relationship was over, and was reaching out in one last bid for Alex to give him something she'd desperately wanted to but now never could.

The one time he'd really needed her, she hadn't been able to help. The only fair thing she could do was set him free. So the family couldn't be tainted by another scandalous pregnancy.

There were more letters, but increasingly less frequent after that. Alex skimmed through their content, noted the bitterness that infused his final words.

He'd finished with her. Who could blame him? She'd betrayed his trust. And all because of a secret— a secret bigger than both of them.

Now that secret was almost eight years old—her one link with happier times and a season of love.

Eight years old. And on every one of those birthdays she'd looked at Jason and wondered if she'd done the right thing, wondered if she should have told Nick, whether she should tell him now.

But she only had to look at the words of his final letters. He didn't want to hear from her. He didn't want anything more to do with her.

And his circumstances hadn't changed. After what his family had been through they would never believe her child was Nick's.

She came back to the roughly scrawled letter and its pained contents, and as she read the words over again her heart squeezed so tight that two plump tears rolled down her face, blurring her vision so she barely noticed it when they landed on the page, her tears mingling with his in the smudged ink.

'Mum—what's wrong?' Jason asked. 'What are all those?'

Alex wiped her eyes with the back of her hand and sniffed. 'Oh, just some old letters from a one-time friend of mine,' she said as she hurriedly scrabbled the papers and envelopes together, without bothering to match letters with envelopes.

'So why are you crying?'

'Because I'm happy thinking about those times, silly.' She rose to her feet, congratulating herself on how light she'd managed to sound, and turned towards her bedroom, the bundle of letters, envelopes and the chocolate box trailing its blue satin ribbon in her arms.

'Mum?' he called after her. 'Who's Nick?'

Alex stopped dead in her tracks, remembering to plaster a bright smile on her face as she wheeled around. 'Why do—' She stopped and felt the smile slide from her face.

Jason was crouched down where she'd been, holding a letter and looking at it quizzically. 'Was he your boyfriend or something?'

She took a step closer, heart in her mouth.

He is your father.

Her mind framed the words but her mouth refused to make the sounds. God, she needed time to work out how to tell him. 'Something like that. It was a long time ago.'

'Before I was born?'

She smiled, and without letting go of her cargo reached out a hand to muss his hair.

'Yes, before you were born.' She hesitated, aware that Jason was handing her the perfect opportunity to tell him all about his father and wondering where to start. 'He was a very special boyfriend, actually. I think you would have liked him.'

But Jason looked as if he'd already lost interest.

'Okay,' he said, shrugging. 'But don't ever think I'm going to write mushy stuff like that to some girl.' He screwed up his face and stuck out his tongue as he handed it to her. 'Totally gross,' he added, heading off back towards the kitchen, then turning. 'Oh, I forgot what I meant to ask you. Matt and Jack said I

could go fishing with them by myself—if it's okay
with you, that is?'

She smiled. 'Of course,' she said. 'And get that
birthday party list worked out too—those invitations
should go out soon.'

'Totally cool!' he said. 'I'll get onto it.'

She watched him happily trot off, confident that all
was right in his world, and then she looked down at
the letter, curious to see which letter her son had
found. It was one of Nick's early letters, and straight
away she caught a glimpse of the lines Jason must
have been referring to.

Nick's words had made her swoon back then. Now
they just made her stomach roll with a sense of fore-
boding she couldn't shake.

CHAPTER SIX

ALEX headed into the office on Monday morning firing on all cylinders. All Sunday, whether doing the housework, kicking a ball around with Jason in the nearby park or catching up on study, she'd been planning exactly what she'd say to Nick and how she'd tell him of their son.

She'd thought of everything. Every line of dialogue, every possible response from him. She had them all covered. She was prepared for every contingency.

Alex took a deep breath as she opened the door. It wasn't going to be easy, certainly, but nothing was going to stop her today from telling Nick the facts of his Australian legacy. The first opportunity she had, she was going to shut herself in his office and explain everything.

She swallowed, her throat suddenly dry at the thought of being shut in an office—*alone*—with Nick. Already her heart had kicked up a beat. Maybe that wasn't such a good idea. Maybe better to take him for coffee in the outdoor café downstairs—find a quiet table. At least it would be public. At least he couldn't back her into a corner there.

After that it would be up to him—if he wanted to

meet Jason she'd speak to him and arrange it. If he refused to acknowledge their boy then so be it. But at least she would have done what she needed to do.

He was there, sitting in what had used to be Aristos's spacious office, when she arrived. The Venetian blinds on the glass walls of his office were slatted open and she knew instinctively, without looking in, that he had noticed her arrival and was watching her.

'Alexandra.' His rich Mediterranean accent confirmed it as it flowed around her from the office. 'Good morning.'

Alex paused outside his open door and looked in. He gazed back from his position behind the wide expanse of timber desk. A small man could get lost behind that desk. Not Nick. The table complemented his dimensions, extending the range of his power and influence. This was a man who knew how to rule. This was a man born to power.

Alex suppressed the burn in her throat. Despite all his apparent strength, there was no time like the present. She dipped her head in acknowledgement, unable to smile.

'Morning,' she said briefly, knowing there was little good about it. She took a small step into his office. 'I need to talk to you. Are you free for the next few minutes?'

'Come in,' he said, pen poised over the documents he'd been signing. 'I need to speak to you today too. I won't be here tomorrow.'

He was leaving. Emotion crashed through her in waves—delight, disappointment and, overwhelmingly, relief. Gone would be the pressure of his everyday presence in the office. Gone would be the memories he brought to life by his touch. Gone would be the need to tell him about Jason...

'You're leaving? Going back to Greece?'

He put the pen down and looked up at her. A bare smile touched his lips. 'You would like that, would you not? For me to return to Greece? To relegate me to the past once more?'

She gulped—his words were far too close to the truth.

'Sorry to disappoint you. I'll be away only a week or so. I think it's time I saw the rest of the Xenophon properties before I make any long-term decisions. How many are there scattered around Australia—twelve or thirteen?'

'Fourteen, all up. If you count the shopping centre in Perth the company has just settled on.'

'Ah, fourteen.' He thought a second. 'Maybe a little longer than a week. I will spend some time in each city, talking to the property managers. I thought Sofia would come with me, but she wants to stay. She has a project she needs your help with.'

She nodded with a touch of resignation, more than used to assisting Sofia with her 'projects'. Past experience told her she'd be doing more of the actual project work herself, rather than merely assisting.

'And Alexandra...?'

His voice had dropped down a level, taken on a more intimate tone, and now he leaned closer, resting his forearms on the desk, hands clasped.

Her dry throat scratched out a shaky response. 'Yes?'

'Look after her for me while I'm gone. Make sure she has everything she needs.'

'Of course,' she said, her voice little more than a whisper. 'Consider it done.'

'Good.' He nodded, unclasped his fingers and stretched back in his chair. 'Now, what did you want to see me about?'

'Oh...' *Where to from here?* If Nick was only going to be away a few days there was no excuse for not telling him the truth about his son right now. And the separation might give him time to get used to the idea. Maybe there was a chance he might like to meet Jason when he got back, before his birthday. Give them time to get to know each other, if that was what they both wanted.

She hesitated. 'It's kind of private.'

Nick's eyebrows rose. 'You want to close the door?'

She shook her head. Even with the blinds open she didn't want to be trapped in that office with Nick, to have to tell him across that wide plain of a desk. He looked far too powerful, too strong.

'No, not here. How about in the courtyard? We'll get a coffee.'

His eyes narrowed a fraction, as if were mentally

assessing her response, and his lips curled up a tad. 'As you wish. Put down your things. I just have one phone call to make and then I'll expect you.'

Alex moved to her office, relieved herself of her laptop and briefcase and took a few calming breaths. There—she was committed. Tilly was right, she could do this.

She picked up her wallet. She'd pay her way. She'd owe Nick nothing.

She had turned to leave the office when Sofia sprang through the door and shut it behind her. She was grinning widely, her lips a bright pink slash across her impeccably made-up face.

'Alex, I need your help.'

Alex's spirits slumped. *Please, not now,* she thought. Not now, when I'm all psyched up for meeting Nick. For *telling* Nick.

'Can it wait a few minutes, Sofia? I have to talk to Nick. He's expecting me.'

She moved to go past, but Sofia threw out her arms, blocking her way. Alex caught a blast of the heavy sandalwood scent Sofia used so liberally.

'No. That can wait. This is too important.'

'I have a meeting…' Alex said, pointedly looking down at her watch.

'Notice anything?' Sofia invited, ignoring her protest.

Alex took a calming breath while her mind searched for whatever it was that was supposedly so apparent. Then it hit her. The blue stretch trousersuit fitted Sofia like a glove.

'Of course—your new suit. Lovely.' It should have registered earlier. Since that conversation last week Sofia had produced an entire new wardrobe. She'd worn something new, and blue, every day.

'No, silly.' She waggled her fingers, still outstretched. 'Notice anything else?'

Alex's eyes followed the gesture. 'No, I—' *Then she saw it.* The diamond was almost as big as Ayers Rock—or so it seemed as every tiny facet dazzled with reflected light in its brilliance. She swallowed. 'Wow. That really is something.'

Sofia theatrically dropped her arms down so that her left hand sat uppermost in her other. She gazed down at the ring, admiring the play of reflected light.

'Thank you. Nick and I will be married as soon as possible.'

Alex's world lurched. *Nick?* It took too much energy to remain standing while her brain tried to process the information. She collapsed into her chair before her knees gave out completely.

'And that's why I need your help. There's so much to do, and I can't bother Nick with it all, with him going away—so will you help me organise the wedding?'

Nick! Getting married! *To Sofia?*

The girl was staring at her expectantly, the illumination of her new engagement bright in her eyes.

'Well…congratulations.' The word came out in a

rush as Alex struggled to make sense of her splintered thoughts. Organise Sofia's wedding? *How?* How would she cope with finding Sofia the perfect flowers, the perfect gown, only to send her down the aisle with the man she'd once dreamed of marrying herself?

'Will you? You know I've got no one else to help,' she pleaded, her head tilted to one side. 'Not any more, anyway.' Suddenly the eyes that a moment ago had been clear and bright misted over, and dampness clung thickly in her long mascaraed lashes.

The change in the girl's mood was instantaneous, and Alex realised how close to the edge Sofia was treading. Her brightness was only a thin veneer, ready to shatter any time and reveal the grieving girl beneath.

She scrabbled to find a gentle response, something that wouldn't hurt Sofia, but could somehow let her back out. 'I'd love to help,' she said, 'but what of my work? There's so much involved in planning a wedding, especially if there's not much time.'

'Nick's taken care of all that. He said he's bringing out his own accountant from Greece, so you should have time to help me.'

Ice flushed through Alex's veins. So that was the plan. This was Sofia's special project. He was keeping her on to help Sofia organise her wedding. What had he asked?

'Look after her for me while I'm gone. Make sure she has everything she needs.'

He was marrying Sofia. He'd asked Alex to be his

mistress for the duration of his stay and then turned around and calmly offered marriage to someone else. Yet still he expected her to help with the wedding plans. What kind of man had he become? Certainly not one she wanted to share her bed with, let alone her son.

Alex thought of her mission, so fixed in her mind just a short while ago.

How was she supposed to tell him now? Everything had changed. Now there wasn't just Nick and Jason to consider. Now Sofia had entered the equation. Telling Nick would just create one whole new set of problems, especially coming so soon after his engagement.

'He has to be told.'

Tilly's words battled their way uppermost in her mind and Alex bit down on her lip, knowing that none of her preceding thoughts counted for anything in the end. No matter what she personally thought of the man, no matter who he was now marrying, she still had to tell him. She could find excuses for ever. But it didn't change the underlying truth that he had a right to know.

'It'll be fun—you'll see.'

She looked up at Sofia, so full of hope, so brimming with excitement and yet so perilously close to despair, and she felt awful. She was being selfish. After the tragedy of the past few weeks Sofia had a right to be happy. Even if Alex couldn't imagine anything less fun, there was at least one way she could help the girl.

'I'm not sure I'd be the best person for the job,' she began, 'but I know a great wedding planner who might be able to help. Do you want me to call her?'

Sofia jumped up and down, clapping her hands, her earlier near breakdown forgotten. 'Cool! I want to get started right away. Can you organise an appointment for me today? Any time—let me know. Only there's so much to do.'

'Sure. I'll give her a call.'

Behind Sofia, Nick opened the door. 'We had a meeting, remember?'

His words sounded short, and his face was dark, as though she'd kept him waiting purposely. Then he saw Sofia and Alex witnessed his face relax, the scowl replaced with a smile as he turned his attention to her.

'I didn't realise you were back in the office. Is everything all right?' He took Sofia's hand and pulled her closer as he leaned down towards her. Sofia raised her face, her beaming love-filled face full of hope and optimism for the future, and Alex saw him smile back, and then she just couldn't watch any more.

She didn't have to look. It was obvious what came next. He was kissing her. He was kissing his future bride—*right in front of her.*

She had to hand it to him. He was one fast operator. He obviously had no intention of waiting six months for his inheritance. He'd earn his half-share right now, by marrying Sofia. And she was more than happy to go along with it.

Alex took a deep breath, trying to regain some perspective. What was her problem? What Nick and Sofia decided was their business. It shouldn't matter. It didn't matter. *So why did it feel so wrong?*

She sensed the couple move apart. 'We've just been discussing my project,' said Sofia, sounding more than a little breathless. 'She's agreed to help me with a few things, just like you promised, but she's all yours now. Don't keep her long, though. She's got a lot to do today.' Sofia winked back over her shoulder on her way out.

Alex picked up her wallet and mobile phone, purposely avoiding Nick's dark eyes and whatever they might tell her. 'Let's go.'

He fell into stride alongside her for the short walk to the café and Alex was choked by his presence. She should congratulate him, but the words wouldn't come, couldn't squeeze past the lump in her chest. *Did he need to be so close?* She could feel the heat emanating from him, could catch a hint of his cologne, and she wondered if it was such a good idea to leave the office after all. When their hands brushed Alex started, the zap as effective as any electric fence.

She covered the movement by folding her arms over her chest, hugging her wallet as she concentrated on keep her breathing calm. *Breathe in. Breathe out.*

Whatever had happened between them was in the past. Now he was getting married. He shouldn't affect her. She wouldn't let him affect her. Not if she was going to be able to tell him the truth. And she would.

They ordered their coffee and chose a table under the shade of a vine-covered pergola, a discreet distance from the other customers. Nick held out a chair and dutifully waited while she sat down. His hands seem to linger for ever on the back of the chair and his breath stirred the loose ends of the twist of hair she had pinned up that morning, sending warm tingles through her skin.

The next moment he had touched the clip holding the coil in place. 'What would happen if this came out?' His warm breath touched her neck, curling into her senses.

Alex's breath stuck as he toyed gently with the edge of the clip. 'My hair would fall down.' She ducked her head a fraction and one hand went up to reassure herself that the style was holding—only to have her hand snared by his.

He moved around the table and sat alongside without letting go. 'I should very much enjoy watching that,' he said, with a look that made her breath catch in her throat.

Alex looked into his dark eyes and not for the first time wished he didn't look quite so damned sexy. Wished he didn't make her feel so uncomfortable— so hot. Wished he wasn't marrying Sofia.

Crazy. She had to stop thinking like that. Who Nick married was not up to her. It shouldn't matter. She should be happy for both of them. And she would be—starting right now. She licked her lips, slipping her hand out of his and tucking it safely away with her other, deep in her lap.

'Sofia is very excited today.' She paused, still struggling to come out with 'that' word. 'I...I guess I should congratulate you. It's lovely to see her so happy after all she's been through.'

His eyes stayed on her, narrowing slightly, while his head tilted a fraction. 'She's a beautiful girl who deserves the best. I want her to be happy...'

Their coffee arrived. Alex, grateful for the interruption, stirred a spoonful of sugar she didn't need into her cappuccino, her spoon making lazy circles in the froth as her mind formed crazy, jagged spikes.

Of course Sofia was beautiful. And she deserved to be happy. But hearing him say those things about someone else, *his fiancée*, rubbed her nerve endings raw.

'So,' he said, after taking a sip of his long black coffee, 'here we are, sharing coffee. What is this private matter that you couldn't tell me in the office?'

Her heartbeat racing, she toyed with the froth on her coffee with her spoon, trying to form the words. 'Nick, I know we got off on the wrong foot, but I have to tell you something...'

He smiled again, and pushed back against his chair. The fine cotton of his shirt did nothing to hide the play of muscle just below the surface and Alex drank in the view. Everything about Nick shouted man, from his rugged olive-skinned jawline to the way his trousers fitted across his muscle-tight thighs. She looked up to realise he was watching her, obviously amused by her interest, and even more than that. He seemed to be *enjoying* her interest.

Cheeks flushed with heat, she pressed on.

'I have certain responsibilities that I need to discuss with you—that you should be aware of.'

He smiled again, wider, with one side tilted up, and he was nodding. It threw her. He didn't look curious or concerned. He looked somehow *satisfied*.

'I knew you would have a change of heart,' he cut in. 'But don't worry. I have taken that into account. You were right to want this meeting outside the office. It's much more discreet.'

Confusion clouded her mind. 'Sorry? I'm not with you.'

'We can't meet at your house, I realise, with your ''responsibilities''.' He moved closer to her, bending his head towards hers. 'I would suggest my apartment, but Sofia has a tendency to drop in whenever she feels like it and I don't want to upset her. I will arrange another apartment for us.'

Alex's eyes rounded as he continued with his plans. *He had to be kidding!* 'No,' she said, interrupting his flow. 'No apartment.'

He brushed aside her protest with a wave of his hand. 'It's more discreet. We can both have a key—'

'*No apartment!* I told you I won't sleep with you. What makes you think I'd change my mind?'

Especially now. Now that she'd been asked to arrange Sofia's wedding. Sofia and Nick's wedding. What kind of man was he, that he could coolly take a mistress while plans for his wedding to another woman were made? Poor Sofia. Did she have any idea what she was letting herself in for? Thinking of the girl just hardened her resolve.

'I won't change my mind.'

'Oh, you'll change your mind,' he said, in a whisper that sounded disturbingly like a threat. 'I'll make it worth your while. You won't have to scratch along on the pitiful wage Aristos paid you.'

She pushed back her chair and stood. '*Nothing* you can offer would make it worthwhile. What's happened to you, Nick, that you can be so callous and hard? When did you stop feeling?'

She picked up her things from the table and moved away, but already he was standing in front of her and blocking her exit.

'Before you go...' he said, leaning closer. He took her shoulder with one hand, and even though she held herself rigid she felt herself being drawn closer to him. His face dipped closer to hers, and for one insane moment she thought he was going to kiss her. She looked up as his face grew nearer, his eyes swirling with the unknown, and her lips parted of their own accord.

Then he gently brushed her upper lip with one finger, leaving her completely and utterly breathless.

'You had chocolate on your lip,' he said, before lifting the finger to his mouth and licking it clean.

For a moment she was too shocked to respond. For one thing the gesture had been completely unnecessary. For another it had been way too intimate. But the worst of it was that she felt cheated.

Because for some insane reason she had found herself wanting that kiss. And it hadn't happened.

'Thank you,' she forced herself to say through gritted teeth, her voice scratchy. Breaking eye contact, and trying to pretend that having cappuccino foam practically licked off her lip was an everyday occurrence, she headed resolutely for the office.

'The pleasure was all mine,' she heard Nick mutter a few paces behind her.

The phone was ringing when she got back to her office.

'So how did it go?' asked Tilly.

'It didn't.'

'You mean you didn't tell him?'

'I couldn't.'

'You chickened out?' Tilly's tone was damning.

'I tried to tell him but he wasn't listening. And things have changed.'

'What's changed?'

'He's marrying Sofia.'

A pause. 'Are you sure?'

'Tilly, he's bought her a diamond the size of Uluru and they've both asked me to help with the wedding. How much more evidence do I need?'

'Oh.' Alex could hear the sound of Tilly sitting down. 'Are you okay about it?'

Alex scoffed. 'Why should it matter? Nick means nothing to me now.'

Liar! Even as she said the words it felt as if someone was twisting a knife inside her. And yet it shouldn't matter, so why the hell did she feel so bad?

'I guess that does complicate things. But he still—'

Alex cut her off, knowing full well what was coming. 'Yeah, I know. I just couldn't do it on top of everything else. Not today.' *Not after he'd offered to set me up in an apartment for sex whenever he felt like it.* She glanced at her watch. 'Listen, sis, I need your help. I can't do this wedding planning thing. I don't have the first idea of how to go about planning a wedding, let alone the extravaganza Sofia will expect—besides which, I have far too much work on my plate already. So I recommended you. Can you do it?'

'So…you're not actually okay about it?'

Alex sighed. 'Look, it's complicated. Let's leave it at that. Now, do you want this job or not?'

Tilly rang off once they'd worked out a time for Sofia to drop by, and Alex worked out that she had better deal with the bank and transfer some money pronto. Sofia's credit card had maxed out—no mean feat, given the gold-plated limit. The new blue wardrobe had obviously taken its toll. She authorised a transfer to ensure there was sufficient credit to cover the inevitable imminent shopping spree and went in search of the blushing bride-to-be.

CHAPTER SEVEN

TIME, like Alex's peace of mind, was wearing thin. It had been a quiet couple of weeks. Tilly had kept Sofia so busy, organising the wedding of her dreams, that she'd hardly been in the office. Nick had extended his trip away, as expected. He was due back tomorrow, in time to collect Dimitri—who was arriving from Athens—from the airport.

Everything was ready. The invoices were up to date. The bank statements reconciled. The management reports were prepared—a neat stack of facts and figures to greet the new administrator, who would need all of this to evaluate the Xenophon Group's operations.

She'd achieved a lot in just a few days—achieved all that she'd set out to do and more. But there was no rush of satisfaction at having met her self-imposed targets. No spring in her step at having smoothed the chaos that had been the office, since Aristos's death, into order and control.

Nick was coming back tomorrow. Somehow the anticipation of that—the dread of that—overpowered everything else.

But that was tomorrow.

She glanced at her watch. It was late, and it was

time she left if she wasn't going to be late picking up Jason from after-school care.

Then she remembered. Sofia had left the copy for her engagement notice for the weekend papers on her desk, wanting it to be faxed to the newspaper today. She made a quick call to the newspaper, checked it wasn't too late, and started keying in the number in the backroom fax. The front office door swung open and clicked shut.

'I'll be right with you,' she called down the hallway, wondering why a courier would be delivering this late in the day.

The fax machine beeped its way through the number and started churning through the page. Satisfied that the copy would make it to the newspaper desk, as promised, Alex turned—only to collide with solid man, solid heat.

'Nick!' she said, bouncing breathlessly off his chest as his hands shot out to steady her. 'I didn't hear you.'

Nick held onto her shoulders, even though she was in no danger of falling now.

'We didn't expect you until tomorrow. Sofia will be pleased.'

He hesitated a second. 'And are you pleased, Alexandra?'

His face was close, the late afternoon stubble on his skin lending a dark, threatening shadow to his jaw. He smelt of coffee, of airline whisky, and man. Pure, unadulterated testosterone. It assailed her senses. It permeated her skin through his touch on her shoulders. It tickled her nose and warmed her lungs, her chest, her body.

She swallowed. 'How did the trip go?'

'You haven't answered my question. Are you pleased I'm back?'

His eyes glinted, challenging her as his words had done a moment before. It made her kick up her chin.

'No. I mean, yes. I mean—'

His eyes lit up and his lips curled. 'Yes *and* no? Some good, some not so good. Tell me how this can be.'

Alex paused. She hadn't meant to be so honest. But how to respond? She gulped. 'Yes, because it's good you're back safely.' *Chicken.* 'And no, because you seem to enjoy making my life difficult.' At least that bit was true.

'I don't mean to make your life difficult. I think you do that yourself.'

'What?' she said, trying unsuccessfully to shrug out of his hands. 'How do you figure that?'

'Because I know what your answer really means.' Alex stilled her struggles. All of a sudden his grip noticeably gentled; now he was stroking languid lines along to her neck. After the strain of a long day assembling reports, the massaging effect was heaven. Her head dipped involuntarily towards his stroking touch.

'You are scared of me. Your head tells you I shouldn't be here, while at the same time your body reaches out for me.'

Her head snapped up.

'Rubbish. I—'

His massage grew more firm, retaining her within his grasp. 'And that's how you make your life more difficult. By denying yourself the pleasure you know you will find with me.'

His arms tightened around her as he moved closer, cupping her head with his hands.

'And there is no doubt you will find pleasure with me.'

She gazed up at him and knew he was right. She was battling the demon of desire and it was sapping her of all her strength. Yes, she would find pleasure with him. Of that there was no doubt. But it was a battle she had to fight. A battle she had to win.

Only now, with his face descending towards hers, passion flaring in those deep, dark eyes as his hands continued to mould her to him, it was hard to remember why.

Her breasts felt him first, her nipples crushing to his chest with a burning need to get closer, ever closer. She let herself be gathered tight in his embrace, pressing herself against the long, strong length of his body, watching him dip his head, slant his lips across hers. They shared a breath between them, shared the air that gave them both life but still wasn't enough to sustain their need.

His lips grazed hers, the barest touch, the hint of recollection strong and hypnotic, and then something like a groan, his need given voice, emanated from deep in his throat and his mouth meshed with hers at last. She responded in kind, parting her lips willingly as his urged her to, his taste in her mouth and his breath taking hers away. His hands splayed at her neck, down her back, sculpting her body as they travelled her length.

For a moment his lips left hers to trail kisses down her neck, and she looked heavenwards, gratefully gasping in much needed oxygen, before they sought her mouth once more and she welcomed him back, her hand raking through his hair. He was so much the same, this man she'd known before. So much the same and yet so different. So much more a man. So much more...

The years melted away under the onslaught of his kisses, banished by a desire that had never changed, never diminished. His touch on her body was electric. Nerve cells kicked into life at his touch, skin goose-bumped and tingled.

All over her feelings were awakening at his touch—exquisite torture as still it was not enough. His lips and tongue duelled with hers while his hands were everywhere—her hair, her neck, her back, her thigh.

Alex gasped as his hand slipped under her raised skirt and slid around to capture her behind. He responded by kissing her deeper, urging her closer against his obvious hardness.

'Alexandra,' he murmured, nuzzling her ear, 'I want you.'

His words fed her own need, even as something inside told this was wrong. A kiss was going too far. And this was way beyond a kiss.

He steered her back towards the desk, jamming her hard against it as his hand lifted the skirt on the other side.

'No,' she whispered, her voice husky and raw. She pulled back, leaning over the desk, away from him, but he only took it as an opportunity for his hand to snare her breast. A sharp intake of air filled her lungs.

'No! Don't, Nick. This shouldn't be happening.'

He pulled back, but only for a moment. 'We've been through all that. This is exactly what *should* be happening.' He leaned closer, aiming for her lips once more. 'It's time to stop fighting it.'

Breath hissed through Alex's clenched teeth.

'This is wrong!'

He moved to kiss her and she swung her head away so his lips collided with her cheek.

'Stop playing games.' His tone was brusque, annoyed, and his hands moved from her thighs to restrain her arms. 'You want this as much as I do.'

She turned her face back to his, painfully aware that her breath was coming in choppy bursts and trying to keep her voice level in spite of it. 'And what does Sofia want? Doesn't that matter too?'

'This doesn't concern her. This is between you and me.'

The anger his words created welled up inside her, giving her a strength she hadn't realised she owned.

She managed to free one hand, pulled it back and cracked it solidly against his cheek.

He recoiled, looking almost amused—except for his eyes. They glinted at her, dark and menacing. She'd taken him by surprise, that much was sure, and he didn't like it.

'How can you say that,' she demanded, 'when your engagement is to be announced in two days?'

Beside her the fax machine beeped into life, snagging Alex's attention. The brief notice spat out. A confirmation.

The *Sydney Daily* had received the announcement she had sent through just minutes before. The day after tomorrow Sofia and Nick's engagement would be official.

For the first time Nick relaxed his hold and leaned back.

'What did you say?' He spun away suddenly, both hands raking through his hair. Alex felt his departure as a sudden absence of heat but couldn't afford to mourn the loss. She took a deep, shuddering breath.

'And this is how you behave.'

She fled to her office to snatch up her things. She was leaving—now! She threw her parting words over her shoulder as she walked out.

'I'm sorry, Nick. Contract or not, I'm not staying in this place another second.'

CHAPTER EIGHT

HE SLOWED the Mercedes Sports to a crawl and came to a halt alongside number nineteen. This was definitely the place. That was her small car there, parked in the narrow driveway.

But who owned the red two-door nestled in close behind? She'd said she didn't have a partner. His gut clenched at the prospect she might have lied to him.

She'd said she had 'responsibilities'. Was that what she'd been trying to tell him at the café—that she had a relationship, that she had a boyfriend she'd been reluctant to admit to?

He watched the house for a few minutes, his window wound down, the light morning breeze puffing through the opening. You could smell the sea from here. Smell it but not see it. She hadn't bought a place right on the sea. Surprising after her love affair with the sea in Crete. She'd loved its deep, bright blue against the stark white of sand or the rubble of rock. Surely she could have found something closer than this? Or was this all she was able to afford?

He looked at the ageing cottage again—there wasn't a lot to it: a single-fronted older style place, built of stone, with flaking wooden fretwork around the small verandah out front, and all topped by a typical red Sydney roof in obvious need of repair. There wasn't much garden—a palm in a pot and a couple of old rose bushes—although a view down the side hinted at the promise of a bigger back garden behind.

Movement at the front door snared his attention. Someone came out—a woman. It had been a long time but still he recognised her. A taller and blonder version of Alexandra. She must be the wedding planner. He watched her wave back towards the house and then turn for her car. The front door closed and the woman made her way to the sporty hatch, curled herself inside and reversed out.

Nick breathed again, waited until the vehicle moved away down the road, eased himself out of the car and approached the front door.

He rang the bell. Nothing seemed to happen for a moment or two. He pushed the button again.

'Okay,' came Alex's voice from inside. 'I'm coming.'

She pulled the door open, 'What did you—?' the words stalled on her lips as her blue eyes widened and rose up to meet his '—lose?'

'My fiancée.'

She stood at the door, wearing the type of clothes he hadn't seen her in since Crete—jeans and a knitted top that fitted her like a second skin, showing off every curve that had been hidden under her work suits. All of a sudden he realised why women weren't supposed to wear jeans to the office. It would be far, far too distracting.

She looked up at him, her lips apart and questioning, and he saw something like a shudder move through her. 'What?' Then she appeared to collect herself, but, still with confusion swirling in her expression, shook her head. 'No, Sofia's not here.'

Nick shook his own head slowly. 'I'm not looking for Sofia.'

Her eyes, once wide and questioning, now pulled tight into a taut frown. 'Then what did you mean?'

He waited a second, tongue poised at his lips as a motorbike roared down the street behind him, then another, yanking his gaze around.

It was next to impossible to be heard over the racket.

'Are you going to invite me in, or do we have to try to discuss this on your doorstep?'

She frowned as her eyes followed the bikes powering down the narrow street. 'I'm sorry about that. The Simpsons from number fifty-two. They're into motorbikes.' She shrugged, as if that explained everything, and then led the way inside.

The living room was not large, just as he had anticipated from his view of the outside, yet still it held a warmth that seemed to wrap itself around him—worn but comfortable chairs; a thin, almost threadbare rug in muted shades; smiling faces peering out at him from the photographs adorning nearly every horizontal surface. Smiling faces of a young boy growing up.

He stopped on impulse, picking one up.

She turned, sensing his stillness, saw what he held in his hands and held her breath.

Time stood still. Would he be able to tell, just from a photograph?

Finally he looked up, his forehead creased. 'Your son?'

She nodded weakly, her mouth dry. *Our son.* 'Jason,' she finally managed, trying to get moisture to her lips so she could say more...

'Good-looking boy,' he said with a nod. 'How could his father do this to you? Leave you with his son all alone? Why would a father not want a son like this? What kind of man is he?'

She swallowed, strangely let down that he hadn't made the connection and that still the onus remained firmly on her to tell him. 'He didn't mean to. It wasn't really his fault.'

His eyebrows drew together in a deep scowl. 'He left you alone. And yet you defend him. Did you love him that much?'

With all her soul. Tears pricked at the corners of her eyes and she turned her head away. It seemed almost laughable now, given the way he'd treated her since his arrival, given the man he'd become. 'I once thought I did.'

'Then don't you hate him for what he's done?'

She looked over at him imploringly and indicated the photo still in his hand. 'How could I ever hate him? Look what he's given me. I still have Jason. At least I have him. I have that much.'

He moved suddenly, thumping the photograph back onto the mantel, and she sensed she'd said the wrong thing—even though she'd spoken only the truth—something had angered him.

She dragged in a deep breath. 'Why are you here?' she asked, clasping her arms with her hands. Then, in case he was here to change her mind, added, 'Because you know I'm not coming back to the Xenophon Group.'

'I assumed that you would say that—even if I told you what Dimitri said.'

Her head tilted one side, curiosity getting the better of her. 'Why? What did he say?'

'He said he couldn't understand why I'd brought him out here when things were being managed so well.'

'He did?'

He nodded. 'There are a few small changes Dimitri would recommend. But on the whole he is happy with the operation and how it has been run.'

Alex digested his words, feeling unexpected pride in the job she'd left. It was worth something that her work had been appreciated, even if not by Nick himself.

'So, then, if it's not to lure me back to the company, why are you here?'

He looked around. 'Where is the boy?'

'Jason's not home. He's gone fishing with some friends.' He seemed to visibly relax, at least a fraction, as if he was no longer concerned about being interrupted by a child. She was sure he wasn't half as relieved as she was. If Nick had dropped by when Jason was home—she shuddered to think about it. She was having enough trouble trying to tell Nick about their son. There was no way she could handle revealing the truth to the two of them together.

'He won't be home for a while,' she prompted when he still just gazed out of the window, not comfortable about telling him that Jason was away for the weekend, but wanting to say something that might prompt him to speak and reveal the reason for his visit.

He turned towards her and she was struck by the sheer force of his presence. Black jeans and a casual shirt did nothing to lessen the impact of his power. It was there. All around him. He carried it like people carried the air in their lungs. He carried it like a birthright.

'I'm not marrying Sofia.'

Alex was grateful for the arm of the chair alongside. It gave her something to cling to. Something welcomingly concrete.

He wasn't getting married. Part of her wanted to jump up and shout that it had been clear from the start that Sofia was never right for him, while another part of her wondered why she should feel so vindicated by the announcement.

But why would he come here to let her know? Did he think it mattered? Unless Nick simply assumed she was the perfect person to cancel the wedding plans for him because her sister was the planner.

'Hold on,' she said. 'What about the notice in the paper today?' She managed the few steps to the table, where the paper lay open at the employment section, checked on the front page for the index to notices and flicked through. 'I placed the notice myself.'

'Did you see the announcement?'

She kept her eyes on the paper. 'No, not yet. I...' In truth she hadn't looked beyond the employment pages. Why confirm what she knew? She had to think about her own future now. Not someone else's.

'I can't find it,' she said, her eyes skimming the engagements section.

'It's not there. I cancelled it.'

'Why? What happened?'

'Simple,' he said. 'I'm not getting married.'

'Then why get engaged in the first place?' she argued, rubbing her forehead with her fingers, feeling annoyed for both Sofia—who'd no doubt be devastated—and for her sister, who'd spent so long planning for the upcoming nuptials. 'Why buy her that ring?'

'I never bought that ring.'

'But...' Alex was about to protest until she recalled that phone call she'd had to make to the bank. The one clearing Sofia's credit card account of an amount hugely over her five-figure limit.

'*Sofia* bought it?'

He shrugged and moved a little closer to the table,

picking up and investigating her bits and pieces along the way. 'I can only presume. Seeing I had nothing to do with it.'

'But you were getting married. All those plans...'

His breath was expelled in one fast, furious motion and he put down the clay kangaroo Jason had crafted in school with a decided thump. Alex started at the sound, relieved the artwork had survived, and then her eyes caught his and she realised there was no such thing as relief when those eyes were on her—not with the way they turned on a switch deep inside, like a kettle, so that her emotions could go from millpond-calm to bubbling turmoil in less than a minute.

'She said she was doing market research into the bridal industry.' He laughed a short, bitter laugh as he raised his eyes to the ceiling. 'I thought she was looking at our tenant mix, to see if we were covering all the bases. It seems she had other ideas.'

'Then you were never getting married? Never even engaged?'

His dark eyes locked back on hers and tripped her internal switch again. 'Never.'

A deep breath filled her lungs. 'Sofia was so sure...'

She'd been so sure! Sofia was marrying Nick. Yet suddenly everything had changed.

He frowned and turned his gaze outside once more. 'Sofia is Aristos's daughter through and through. She wants exactly what her father wanted for her—marriage to someone he approved of, and preferably someone with links to the family. She assumed I was that person and somehow that helped to ease her grief.'

'But I congratulated you. You told me...' She thought about his words. He wanted Sofia to be happy. He wanted her to have the best. But not once had he said he was going to marry her. She'd taken Sofia's fantasy and turned it into her own reality.

Nick just shook his head. 'She's all alone. I know what that's like. She needs looking after and I intend to get her help in coming to terms with her father's death. But even if I was interested spending my life with Sofia, I'm the least qualified person to build any sort of family with.'

She couldn't let his last statement lie. He'd said the words as a cold statement of fact, without a hint of self-pity. It was clear he really believed it, and Alex couldn't help but bridge the few steps between them. 'Nick, I'm sure that's not true.'

Her hand found his bare forearm, intending to console, but the second she made contact any altruistic intention flew from her head. His flesh was rock-firm beneath her touch, yet strangely at odds with the softer, springier coating of hair. Her fingers were fascinated by the contrast. Hard and yet soft. Different parts of the same thing. Was that how Nick himself was? Different parts of the same thing? Only in Nick's case he seemed to be harder on the outside, where it showed to the world. Hard and decisive and unforgiving.

Did he have a softer inside lurking below that harsh public exterior, hidden deep below?

She wanted to believe so.

'It doesn't matter,' he said, his brow knotting as he gazed down at her hand. 'I just came to tell you that I'm leaving. I'm going home to Greece, and for good now that Dimitri is here to manage the operation. It was a long shot, but I just wanted you to know that if you wanted your old job back—'

She pulled her arm away.

'My job? After all you've done to ensure it goes to someone else? What is this, some last-ditch attempt to buy me now that Sofia doesn't stand in the way?'

Without taking a step it felt he was closer. Heat emanated from him and his eyes focused on hers until even the air between them dissolved. 'I don't need to buy you.'

Breath rushed through her. He was too close, too threatening, too dangerous. But she he couldn't let him get away with that. She had to ask. She swallowed, kicking her chin up a notch.

'What makes you so sure of yourself?'

In a breath he was there, right next to her, filling her body with heat simply by his proximity. He looked down at her, making her skin tingle with just his gaze, his eyes certain and his words just as sure. 'Because there's never been any question. You have always been mine.'

Her intake of breath was arrested by his lips, his mouth slanting over hers as his arms surrounded her and gathered her into his chest. Everywhere they made contact her body felt the heat, responded to it as every cell swelled and firmed and sought to get even closer to him. His hands swept her back as his mouth magicked hers, weaving a spell of want and need.

For a moment she thought of arguing the point. But only for a moment. The way her body responded he'd know in an instant she was lying. She had always been his. There'd never been another she'd even looked at. She had never wanted anyone else. In nine years there had been only one man who had haunted her dreams and filled her nights with want. Only the man holding her now. Only Nick. Only ever Nick.

It was impossible not to respond, not to match his passion with her own pent-up desire. He wasn't marrying Sofia! Her heart sang with the knowledge, though there was no time to analyse why. Not with Nick's taste in her mouth, his breath merged with hers and his touch set her body alight.

Her hand found a gap between shirt and jeans and her fingers immediately took advantage, seeking the skin beneath. A deep sound issued from his throat as she found the hot flesh beneath and found what she was looking for—skin-to-skin contact. She forced the shirt higher, until both her hands could roam his back, feeling the tight play of muscles as his arms moved over her.

'Today we will make love.' His voice was a husky

whisper against her ear, so that she felt it more as vibration than as sound.

She wasn't about to argue. His simple statement of fact was beyond argument. They both knew it. This time they would make love. A small tremor, filled with expectation and promise, moved through her.

His head pulled back a fraction from hers. His eyes were dark and smoky with desire. Desire for her. She saw the eyes of the young man on Crete all those years ago and breath caught in her throat. The eyes he'd turned on her back then were hers again.

And she knew in that instant that she still loved him. Totally, utterly, completely. She loved him and she'd never stopped loving him through all the years. It wasn't just her body that was Nick's. Her heart belonged to him too.

'Your boy—when is he due home?'

She swallowed, reluctant to break the mood but knowing that this secret between them had to be revealed. 'Nick, I have to tell you something. I—'

'When will he be home?'

'Tomorrow—he's gone camping overnight.'

She caught the gleam in his eye, the smile that rocked the corners of his mouth. He gently shook his head and shooshed her with a finger to her lips. 'We've both said too many words.' In one easy movement he lifted and swung her into his arms. 'Tell me tomorrow. Now it is time we made love.'

He kissed her again, and she kissed him back,

grateful that now nothing was going to stop their inevitable, inescapable date with destiny.

Today they would make love.

And tomorrow she would tell him about his son.

Still kissing her, he headed down the narrow side
hallway. The kitchen waited at the end of the hall and
two doors led off to the left in between. He paused
at the first door and she shook her head under his lips.
He continued to the next.

She pushed it open with her foot and he carried her
inside the high-ceilinged room, decorated in Victorian
shades and dominated by an old iron-framed double
bed. She shuddered against him as she thought of the
bed, of Nick with her, and he squeezed her tightly,
as if sensing her nervousness.

Then he eased her down gently, so gently, as if she
might break, in the centre of the bed and gazed deeply
into her eyes, into her soul. 'I want to see you naked,'
he said. 'I want to see your skin. But first...' He
reached behind her head to prise open and slip out
the clip holding her hair in its tight, twisted knot.
With his other hand he shook the hair free, until it
spilled around her shoulders in a wave of blonde
foam.

He made a rough sound of approval, deep in his
throat, held her face in his two hands and kissed her
gently on the lips. 'And now to feel your skin.' He
sat alongside her on the bed and eased her light knitted top over her head. He threw it to one side and
stopped, riveted, his eyes hotly on her.

She sat there, his intense dark gaze upon her, recognising the appreciation and sheer desire therein. As if spellbound, he reached out a hand and touched her skin. Her breath tracked in sharply and he sighed as her chest swelled in response. Lightly his finger traced the line of her champagne lace bra, burning her skin as his fingers followed the strap down from her shoulders, circling each breast so gently she thought she would explode. He took his hand away and his knuckles brushed one nipple—instinctively her back arched in response and in a second both hands were gone. She knew just where a second later when she felt her bra relax, its rear clip manipulated open. A moment later her breasts felt the freedom of the air as he swept all trace of the bra away.

His following swift intake of air empowered her. He wanted her. Exposed to his appreciative gaze, her nipples hardened in the firm, goosebumped skin of her breasts. As much as she wanted his eyes to drink her in, her breasts craved the touch of his hand, his mouth.

She took one of his hands and held it against her. He smiled, squeezing his fingers around her flesh and following likewise with the other hand. He shifted his grip so that one hand supported her behind her back while he kissed her and eased her down flat on the bed. His kiss deepened, his hands once again exploring her breasts. It wasn't enough. Just as he wanted to look at her skin, to feel her skin, she needed that contact too. As his lips traced down the line of her neck she scrabbled with the buttons on his shirt.

In a final flurry the sides of his shirt flew apart and she pulled him down on her so that her skin met his. Her senses sizzled as their warm flesh meshed and merged. Everywhere they touched felt like paradise, and a whole lot of reason to go on. When he suddenly pushed her away she felt cold, a sense of abandonment. But in a second he'd discarded the shirt and his mouth was back, seeking out the flesh of her breast, taking her nipple in his mouth, rolling its tight bud around with his tongue and sucking with such gentle, even pressure that she felt the layers of her old life being stripped away, leaving only that which Nick had tasted before.

He caressed each nipple in turn, the warmth of his mouth rendering them harder and more insistent, sending shards of sensation down to the base of her deepest need.

And while his tongue went to work her own hands explored his body, stroking and massaging his shoulders, his ribs, his stomach—wherever they could reach.

She felt each sculpted dip between his ribs, felt the play of muscle under skin and the touch of his satiny olive skin. And still it wasn't enough. It wasn't enough to be close. It wasn't enough to touch.

For eight long years she had tried to shut this man out of her mind, tried to shut him out of her heart. But there was no denying the truth of how she felt.

Now her body prepared to welcome him back inside, where she wanted him, where she needed him more than anything else.

He eased down the zip of her jeans and peeled them down her legs, collecting her panties and flicking off her sandals in the same desperate movement. His hands glided down her legs, gentle in touch but electric in intensity. Everywhere he touched sparked and fused. Desire rippled through her as the inevitable nearness of their union struck home.

He kneeled over her and took a deep breath, one hand now skimming over the skin of her stomach. She flinched slightly, knowing she was different from that girl who'd made love to him as a teenager. Since then this body had stretched, had borne a child, and she knew more than anyone of the telltale, even if somewhat faded proof of that. How would he react to that?

'So beautiful, Alexandra. You are more beautiful than I remember.'

His words swelled her chest, bringing a smile to her mouth that was a mixture of pride and gratitude that he found her this way, that his eyes worshipped her. 'Make love to me,' she said, suddenly sitting up and stretching one hand out to him.

His actions spoke loud in response as, without taking his eyes from her, he unbuckled his belt and shucked off his jeans. And then he was naked, and it was her turn to catch her breath. All the dreams she'd had, all the nights she'd imagined Nick in her thoughts—they were nothing compared to the sight of the man who stood before her now.

She'd asked him to make love to her and only now did she realise what that entailed. She gulped down both wind and courage as she registered the sheer physical presence of him next to her. His abdomen, tight and muscular, the olive skin smooth and sheened, his hips, lean and strong, promising delivery of satisfaction—and beyond.

He reached out and took her hand. 'Alexandra,' he said, his voice husky, almost catching as he lowered himself down alongside her. He held her hand to his mouth and kissed the palm of her hand—a gesture so simple yet somehow so intimate that she was moved by the depth of feeling it inspired in her.

'Nick…' she said, before his lips found hers once more and there was no need for words of any kind. Their bodies spoke a language known only to them, his body wooing her with his strength and mastery, and her body responding to every subtle intonation and expression. His hands spoke of rediscovery, and her body sang with reawakening. His body spoke of his need, and hers answered it.

Pressure mounted within her until only one thing mattered and that was to have Nick fill her, to make the last nine years disappear in a blur of passion and desire. She clutched him, felt the slick sheen of his sweat at his lower back, and wished for him to fill her.

He kissed her and growled deep and low, pulling

away. 'One moment,' he said, and then he was back—and when she realised what he was doing she almost cried out with relief. He was protecting her. While she was touched by his consideration, there was much more immediate cause to celebrate. At last! Soon he would be inside her and this long, dragging ache inside her would be gone.

He positioned himself between her legs, his hands at her hips. Without thinking she raised them in greeting and he accepted her invitation, nudging gently at first, then more insistently, before finally driving home the full glorious length of him.

Both of them stopped for a second, as if in awe of the moment. Alex felt her eyes widen with shock and pleasure combined. The moment held such clarity and purpose, as if both had been waiting too long for this moment to arrive and it was here.

Slowly at first he started moving, withdrawing, teasing, before filling her once more with his next thrust.

Alex moved under him, pleasure mounting into delicious torture, and she looked for release. It came in his next surging thrust and her immediate world exploded, again and again, as he filled every space inside her, just as he filled her heart.

They rocked together, feeling the tremors diminish, their breathing subside, their sweat-slicked bodies at last gentling, and Alex knew there would only ever be one man for her. How she'd managed to try and ignore the fact for the last nine years she had no idea.

For now it was crystal-clear that there would never be room in her heart or her bed for any man other than Nick.

And he was leaving.

Breath stopped in her chest. He hadn't said when, just that he was going back to Greece. In a few days or a few hours he'd be gone, and she would have lost him to another hemisphere once again.

His hand pushed some hair from her eyes, and, surprised, she turned to meet Nick's dark eyes on her.

'You are thinking,' he said. 'Tell me what you are thinking of.'

She smiled. 'Just—thank you.' It was the truth too. She did owe him thanks—thanks for showing a gentler side of him, a side she'd thought lost completely under the bitter armour he'd built up around himself over the last few years, thanks for showing her that the man she'd thought lost was still there, deep down inside him.

His eyebrows and lips rose together, and his hand drew a line down the side of her face and down to her breast, circling the nipple.

'Thank you for asking me. Now it is my turn to ask you.' His hand traced down to her navel, again circling. In spite of its recent release, her body stirred in delicious response. 'Make love to me, Alexandra.'

She felt him harden alongside her, felt the nudge of his erection against her thigh, and anticipation rose in her once more. His mouth sought hers and she didn't need words to give her agreement. She conveyed it in her kiss, in the touch of her hands, and in her body's response.

He was going home to Greece. But before he went she would ensure she had enough memories to take her through the long, lonely nights of the future. Memories of Nick. Memories of love.

She made love to him, and morning moved into afternoon and then into evening. They stopped to eat, sharing a salad and bread and memories of Crete, then shared an evening walk, hand in hand, along the beach, before falling into bed again as evening became night.

Alex yawned after their latest lovemaking and nestled into the space between his arm and his body. With his free arm he stroked her shoulder, almost hypnotising her. It had been a perfect day. Her body felt exhausted, yet at the same time exhilarated. Muscles she'd long forgotten about already voiced their protest.

She was deliciously close to sleep. 'When are you leaving?' she asked softly.

His hand stopped and pulled away to rub his forehead. 'A few days.'

Alex felt her heart squeeze tight. She'd known he was leaving, but still disappointment consumed her. But why should one day's lovemaking make any difference to his plans? She'd never believed it would—had she?

But what of a son? Would he stay if he knew about his son?

She licked her swollen lips. 'Is there anything that might make you reconsider?'

'I have businesses back in Greece. Now that Dimitri is here, there is no reason for me to stay. I have to go.'

He didn't hesitate with his response. She should feel grateful he'd made his intentions clear. She closed her eyes and nodded into his shoulder. 'I know.'

So he was going. And tomorrow she would tell him about Jason. At least they would have a chance to meet each other before he left. Tomorrow. First thing tomorrow...

He was gone. Alex looked at the pillow next to her, devoid of everything but the impression of Nick's head. Her ears strained for sounds of running water— the shower—a kettle? But there was nothing to hear. The silence of an otherwise empty house wrapped around her. Only the sounds of early-morning bird calls drifted in from outside, like the bright needles of sunlight squeezing through the gaps in the curtains.

She reached out an arm. The bed was cold. Where was he? She sat up, looking over the edge of the bed, but the floor only held her own discarded clothes.

Suddenly wide awake, she jumped up and scrabbled into her robe, trying to ignore the ache of rarely used muscles. She checked the kitchen and bathroom. She kneeled on the sofa and looked through the front curtains. But even a peek out of the front window revealed nothing but her own car in the driveway.

She looked around the room for a note or message. But there was nothing.

Nick and every trace of him had disappeared. She collapsed down onto the sofa. Some time early in the morning he'd sneaked out of her bed and out of her life.

'You're a fool, Alex Hammond, a prize fool,' she told herself, anger replacing her shock at discovering his undercover departure. 'How could you have fallen for that?'

After all, ever since his arrival he'd been after her to jump into bed. Now she had, and where was he? Gone. Long gone.

It was clear he'd got what he wanted.

Tears pricked at her eyes, but anger at her own actions forced them back. She sniffed. 'A silly fool,' she repeated, heading off to the kitchen to put on the kettle. He'd conned her well and good. All that stuff about leaving any talk until tomorrow—well, he clearly wasn't interested. He'd had no intention of staying and hearing any of it. Clearly wasn't interested in her or her life. He never wanted to know— otherwise why wouldn't he have stuck around?

Now he would go back to Greece and never know about his son. Well, it would serve him right.

Alex jiggled a teabag while her teeth toyed with her bottom lip. Only that didn't solve anything. Nick still needed to know he had a son. But with Jason's birthday tomorrow there was no way he was going to know before the event.

She flicked the teabag out into the sink and sat down at the table, trying to get her thoughts under some sort of control.

She should have insisted on telling him about Jason before they'd made love—only it had been easier not to. She hadn't taken much convincing. There was little chance he'd have wanted to make love to her after a revelation like that, and at the time that had seemed the most important thing. Amazing how your hormones could replace logic with lust.

The phone rang and she jumped. Just maybe…

But it was Tilly, confirming what time she should arrive for the party tomorrow. Alex recited the details, trying not to sound too disappointed, and briefly explained that Sofia's 'wedding' was off. She rang off and checked the time on the wall clock, and clunked her brain out of what-ifs and back into reality.

Jason was due back after lunch. Since she'd written off yesterday she now only had a few hours to do what she needed to get done for tomorrow's holiday Monday party. She had to get moving.

CHAPTER NINE

THEY were all there. Jason and seven of his school-friends, including Matt and Jack, took turns at slapping the *piñata* hanging from the clothesline with a broomstick while Alex and Tilly escaped inside to put the final touches to the party food.

Her parents had already called from Perth, to wish Jason happy birthday and good fortune. Alex wished they could be here, but it wasn't too long until Christmas, which would be even better.

The cake was all ready—a huge chocolate mud cake, iced to resemble a soccer ball—with eight candles positioned all around, ready to be lit at the right time. She'd take that outside when they'd finished with afternoon tea.

Alex smiled to herself as she heated the last of the sausage rolls. Everything was going so well. It was a bright day, Jason was having the time of his life and the kids were all having fun. Just perfect.

The doorbell rang as she was carrying the last of the food out to the outdoor seating on the rear verandah. She hesitated, sure all the invitees were accounted for.

'I'll get it,' Tilly called. 'It's probably just someone collecting money for a good cause. You go on.'

Alex smiled gratefully and backed out through the screen door, carrying her load in both hands, to be met with squeals and yells of triumph. The final blow had been delivered to the *piñata* and sweets rained out over them. Eight boys immediately dropped to the ground, scrabbling for the most booty. She couldn't help but laugh at the sight.

She heard footsteps coming through the kitchen. 'Tilly,' she called, 'come and see. This is too funny.'

Tilly stepped through the door. 'It seems we have another guest.'

Alex turned, only to see Nick follow Tilly onto the verandah. Blood drained from her face to congeal in her gut. At just one glimpse of him memories of their lovemaking surged back, memories of being close, of how he'd pleasured her, how she'd pleasured him...

Everything had been so perfect. So why had he left? And why was he back? She tossed up her chin and looked from one to the other. 'What's going on?'

Tilly scowled at her sister. 'Hey, don't be like that. Nick just apologised for losing me the best contract I'd ever had. And he's brought Jason a present— look.'

Alex dragged her eyes down to the package he held, frowned, and then looked back to his face.

'What are you doing here?'

'I came to see you, as it happens, and I remembered what you'd said about your son's party. I hope you don't mind, only I don't have much time before I leave.'

'Of course she doesn't mind,' said Tilly. 'Lovely of him to think of Jason—don't you think, Alex?'

Alex looked at Tilly, who was smiling too encouragingly.

'I'm sure Jason will appreciate the gesture,' she went on, and Alex could swear she could just about hear Tilly's teeth grating, forcing her to respond in the affirmative.

She swallowed and forced a bare smile to her face. 'Thanks. I'm sure he'll be very pleased.'

She looked over to the boys, who were now busily comparing the spoils of war, and sought out her son. He was there, in the middle, and pain knifed through her heart. She stole a breath and found a new emotion filling the gouge the knife had made—exhilaration. After eight long years father and son would finally meet.

Would they like each other?

She called out to Jason and he looked up, noticing for the first time the stranger beside her. He stuffed the sweets into his pockets and ran over, looking curiously at the visitor.

'Jason,' she said, with one hand around his waist, as he was already getting too tall to put her arm comfortably around his shoulders any more, 'this is Mr Santos, a—colleague of mine. He wants to meet you.'

'Pleased to meet you, Jason. Happy birthday.'

He looked up at Nick, then down at the present, and then over to his mother as if checking it was okay. She smiled and nodded her head and he seemed to relax, shaking Nick's hand and saying hello.

'I forgot to get a card; I hope you don't mind,' said Nick, handing over the present.

'Nah, that's cool. Thanks, Mr Santos.'

'Call me Nick.'

Jason looked up curiously from his unwrapping. 'Sure—thanks, Nick.' Then his attention went back to the present. 'Oh, cool! Guys! Check this out. Wow! A World Cup soccer ball. Who wants to have a kick?' He turned away to share his prize with his friends and then turned back. 'Gee, thanks Mr Sa— I mean, thanks, Nick.'

Nick smiled and reached out a hand to ruffle his hair.

'My pleasure. Go and have a kick with your friends. I hear you're pretty good. I used to play a bit myself.'

Jason looked sideways up at him. 'You want a kick too?'

Nick nodded. 'Sounds good to me,' he said, heading off after Jason. Before long the small backyard was full of eight kids and Nick, standing as far apart as they could get in the tiny space, kicking the ball to each other, dribbling it around the lawn, and practising headers between them. While they practised their tackling Nick was doing some pretty fancy footwork, successfully evading the kids trying to tackle him.

Alex could do nothing but stare after them, wondering what on earth was happening. 'Close that mouth,' Tilly suggested, 'before some bird builds a nest in it.'

Alex looked at her. 'Did you see that?'

'Yep. They say boys never grow up. Looks like they're right. Now, help me get some covers for this food. I suspect afternoon tea is going to be late.'

Ten minutes later the two women sat down and watched the others play while they enjoyed a cup of coffee. Alex was glad for the chance to think. Nick had said he'd come to see her—what was that all about? Or had he remembered she wanted to talk— was that why he'd come back?

In the past day she'd tried unsuccessfully to put him out of her mind. She'd tried to come to terms with the thought she might never see him again, and yet here he was.

But in reality what chance had she had to put him out of her mind? Forty-eight hours ago they'd been in the throes of lovemaking. Just watching him made her body ache for more. Heat built up inside her and she crossed her legs, trying to suppress her growing need. It didn't seem right to think such thoughts at a child's birthday party.

Finally the players collectively decided they'd had enough. They all drifted up to the table, puffing and with sweat-spiked hair, eager for cordial and sustenance.

'Wow,' said Jason turning to Nick as he reached for a cup, 'where'd you learn to play like that?'

'Back in Greece, where I grew up.'

'You're from Greece?' He looked at his mother strangely, then focused back on Nick. *'Kalimera,'* he said. *'Kalimera,* Kyrios Santos.'

Nick stopped pouring cordial into the cups held out around him. *'Kalimera,* Jason. You speak Greek?'

'I'm learning at school. My teacher says we should practice whenever we meet someone from Greece.'

'Sounds like good advice,' he said, and resumed pouring cordial. 'Are you all learning Greek?'

A chorus of 'no' went up, with cries of 'French' and 'Spanish'.

'Why did you choose Greek, Jason?'

He shrugged as he piled up his plate with four sausage rolls, three pieces of pizza and a half-dozen cocktail frankfurters, over all of which he squeezed an unhealthy spurt of tomato sauce. 'Mum picked it. But that's okay. I like it.'

Alex was anxious to change the subject. 'Nick, I don't expect you want cordial. Can I get you something stronger—a beer or some wine, maybe?'

He looked at her, eyes narrowed. 'Thanks, but cordial is fine—really.'

She shivered as his eyes bored into her. Was he working it all out? Good for him. Whatever happened he wasn't going to be able to say she had denied her son his heritage.

'Did you two want to talk?' Tilly asked. 'I can always look after these guys for a while. They won't be getting into much mischief with their mouths full.'

'There's no need—'

'We'd appreciate it—'

Tilly looked from one to the other, smiling. 'Well, what's it to be, then?'

Alex shrugged, knowing when she was beaten and realising that the time had finally come. 'Okay,' she said, heading into the kitchen, 'follow me.'

'It will be my pleasure,' she heard him say behind her, in a way that put ripples down her spine.

It was dark inside, and it took a moment for his eyes to adjust. He'd enjoyed the determined sway of her hips as she led him into the room, and now she'd turned with her back to the kitchen sink he was enjoying the way her bust filled the soft scoop-neck T-shirt. The soft floral skirt she was wearing floated around the top of her knees, giving only a hint of the smooth legs beneath.

'Jason seems to like his present. Thank you for that.'

He shrugged. 'It was no trouble—seeing I crashed his party.' Now that his eyes had adjusted to the dim light he could see more clearly. He was about to lean against the kitchen table but thought better of it when he saw the soccer ball birthday cake sitting in pride of place. 'Nice cake,' he said, though there was something about it that jagged in his mind, something not quite right.

'I didn't expect to see you again.'

He looked up at her voice. He hadn't expected to be here. 'No, I guess not.'

'But we do have to talk...' She'd wanted to get her head around how she was going to introduce the subject of their son, but instead blurted out the first thing that came to mind. 'Why did you sneak off like that?'

Good question, he thought. *Because it was easier.* 'I thought it would be better for both of us.'

'Well, it wasn't. I had something to tell you and you didn't give me the chance.'

'I forgot.'

Truth was, he'd wanted out of there—fast. He'd known he'd enjoy the lovemaking, but that day had been something else. The sex had been incredible. Though it had gone beyond that. The day he'd spent with her had taken him back to a time he'd thought he'd never experience again. It had scared him, and his first reaction had been to run. That wasn't what he'd intended. He turned his eyes back to her and remembered what he'd been saying.

'How could I not forget—in the *heat* of the moment?'

She felt it too. He could see by her widening eyes and the way her grip tightened on the counter behind. She could feel this indefinable heat that accompanied her presence.

She cleared her throat, her hands clinging to the counter in their white knuckled grip. 'Then I'm glad you came back.'

'What is it?' he asked, curious about what was so important, and more curious about that cake, done up like a soccer ball.

Something about it didn't seem right. He looked over at it once more and it hit him.

Breath hissed in through his teeth.

'When is Jason's birthday?'

She looked taken aback for a second. She blinked and he saw her throat move as she swallowed. 'Today.'

'No,' he said, 'not his party. His birthday.'

'Today.'

Today! The anniversary of Stavros's death. What kind of coincidence was that?

'But he's seven today—correct? I thought he was seven.' Seven candles would confirm what he suspected. She'd met someone else when she'd come home and it had been his baby she'd delivered a year or so later. He indicated the cake. 'Yet I count eight candles. Did someone make a mistake?'

She looked at him and nodded, but instead of making him relieved, the look on her face made his gut clench tighter with every dip of her head.

'*I* made a mistake. I should have told you earlier.' She hesitated. 'I'm sorry, Nick. Jason is your son.'

Silence, and the seconds spun out, encompassing them both as their eyes locked true to each other.

Until finally the screen door slammed and the subject of their conversation skidded to a halt in the middle of the kitchen between them.

'Aunt Tilly says it's time for cake, before the guys have to go home.' He looked from one to the other. 'Are you guys okay? You both look kind of funny.'

Alex roused herself first. She took a deep breath and flexed her shoulders, trying to ease the building strain. 'Fine, Jason. We were just talking. I'll get the cake.'

'Okay,' he said, running once more for the door. 'Hey, guys!' he yelled before he'd cleared the door. 'Here comes the cake.' Cheers drifted in from outside.

She moved to the table, almost in slow motion, trying to keep as far away as possible from Nick as she could. *Say something,* she screamed inside. *Say anything.* But Nick didn't move a muscle until she was leaning over the cake and then he suddenly edged her aside.

'I'll do it,' he said in a voice that invited no argument. 'It's about time I was allowed to do something for my son.'

He swept the cake off the table and strode outside. Alex was left following, teeth jammed into her bottom lip. He was talking, and he was at least civil. That was something, given the circumstances. But she could see he was tightly wound up, and she just prayed he wouldn't unwind right now. She still had to tell Jason after all.

She followed him out through the door and noticed Tilly's raised eyebrows at the strange procession. Nick put the cake down on the table, to delighted oohs and aahs from the boys, and looked around.

Alex held out her hand. 'Do you want to light the candles?'

'Thank you,' he said, his words polite but his eyes cold and damning as he took the matches from her.

Tilly looked over at her, her eyes questioning. Well? she mouthed. Alex gave a brief nod and looked away, before Tilly or anyone else might see the moisture welling there.

The candles lit, Nick started the boys singing 'Happy Birthday'. Alex remembered her camera at the last minute and managed a shot of Jason blowing out each and every candle in one go. For once she didn't have to reach for the video camera. Nick was here to witness this birthday party after all.

'Now,' said Nick, after the cheers had subsided, 'make a wish.'

The boy looked at Nick, this man who all of a sudden seemed to be the one in control, a slight frown puckering his young eyebrows. Then he looked at his mother. Alex smiled and he seemed to relax a little. Then he squeezed his eyes shut for a good ten seconds.

Then he opened them and yelled, 'Bags the biggest bit.'

Nick sliced the cake into man-sized portions the boys appreciated, and before the last one had finished parents were arriving to collect their exhausted and chocolate-smeared children.

Soon only the four of them remained. Alex dreaded what was coming as she started the cleaning up. She could sense the volcano that was building inside Nick, could see the tension rising in his dark eyes, and though all remained calm on the exterior, she knew he was going to blow.

Tilly sensed it too, as they were washing up the last of the dishes in the kitchen. Nick was gazing out of the window at his son, still kicking the new soccer ball around. 'I might wander off, sis, in a little while,' she said, drying her hands on a towel. 'Do you think Jason might like to come to my place for a while?'

Nick looked up sharply. 'No!'

Tilly recoiled as if she'd been slapped. 'We'll be back, if that's what you're worried about. It just looks like you two have some unfinished business. Maybe it's better if you sort that out first, before involving my nephew.'

Nick looked at Alex. Did he really think she would try and spirit Jason away when at last they had finally met? But in his position maybe she'd be nervous about exactly the same thing. She didn't have a shiny track record in the keeping-him-informed stakes. 'They'll be back. I promise.'

He grunted something about a couple of minutes and strode outside in time to pick up a deftly aimed pass from Jason. She watched him out of the window, noticed the tension dissolving in his shoulders as his muscles freed up and they kicked the ball to each other.

And it hit her like a soccer ball into her gut. Father and son together. The picture she'd never had in her mind was now being played out in the backyard. They could be any normal family on a public holiday weekend. Father and son kicking around a football while Mum cleaned up inside. The cliché brought a sardonic smile to her face.

Tilly picked up her bag and keys. 'You be all right?'

She nodded. 'Sure. Best to get it over with. It had to happen one day, I guess.'

Tilly kissed her sister on the cheek, gave her arm a squeeze and smiled. 'I'll be back in an hour—okay? But call me on my mobile before if you need to.' She called to Jason and he came running, soccer ball in his arms. After a quick peck on his cheek, they were gone.

Alex waved from the front door and knew the moment he stepped up behind her—knew by the prickle of her skin, by the scent of man—hot, angry man. Every nerve cell screamed his presence. Except this time it was for all the wrong reasons.

This time she felt afraid.

'Thank you for inviting me to my son's eighth birthday,' he said from behind her.

She closed her eyes, made a mental prayer for strength, and turned to face him.

'I would have, if you hadn't bolted from my bed without a word.'

He glared at her. 'You say that now. How am I supposed to believe you? You have lied to me for eight years—even longer! Why should you start telling the truth now?'

'I never lied to you!'

'So what do you call more than eight years of silence? Eight years of hiding my son from me. Eight years of depriving me of seeing my son grow up. What is that if not a lie?'

'I didn't lie—'

'And when would you have told me if I hadn't turned up in Sydney? If I hadn't turned up on your doorstep today? How much longer would you have made me wait for the truth? I would never have found out about Jason being my son. You would never have told me.'

He took a few steps around the room, picking up a photograph at random and moving on to the next.

'I've already missed out on eight years of his life. How much more would you have had me miss?'

Suddenly she moved to an old chest of drawers in the corner of the room. She pulled out the bottom drawer. 'Look,' she said, holding one of the stash of folders contained within. 'I have photos—lots of photos—and...' She pulled out the next drawer. 'Videos. Every birthday. Jason when he was newborn, in the bath, his first steps. I have them all on video...'

'You have had my son for eight years and all you offer me is videos?'

She dropped the folder back in the drawer and pushed it shut, realising how pathetic her offer sounded. He was right. She'd been a fool all these years, thinking that somehow a picture every now and then or a few minutes of film was going to somehow make up for years of absence.

'And where is his father in these videos? You have deprived my son of a father for eight years. How could you be so selfish?'

Selfish! After eight years of struggling by herself to create some sort of security for her child—years when her own youth had been put aside so she could be a young mother to a child no one had asked for but was there to be cared for and loved nonetheless—to hear that word used about her stung deep. She swallowed down the burn at the back of her throat, fought the prick of tears that was threatening. She sniffed.

'He's my son too, don't forget.'

'How could I forget? He must be your son. Not once did you intimate that I might be involved.' He paused for a second, revelation bright in his eyes. 'That's why you resigned, isn't it? So you wouldn't have to tell me. So I would never find out.'

She gulped, shook her head. 'It wasn't like that... I can explain...'

In three strides he had crossed the room between them and stood before her, gripping her arms and glaring down at her so that she felt small and powerless.

'Then what was it like? Why did you never tell me? Why did you let me believe he was another man's child? Why did you never tell me when he was born?'

'I didn't think you'd believe me.'

'What?'

'We used a condom. He shouldn't have happened. Why would you believe me?'

'But a baby. How could you keep that secret from his father?'

She swallowed back a sob. 'I know. I rang the day he was born—remember. I rang to tell you. But it was the day—'

'The day Stavros died,' he finished, dropping her arms and wheeling around. 'We could have done with some good news that day.'

She laughed—a harsh, brittle laugh that sounded as if at any moment it would fracture in the tense, heated air between them.

She rubbed her arms where they still stung, as if he had branded her. 'It wouldn't have been good news—not to your family.'

'Not good news? My family lurched from one nightmare to the next after that. Don't you think we deserved a bit of happiness? Something to look forward to—a child for me—a grandchild for my parents?'

'An *illegitimate* grandchild for your parents. The second—remember?'

He brushed her words away with a firm sweep of his arm.

'That child was never Stavros's!'

'But Stavros believed he was. He went against your parents' wishes. He married the mother, believing he was doing the right thing.'

'She wanted his money—'

'Yes, and so did her boyfriend. He wanted the family to pay up—hush money. But the plan went wrong and Stavros acted from the heart. So she won a bigger prize—she married into the Santos family and drove her boyfriend crazy with jealousy until he couldn't stand that she wasn't coming back and killed Stavros.'

'What has this to do with you not telling me?'

She looked at him, momentarily dumbstruck.

'Don't you remember how you felt all the months leading up to Stavros's death? Month after month you would tell me how the situation had worsened. How your parents would not accept the girl. How she flouted Stavros's will and spent his money as fast as she could, leaving the baby in the care of full-time nanny.'

She took a deep breath.

'Then you told me how Stavros had realised what a mistake he had made. When I found out I was pregnant they had only just been married. I thought it was so romantic of him to defy his parents and marry for love. But I knew how much his family, including you, were against the marriage. And there was me, wanting so much for their marriage to work out.'

She stopped talking but he remained silent, totally unresponsive to her story. What impact her words had had she couldn't tell. His jawline remained firm and set and his eyes glinted with anger still. She ran her tongue over dry lips.

'But things didn't improve. They got worse. And

as they grew worse I grew more and more afraid to tell you. I knew your parents would never believe me. I knew you would never believe me.'

'How can you say that?'

'Because you never believed her story either. Stavros had used protection, you told me. You thought she was lying. Why, then, should you believe me?'

'She was lying!'

Her chin lifted a tad. 'Absolutely. So you weren't about to fall for that old trick again.'

She could see his jaw working as his teeth ground together.

'I still had a right to know!' he said at last.

She nodded in agreement, and when she spoke her voice was more resigned. She picked up one of the photos sitting on the mantel nearby. Jason had only been two days old, wrapped in his blue hospital shawl, his alert dark eyes absorbing everything. She smiled.

'I know. That's why I rang the day Jason was born. I looked into his beautiful face and knew you had to be told. So I rang—' Her voice cracked as she remembered that day, the stresses, the excitement and afterglow of birth, and the anticipation of speaking to Nick and sharing their wonderful news. Only to hear of the family's shocking tragedy first.

When she looked up his eyes were shiny, blurred behind tears of pain, and she knew he was remembering too.

'Do you think your family—you included—would have been interested in my news?' She hesitated. 'You had suddenly become the heir. When you were the younger brother I had thought it possible—maybe, if Stavros could make it work—that you and me—and Jason—might make a go of it together. But when Stavros died I couldn't do it to you—not after that.'

'So it seems Stavros and I have something in common. We both fell for women who were born liars.'

She shook her head.

'She lied to trap Stavros. I never tried to trap you. I did everything I could to protect you.'

He spun on his heel and looked to the ceiling, his hands clasped behind his head and his chest heaving in air. It seemed like for ever before he turned, and by then the sheen in his eyes had gone and pure steel blazed out from them.

'But eight years! In eight years you haven't tried to set that to rights. You have made no attempt to call or send news or even any of this vast photograph collection you claim to have been keeping for me. You have kept my child from me.'

She looked away, hanging her head. 'I guess that's how it looks.' Then she looked up. 'But that wasn't my intention, Nick. Never my intention. You have to believe me.'

'No. I don't think I should believe anything you say. It seems you have hidden this secret for eight years. What else are you hiding?'

'I don't know what you mean.'

'Is there more you should tell me that you haven't? Has the boy suffered any serious medical conditions? Is he having trouble at school?'

'What? You've seen for yourself he's perfectly well. And his grades are in the top ten per cent for his age. I have a folder with his school results. Do you want to see those?'

He waved her offer aside with a flick of his wrist. 'Don't be so outraged. I can't trust you to tell me the truth. It's no wonder I have to ask directly. Expect many more questions as I come to learn about my son.'

'*Our* son.'

His lips curled into a sardonic smile as he took a couple of steps towards her. 'Oh? So now he's "our" son? How very generous of you.'

She shrugged off his sarcasm. He had a right to feel aggrieved, after all. Though that was no reason to forget Jason was still her son too. 'I know you have some catching up to do. We'll have to make some arrangements. You can visit any time you like. I'm sure Jason would like that.'

He raised an eyebrow. 'I'm sure he would. But I think after all this time we both deserve more.'

A cold sliver of fear wedged its way down her spine. 'What do you mean?'

'Simple. You've had my son for eight years. Now it's my turn. I'm taking him home to Greece.'

CHAPTER TEN

'No! You can't do that!'

Pure dread clutched at her heart.

'Why not? I see a certain symmetry in the plan—a certain equity, wouldn't you say? Eight years with you—eight years with me. You can come and collect him on his sixteenth birthday—if he still remembers you.'

'You can't mean that!'

His lip curled at the edge and he shook his head fractionally. 'You really believe I have become such a monster? Well, maybe I have.'

He turned his head away, so he wouldn't be distracted by the panic in her eyes, the ice-blue terror he could see welling there. But there was no other way. She'd given him no choice—not after what she'd done.

He would make it as easy as possible for the boy—Dimitri would have contacts. He'd arrange the best care, the best school. He'd find the top soccer coaches. His son would have the best of everything.

And he would have his son.

He turned back, his mind made up.

'The boy will come with me.'

'All the way to Greece? How can you do that to

him? Don't you realise what a shock that will be for him?'

'But, my dear Alexandra, don't you appreciate what a good job you've done in preparing him for this? He plays soccer, our national sport, and he's already speaking Greek. He will be right at home.'

'But this is his home!'

He looked around, as if assessing and finding it lacking. 'I can give him more. I can give him his birthright. He doesn't need to live like this.'

Fingernails biting into her palms, Alex struggled to remember to breathe.

'Like *what*, exactly?'

He shrugged. 'All these years you've been doing it tough, getting by with what you have. Jason deserves better—he could have so much more—he *should* have so much more. I can give it to him.'

'That's not fair. There's more to life than money.'

'Don't talk to me about fair! You kept my child secret for eight years. Denied me what is rightfully mine. You're the *least* qualified person to decide what is and what isn't fair. My son is coming to Greece. It's settled. I'll make the arrangements.'

'You can't just do that. He can't go. He doesn't even have a passport.'

That took him by surprise, she could see. He wouldn't have imagined for a minute that Jason wouldn't have a passport.

'How long will it take to get one?'

'One week, maybe two—*if* I agree to sign the papers.'

He moved up next to her and held the back of her head with his hand, so that she couldn't look anywhere but into his deep, dark eyes. Her hands pressed against his chest. She could feel the hard nub of his nipples with her fingers as she tried to stop her body colliding full length with his.

She could feel his heartbeat, slow and strong under her fingers, and knew that her own was beating crazily at least at twice the rate. For a second she thought he was going to kiss her, and confusion muddied her thoughts. Her lips parted, though whether it was from anticipation or the shock of his sudden proximity she couldn't be sure.

But instead of his mouth he brushed one finger over her lips, and breath infused with the scent of him stuck in her throat.

'Oh, you'll sign. You've got a lot to make up for.'

From outside came the sound of a car pulling into the driveway. Nick's eyes were drawn to the window, but Alex didn't need to look to realise Tilly and Jason were back already.

'Ah, my son is back,' announced Nick, letting her go and moving away. 'I take it you haven't told Jason anything?'

Still too disturbed by his touch, she confirmed it with a nod of her head.

'Then it's time we did.'

Alex raced after him as he headed for the door.

Five minutes later Tilly had departed and Jason had been settled on the sofa with a glass of milk, his free hand patting the soccer ball alongside.

'We've got something to tell you, Jason,' Alex started, kneeling on the carpet near where he sat, her hands tightly clasped together to resist the temptation to reach out and flick the blade of grass welded to his knee. If she touched him now she'd be too tempted to pull him into her arms and protect him for ever from secrets and their consequences. But one sidelong look at Nick and it was clear nothing would protect either of them.

He shifted alongside, showing his impatience at her hesitation. She pressed her lips together, concentrating on the words to come. 'Only it might come as a bit of a shock.'

Jason looked at them both in turn, his serious expression completely at odds with the milky-white smile left by his drink. Without saying a word he leaned forward, settled the glass on the coffee table in front of him, and sat back, his breath coming out in a huff. 'Is this anything to do with Mr Sant— I mean, Nick being my dad?'

Alex reeled back, but still caught the shock flash across Nick's face. 'Yes…but how did you know?'

'I made a wish when I blew my candles— Er, am I allowed to tell you that, now that it's come true?' he asked sheepishly.

She mussed his hair. 'Of course.'

'Is he the man in those letters?'

'Ah.' She licked her lips and looked to the floor.

Nick frowned. 'What letters?'

'Mum's got a box of letters in the cupboard from someone called Nick. She said he was her boyfriend before I was born. That was you—wasn't it?'

He looked at Jason and nodded. 'That was me.' Then he looked at Alex, who shook her head.

'I was…cleaning up. Had forgotten they were there.'

His face impassive, he looked back to his son and smiled. 'So, Jason, how would you like to come and visit Greece with me—get some real practice with your Greek language skills?'

'Greece? You mean it? That would be so cool. Wait till I tell the guys at school.'

'Only if you're sure, Jason. It's a long way to go, and you might stay there for a while. You might want to wait till end of term?'

'No way. How soon do we go?'

Alex tried to smile, but it was so hard, with her heart tearing its way through the floor, leaving jagged edges and bleeding veins in its wake.

Suddenly he threw himself forward, winding his arms around his mother's neck. 'Thanks, Mum. This is the best birthday ever. Can I take my soccer ball?'

She sniffed and hung on tight, and tried to ignore the threatening stab of tears. 'I'm sure you can,' was all she could manage.

'Cool.' As quickly as he had jumped on her he

released her and picked up the ball. 'Can I go play out in the back now?'

Alex nodded—it was easier than speaking with this huge sense of loss hovering at the back of her throat.

As much as she hated the idea of him leaving her, there was no way she could deny him a passport and the chance to see his other home. It was only fair that he knew both.

She would lose him as quickly as he had run out through that door. In a week or two, or however long it took, Jason would leave for the other side of the world and Alex would be left with nothing.

'I hope you're satisfied,' she said at last, wiping the tears from her eyes with the back of her hand.

Nick grunted and slapped his legs with his hands. 'So—tomorrow I want you to make arrangements for a passport. I'll arrange the tickets.'

She sniffed. 'And then you will take my son away from me.'

'Like you took him from me.' His words came as a harsh grating sound.

'No. It's not the same thing. You didn't know he existed until now. I have loved this child for more than eight years—nurtured him, held him when he was sick and cheered with him when he achieved every new goal.' Her voice was a bare whisper but she had to continue. She had to make him realise what he was costing her. 'For you to take him from me now, after all that, it's much, much worse.'

Her voice threatening to break, she had to stop.

Had to get out of the space Nick was consuming and into the kitchen. He had come into her house and consumed her and her life like a vacuum. He had sucked her life dry.

A month ago she'd had a job, a new home and a son she loved more than anything. Nick had turned all of that upside down. Now she had to find another job, some way of meeting her home-loan repayments. Now she'd lost her self-respect after a day of love-making that had left her with nothing but bittersweet memories. And now she was going to lose Jason, the brightest light in her life and the person who gave her a reason to go on. Nick was taking him away.

To think that two days ago she'd finally admitted she still loved Nick. What good had that realisation done her?

Nick had always been going to go back to Greece, and she had looked forward to the day with a mixture of anticipation and sorrow. His departure would have been bad enough to bear—to lose him for the second time. But now that pain would be surpassed by a greater, more devastating agony. Now he was taking their son with him.

Now she would lose them both.

Nick spent every chance he could in the following days to be with Jason and get to know him better. He even chose to play babysitter when Alex had her night classes. It was hard to begrudge him his presence as it was clear he was genuinely interested in their son.

On the weekend Nick decided on an outing—a 'family outing', he'd said—and chose the zoo. Jason responded with his usual zeal for everything about Nick. Nick could do no wrong in Jason's eyes, ever since he'd appeared bearing his soccer ball gift.

'Beware of Greeks bearing gifts.' The old proverb ran through her mind. How appropriate, she reflected, just a bit too late.

But part of her knew this was right. It was the way things should be between a father and a son, and Nick was taking to the role of father as if he'd been born to it. As for Jason, he was revelling in it. It was as if all his dreams had come true.

Alex suppressed a sigh. For her the nightmare was about to begin. In a few days Jason's passport would be ready and he would leave. She had no idea how she was going to survive after that. She could have avoided coming today, but she didn't want to miss a chance of being with Jason before he left.

She looked around, scanning the crowd for Nick, who'd gone to buy ice creams while Jason was entertained by the antics of a wild-haired orang-utan, climbing up and then jumping off his pole. Again and again he did the same routine, clapping when he reached the top of the pole, encouraging his audience to applaud likewise.

Jason gripped her hand tightly, pointing at the animal and laughing madly.

Without notice the orang-utan suddenly changed his routine. He jumped down from the pole, but instead of climbing right back up he made a dash towards his audience, took a flying leap, and crashed into the perimeter fence right in front of them. The entire crowd gasped and instantly recoiled, before spontaneously breaking out into laughter. Jason was no exception—he had all but leaped into his mother's arms—and shook with laughter as the orang-utan bobbed up and down in front of them, obviously feeling very self-satisfied.

Nick stood holding the ice creams just to one side, watching Alex hold Jason. She was laughing out loud, laughing so hard she had to wipe the tears from her eyes.

It was good to see her laugh. She hadn't been doing much of it lately. Her face looked drawn and her eyes were shadowed and dull. But for now she was laughing, her face bright and beautiful, her hands on Jason's shoulders as his own laughter subsided.

And something shifted inside Nick—something vague and harsh-edged tilted and swung, lodging into a place deep inside and grating with every intake of breath so that he felt himself frown.

He still wanted her, and after last week's lovemaking he wanted her more than ever. That surprised him. But what was more surprising was that he wasn't angry with her any more. Last week's cold fury had been replaced by something else—something that felt more like regret, that things hadn't worked out differently all those years ago.

Alex turned, the smile still on her face where it

froze, only her eyes showing surprise that he was watching them. He shook off the frown and the mess of unusual emotions crashing through him and smiled back, holding up the ice creams triumphantly. Finally her smile edged up near her eyes and she moved Jason's shoulders around so he could see what was coming.

'Ice cream!' he yelled. 'Cool!'

They wandered around the zoo, eating their ice creams and watching the animals. And when they'd finished their ice creams they walked hand in hand, Jason between them, around the park. They shared a picnic under shady trees with all the other families, and then Jason showed Nick how to feed the kangaroos and Alex took photos of the two of them until a man took the camera and snapped the three of them together. Then they walked some more, and somehow Nick ended up between Jason and Alex, holding hands as they strolled around.

It was nine-thirty before they were home and Jason had finally gone to bed, and Nick suggested a glass of wine to finish the evening.

She nodded. 'Please,' she replied, feeling tired and dreamy. Usually she couldn't wait for Nick to leave, but today had been such a wonderful day—a day when they'd come the closest ever to being a family. It couldn't last—she knew that—and because of that she was reluctant to let it end.

In the still warm air they sat on the verandah, moths dancing around the soft outside light to the accompaniment of the noises of a suburb settling down to sleep, and the distant whoosh of the slip of waves across the shore.

He set the wine glasses down on the table between them and sat down alongside. Neither spoke for a long time.

She was weary, but comfortable, and for once felt relaxed in Nick's presence. It was as if she had worked out her tension in the exertions and laughter of Taronga Zoo, and now she was content to just be there. Whatever happened, whatever her future, she would treasure today's memories for a long time.

And she could honestly say that she was happy with the way things were working out between Nick and Jason. She could never have let Jason go to Greece if he hadn't liked his newfound father, or if Nick hadn't treated him well. But things were working out better than anyone could possibly have predicted. Despite all the cynicism Nick had shown towards family life, he'd taken to his new role admirably. It was clear the two had built a solid foundation on which to develop their relationship further in Greece. That at least was some consolation. For some time soon she'd have to tell Jason that he was going to Greece without her. The better he got to know Nick before then, the more comfortable he'd feel with the whole arrangement.

She sighed and reached for her glass.

'Tired?' he asked, his voice soft and husky, as if he was trying not to interrupt the evening quiet.

She looked over at him and nodded, surprised he was so in tune with her mood. With the light behind him, his face was in shadow. It should have had the effect of making him more dangerous, but tonight it softened his features, so that they blended in the dim light, and instead of feeling threatened by him she felt warm and comfortable and relaxed.

Maybe it was the wine. The wine combined with a long, exhausting day. Maybe she'd had enough. She put her glass back down, letting her arm rest over the arm of the chair for a second. His hand closed over hers, coaxing her fingers away from the stem of the glass so that his hand completely surrounded hers.

She wasn't surprised. They'd held hands today, just like friends. It was nice, that was all.

His hand was warm. Warm and comfortable, just like he looked, and his thumb gently stroked the back of her hand, matching the rhythm of the waves so that it was almost as if it was the foam from the waves caressing her skin. She closed her eyes and let the sensation wash through her. His gentle massage was as intoxicating as the wine—gentle, slightly sweet, and with an afterglow that warmed her to the core.

He changed grip and let his fingers dance across her palm, tickling and sending waves of tingling sensation up her arm. His hand stroked the skin of her wrist, tracing a line up to her elbow and heating the blood in her veins lying underneath. She breathed deeply, feeling the flesh of her breasts firm and peak, realising that something was changing. This was suddenly much more than holding hands.

She opened her eyes to see him staring at her. He'd changed too. Now he didn't look warm and comfortable any more. Even with his face in shadow his eyes sparked with desire, and the look he sent her was laden with white heat. Breath caught in her throat as her own desires kicked up a notch in response.

He wanted her. It was in his eyes and in his touch. And if he kept looking at her that way, touching her that way, then he'd know she wanted him too.

And she didn't want him to know that. Didn't want him to know that even when he was taking her son away from her she was still not immune to his body. It was bad enough facing up to it herself. The last thing she wanted was for him to know it too.

His face dipped to her hand and his mouth brushed her skin, a warm dance of lips and heated breath before settling into a kiss that suggested so much more. She gasped, her heart skipping a beat, as his tongue grazed her skin and promised more heat, more moisture, more contact.

Desire and panic welled up inside her in equal measure. She sat up, tugging her arm from his, and rose unsteadily to her feet.

'I think it's time you left.'

He looked up at her, his eyes telling her he didn't believe a word. Her own pleaded back.

'Please,' she stressed.

Then he nodded and rose, smoothing the denim of his jeans. 'As you wish.'

Her eyes followed the movement and she almost wished they hadn't. The swell of his jeans both inflamed her and told her she'd been right to stop. There was only one place they'd been heading. She'd been there before. For a few brief moments there would be paradise, a world of passion and heightened sensations beyond belief, but afterwards would come regret, the bitter taste of hollow lovemaking, of wasted emotion and empty tomorrows.

So why did she still want him? Shouldn't it be easier than this, knowing she was right?

He took her hand and she looked up at him, surprised. 'Come on,' he said, 'you can still see me to the door.'

She nodded, not trusting herself to speak with the mess of emotions swirling inside, and obediently followed him inside.

He paused outside Jason's room. The door was ajar and a slant of moonlight cut across his bed, glowing across his sleeping face, his lips slightly parted. One arm tucked his teddy in close, the other was flung back, as if reaching for Nick's soccer ball, resting nearby.

They stood shoulder to shoulder in the doorway, watching him sleep, watching his steady breaths and angelic child's face.

And when she looked up at Nick he was staring

down at her with so much unspoken in his eyes that it passed, tremor-like, through her.

'He is a beautiful boy,' he whispered. 'Beautiful, like his mother. And strong. You have done a good job looking after him.'

She swallowed as his eyes continued to hold hers. She wanted to say that she hadn't just been looking after him, that bringing up Jason had been her life, her mission, but she didn't want to argue the point. The day had been far too special to spoil it by bickering.

And she had more to think about besides, as his fingers left hers and smoothed across her jeans, gently but insistently pulling her around and closer, so that she soon pressed up against him, so close that she could feel him harden against her belly. Even as her shoulders reared back his mouth came down and claimed hers.

She had expected his kiss to be hard and strong, expected him to try to subdue her with his sudden attack. But as his lips met hers there was no ferocity, no ambush. Instead his mouth gentled, his lips caressed hers, coaxing them to open, inviting her to join with him. The passion was there. She could feel it under the surface. But he was waiting for her.

Somehow that was the most wonderful thing. Maybe he'd stopped thinking of her as an easy target. Maybe he felt something for her after all, even if it was only as the mother of his son. Maybe he didn't just want to take her at his child's door.

Whatever, he was waiting for her to decide, and his generous gesture squeezed her heart, forcing two tears from her eyes.

It wasn't that she didn't want to make love to him. But hadn't he taken enough? Why did he want more? There was no more she could give without losing herself entirely.

Finally, as if sensing her lack of response, he pulled back and sucked in a deep breath, looking down at her, his eyes warm and enquiring. His fingers brushed her face, wiping away the tears. He frowned, and to avoid the questions in his eyes she glanced at Jason.

'You should go,' she whispered, breathless and dizzy and hoping he would take her advice, and knowing that if he argued the point she would be lost.

He chose not to argue, but let her go and led her to the front door, where he stopped for a moment before turning back. 'I want you to know Jason will be in excellent hands back in Greece. Dimitri has recommended someone excellent to look after the boy.'

Her back stiffened and she crossed her arms. 'What do you mean?'

'Just that I've been away a long time. I have a business to take care of. Obviously I won't be able to spend as much time with him as I would like—at least for a while.'

The comfortable and warm feelings he'd been stirring in her all evening began to slide off. Visions of Jason, alone and abandoned or, even worse, with a stranger in some huge empty mausoleum of a house plagued her mind. That wasn't the picture Nick had been selling to them both. How could he do that to their son?

'Maybe you should have thought about that before you decided to steal him away from me.'

It was clear from his eyes what he thought of that, and his words confirmed it. 'It is hardly stealing to take what is already mine.'

'But why do it if you know you can't look after him? Why rip him away from his home, his school, his friends, from *me*, when you know you don't have the time to commit to him? Do you really think it's fair to do all that to an eight-year-old boy?'

'He will have a new school, make new friends, and, as I said, he will have the best carer.'

'If you have to do that, why not let me come and I'll look after him?'

The thought had sprung from nowhere, but she would do anything to prevent Jason being left alone and afraid in a foreign country. She had no doubt that Nick would treat him well when he was there. They both got on so well with each other. But Nick's cool announcement that he would not have time to devote to Jason terrified her.

Who was this stranger he was about to entrust their child to? He had no idea himself.

'No.' Nick's abrupt denial cut through her like a frozen knife. 'That is not an option.'

'What do you mean—it's ''not an option''? You need someone to look after Jason. He'll be happy with me there. And I'm available.' Couldn't he see how perfect it was? She didn't have to lose Jason. Nick could have him, but she didn't have to lose him. She choked back an ironic laugh. 'Let's face it, I've no job any more. No way of paying for this house. And when you take Jason I'll have nothing left. It's a perfect option.'

He shook his head. 'No.'

'But why?'

He stared, his face angled against the harsh street-light so that the hard planes, the cold eyes, were back. 'You need to ask?'

'So you're punishing me? This is my payback for bringing up Jason by myself? For struggling to give him a home?'

'Drop the martyr act, Alexandra, it doesn't suit you. If you like it's your payback for keeping my son a secret. For denying me my son for eight years.'

'Come on! Do you really believe you would have welcomed him back then?'

'I guess we'll never know—seeing you never bothered to give me the opportunity.' He pulled his car keys from his pocket. 'I want to know as soon as that passport arrives.'

With that he turned and pointed the remote at his car, unlocking the doors. Then he was gone, in a cloud of rich petrol fumes and burning rubber.

Alex stood at the door for a while, her soul bruised and bloodied and her blood boiling after their latest run-in. So much for not wanting to bicker and risk spoiling the day. The day and the mood it had engendered in her had been completely and utterly ruined.

Would he never forgive her? Today at times he had felt like a friend, a very good friend, and not long ago she could have led him to her bed if she had so wished.

Clearly he was still attracted to her—enough to share a bed while he was here at least. It was disappointing that her earlier impressions of him were so spot-on.

He wanted her body. He wanted their son. But there was nothing beyond that. He didn't want her.

He drove along the coast a long way, not caring where he was going, just wanting the wind to blow away the anxiety churning through his mind and the heat pooling in his groin.

Not that the combination was so much of a novelty. Both conditions seemed to go hand in hand with his dealings with Alexandra.

He hadn't realised how angry he still was. For a while lust had overridden that. Spending all day alongside her had almost been too much to bear. And she would have made love tonight if he had pressed, he was sure—what had stopped her?

Even after their final heated words, he still burned for her. Wanting her was like an ache that never went. Even those years they were apart—the pain had been duller, but it had still been there, brought into sharp and stark relief the minute she'd walked into the office that morning. If he'd thought last week's day of lovemaking would take away the burning need for her, he had been wrong. The pain was there, like a needle, only growing sharper with every fix.

Her refusal this evening had honed the edge, and even her fiery words as they'd parted couldn't dull the ache. He wanted her, whatever she had done. To deny it was to deny his very existence. But did that mean he had to forgive her?

He'd already missed out on eight years of his son's life. How much more would he have missed if not for his uncle's strange bequest?

And all because she'd lied to him. She'd kept their son a secret—a secret he might not know about now if he hadn't arrived so unexpectedly.

Why was it that lies and secrets featured so strongly in the Santos family line? First his brother and now him. Stavros's wife's lies had cost him his life. Stavros had believed her, had fallen for her lies and paid the ultimate price.

Nick's hands tightened on the steering wheel. His brother had been crazy for the woman, refusing to listen to anyone, to believe anything other than her sordid lies. He'd had to be crazy to accept her claims he was the father. He had been so blind with lust and love he hadn't even insisted on DNA testing, as everyone had advised.

She was a lying, scheming witch and he would make sure she rotted in prison along with her jealous lover. It was the only thing he could do for his brother now.

They were all the same. Stavros's wife and Alexandra—women who lied their way to what they wanted. Women who made you burn with need and took what they wanted.

She was right. It was payback time. Women like her deserved to be paid back for the lies they had told, for the truths not disclosed, for the harm they had done.

She deserved it.

He knew that, recognised it as truth, and still it didn't ease the congestion in his mind. Still something didn't make sense.

Because one woman had lied to marry into his family, while the other had done all she could to stay right away. One woman had schemed to win money and influence and power, while the other had spent her life scraping by, living on the margin as a single mother. Why would she do that when Nick could have provided for them both?

He changed down a gear and manoeuvred the sports car to a halt, suddenly annoyed with the direction both his car and his thoughts were now taking.

It was late. The moon slanted low in the sky and the stars winked down at him knowingly. He looked at them—the answer was out there, somewhere. Just like those stars that looked as if he could reach out a hand and take his pick—the answer was there, almost within his grasp but not quite.

He dropped his head and rolled his neck, trying to ease the tension in his shoulders. The drive was supposed to relax him, help him unwind, but it wasn't working. He turned the key in the ignition, heard the powerful purr of the engine and threw the car into first.

Soon he'd be home, back in Greece and with his son. He was wasting his time even thinking about anything else.

Alex was kneeling on the floor, attempting to pack the remaining piles of gear in Jason's bedroom. It wasn't all going to fit. She'd have to rearrange it or leave some things behind.

The passport had arrived early in the week. She'd lifted the unmistakable envelope from the mailbox and felt the bands around her heart tighten. The last barrier to Jason leaving was gone. The last barrier to Nick leaving was gone.

They would both be gone the day after tomorrow.

It was impossible not to think about it. Not to wonder how her life could go on without Jason's presence, not to wonder how she could go on alone.

She had three months until her first visit. Nick had at least conceded she could do that, but it was going to be the longest three months of her life.

She heard a car pull up in front. 'He's here!' yelled Jason. But Alex didn't need to be told. She knew it was him, could feel his presence in the prickle of the hairs of her neck and the sudden alertness of every cell in her body.

The front door opened and she heard Jason greeting his father in their now familiar Greek, crashing into his arms. She was going to miss her boy and the way he did everything at top speed and at full volume. Life was about to get one whole lot quieter, that was for sure.

And then they were there, at the doorway. Nick was casually dressed in black jeans and an open-necked white shirt that only accentuated his olive skin and dark features. She swallowed, as always affected by the impact of his sheer presence, and tucked a strand of hair back behind her ears.

'Hi,' she managed.

He swung a brand-new suitcase into the room. 'I wondered if you needed this? Jason seems to have a lot of gear.'

'He does,' she responded. 'I'm a bit overwhelmed by how much there is. Thanks.'

'And she hasn't even started packing her own stuff yet, have you, Mum?'

Nick frowned and flashed her a questioning look. She shook her head at Nick and flashed Jason a smile. 'Don't worry. What time is Matt's dad picking you up for your playover?'

'He's late already.' He cocked an ear as a car horn tooted. 'Oh, hang on.' He disappeared down the hall-way and was back in a second. 'Gotta go—see you later, guys.'

He dashed for the front door, with Alex following him out to talk to Matt's father about what time they'd be back. And then they were gone and Alex turned back into the house.

Nick was waiting for her, angled against the doorframe with his hands and legs crossed. He didn't look happy.

'Thanks for the suitcase,' she offered, trying to work out how she was going to get by without touching him. 'I was wondering how I was going to fit everything in.'

'Avoiding the truth again?'

'What do you mean?'

'When were you thinking of telling him?'

Alex's mind hit onto his wavelength. 'Oh, I thought I would tomorrow.'

'You're sure about that? You weren't planning on telling him you wouldn't be coming just before he was about to get on the plane with me?'

'Now what are you talking about?'

'Maybe you were hoping to create a scene at the airport—*Boy ripped from mother's loving arms by foreign father*? Is that what you had in mind? The local press would love that.'

'Forget it, Nick. If I'd wanted to stop you leaving then I never would have signed his passport application.'

'Unless you want me to be embarrassed.'

'You're crazy,' she said, and pushed past him, not even trying to avoid touching him she was so angry.

He lashed out and grabbed her arm. 'Am I? You seem to have a singular ability to avoid telling the truth until it slaps you in the face. Why wouldn't you tell him, unless you were planning to embarrass me? Why leave it so late? Unless avoiding the truth really has become habit-forming for you?'

Using all the fury she felt, she yanked her arm out of his grip.

'Why wouldn't I tell him? He's my son—'

'And mine!'

'Yes! But he's a child, not a possession. And I know him. Yes, I could have told him a week ago— but why would I tell him he's being sent to Greece with a father he's never known and all by himself? Why do that to him before he's had a chance to get to know that person?'

'We get on fine.'

'I know. I think you have the makings of an excellent relationship. But any relationship takes time to develop and that's why I waited. Even when I tell him it's probably going to come as a shock that I won't be on that plane. He's spent the last eight years of his life with me and he's known you for—what? Ten days? Yes, he's going on a wonderful adventure with someone he's grown to like. But he's going to feel less secure than if I'm with him.'

'When is he returning?'

She looked up cautiously, feeling her eyes narrow. 'Why?'

'Because you are incapable of telling the truth. I will tell him myself.'

'Oh, and which version of the truth will you tell him?'

'The only one. There is only one truth here, and that is that he is coming to Greece with me—alone.'

'And will you tell him that he is going to be looked after by a nanny, a stranger, because you will be too busy to spend time with him? Will you tell him that when I suggested I should come along you refused me? And if—no, in fact *when* he wants me to come, can you imagine how learning that will make him feel? Will you tell him everything, or just the part you want him to know?'

Something harsh like a snarl erupted from deep inside him, and he closed the space between them and grabbed her arms.

'Now suddenly I'm to believe you're the expert on what constitutes truth?'

'No. I never claimed to be an expert. I'm simply saying that sometimes the truth is not so easy to define. Sometimes there's more than one truth. Sometimes there's a different take on truth.'

'I know what you're saying, but you don't get out of keeping my son a secret that easily. Your version of the truth is no better than a lie.'

'I never lied to you. I didn't think your family was ready to hear the truth back then. Maybe it was a bad call, and it made revealing the truth later on that much harder, but it was my call.'

'Just like that woman claiming Stavros was her child's father. That was her call. That was a bad call too.'

She looked at him, saw the anger and pain mixed in his eyes and realised just how much his family's tragedies had affected him. He wielded the scars like shields.

'I didn't kill Stavros, Nick. When are you going to stop blaming me? When are you going to stop punishing me for it?'

CHAPTER ELEVEN

HE LET her go as quickly as he had grabbed hold of her, wheeling away. 'That doesn't make sense.'

'Doesn't it?' She shook her head and rubbed her arms where he had branded her. 'I'm on your side, Nick. What that woman did to Stavros was beyond belief. She lied to Stavros for one reason—she wanted your family's money.'

'But you said you wanted their marriage to succeed.'

'Of course I wanted that—in the beginning. I was pregnant myself by that stage. I thought that if Stavros, the heir, could have a successful marriage on such a foundation as an unexpected baby, then there was hope for our relationship—for you and me and for our baby. I had no idea she was lying. And I saw what her betrayal did to your family. I saw it in your letters. I felt it in your words.

'The worse things got with Stavros, the harder it was for me to tell you. You hated her. Hated her for tricking him into marriage. Hated her for cheating her way into the family on the basis of a suspect pregnancy.

'You talk of speaking the truth. Of course I wanted to share the news of my pregnancy with you—but would you yourself have been prepared to announce another unexpected pregnancy in such an atmosphere? In a family already divided and pained with mistrust, savage emotion and ultimately tragedy? I doubt it. The Nick I knew then would have wanted to save his family any more pain.'

She stopped, as much to allow her to catch her breath as to see if her words were getting through, and she realised she'd made herself sound far too noble.

'Besides, I was a coward.' He looked up sharply, but she bade him to remain silent while she finished. 'I was scared of your family's reaction. Scared they'd hate me for what had happened. Scared they'd brand me a liar and a gold-digger and forbid me from ever having anything to do with you again.'

She exhaled on a sigh, shrugging.

'So I took the easy route. I kept Jason my secret, because I knew he was yours and I had loved our time on Crete and I would always have Jason to remind me of those days.'

He stared at her, dark eyes direct and purposeful, 'You're no coward, Alexandra. I have never met a stronger woman.'

She brushed off his comment. 'Hardly strong. I became more of a coward as Jason grew. I wanted you to know about him but I was so scared you'd take him away from me.' She looked up at him through damp lashes. 'And I was right to be scared.'

'But you're letting him go.'

She nodded reluctantly. 'I don't want to. But it's time. It's only fair you get to share in our child. We both had a hand in making him after all.'

Silence fell in the room as both remained motionless for a time. Finally Nick expelled one long breath and moved across the room to face her, reaching out one hand to her face. 'You see what I mean? I've never met a woman with such inner strength.'

Without thinking her face leant into his warm hand automatically and she accepted the caress.

'Single-handedly you've raised our son, struggling through the years. And now you're going to hand him over.'

A lump formed at the back of her throat that swallowing wouldn't budge. Another day his words would have been an accusation. Today they sounded like something approaching respect. Something had changed, something that suddenly gave her the hope and the courage to continue.

'I was wrong,' she started, her voice faltering. 'I believed I was right not to tell you, but it just made things so much more complicated later on. I'm so sorry, Nick—' She dipped her head as tears threatened to fall, and he wound his arms around her and pulled her into his chest.

He stroked her back while his other hand brushed her cheek, feeling the hint of dampness clinging to her soft skin and her harsh, choppy breath puff in short staccato bursts against his skin.

But she didn't burst into tears, as he'd expected

when he'd brought her to his chest, and he could feel the control she was exerting over herself in every ragged breath. No matter what Alexandra herself thought, she was strong. He was tearing her apart inside with his plans to take Jason back to Greece, and yet still she was holding together.

Even though she was right.

He shoved that thought aside. There was no point thinking of the past. Instead he should concentrate on the future, with his son, back in Greece. Though even that thought didn't give him the rush of warmth he was seeking.

Stavros was gone. Jason would have no uncle to welcome him, no *nonna* or *poppo* to spoil their only grandchild.

If they would have spoiled him.

How would they have reacted? To suddenly discover a long-lost grandchild who'd been living half a world away—surely he could have convinced them?

Just as Stavros hadn't?

So what? Stavros had been lied to. Stavros had believed the woman. He hadn't been able to convince their parents.

Would they have believed Jason was Nick's son? It wasn't as if he was a baby any more, where there might have been doubt, surely they would have seen the resemblance.

The emotions of that time came swirling back—the acrimony, the accusations, the harsh words—all of them ugly, only his brother's faith and insistence a bright, though ill-founded light.

And the implicit logic in her words struck home.

They hadn't believed that other child was Stavros's. Why would they have believed Jason was Nick's?

Suddenly the harsh-edged plate that had been lurching inside him cut loose, clattering away and finally clearing his view of history, revealing the truth of her words.

His parents would have been devastated. A replay of the tragedy of their first son's death would have destroyed them. They would never have allowed Alexandra into the family in the wake of what had transpired. She would never have stood a chance.

Even if Nick had believed her.

His gut squeezed even as he sucked in a breath.

There should be no question he would have believed her. He had loved her then. How could he not have believed her?

Though in the atmosphere of that time...

He looked down at the woman in his arms, felt her warm breath through the fine weave of his shirt, absorbed the press of her breasts into his chest and breathed in her fresh woman's scent. He dipped his head, kissing the top of her head.

'It's no wonder you acted as you did,' he said softly. 'You have no need to apologise.'

He felt her reaction like a twitch to start with. She stirred in his arms, lifting her head a fraction, stretching her arms and unfurling from his chest like a butterfly making its first tentative moves out of the chrysalis.

Slowly she turned her face up to meet his. She sniffed back one last gulp of air, blinked her questioning eyes clear of moisture and stared up at him.

'Do you mean that?' she asked, almost as if she was afraid she'd misunderstood.

Even with her hair mussed from their contact, the salty tracks on her cheeks evidence of her tears and her lips slightly parted, she'd never looked more beautiful. So strong and yet so vulnerable.

A base primal need to take this woman, to possess her and claim her for ever, overwhelmed him, and a deep, guttural groan that said all of those things welled up from inside—only to be cut off when his lips meshed with hers.

Gently, tenderly, his mouth moved over hers, answering her question the best way he could, trying to obliterate the pain of these last years, attempting to ease all the hurt and anguish she'd suffered at the hands of his family.

Tentatively at first her mouth started to move under his, responding with a gentle pressure of her own until on a sigh her lips parted, welcoming him inside.

Any sense of time was lost as he accepted her invitation, her taste in his mouth fuelling his passion, increasing the intensity of both what he was experiencing and what he was giving. And now he wasn't just trying to ease her pain. Now he was seeking his own absolution.

As if aware of his needs, she kissed his mouth, his lips, his face and eyes, her lips simultaneously soothing yet inflaming wherever they made contact. Her body pressed against his in a way that left no doubt as to where her skin dipped and curved, the sweet concave arc of her waist and the delicious flare of her hips. His hands traced the lines, sculpting her to him as he pressed her even closer.

She would be in no doubt as to his arousal. It was there, pushing out to her even as she seemed to press into its bulge. Her hands scrabbled with his shirt, freeing the fabric from his jeans so that her hands could roam the skin of his back, holding him so firmly he could feel the press of her nails into his skin.

He groaned with the pleasure and the pain and the frustration of the barrier of their clothes. Now his need had grown into something far more insistent, something far more carnal, and skin was what he too needed. The highly charged encounter of skin against skin.

His hands traced behind her, down the slinky fabric of her tiered skirt. Bunching the fabric in his thumbs, he drew the sides of the skirt up, sliding his hands up the backs of her legs as they rose. She gasped in his mouth, shifting her weight so that her legs parted slightly, allowing him access to direct his touch between her legs, up to where they met, her stretch lace panties the only remaining barrier. Her *damp* stretch lace panties. He groaned.

She was fire in his hands, liquid fire, setting him alight with her touch and her taste and her smell, setting his senses reeling and his internal thermostat out of orbit. And she was as aroused as he was. Knowing that threatened to send him off the scale.

Her hands dropped, her fingers inside his belt tugging, insistent.

He took her chin in his hand, forcing her to look up at him. 'Jason?' he asked.

'He'll be gone hours,' she replied, her breath choppy, her eyes dilated and almost luminous in their intensity.

He kissed her then, knowing she'd just answered his unspoken question in the affirmative as her hands continued to scrabble with his belt, forcing their way in to work at the buckle. He leaned over, to give her more room. He ached to be freed, and every time her hands brushed over him, even through the stout denim, her movements drove him crazy.

Now he had better access behind her. His hand slid under the fabric of her panties and he held the goose-bumped flesh of one round cheek of her bottom in one hand. She quivered against him, and hurried her actions. Then his buckle was gone and she worked at the zip, easing the catch over the distended fabric.

He slid his hand down, into the cleft between her legs, into the moist, hot place there. When he slid first one and then two fingers inside her she moaned, her back arching as her breath came fast and urgent.

Almost frantically she pulled aside his jeans and put one palm to the semi-released hardness beneath as the other eased the band of his underwear over. And then he was freed and it was his turn to gasp, her hands searing his skin and inflaming his senses.

Suddenly it wasn't enough for his fingers to be there; he needed to be inside her—all of him. He wrenched down her panties and lifted her skirt away, so that he could feel the spring of her curls against the base of his erection as it pressed into her belly. And he moved her back, bracing her against the wall.

She wound her arms around his neck tightly for support as he lifted her, wrapping her legs around him. One hand braced on the wall, with the other he found her, ready for him, and he placed the tip at her opening.

She cried out something, the words indiscernible, but they spoke to him of her need, her desires, her passion, and he knew that his own matched all of those. He entered her with one long thrust that had her throw back her head against the wall, her eyes wide, her mouth open in shock and delight.

He pulled back, waited on the brink, and thrust again, deeper this time, beads of sweat stinging his eyes and compounding the pain-ecstasy mix. Then faster. She bucked her hips against him, as much as she could in her position, matching every thrust with a tilt of her hips to welcome him, to guide him deeper inside her, into that place where the past would be eradicated, where hurt and blame would be wiped away for ever.

Again and again he withdrew, only to slam into her. Each time the need inside him was building, a hot and urgent thing, unavoidable, unstoppable. She peaked under his onslaught and cried out, the tremors inside her clenching him tightly and forcing his own climax, pumping in his own shattering release.

They huddled together as their shaking subsided, their bodies humming, their breath recovering, her legs finally sliding down to the ground. Her knees buckled and he steadied her, nuzzled the area just below her ear. She tasted salty and warm, the damp tendrils of her hair tickling his nose.

She stood there, her back still pressed against the wall, her arms around his neck, feeling her heartbeat calm as his breath steadied against her hair. She'd thought last week's lovemaking could not be bettered, but this time she was shattered, mentally and physically. And still she wanted him again.

Even as some sense of normality returned to her body, the hunger was there, the need to be close to him, to enclose him in her body.

He'd said she was strong. How wrong could he be? She was lost in his arms, knowing the pleasures to be found there. There was no earthly way she could deny herself those sensations.

Not when she loved him. And he must feel something for her, surely? He'd said she didn't have to apologise, but they hadn't taken the time for him to explain. Were his views softening towards her? Maybe now he would take the opportunity to expand on his words. Maybe now that they had satisfied their physical selves there would be time to talk.

As if sensing her mood, he sighed sharply, his breath a warm blast against her neck, but then he raised his head and pounded one solid fist into the wall. She flinched at the sudden action, at the dull boom just above her head.

'I must be mad.' He wheeled away, zipping up his jeans.

Alexandra stood stock still for a moment, chilled at both the sudden rush of cold where his body had just been and at his words. Her panties lay on the floor in front of her, unmistakable evidence of her folly. She pushed herself shakily off the wall, snatched up the offending article and started for her room. 'If you're mad, then I guess that makes me just plain stupid.'

She ran from the room, waiting for the prickle of tears, but there was none. Instead it was white-hot anger that infused her veins.

He caught up with her in the hall, his hand on the wrist holding her panties, spinning her around.

His eyes looked wild and tortured. 'Maybe we were both stupid. But I'm talking about not using protection. I'm sorry, Alexandra. That's never happened to me before.'

'You're worried I could get pregnant?' She thought

the idea over. It was probably too late in her cycle—
her period was due in a day or so—but there was
always the chance. The possibility brought a brief
smile to her face. To be made pregnant by the same
man who was now taking their first child away—it
was almost too ironic.

'That's not the only concern. There are other risks
too.'

'Well, if it's any consolation,' she said, looking
down at his hand on her arm, 'there's no chance
you'll catch anything from me. I can assure you of
that.'

'Even if I was concerned, how can you be so sure?'

'Because there's never been anyone else, Nick.
You've been the only one.' She raised an eyebrow.
'Can you say the same thing?'

He dropped her wrist. 'I'm a man. What do you
think?'

Her chin kicked up a notch. 'Oh, I think you're a
man.' She purposely misinterpreted his question.
'Didn't you just prove it? But there's probably no
need to worry. So don't. I'll let you know if there's
a problem—and I *will* let you know.'

'I can't go back to Greece and leave you here—
not knowing—like this.'

'I'll be okay, Nick. I'll probably have my period
before you get on the plane.' She shrugged. 'Simple
as that—problem solved.'

'No. You should come with us. Back to Greece.'

She rubbed her forehead with one hand and stepped

into her room. She couldn't face him like this, naked under her skirt. By the time he'd followed her in she had slipped back into her panties. Somehow it made her feel she was more in control.

'Back to Greece? Why should I do that on the off-chance I could be pregnant? I can't just traipse off to Greece on a whim. I have a life here. Responsibilities. My parents are coming for Christmas—how can I just abandon them? It will be hard enough explaining why Jason has gone—how can I just take off too? Have you just changed your mind about me coming over so that I can look after Jason for those times you won't be there? Or maybe you just like having your sex on tap. Let's face it, I fall so easily into your bed lately—not that I can pretend I don't enjoy it—there's bound to be a bit of sex on the side in it for you.'

He hesitated a fraction, and Alex would just about have sworn she could see the machinations taking place in his mind.

'So marry me,' he said at last. 'Come as my wife!'

CHAPTER TWELVE

'IS THAT a proposal?' She shook her head, disbelieving.

After everything that had happened the idea was too ridiculous. Everything he had done to date suggested he wanted to get as far away as possible from her. He didn't want her to come to Greece to look after Jason and it was patently clear he didn't really want her for his wife.

All this because of the minuscule chance she could be pregnant? Did he still not trust her to the extent that he would marry her rather than risk her hiding another secret pregnancy?

Hadn't he learnt anything?

'It makes perfect sense,' he said, as if his mind was made up. 'You will come to Greece with us. It solves all our problems. We will marry, either here or in Greece. It makes no difference to me.'

'As it makes no difference to me where we will *not* marry.'

'You are refusing to marry me? You surprise me. You would have security—our child, our *children* would be provided for. Isn't that what you want?'

Security. She laughed. Financially she'd be secure, sure. But her heart? How could that ever feel secure, knowing his was lost to her for ever? 'No, Nick. I don't want that.'

'Then what?'

'It's ironic, but the only thing I want from you is the one thing you're incapable of giving.' She paused, picked up the photo of the three of them the stranger had taken that day at the zoo, all smiling, looking for all the world like the happiest family on earth—and it was all a fraud.

She put the photo back down onto the dressing table and sighed. That family didn't exist—couldn't exist—in the vacuum that was his heart.

'I love you, Nick. And all I ask is that you love me in return.' She looked up into the swirling depths of his eyes, saw the tangle of emotions at play, and knew the answer she wanted wasn't there.

'Alexandra...I admit I underestimated you. You're a good mother. I have a lot of respect for you.'

'But you don't love me. You don't trust me. At times I think you even hate me. I can't think why you want to marry me—unless it's to keep me so close there would be no chance I could take Jason away from you again.'

Nick's face hardened and grew dark. 'Then don't come!' His voice boomed in the small room. 'I will take Jason to Greece and you will stay here alone. Alone and bitter. Maybe then you will appreciate—'

There was a movement behind Nick, at the door— a sound—a *cry*. A glimpse of a face, crumpled and agonised, and then he was gone.

'Jason!' Alex shouted as she burst past Nick and out of the room. He was already powering through the front door, his legs like pistons, and his sobs tore at her heart as she tried to catch up.

How much had he heard, standing by the doorway? She had love—her son's love—and pride was going to lose it for her. Stupid pride that wouldn't allow her to be with her son just because his father didn't love her. What the hell was wrong with her?

Over the front verandah he flew, across the patch of front garden and past the car waiting in the driveway. Matt's father's car—they were back early.

'Jason! Stop!'

Out of the corner of her eye she saw Matt's father step out of the car, the question on his face, but there was no time to acknowledge him, no time to explain what was wrong, as Jason sprinted away down the footpath. Behind her the screen door slammed. Nick had joined the chase.

She was gaining. He could outrun her in the end, but for now she was gaining ground, despite her slip-ons flapping, threatening to trip her up at each step.

Her lungs were choked, her heart beating loud in her ears, beating time with the thunder of the two motorbikes accelerating down the street. He looked back at her. She saw his face contorted, eyes squeezed in pain and chin back, as he tried to focus through the tears, and then he turned, blundering on past a parked car and dashing for the road.

'Jason, no!'

There was nothing she could do.

He was so small. So small and so fast they'd never see him in time. Never expect a child to run out from behind the car. Never have time to stop, not this close.

But they might see her. She cut across the footpath and stepped onto the road.

'*Noooooo!*'

Nick's cry melded with the roar of the machines, the roar that became a storm as the black-leathered riders thundered closer—so close that she could see the panic hit their faces when they saw her on the side of the road, when they saw Jason frozen in fear directly in their path and when their reactions finally allowed them to attempt to stop.

It all happened so quickly. One bike snaked wildly as its rider battled to reign in the whining machine, finally coming to a screeching, smoking halt just inches from the white-faced boy. The other locked its front wheel, sliding out so both rider and machine screamed a path of destruction along the asphalt, tearing and scraping and mangling, and finally collecting the woman who had chosen to run the wrong way.

Not slow motion. *Slow terror.*

The slow, agonising terror of not knowing whether the woman who lay so still and lifeless on the ground was alive or dead. The terror of thinking...

He raced to her side. She looked like a doll—a beautiful sleeping doll, until he got closer and saw the blood pooling onto the road below her head and the leg buckled back on itself beneath her.

Nearby someone groaned and swore—the biker— and Jason, at last able to move, threw himself down next to his mother. Nick gathered the shaking boy into his arms and held on tight as running footsteps sounded behind him.

He touched the fingers of his free hand to her motionless white throat, desperately searching for a pulse. *She had to be alive.*

'Call an ambulance!' he yelled.

He hated hospitals. Hated their antiseptic smell, their long straight corridors, their stark, clinical quality. Hated the way that tucked deep down in the basement would be the morgue, that secret place where they hid the non-living, away where you couldn't see them— unless it was your job to identify them.

Hospitals meant death.

Just stepping inside had made his gut clench in equal measures of revulsion and panic, and only the small, trembling hand he held had stopped him from turning around and walking straight out again. That, and the woman who lay somewhere behind closed doors. The woman who had risked her own life to save that of her son—*their son.*

The woman he loved.

But was it too late?

Anguish welled up inside him. She couldn't die—

not now—not when there was so much he had to make up for.

On the vinyl chair beside him in the cold, bare box that was the waiting room his son sobbed quietly. He undid the damp knot of their hands and wrapped his arm around the boy, nestling him in against his chest. Jason sniffed and swiped his nose with the back of his wrist. Nick pulled a handkerchief from his pocket and passed it to him.

'Do you think...? I mean, what happens if...?' Nick squeezed his son closer as he blew his nose. 'Is Mum going to die?'

Something deep inside Nick that had already been stretched to breaking point fractured as his son gave voice to the question that was his own greatest fear.

'No.' His voice was a bare croak.

'How do you know?' He lifted his tear-stained face and Nick's heart nearly broke at the hope he saw flickering in his eyes—hope he wished with all his soul wasn't false.

'Because we won't let her.'

The boy studied his face, as if judging whether he should believe him, then he blinked and sniffed again and looked back into his lap.

'It's all my fault.'

'No. Don't think that.'

'But if I hadn't run—'

'No,' said Nick, firmer this time. 'It's my fault. I was angry and said some stupid things to your mother. Stupid things I didn't mean. That's why you ran, isn't it?'

The voice, when it came, was so thin and frail it sounded as if it would snap. 'I don't want Mum to be alone.'

Nick cursed inwardly. How much damage had he done? And how could he make it right?

'Neither do I,' he said at last, promising himself he'd do everything in his power to ensure she'd never be alone. Whatever it took, he'd make things right. 'Neither do I.'

Heels clacked on the tile floor and the two of them looked up in the same instant. 'Tilly!' yelled Jason, jumping out of his chair and barrelling down the corridor. 'Aunt Tilly.' He buried his face in her jacket as she hugged him close. The smile she directed to Nick was thin and strained.

'I came as fast as I could. Any word?'

Nick stood, shaking his head and raking hands through his hair. 'Nothing. She was still unconscious when she came in. All we know for sure is she's got a broken leg. They're doing a brain scan and X-rays—checking for internal injuries.'

And it was taking for ever. Someone must know something. Why the hell couldn't they tell them?

As if on cue a middle-aged man wearing scrubs pushed his way through the swing doors and looked around at them, his gaze settling finally on Nick.

'You came in with Alexandra Hammond?'

'That's right.' They all gathered close around the doctor. 'How is she?'

'Well, Mr Hammond, your wife is one very lucky woman.'

Collectively Nick and Tilly sighed their relief, expelling the breath they'd been holding.

'She's going to be okay, then?' Tilly asked.

'She's sustained multiple fractures to her right tibia,' the doctor continued, smiling at their relieved faces, 'and she needed a few stitches to patch up that cut to her head. But other than that we can't find anything too wrong with her. And you'll be very happy to know she's regained consciousness—though she's going to have a bit of a headache for a while.'

'Can we see her?' asked Nick.

'Well, we'll be prepping her for Theatre to set that leg, but I think a five-minute visit will be in order.'

Jason gazed up at the doctor, a perplexed look on his face. 'Excuse me?'

The doctor looked down at the child. 'Yes, son. What is it?'

'He's not called Mr Hammond. His name is Nick Santos.'

The doctor looked back at Nick, confused. 'You're not next of kin?'

'Not *officially*,' he said.

'He's my father,' offered Jason.

'He's family,' said Tilly, nodding.

Nick smiled, hoping for the best. 'Now I just have to convince her.'

*   *   *

She lay in the bed, bruised and battered, her eyes closed and her slumbering body attached to an array of equipment, beeping and flashing. Nick stood stock still, his progress arrested at the door as he watched their son edge slowly towards the bed. Ashen-faced, he crept up to his mother's side, leaned over and kissed her gently on the cheek.

'I love you, Mum.'

Everyone in the room seemed to hold their breath until Alex's eyelids finally fluttered open, and though her blue eyes were dull with painkillers and shock the wan smile she returned was real enough. 'Jason.' She lifted a hand to reach him. 'I love you, too.'

Tilly moved closer. 'Hey, sis. Don't you know it's dangerous, fooling around with motorbikes?' She planted a gentle kiss on the unblemished side of her sister's bruised forehead. 'Gee, you had us worried there for a while.'

'The Simpson boy—is he okay?' Alex's voice was whisper soft. 'I feel so bad...'

'Don't feel bad,' said the doctor, finally following the party into the room and rechecking all the equipment. 'His leathers saved him from any serious damage. And from what I've heard, right now I suspect he and his brother are more worried about what the police will have to say. Now, if everyone would like to excuse us, I think it's time we were getting Alex over to Theatre to fix that leg.'

Nick cursed softly under his breath, but already the doctor had a hand under Tilly's elbow, ushering both her and Jason towards the door. The doctor then made a move to remove Nick likewise.

'No,' he said firmly, but softly enough not to alarm Alex. 'I must have just one minute alone with her.'

The doctor hesitated.

'It's important.'

'Very well,' the doctor conceded with a brief nod. 'Just one minute.' He moved back to the bed. 'Alex, it seems your *Mr Hammond* wants to have a quick word with you.'

Nick moved to the side of the bed and sat down on the edge, picking up Alex's hand and holding it gently within his own, so as not to disturb the canula taped into the vein.

'Oh, Nick,' she said, finally opening her eyes. 'It's you. I thought my father must be here.'

It was an acknowledgement. Not a greeting. Not a welcome. She was protecting herself, and it stung that she would need to. But it was no wonder. After the way he'd treated her, he didn't deserve more.

Then a tiny wrinkle appeared between her brows. 'But why did he call you Mr Hammond?'

A wry smile came to his lips. 'I suspect the good doctor believes I am your husband.'

'Imagine that,' whispered Alex tightly, turning her head away.

'I'm imagining,' said Nick, drawing her chin gently back to face his. 'And I'm hoping.'

'You are? Even after me turning you down before?' She hesitated, biting her lip. 'I keep thinking this is all my fault. If I'd agreed to marry you then the life of our son would not have been threatened—none of this would have happened.'

He shrugged. 'You could have said yes then. But whatever has happened I would much prefer you to say yes now.'

'After all this—how can you say that?'

'Because now, unlike before, when I demanded that you marry me, now I would like to *ask* you, not tell you what to do. So you can decide for yourself. And so we can give Jason a real family, with a mother and a father who love each other.'

Alex's eyelids flickered. 'But...but that would mean...'

'Exactly.' He smiled and touched her face with his fingers, stroking her skin so that she leant into his gesture.

'I love you, Alexandra. The bitterness I felt at losing my family wouldn't let me see that until now. I had no way of realising just how much I loved you until I'd nearly lost you. And now I know I cannot live without you, without your love. Please don't make me.'

He dropped down suddenly beside the bed, onto one knee. 'Alexandra Hammond, my love, my destiny, will you marry me?'

Misty tears filmed her eyes as the impact of his words hit home.

'Yes,' she whispered. 'Yes, of course I will marry you.'

His lips curled up, almost in grateful thanks, and he kissed her then, so gently and so sweetly, but with such innate power and emotion that a tear squeezed from her eye as her soul recognised that this was right, that the two of them belonged together and their love was for ever.

EPILOGUE

'CATCH me, Dad!' Jason screamed with laughter as he ran along the stony shore, Nick in hot pursuit, as the sun shone down on them from the limitless Aegean sky. It was a perfect Cretan early spring day, the weather fine, with the promise of rain coming later.

Alex watched from her recliner chair, laughing along with them as Nick made unsuccessful dive after dive for his son. It was so good to watch them play together.

But her happiness went deeper than that. Watching the two of them, the two loves of her life, she knew that things could not have turned out better—for all of them.

Jason loved Nick; that was so clear. It was as if his every dream had come true. She thought back to her wedding day, after the ceremony, when Jason had asked Nick if he could call him Dad. Nick had shaken his hand solemnly and thanked him, and told him he could never have received a better wedding present. Then he'd hugged him tightly and she'd seen the sheen blur his eyes even as he'd blinked it away.

As she blinked it away now, laughing again as Nick made one last rush, collecting a screaming Jason up over his head and declaring himself the victor. Jason giggled and squirmed in his arms before being tossed over Nick's shoulder and escaping to the shore to look for treasure from the sea.

Nick ran up puffing to her side, his glossy olive skin rising and falling in a way that held her mesmerised.

Even after being married for two months she was still struck by the beauty of the man, his sheer masculine form, that always brought a rush of blood and lust through her veins.

She shifted position slightly, noticing his own appreciative gaze on her. He made her feel so beautiful, so incredibly sexy, merely with a glance or a smile.

He squatted down alongside her and kissed her, one hand caressing her once damaged leg, sending sparks through her skin.

'Is your leg all right? Can I get you anything?'

She smiled back at him. He was so concerned for her welfare. She wasn't used to having someone look after her, and she felt spoilt and special and very, very loved. And while he'd been disappointed at first that she hadn't become pregnant that time, before they were married, it had given the three of them a special time to bond together as a family at last.

'I'm fine—just being lazy. I was thinking about Christmas. There was something special about having Tilly and my parents over for our wedding, and for a real Greek Christmas. A double celebration. I know we all enjoyed it. Thank you for making all that possible.'

'You've already thanked me, Alexandra. Not that you need to—I think families are the most important thing, and I don't think I would appreciate that as much if I hadn't lost almost everything.'

'I'm glad Sofia could join us. She looks so much happier now. Do you think she and Dimitri will marry?'

Nick raised his eyebrows. 'I don't know. Though I think she's realised herself that she needs time to get over her father's death before she commits to any one man.'

He traced the back of one finger down the side of her face and she drew in breath, smiling as she realised he would always have this effect on her. He would always be able to move her soul and rock her emotions, just with one touch, one word.

'It's lovely to see you smile,' he said. 'To see you smile without worries. In the last few weeks, even in the last few days, you have looked more beautiful than ever.'

His words fired her heart, tugged at her senses. Would she never get used to the impact he made on her?

'That's because I'm so happy. Happy to be with you. And happy to be back here again. Thank you for deciding on Crete for this holiday.'

'Where else could we go? This is where we began.'

She smiled. 'Back where it all started. Back where Jason began.'

His eyes flared. 'That thought had crossed my mind. Do you suspect you might be more fertile in Crete?'

She knew what he had in mind, and the sparks he had generated inside her moved up to a slow burn. 'I don't know, but it's a good theory.'

He picked up her hand and kissed it softly, looking up at her through his dark lashes.

'A theory I intend to test thoroughly.'

She moistened her lips, knowing just what was in store and looking forward to it as his lips descended purposefully towards hers.

She wrapped her arms around his neck and pulled him closer.

'I was hoping you might say that.'

* * *

Trish Morey brings you a passionate prince and a secret baby in Forced Wife, Royal Love-Child.
Available next month, in Mills & Boon® Modern™.

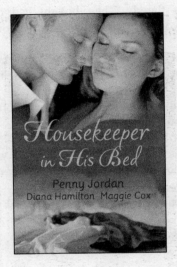